Dark places

Gillian Flynn

Weidenfeld & Nicolson

LONDON

First published in Great Britain in 2009
by Weidenfeld & Nicolson
An imprint of the Orion Publishing Group
Orion House, 5 Upper St Martin's Lane,
London WC2H 9EA

An Hachette UK Company

First published in the USA in 2009
by the Crown Publishing Group

1 3 5 7 9 10 8 6 4 2

A CIP catalogue record for this book
is available from the British Library

ISBN 978 0 297 85157 8 (cased)
ISBN 978 0 297 85287 2 (export paperback)

Printed in Great Britain by Clays Ltd, St Ives plc

The Orion Publishing Group's policy is to use papers that
are natural, renewable and recyclable products and made
from wood grown in sustainable forests. The logging and
manufacturing processes are expected to conform to the
environmental regulations of the country of origin.

www.orionbooks.co.uk

To my dashing husband, Brett Nolan

The Days were a clan that mighta lived long
But Ben Day's head got screwed on wrong
That boy craved dark Satan's power
So he killed his family in one nasty hour

Little Michelle he strangled in the night
Then chopped up Debby: a bloody sight
Mother Patty he saved for last
Blew off her head with a shotgun blast

Baby Libby somehow survived
But to live through that ain't much a life

—SCHOOLYARD RHYME, CIRCA 1985

Dark places

Libby Day

NOW

I have a meanness inside me, real as an organ. Slit me at my belly and it might slide out, meaty and dark, drop on the floor so you could stomp on it. It's the Day blood. Something's wrong with it. I was never a good little girl, and I got worse after the murders. Little Orphan Libby grew up sullen and boneless, shuffled around a group of lesser relatives—second cousins and great-aunts and friends of friends—stuck in a series of mobile homes or rotting ranch houses all across Kansas. Me going to school in my dead sisters' hand-me-downs: Shirts with mustardy armpits. Pants with baggy bottoms, comically loose, held on with a raggedy belt cinched to the farthest hole. In class photos my hair was always crooked—barrettes hanging loosely from strands, as if they were airborne objects caught in the tangles—and I always had bulging pockets under my eyes, drunk-landlady eyes. Maybe a grudging curve of the lips where a smile should be. Maybe.

I was not a lovable child, and I'd grown into a deeply unlovable adult. Draw a picture of my soul, and it'd be a scribble with fangs.

———

IT WAS MISERABLE, wet-bone March and I was lying in bed thinking about killing myself, a hobby of mine. Indulgent afternoon daydreaming: A shotgun, my mouth, a bang and my head jerking once, twice, blood on the wall. Spatter, splatter. "Did she want to be buried or cremated?" people would ask. "Who should come to the funeral?" And no one would know. The people, whoever they were, would just look at each other's shoes or shoulders until the silence settled in and then someone would put on a pot of coffee, briskly and with a fair amount of clatter. Coffee goes great with sudden death.

I pushed a foot out from under my sheets, but couldn't bring myself to connect it to the floor. I am, I guess, depressed. I guess I've been depressed for about twenty-four years. I can feel a better version of me somewhere in there—hidden behind a liver or attached to a bit of spleen within my stunted, childish body—a Libby that's telling me to get up, do something, grow up, move on. But the meanness usually wins out. My brother slaughtered my family when I was seven. My mom, two sisters, gone: bang bang, chop chop, choke choke. I didn't really have to do anything after that, nothing was expected.

I inherited $321,374 when I turned eighteen, the result of all those well-wishers who'd read about my sad story, do-gooders whose *hearts had gone out to me.* Whenever I hear that phrase, and I hear it a lot, I picture juicy doodle-hearts, complete with bird-wings, flapping toward one of my many crap-ass childhood homes, my little-girl self at the window, waving and grabbing each bright heart, green cash sprinkling down on me, *thanks, thanks a ton!* When I was still a kid, the donations were placed in a conservatively managed bank account, which, back in the day, saw a jump about every three–four years, when some magazine or news station ran an update on me. Little Libby's Brand New Day: The Lone Survivor of the Prairie Massacre Turns a Bittersweet 10. (Me in scruffy pigtails on the possum-pissed lawn outside my Aunt Diane's trailer. Diane's thick tree-calves, exposed by a rare skirt, planted in the yellow grass behind me.) Brave Baby Day's Sweet 16! (Me, still miniature, my face aglow with birthday candles, my shirt too tight over breasts that had gone D-cup that year, comic-book sized on my tiny frame, ridiculous, porny.)

I'd lived off that cash for more than thirteen years, but it was almost gone. I had a meeting that afternoon to determine exactly how gone. Once a year the man who managed the money, an unblinking, pink-cheeked banker named Jim Jeffreys, insisted on taking me to lunch, a "checkup," he called it. We'd eat something in the twenty-dollar range and talk about my life—he'd known me since I was this-high, after all, heheh. As for me, I knew almost nothing about Jim Jeffreys, and never asked, viewing the appointments always from the same kid's-eye view: Be polite, but barely, and get it over with. Single-word answers, tired sighs. (The one thing I suspected about Jim Jeffreys was that he must be Christian, churchy—he had the patience and optimism of someone who thought Jesus was watching.) I wasn't due for a "checkup" for another eight or nine months, but Jim Jeffreys had nagged, leaving phone messages in a serious, hushed voice, saying he'd done all he could to extend the "life of the fund," but it was time to think about "next steps."

And here again came the meanness: I immediately thought about that other little tabloid girl, Jamie Something, who'd lost her family the same year—1985. She'd had part of her face burned off in a fire her dad set that killed everyone else in her family. Any time I hit the ATM, I think of that Jamie girl, and how if she hadn't stolen my thunder, I'd have twice as much money. That Jamie Whatever was out at some mall with my cash, buying fancy handbags and jewelry and buttery department-store makeup to smooth onto her shiny, scarred face. Which was a horrible thing to think, of course. I at least knew that.

Finally, finally, finally I pulled myself out of bed with a stage-effect groan and wandered to the front of my house. I rent a small brick bungalow within a loop of other small brick bungalows, all of which squat on a massive bluff overlooking the former stockyards of Kansas City. Kansas City, Missouri, not Kansas City, Kansas. There's a difference.

My neighborhood doesn't even have a name, it's so forgotten. It's called Over There That Way. A weird, subprime area, full of dead ends and dog crap. The other bungalows are packed with old people who've lived in them since they were built. The old people sit, gray and pudding-like, behind screen windows, peering out at all hours. Sometimes they walk to their cars on careful elderly tiptoes that make me feel guilty, like I should go help. But they wouldn't like that.

They are not friendly old people—they are tight-lipped, pissed-off old people who do not appreciate me being their neighbor, this *new* person. The whole area hums with their disapproval. So there's the noise of their disdain and there's the skinny red dog two doors down who barks all day and howls all night, the constant background noise you don't realize is driving you crazy until it stops, just a few blessed moments, and then starts up again. The neighborhood's only cheerful sound I usually sleep through: the morning coos of toddlers. A troop of them, round-faced and multilayered, walk to some daycare hidden even farther in the rat's nest of streets behind me, each clutching a section of a long piece of rope trailed by a grown-up. They march, penguin-style, past my house every morning, but I have not once seen them return. For all I know, they troddle around the entire world and return in time to pass my window again in the morning. Whatever the story, I am attached to them. There are three girls and a boy, all with a fondness for bright red jackets—and when I don't see them, when I oversleep, I actually feel blue. Bluer. That'd be the word my mom would use, not something as dramatic as *depressed*. I've had the blues for twenty-four years.

I PUT ON a skirt and blouse for the meeting, feeling dwarfy, my grown-up, big-girl clothes never quite fitting. I'm barely five foot—four foot, ten inches in truth, but I round up. Sue me. I'm thirty-one, but people tend to talk to me in singsong, like they want to give me fingerpaints.

I headed down my weedy front slope, the neighbor's red dog launching into its busybody barking. On the pavement near my car are the smashed skeletons of two baby birds, their flattened beaks and wings making them look reptilian. They've been there for a year. I can't resist looking at them each time I get in my car. We need a good flood, wash them away.

Two elderly women were talking on the front steps of a house across the street, and I could feel them refusing to see me. I don't know anyone's name. If one of those women died, I couldn't even say, "Poor old Mrs. Zalinsky died." I'd have to say, "That mean old bitch across the street bit it."

Feeling like a child ghost, I climbed into my anonymous mid-sized car, which seems to be made mostly of plastic. I keep waiting for someone from the dealership to show up and tell me the obvious: "It's a joke. You can't actually drive this. We were kidding." I trance-drove my toy car ten minutes downtown to meet Jim Jeffreys, rolling into the steakhouse parking lot twenty minutes late, knowing he'd smile all kindly and say nothing about my tardiness.

I was supposed to call him from my cell phone when I arrived so he could trot out and escort me in. The restaurant—a great, old-school KC steakhouse—is surrounded by hollowed-out buildings that concern him, as if a troop of rapists was permanently crouched in their empty husks awaiting my arrival. Jim Jeffreys is not going to be The Guy Who Let Something Bad Happen to Libby Day. Nothing bad can happen to BRAVE BABY DAY, LITTLE GIRL LOST, the pathetic, red-headed seven-year-old with big blue eyes, the only one who survived the PRAIRIE MASSACRE, the KANSAS CRAZE-KILLINGS, the FARMHOUSE SATAN SACRIFICE. My mom, two older sisters, all butchered by Ben. The only one left, I'd fingered him as the murderer. I was the cutie-pie who brought my Devil-worshiping brother to justice. I was big news. The *Enquirer* put my tearful photo on the front page with the headline ANGEL FACE.

I peered into the rearview mirror and could see my baby face even now. My freckles were faded, and my teeth straightened, but my nose was still pug and my eyes kitten-round. I dyed my hair now, a white-blonde, but the red roots had grown in. It looked like my scalp was bleeding, especially in the late-day sunlight. It looked gory. I lit a cigarette. I'd go for months without smoking, and then remember: I need a cigarette. I'm like that, nothing sticks.

"Let's go, Baby Day," I said aloud. It's what I call myself when I'm feeling hateful.

I got out of the car and smoked my way toward the restaurant, holding the cigarette in my right hand so I didn't have to look at the left hand, the mangled one. It was almost evening: Migrant clouds floated in packs across the sky like buffalo, and the sun was just low enough to spray everything pink. Toward the river, between the looping highway ramps, obsolete grain elevators sat vacant, dusk-black and pointless.

I walked across the parking lot all by myself, atop a constellation of crushed glass. I was not attacked. It was, after all, just past 5 p.m. Jim Jeffreys was an early-bird eater, proud of it.

He was sitting at the bar when I walked in, sipping a pop, and the first thing he did, as I knew he would, was grab his cell phone from his jacket pocket and stare at it as if it had betrayed him.

"Did you call?" he frowned.

"No, I forgot," I lied.

He smiled then. "Well, anyway. Anyway, I'm glad you're here, sweetheart. Ready to talk turkey?"

He slapped two bucks on the bartop, and maneuvered us over to a red leather booth sprouting yellow stuffing from its cracks. The broken slits scraped the backs of my legs as I slid in. A whoof of cigarette stink burped out of the cushions.

Jim Jeffreys never drank liquor in front of me, and never asked me if I wanted a drink, but when the waiter came I ordered a glass of red wine and watched him try not to look surprised, or disappointed, or anything but Jim Jeffreys–like. *What kind of red?* the waiter asked, and I had no idea, really—I never could remember the names of reds or whites, or which part of the name you were supposed to say out loud, so I just said, *House.* He ordered a steak, I ordered a double-stuffed baked potato, and then the waiter left and Jim Jeffreys let out a long dentist-y sigh and said, "Well, Libby, we are entering a very new and different stage here together."

"So how much is left?" I asked, thinking *saytenthousandsayten thousand.*

"Do you *read* those reports I send you?"

"I sometimes do," I lied again. I liked getting mail but not reading it; the reports were probably in a pile somewhere in my house.

"Have you *listened* to my messages?"

"I think your cell phone is messed up. It cuts out a lot." I'd listened just long enough to know I was in trouble. I usually tuned out after Jim Jeffreys' first sentence, which always began: *Your friend Jim Jeffreys here, Libby . . .*

Jim Jeffreys steepled his fingers and stuck his bottom lip out. "There is 982 dollars and 12 cents left in the fund. As I've mentioned before, had you been able to replenish it with any kind of regular work, we'd have been able to keep it afloat, but . . ." he tossed out his hands and grimaced, "things didn't work out that way."

"What about the book, didn't the book . . . ?"

"I'm sorry, Libby, the book did not. I tell you this every year. It's not your fault, but the book . . . no. Nothing."

Years ago, to exploit my twenty-fifth birthday, a publisher of self-help books asked me to write about how I'd conquered the "ghosts of my past." I had in no way conquered much of anything, but I agreed to the book anyway, talking over the phone with a woman in New Jersey who did the actual writing. The book came out at Christmas time, 2002, with a cover photo of me sporting an unfortunate shag haircut. It was called, *Brand New Day! Don't Just Survive Childhood Trauma—Surpass It!* and it included a few childhood snapshots of me and my dead family, packed between two hundred pages of gloppy, positive-thinking porridge. I was paid $8,000, and a smattering of survivors' groups invited me to speak. I flew to Toledo for a meeting of men who'd been orphaned young; to Tulsa for a special gathering of teenagers whose moms had been killed by their dads. I signed my book for mouth-breathing kids who asked me jarring questions, like did my mom cook pies. I signed the book for gray, needful old men peering at me from behind bifocals, their breath blasting burnt coffee and stomach acid. "Start a New Day!" I'd write or "A New Day Awaits!" How lucky to have a pun for a last name. The people who came to meet me always looked exhausted and desperate, standing uncertainly near me in loose packs. The groups were always small. Once I realized I wasn't getting paid for any of this, I refused to go anywhere. The book had already bombed anyway.

"It seems like it should have made more money," I mumbled. I really wanted the book to make money, in an obsessive childish way—that feeling that if I wanted it enough, it should happen. It should happen.

"I know," Jim Jeffreys said, having nothing more to say on the subject after six years. He watched me drink my wine in silence. "But in a way, Libby, this presents you with a really interesting new phase of your life. I mean, what do you want to be when you grow up?"

I could tell this was supposed to be charming, but it brought a burst of rage up in me. I didn't want to be anything, that was the fucking point.

"There's no money left?"

Jim Jeffreys shook his head sadly, and started salting his newly arrived steak, the blood pooling around it like bright Kool-Aid.

"What about new donations—the twenty-fifth anniversary is coming up." I felt another splash of anger, for him making me say this aloud. Ben started his killing spree around 2 a.m. on January 3, 1985. The time stamp on my family's massacre, and here I was looking forward to it. Who said things like that? Why couldn't there have been even $5,000 left?

He shook his head again. "There's no more, Libby. You're what, thirty? A woman. People have moved on. They want to help other little girls, not . . ."

"Not me."

"I'm afraid not."

"People have moved on? Really?" I felt a lurch of abandonment, the way I always felt as a kid, when some aunt or cousin was dropping me off at some other aunt or cousin's house: *I'm done, you take her for a while.* And the new aunt or cousin would be real nice for about a week, try real hard with bitter little me, and then . . . in truth it was usually my fault. It really was, that's not victim-talk. I doused one cousin's living room with Aqua Net and set fire to it. My aunt Diane, my guardian, my mom's sister, my beloved, took me in—and sent me away—half a dozen times before she finally closed the door for good. I did very bad things to that woman.

"There is always a new murder, I'm afraid, Libby," Jim Jeffreys was droning. "People have short attention spans. I mean, think how crazy people're going about Lisette Stephens."

Lisette Stephens was a pretty twenty-five-year-old brunette who'd disappeared on the way home from her family's Thanksgiving dinner. All of Kansas City was invested in finding her—you couldn't turn on the news without seeing her photo smiling at you. The story had gone national in early February. Nothing at all had happened in the case for a month. Lisette Stephens was dead, and everyone knew that by now, but no one wanted to be the first to leave the party.

"But," continued Jim Jeffreys, "I think everyone would like to hear you're doing well."

"Awesome."

"What about college?" he chewed off a hunk of meat.

"No."

"What about we try to set you up in some sort of office job, filing and whatnot?"

"No." I folded in on myself, ignoring my meal, projecting glumness. That was another of my mom's words: *glum*. It meant having the blues in a way that annoyed other people. Having the blues aggressively.

"Well, why don't you take a week and do some thinking on it?" He was devouring his steak, his fork moving up and down briskly. Jim Jeffreys wanted to leave. Jim Jeffreys was done here.

HE LEFT ME with three pieces of mail and a grin that was supposed to be optimistic. Three pieces, all looking like junk. Jim Jeffreys used to hand me bulging shoe boxes full of mail, most of them letters with checks inside. I'd sign the check over to him, and then the donor would receive a form letter in my blocky handwriting. "Thank you for your donation. It is people like you who let me look forward to a brighter future. Your truly, Libby Day." It really did say "your" truly, a misspelling that Jim Jeffreys thought people would find poignant.

But the shoe boxes of donations were gone, and I was left with a mere three letters and the rest of the night to kill. I headed back home, several cars blinking their headlights at me until I realized I was driving dark. Kansas City's skyline glimmered to the east, a modest, mid-rise Monopoly scatter, radio towers spiking here and there. I tried to picture things I could do for money. Things that grown-ups did. I imagined myself in a nurse's cap, holding a thermometer; then in a snug blue cop's uniform, escorting a child across the street; then wearing pearls and a floral apron, getting dinner ready for my hubby. *That's how screwed up you are,* I thought. *Your idea of adulthood still comes from picturebooks.* And even as I was thinking it, I saw myself writing ABCs on a chalkboard in front of bright-eyed first graders.

I tried to come up with realistic occupations—something with computers. Data entry, wasn't that some sort of job? Customer service, maybe? I'd seen a movie once where a woman walked dogs for a living, dressed in overalls and sweater sets and always holding flowers, the dogs slobbery and loving. I didn't like dogs, though, they scared me. I finally thought, of course, about farming. Our family had been farmers for a century, right down to my mom, until Ben killed her off. Then the farm got sold.

I wouldn't know how to farm anyway. I have memories of the place: Ben mucking through the cold spring mud, swatting calves out of his way; my mom's rough hands digging into the cherry-colored pellets that would blossom into milo; the squeals of Michelle and Debby jumping on haybales in the barn. "It itches!" Debby would always complain, and then jump in again. I can never dwell in these thoughts. I've labeled the memories as if they were a particularly dangerous region: Darkplace. Linger too long in an image of my mom trying to jury-rig the blasted coffeemaker again or of Michelle dancing around in her jersey nightgown, tube socks pulled up to her knees, and my mind would jerk into Darkplace. Maniacal smears of bright red sound in the night. That inevitable, rhythmic axe, moving as mechanically as if it were chopping wood. Shotgun blasts in a small hallway. The panicked, jaybird cries of my mother, still trying to save her kids with half her head gone.

What does an administrative assistant do? I wondered.

I pulled up to my house, stepped onto a slab of sidewalk where someone had scraped "Jimmy Loves Tina" in the concrete decades ago. Sometimes I had flashes of how the couple turned out: He was a minor-league baseball player/she was a housewife in Pittsburgh, battling cancer. He was a divorced fireman/she was a lawyer who drowned off the Gulf Coast last year. She was a teacher/he dropped dead of an aneurysm at twenty. It was a good, if gruesome, mind game. I had a habit of killing off at least one of them.

I looked up at my rented house, wondered if the roof was lopsided. If the whole thing crashed in, I wouldn't lose much. I owned nothing of value but a very old cat named Buck who tolerated me. As I hit the soggy, bowed steps, his resentful mews reached me from inside the house and I realized I hadn't fed him today. I opened the door and the ancient cat moved toward me, slow and crimped, like a jalopy with a busted wheel. I didn't have any cat food left—that had been on the to-do list for a week—so I went to the fridge, pulled out some slices of hardened Swiss cheese, and gave those to him. Then I sat down to open my three envelopes, my fingers smelling like sour milk.

I never made it past the first letter.

Dear Ms. Day,

I hope this letter reaches you, as you seem to have no website. I have read about you and followed your story closely over the years, and am very interested to hear how you are doing and what you are up to these days. Do you ever do appearances? I belong to a group that would pay you $500 just to show up. Please contact me and I will happily give you more information.

Warmly,
Lyle Wirth

PS This is a legitimate business offer.

Stripping? Porn? Back when the book came out, with its section of Baby Day Grows Up photos, the most notable was me at seventeen, my wobbly, woman-breasts barely held in by a white-trash halter top. I'd received several propositions from fringe nudie mags as a result, none of them offering enough money to make me think hard. Even now five hundred wouldn't quite do it, if these guys did want me to get naked. But maybe—*think positive, Baby Day!*—maybe it really was a legit offer, another of those mourners' groups, needing me to show up so they had a reason to talk about themselves. Five hundred for a few hours of sympathy was a doable exchange.

The letter was typed, except for a phone number that had been inked at the bottom in assertive script. I dialed the number, hoping for voicemail. Instead, a cavernous pause came on the line, a phone picked up, but not spoken into. I felt awkward, as if I'd called someone in the middle of a party I wasn't supposed to know about.

Three seconds, then a male voice: "Hello?"

"Hi. Is this Lyle Wirth?" Buck was nosing around my legs, anxious for more food.

"Who's this?" Still in the background: a big loud nothing. Like he was at the bottom of a pit.

"This is Libby Day. You wrote me."

"Ohhhh holy cow. Really? Libby Day. Uh, where are you? Are you in town?"

"Which town?"

The man—or boy, he sounded young—yelled something at someone back behind him that included the phrase, "I already did them," and then groaned into my ear.

"You in Kansas City? You live in Kansas City, right? Libby?"

I was about to hang up, but the guy started yelling *hel-ooo-o? hel-ooo-o?* into the line, like I was some dazed kid not paying attention in class, so I told him I did live in Kansas City and what did he want. He gave one of those *heheheh* laughs, those *you-won't-believe-this-but* laughs.

"Well, like I said, I wanted to talk to you about an appearance. Maybe."

"Doing what?"

"Well, I'm in a special club . . . there's a special club meeting here next week, and . . ."

"What kind of club?"

"Well, it's kind of different. It's sort of an underground thing . . ."

I said nothing, let him twist. After the initial bravura, I could feel him get uneasy. Good.

"Oh crap, it's impossible to explain over the phone. Can I, uh, buy you a coffee?"

"It's too late for coffee," I said, and then realized he probably didn't even mean tonight, probably meant sometime this week, and then I wondered again how I'd kill the next four or five hours.

"A beer? Wine?" he asked.

"When?"

Pause. "Tonight?"

Pause. "Fine."

LYLE WIRTH LOOKED like a serial killer. Which meant he probably wasn't one. If you were chopping up hookers or eating runaways, you'd try to look normal. He was sitting at a grimy card table in the middle of Tim-Clark's Grille, a humid dive attached to a flea market. Tim-Clark's had become famed for its barbeque and was now being gentrified, an uneasy mix of grizzled old-timers and flop-haired dudes in skinny jeans. Lyle was neither: He was somewhere in his very early twenties, with wavy, mousy hair he'd tried to tame with too much gel in all the wrong places, so that it was half fuzzy, half shiny points. He wore wireless glasses, a tight Members Only windbreaker, and jeans that were skinny, but not in a cool way, just in a tight way. He had features that were too delicate to be attractive on a man. Men shouldn't have rosebud lips.

He caught my eye as I walked toward him. He wasn't recognizing me at first, just assessing me, this lady-stranger. When I'd almost reached the table, it clicked for him: the freckles, the baby-bird skeleton, the pug nose that got pugger the longer someone held eye contact.

"Libby!" he started, realized it was too familiar, and added, "Day!" He stood up, pulled out one of the folding chairs, looked like he regretted the chivalry, and sat back down. "Your hair's blond."

"Yup," I said. I hate people who start conversations with facts— what are you supposed to do with that? *Sure is hot today. Yes, it is.* I peered around to signal for a drink. A miniskirted waitress with voluptuous black hair had her pretty backside to us. I table-tapped my fingers til she turned around, gave me a face that had to have been at least seventy years old, her pancake makeup pooling in the crepe of her cheeks, purple veins marbling her hands. Some part of her creaked as she bent down for my order, snuffing when I asked for just a PBR.

"The brisket is really good here," Lyle said. But he wasn't having it either, just sipping on the dregs of something milky.

I don't eat meat, really, not since seeing my family sliced open— I was still trying to get Jim Jeffreys and his sinewy steak out of my head. I shrugged no, waited for my beer, looking around like a tourist. Lyle's fingernails were dirty, first thing I noticed. The old waitress's black wig was ajar: Strands of sweaty white hair stuck to her neck. She tucked a few back under as she grabbed a packet of fries sizzling beneath the heat lamp. A fat man sat by himself at the next table, eating short ribs and examining his flea-market purchase:

a kitschy old vase with a mermaid on it. His fingers left grease marks on the mermaid's breasts.

The waitress said nothing as she set the beer squarely in front of me and then purred over to the fat man, calling him Honey.

"So what's with the club?" I prompted.

Lyle turned pink, his knee jittery beneath the table.

"Well, you know how some guys do fantasy football, or collect baseball cards?" I nodded. He let out a strange laugh and continued. "Or women read gossip magazines and they know everything about some actor, know like, their baby's name and the town they grew up in?"

I gave a wary incline of the head, a be-careful nod.

"Well, this is like that, but it's, well, we call it a Kill Club."

I took a slug of beer, sweat beads popping on my nose.

"It's not as weird as it sounds."

"It sounds pretty fucking weird."

"You know how some people like mysteries? Or get totally into true-crime blogs? Well, this club is a bunch of those people. Everyone has their crime that they're obsessed with: Laci Peterson, Jeffrey MacDonald, Lizzie Borden . . . you and your family. I mean you and your family, it's huge with the club. Just huge. Bigger'n JonBenét." He caught me grimacing, and added: "Just a tragedy, what happened. And your brother in jail for, what, going on twenty-five years?"

"Don't feel sorry for Ben. He killed my family."

"Heh. Right." He sucked on a piece of milky ice. "So, you ever talk with him about it?"

I felt my defenses flip up. There are people out there who swear Ben is innocent. They mail me newspaper clippings about Ben and I never read them, toss them as soon as I see his photo—his red hair loose and shoulder-length in a Jesus-cut to match his glowing, full-of-peace face. Pushing forty. I have never gone to see my brother in jail, not in all these years. His current prison is, conveniently, on the outskirts of our hometown—Kinnakee, Kansas—where he'd committed the murders to begin with. But I'm not nostalgic.

Most of Ben's devotees are women. Jug-eared and long-toothed, permed and pant-suited, tight-lipped and crucifixed. They show up occasionally on my doorstep, with too much shine in their eyes. Tell me that my testimony was wrong. I'd been confused, been coerced, sold a lie when I swore, at age seven, that my brother had been the killer. They often scream at me, and they always have plenty of saliva. Several have actually slapped me. This makes them even less convincing: A red-faced, hysterical woman is very easy to disregard, and I'm always looking for a reason to disregard.

If they were nicer to me, they might have got me.

"No, I don't talk to Ben. If that's what this is about, I'm not interested."

"No, no, no, it's not. You'd just come to, it's like a convention almost, and you'd let us pick your brain. You really don't think about that night?"

Darkplace.

"No, I don't."

"You might learn something interesting. There are some fans . . . experts, who know more than the detectives on the case. Not that *that's* hard."

"So these are a bunch of people who want to convince me Ben's innocent."

"Well . . . maybe. Maybe you'll convince them otherwise." I caught a whiff of condescension. He was leaning in, his shoulders tense, excited.

"I want $1,000."

"I could give you $700."

I glanced around the room again, noncommittal. I'd take whatever Lyle Wirth gave me, because otherwise I was looking at a real job, real soon, and I wasn't up for that. I'm not someone who can be depended on five days a week. Monday Tuesday Wednesday Thursday Friday? I don't even get out of bed five days in a row—I often don't remember to eat five days in a row. Reporting to a workplace, where I would need to stay for eight hours—eight big hours outside my home—was unfeasible.

"Seven hundred's fine then," I said.

"Excellent. And there'll be a lot of collectors there, so bring any souvenirs, uh, items from your childhood you might want to sell. You could leave with $2,000, easy. Letters especially. The more personal the better, obviously. Anything dated near the murders. January 3, 1985." He recited it as if he'd said it often. "Anything from your mom. People are really . . . fascinated by your mom."

People always were. They always wanted to know: What kind of woman gets slaughtered by her own son?

Patty Day

He was talking on the phone again, she could hear the cartoonish *mwaMWAwa* of his voice murmuring behind his door. He'd wanted an extension of his own—half his schoolmates, he swore, had their own listings in the phone book. They were called Children's Lines. She'd laughed and then got pissed because *he* got pissed at her for laughing. (Seriously, a children's phone line? How spoiled were these kids?) Neither of them mentioned it again—they were both easily embarrassed—and then a few weeks later he'd just come home, head tucked down, and showed her the contents of a shopping bag: a line splitter that would allow two phones to use the same extension and a remarkably light plastic phone that didn't seem much different from the pink toy versions the girls used to play secretary. "Mr. Benjamin Day's office," they'd answer, trying to pull their older brother into the game. Ben used to smile and tell them to take a message; lately he just ignored them.

Since Ben brought home his goodies, the phrase "goddang phone cord" had been introduced to the Day home. The cord corkscrewed from the kitchen outlet, over the counter, down the hall, and crimped under the crack of his door, which was always closed.

Someone tripped on the cord at least once a day, and this would be followed by a scream (if it was one of the girls) or a curse (if it was Patty or Ben). She'd asked him repeatedly to secure the cord against the wall, and he'd just as repeatedly failed to do it. She tried to tell herself this was normal teenage stubbornness, but for Ben it was aggressive, and it made her worry he was angry, or lazy, or something worse she hadn't even thought of. And who was he talking to? Before the mysterious addition of the second phone, Ben hardly ever got calls. He had two good friends, the Muehler brothers, overalled Future Farmers of America who were so reticent they sometimes just hung up when she answered—and then Patty would tell Ben that Jim or Ed just called. But there had never been long conversations behind closed doors until now.

Patty suspected her son finally had a girlfriend, but her few hints in that direction made Ben so uncomfortable his pale skin turned blue-white and his amber freckles actually glowed, like a warning. She'd backed off completely. She wasn't the kind of mother to jam open her kids' lives too wide—it was hard enough for a fifteen-year-old boy to get privacy in a house full of women. He'd installed a padlock on his door after he'd returned home from school one day to find Michelle squirreling through his desk drawers. The lock installation, too, was presented as a done-deal: A hammer, some banging, and there it suddenly was. His own boy-nest, secured. Again, she couldn't blame him. The farmhouse had gone girly in the years since Runner left. The curtains, the couches, even the candles were all apricot and lace. Little pink shoes and flowered undies and barrettes cluttered drawers and closets. Ben's few small assertions—the curlicue phone cord and the metallic, manly lock—seemed understandable, actually.

She heard a shot of laughter coming from behind his door, and it unnerved her. Ben wasn't a laugher, not even as a kid. At age eight he'd looked at one of his sisters coolly and announced, "Michelle has a case of the giggles," as if it was something to be fixed. Patty described him as stoic, but his self-containment went beyond that. His dad certainly didn't know what to do with him, alternating between roughhousing (Ben stiff and unresponsive as Runner crocodile-rolled him on the floor) and recrimination (Runner complaining loudly that the kid was no fun, weird, girlish). Patty hadn't fared much better. She'd recently bought a book about mothering a teenage boy, which she'd hidden under her bed like pornography. The author said to be brave, ask questions, demand answers from your child, but Patty couldn't. Much more than a graze of a question pissed Ben off these days, triggered that unbearably loud silence from him. The more she tried to figure him out, the more he hid. In his room. Talking to people she didn't know.

Her three daughters were already awake too, had been for hours. A farm, even their pathetic, overleveraged, undervalued one, demanded early rising, and the routine stuck through the winter. They were now fluffing around in the snow. She'd shooed them out like a pack of puppies so they wouldn't wake up Ben, then got annoyed when she heard his voice on the phone, realized he was already up. She knew that was the reason she was fixing pancakes, the girls' favorite. Even the score. Ben and the girls were always accusing her of taking sides—Ben forever being asked to have patience with the small, ribboned creatures, the girls forever being begged to hush now, don't bother your brother. Michelle, at ten, was the oldest daughter, Debby was nine, and Libby seven. ("Jesus, Mom, it's like you dropped a litter," she could hear Ben admonish.) She peeked out a filmy curtain to view the girls in their natural animal state: Michelle and Debby, boss and assistant, constructing a snow fort from plans they hadn't bothered to share with Libby; Libby trying to nose into the side of the action, offering snowballs and rocks and a long, waggly stick, each rejected with barely a glance. Finally Libby bent at the legs for a good scream, then kicked the whole thing down. Patty turned away—fists and tears were next, and she wasn't in the mood.

Ben's door creaked open, and his heavy thumps at the end of the hall told her he was wearing those big black boots she hated. Don't even look at them, she told herself. She said the same thing whenever he wore his camo pants. ("Dad wore camo pants," he sulked when she'd complained. "Hunting, he wore them hunting," she'd corrected.) She missed the kid who used to demand unflashy clothes, who wore only jeans and plaid button-downs. The boy with dark red curls and an obsession with airplanes. Here he came now, in black denim jacket, black jeans, and a thermal hat pulled down low. He mumbled something and aimed for the door.

"Not before breakfast," she called. He checked, turned only his profile to her.

"I gotta get a few things done."

"That's fine, have some breakfast with us."

"I hate pancakes. You know that." Dammit.

"I'll make you something else. Sit." He wouldn't defy a direct order, would he? They stared each other down, Patty about to give in, when Ben sighed pointedly, then slumped onto a chair. He started fiddling with the salt shaker, pouring the granules on the table and plowing them into a pile. She almost told him not to do it, but stopped. It was enough for now that he was at the table.

"Who were you talking to?" she asked, pouring him some orange juice she knew he'd leave untouched to spite her.

"Just some people."

"People, plural?"

He only raised his eyebrows.

The screen door scissored open, then the front door banged against the wall, and she could hear a series of boots tumbling onto the floor mat—well-trained, untracking daughters that they were. The fight must have been settled quickly. Michelle and Debby were already bickering about some cartoon on TV. Libby just marched right in and hurled herself on a chair next to Ben, shook some ice off her hair. Of Patty's three daughters, only Libby knew how to disarm Ben: She smiled up at him, gave a quick wave, and then stared straight ahead.

"Hey, Libby," he said, still sifting salt.

"Hey, Ben. I like your salt mountain."

"Thanks."

Patty could see Ben visibly re-shell himself when the other two entered the kitchen, their bright, harsh voices splattering the corners of the room.

"Mom, Ben's making a mess," Michelle called out.

"It's fine, sweetie, pancakes are almost ready. Ben, eggs?"

"Why does Ben get eggs?" Michelle whined.

"Ben, eggs?"

"Yeah."

"I want eggs," Debby said.

"You don't even like eggs," Libby snapped. She could always be depended on to side with her brother. "Ben needs eggs cause he's a boy. A man."

That made Ben smile the slightest bit, which made Patty select the most perfectly round pancake for Libby. She piled the cakes onto plates while the eggs spat at her, the fine calibrations of breakfast for five going surprisingly well. It was the last of the decent food, left over from Christmas, but she wouldn't worry right now. After breakfast, she'd worry.

"Mom, Debby has her elbows on the table." Michelle, in her bossy mode.

"Mom, Libby didn't wash her hands." Michelle again.

"Neither did you." Debby.

"Nobody did." Libby laughing.

"Dirty bugger," Ben said, and poked her in her side. It was some old joke with them, that phrase. Patty didn't know how it had started. Libby tilted her head back and laughed harder, a stage laugh designed to please Ben.

"Mother hugger," Libby giggled wetly, some sort of response.

Patty soaped up a rag and passed it around to each so they could all stay seated at the table. Ben bothering to tease one of his sisters was a rare event, and it seemed like she could hold on to the good mood if everyone just stayed in their place. She needed the good mood, the way you need sleep after an all-nighter, the way you daydream of throwing yourself into bed. Every day she woke up and swore she wouldn't let the farm weigh her down, wouldn't let the ruination of it (three years she was behind in the loan, three *years* and no way out) turn her into the kind of woman she hated: mirthless, pinched, unable to enjoy anything. Every morning she'd crick herself down onto the flimsy rug by her bed and pray, but it was actually a promise: *Today I won't yell, I won't cry, I won't clench up into a ball like I am waiting for a blow to level me. I will enjoy today.* She might make it to lunch before she went sour.

They were all set now, everyone washed, a quick prayer, and all was fine until Michelle spouted up.

"Ben needs to take off his hat."

The Day family had always had a no-hat rule at the table, it was such a non-negotiable regulation that Patty was surprised to even have to address it.

"Ben does need to take off his hat," Patty said, her voice a gentle prod.

Ben tilted his head toward her and she felt a pinch of worry. Something was wrong. His eyebrows, normally thin rusty lines, were black, the skin beneath stained a dark purple.

"Ben?"

He took off his hat, and on his head was a jet-black crown of hair, ruffed like an old Labrador. It was such a shock, like swallowing ice water too quickly, her red-headed boy, Ben's defining characteristic, gone. He looked older. Mean. As if this kid in front of her had bullied the Ben she knew into oblivion.

Michelle screamed, Debby burst into tears.

"Ben, sweetheart, why?" Patty said. She was telling herself not to overreact, but that was just what she was doing. This stupid teenage act—that's all it was—made her entire relationship with her son feel suddenly hopeless. As Ben stared down at the table, smirking, force-fielding himself from their female commotion, Patty worked up an excuse for him. He'd hated his red hair as a kid, been teased for it. Maybe he still was. Maybe this was an act of assertion. A positive thing. Then again, it was Patty who'd given Ben her red hair, which he'd just obliterated. How was that not a rejection? Libby, her only other redhead, clearly thought so. She sat holding a piece of her hair between two skinny fingers, staring at it morosely.

"All right," Ben said, slurping an egg and standing up. "Enough drama. It's just stupid hair."

"Your hair was so handsome, though."

He paused at that, as if he was really considering it. Then shook his head—at her comment, at the whole morning, she didn't know—and stomped toward the door.

"Just calm down," he called without turning around. "I'll be back later."

She was guessing he'd slam the door, but instead he shut it quietly, and that seemed worse. Patty blew at her bangs and glanced around the table at all the wide blue eyes, watching her to see how to react. She smiled and gave a weak laugh.

"Well, that was weird," she offered. The girls perked up a bit, visibly sitting higher in their chairs.

"He's so weird," Michelle added.

"His hair matches his clothes now," Debby said, wiping her tears on the back of her hand, and forking some pancake into her mouth.

Libby just looked at her plate, shoulders caved in toward the table. It was a look of dejection only a kid could pull off.

"It's OK, Lib," Patty said, and tried to pat her casually without getting the other girls going again.

"No it's not," she said. "He *hates* us."

Libby Day

Five nights after my beer with Lyle, I drove down the bluff from my house, and then down some more, into the trough of Kansas City's West Bottoms. The neighborhood had thrived back in the stockyard era and then spent many decades the-opposite-of-thriving. Now it was all tall, quiet brick buildings, bearing names of companies that no longer existed: Raftery Cold Storage, London Beef, Dannhauser Cattle Trust. A few reclaimed structures had been converted into professional haunted houses that lit up for the Halloween season: five-story slides and vampire castles and drunk teenagers hiding beers inside letter jackets.

In early March, the place was just lonesome. As I drove through the still streets, I'd occasionally spot someone entering or leaving a building, but I had no idea what for. Near the Missouri River the area turned from semi-empty to ominously vacant, an upright ruin.

I felt a bulb of unease as I parked in front of a four-story building labeled Tallman Corporation. This was one of those moments where I wished I had more friends. Or, friends. I should have someone with me. Barring that, I should have someone who'd be waiting to hear from me. As it was, I'd left a note on the stairs inside my house, explaining where I was, with Lyle's letter attached. If I disappeared, the cops would have a place to start. Of course, if I had a friend, maybe the friend would tell me, *No way am I letting you do that, sweetie,* the way women always said things, in that protective voice.

Or maybe not. The murders had left me permanently off-kilter in these kinds of judgment calls. I assumed everything bad in the world could happen, because everything bad in the world already did happen. But, then, weren't the chances minuscule that I, Libby Day, would meet harm on top of it? Wasn't I safe by default? A shiny, indestructible statistic. I can't decide, so I veer between drastic overcaution (sleeping with the lights on at all times, my mom's old Colt Peacemaker on my bedside table) to ridiculous incaution (venturing by myself to a Kill Club in a vacant building).

I was wearing boots with big heels, to give myself another few inches, the right one fitting much looser than the other because of my bad foot. I wanted to crack every bone in my body, loosen things up. I was tight. Pissed, my teeth gritted. No one should need money this badly. I'd tried to cast what I was doing in an inoffensive light, and in brief flashes over the past day, I'd turned myself into something noble. These people were interested in my family, I was proud of my family, and I was allowing these strangers some insight they wouldn't otherwise have. And if they wanted to offer me money, I'd take it, I wasn't too good for that.

In truth though, I wasn't proud of my family. No one had ever liked the Days. My dad, Runner Day, was crazy, drunk, and violent in an unimpressive way—a small man with sneaky fists. My mom had four kids she couldn't take proper care of. Poor, farm-bust kids, smelly and manipulative, always showing up at school in need: breakfast skipped, shirts ripped, snotty and strep-throat ridden. Me and my two sisters had been the cause of at least four lice infestations in our short grade-school experience. Dirty Days.

And here I was, twenty-some years later, still showing up to places, needing things. Money, specifically. In the back pocket of my jeans was a note Michelle had written me a month before the murders. She'd ripped it from a spiral notebook, the fringe carefully trimmed away, then folded it elaborately into the shape of an arrow.

It talked about the usual things that filled Michelle's fourth-grade mind: a boy in her class, her dumb teacher, some ugly designer jeans that some spoiled girl got for her birthday. It was boring, unmemorable—I had boxes of this stuff I crated from house to house and never opened until now. I'd need $200 for it. I had a quick, guilty burst of glee when I thought of all the other crap I could sell, notes and photos and junk I'd never had the balls to throw out. I got out of my car and took a breath, popped my neck.

The night was cold, with balmy pockets of spring here and there. An enormous yellow moon hung in the sky like a Chinese lamp.

I climbed the soiled marble stairs, dirty leaves crunching beneath my boots, an unwholesome, old-bones sound. The doors were a thick, weighty metal. I knocked, waited, knocked three more times, standing exposed in the moonglow like a heckled vaudevillian. I was about to phone Lyle on my cell when the door swung open, a tall, long-faced guy looking me up and down.

"Yeah?"

"Uh, is Lyle Wirth here?"

"Why would Lyle Wirth be here?" he said without a smile. Screwing with me because he could.

"Oh, fuck you," I blurted, and turned away, feeling idiotic. I got three steps when the guy called after me.

"Jeez, wait, don't get bent out of shape."

But I was born bent out of shape. I could picture myself coming out of the womb crooked and wrong. It never takes much for me to lose patience. The phrase *fuck you* may not rest on the tip of my tongue, but it's near. Midtongue.

I paused, straddled between two steps, heading down.

"Look, I know Lyle Wirth, obviously," the guy said. "You on the guest list or something?"

"I don't know. My name's Libby Day."

He dropped his jaw, pulled it back up with a spitty sound, and gave me that same checklist look that Lyle had given me.

"Your hair's blond."

I raised my eyebrows at him.

"Come in, I'll take you down," he said, opening the door wide. "Come on, I won't bite."

There are few phrases that annoy me more than *I won't bite.* The only line that pisses me off faster is when some drunk, ham-faced dude in a bar sees me trying to get past him and barks: *Smile, it can't be that bad!* Yeah, actually, it can, jackwad.

I headed back up, rolling my eyes goonily at the door-guy, walking extra slow so he had to lean against the door to keep it open. Asshole.

I entered a cavelike foyer, lined with broken lamp fixtures made of brass and shaped to look like stalks of wheat. The room was more than forty feet high. The ceiling had once been painted with a mural—vague, chipped images of country boys and girls hoeing or digging. One girl, her face now vanished, looked like she might be holding a jump rope. Or a snake? The entire western corner of the ceiling had caved in at some point: where the mural's oak tree should have exploded into green summer leaves, there was instead a patch of blue night sky. I could see the glow of the moon but not the moon itself. The foyer remained dark, electricity-free, but I could just make out piles of trash swept into the corners of the room. The partygoers had hustled off the squatters, then taken a broom to the place, tried to spiff it up. It smelled like piss anyway. An ancient condom was spaghetti-stuck to one wall.

"You guys couldn't have sprung for, like, a banquet hall?" I mumbled. The marble floor hummed beneath me. Clearly all the action was happening downstairs.

"We're not exactly a welcome convention," the guy said. He had a young, fleshy face with moles. He wore a tiny turquoise stud earring I always associated with Dungeons and Dragons types. Men who own ferrets and think magic tricks are cool. "Plus this building has a certain . . . ambiance. One of the Tallmans blew his brains out here in 1953."

"Nice."

We stood looking at each other, his face shapeshifting in the gloom. I couldn't see any obvious way to get downstairs. The elevator banks to the left were clearly not working, their tarnished counters all frozen between floors. I pictured a workforce of ghost-men in business suits waiting patiently to start moving again.

"So . . . are we going anywhere?"

"Oh. Yeah. Look I just wanted to say . . . I'm sorry for your loss. I'm sure even after all this time . . . I just can't imagine. That's like, something out of Edgar Allan Poe. What happened."

"I try not to think about it much," I said, the standard answer.

The guy laughed. "Well, you're in the wrong place, then."

He led me around the corner and down a hallway of former offices. I crunched broken glass, peering into each room as we passed: empty, empty, a shopping cart, a careful pile of feces, the remains of an old bonfire, and then a homeless man who said *Hiya!* cheerfully over a forty-ounce.

"His name's Jimmy," the kid said. "He seemed OK, so we let him stay."

How gracious, I thought, but just nodded at Jimmy. We reached a heavy firewall of a door, opened it, and I was assaulted by the noise. From the basement came competing sounds of organ music and heavy metal and the loud hum of people trying to yell over each other.

"After you," he said. I didn't move. I don't like people behind me. "Or, I can . . . uh, this way."

I thought about retreating right then, but the nastiness reared up in me when I pictured this guy, this fucking Renaissance Fest *juggler,* going down and telling his friends: *She freaked, she just ran away!* And them all laughing and feeling tough. And him adding: *She's really different from what I thought she'd be.* And holding his hand up about yay-high to show how little I'd stayed. Fuckyoufuckyoufuckyou, I chanted, and followed him.

We walked down the one floor to a basement door plastered with flyers: Booth 22: Hoardin' Lizzie Borden! Collectible items for sale or swap! Booth 28: Karla Brown—Bite Marks Discussion. Booth 14: Role Play—Interrogate Casey Anthony! 15: Tom's Terrible Treats—Now serving Jonestown Punch and Sweet Fanny Adams!

Then I saw a grainy blue flyer with a xeroxed photo of me in one corner: Talk About a Bad *Day*! The Kinnakee Kansas Farmhouse Massacre—Case Dissection and a Special, Special GUEST!!!

Again I debated leaving, but the door flung open and I was sucked inside a humid, windowless basement crowded with maybe two hundred people, all leaning into each other, yelling in ears, hands on shoulders. At school once, they showed us a film strip of a grasshopper plague hitting the Midwest, and that's what I flashed to—all those goggling eyes looking at me, mouths chewing, arms and elbows askew. The room was set up like a swap meet, divided into rows of booths created from cheap chain-link fencing. Each booth was a different murder. I counted maybe forty at first glance. A generator was barely igniting a string of lightbulbs, which hung from wires around the room, swaying in uneven time, illuminating faces at gruesome angles, a party of death masks.

On the other side, Lyle spotted me and started arrowing through the crowd, leading with a shoulder, scooting along sideways. Glad-handing. He was, apparently, an important guy in this crowd—everyone wanted to touch him, tell him something. He leaned down to let some guy whisper in his dainty ear, and when he pulled himself upright, his head hit a flashlight, and everyone around him laughed, their faces glowing off and on as the light rotated like a police car's. Men's faces. Guys' faces. There were only a few women in the entire place—four that I could see, all bespectacled, homely. The men were not attractive either. There were whiskery, professorial fellows; non-descript, suburban-dad types; and a goodly amount of guys in their twenties with cheap haircuts and math-nerd glasses, men who reminded me of Lyle and the guy who'd led me downstairs. Unremarkable, but with a brainy arrogance wafting from them. Call it AP aftershave.

Lyle reached me, the men behind him grinning at his back, studying me like I was the new girlfriend. He shook his head. "Sorry, Libby. Kenny was supposed to phone my cell when you got here so I could bring you down myself." He eyed Kenny over my head and Kenny made a shruggy noise and left. Lyle was steering me into the crowd, using an assertive finger to the back of my shoulder. Some people were wearing costumes. A man with a black waistcoat and tall black hat pushed past me, offering me sweets and laughing. Lyle rolled his eyes at me, said, "Frederick Baker freak. We've been trying to push out the role players for the past few years, but . . . too many guys are into that."

"I don't know what that means," I said, worried I was about to lose it. Elbows and shoulders were jostling me, I kept getting pushed back every few feet I moved forward. "I really, seriously, don't understand what the fuck is going on."

Lyle sighed impatiently, looked at his watch. "Look, our session doesn't start til midnight. You want me to walk you around, explain more?"

"I want my money."

He chewed at his lower lip, pulled an envelope out of his back pocket, and stuck it in my hand as he leaned into my ear and asked me to count it later. It felt fat, and I calmed down a bit.

"Let me show you around." We walked the perimeter of the room, cramped booths on our left and right, all that metal fencing reminding me of kennels. Lyle put that finger on my arm again, prodding me onward. "The Kill Club—and by the way, don't lecture, we know it's a bad name, it just stuck. But the Kill Club, we call it KC, that's one reason we have the big meeting here every year, Kansas City, KC, Kill Club . . . uh, like I said, it's basically for solvers. And enthusiasts. Of famous murders. Everyone from, like Fanny Adams to—"

"Who is Fanny Adams?" I snapped, realizing I was about to get jealous. I was supposed to be the special one here.

"She was an eight-year-old, got chopped to bits in England in 1867. That guy we just passed, with the top hat and stuff, he was playing at being her murderer, Frederick Baker."

"That's really sick." So she'd been dead forever. That was good. No competition.

"Well, that was a pretty notorious murder." He caught me grimacing. "Yeah, like I said, they're a less palatable section. I mean, most of those murders have already been solved, there's no real mystery. To me, it's all about the solving. We have former cops, lawyers—"

"Are there role players for . . . mine? My family, are there role players here?" A beefy guy with highlighted hair and an inflatable doll in a red dress paused in the crowd, nearly on top of me, not even noticing me. The doll's plastic fingers tickled my cheek. Someone behind me yelled *Scott and Amber*! I pushed the guy off me, tried to scan the crowd for anyone dressed as my mother, as Ben, some bastard in a red wig, brandishing an axe. My hand had balled into a fist.

"No, no of course not," Lyle said. "No way, Libby, I would never let that happen, the role play . . . it. No."

"Why is it all men?" In one of the booths nearby, two tubby guys in polo shirts were snarling at each other over some child murders in the Missouri bootheel.

"It's not all men," Lyle said, defensive. "Most of the solvers are men, but I mean, go to a crossword-puzzle convention and you'll see the same thing. Women come for the, like, networking. They talk about why they identify with the victims—they've had abusive husbands or whatnot—they have some coffee, buy an old photo. But we've had to be more careful because sometimes they can get too . . . attached."

"Yeah, better not get too human about it," I said, me being a fucking hypocrite.

Thankfully Lyle ignored me. "Like, right now, they're all obsessed with the Lisette Stephens thing." He motioned back behind him, where a small cluster of women were huddled around a computer, necks stretched downward, henlike. I moved past Lyle toward the booth. They were all looking at a video montage of Lisette. Lisette and her sorority sisters. Lisette and her dog. Lisette and her look-alike sister.

"See what I mean?" Lyle said. "They're not solving, they're just looking at stuff they could see online at home."

The problem with Lisette Stephens was there was nothing to solve: She had no boyfriend, no husband, no upset coworkers, no strange ex-cons doing repair work in her home. She just vanished for no reason anyone could think of, except she was pretty. She was the kind of girl people noticed. The kind of girl the media bothered to cover when she disappeared.

I nudged into a spot next to a stack of sweatshirts bearing iron-on decals that read Bring Lisette Home. Twenty-five bucks. The group, however, was more interested in the laptop. The women clicked through the website's message boards. People often attached photos with their notes, but the photos were jarring. "We love you Lisette, we know you will come home," popped up alongside a picture of three middle-aged women at the beach. "Peace and love to your family in this time of need," surfaced next to a photo of someone's

Labradoodle. The women returned to the homepage, and up came the picture the media liked the most: Lisette and her mother, both arms wrapped around each other, cheek-to-cheek, beaming.

I shrugged, trying to ignore my worry about Lisette, who I didn't know. And also fighting the jealousy again. Out of all these murders, I wanted the Day booth to be the biggest. It was a blush of love: my dead people were the best. I had a flash of my mother, her red hair tied back in a ponytail, helping me tug off my flimsy winter boots, and then rubbing my toes one by one. *Warming up big toe, warming up baby toe.* In this memory, I could smell buttered toast, but I don't know if there was buttered toast. In this memory I still had all my toes.

I shivered hard, like a cat.

"Wow, someone walk over your grave?" Lyle said, and then realized the irony.

"So what else?" We hit a traffic jam of people in front of a booth marked Bob's Bizarre Bazaar, manned by a guy wearing an oversized black mustache and slurping soup. Four skulls lined up on a plank behind him with a sign that read The Final Four. The guy was hollering at Lyle to introduce him to his little friend. Lyle started to wave him off, tried to pull us through the milling crowd, then shrugged, whispered *role player* to me.

" 'Bob Berdella,' " Lyle said to the man, making a winky joke of the name, "this is Libby Day, whose family was . . . of the Kinnakee Kansas Farmhouse Massacre. The Days."

The guy leaned across the table at me, a drooly piece of hamburger hanging off his tooth. "If you had a cock, you'd be in pieces in my garbage right now," he said and then gunned out a laugh. "Little, tiny pieces."

He swatted at me. I skittered back involuntarily, then I lurched back toward Bob, my fist up, rageful, as I always got when I had a fright. Go for the nose, make him bleed, smack that piece of chili meat right off his face, then hit him again. Before I could get to him, Bob shoved his seat back, hands up, muttering not to me but to Lyle, *dude I was only playing, no harm, man.* He didn't even look at me as he apologized, like I was some child. As he yammered at Lyle, I went for him. My fist couldn't quite connect, so I ended up giving him a hard smack against his chin, the way you'd punish a puppy.

"Fuck you, asshole."

Then Lyle snapped to, muttering apologies and steering me away, my fists still tight, my jaw set. I kicked Bob's table with my boot as I walked away, just enough so it wobbled once, severely, and dumped the guy's soup on the floor. I was already regretting that I hadn't just shot over the table. Nothing more embarrassing than a short woman who can't land a punch. I might as well have been carried away, my feet baby-kicking in the air. I glanced behind us. The guy just stood there, his arms slack, his chin pink, trying to decide if he was contrite or angry.

"OK, that wouldn't have been the first fistfight at Kill Club, but it might have been the weirdest," Lyle said.

"I don't like being threatened."

"He wasn't really . . . I know, I know," Lyle muttered. "Like I said, at some point these role-play guys will splinter off and leave the serious solvers alone. You'll like the people in our group, the Day group."

"Is it the Day group, or the Kinnakee Kansas Farmhouse Massacre group?" I grumbled.

"Oh. Yeah, that's what we call it." He tried to squirm through another bottleneck in the cramped aisle, ended up smushed to my side. My face was stuck just a few inches shy of a man's back. Blue oxford shirt, starched. I kept my eyes on the perfect center crease. Someone with a big hobo-clown gut was pushing me steadily from behind.

"Most people work Satan in there somehow," I said. "Satan Farmhouse Massacre. Kansas Satan Killings."

"Yeah, we don't really believe that, so we try not to use any Devil references. Excuse me!" he said, wriggling ahead.

"So it's a branding issue," I sniped, eyes fixed on the blue shirt. We pushed around a corner into the coolness of open space.

"Do you want to see any more groups?" He pointed to his immediate left, toward a bunch of men in Booth 31: quickie haircuts, a few mustaches, a lot of button-downs. They were arguing intensely at a low volume. "These guys are pretty cool, actually," Lyle said.

"They're basically creating their own mystery: They think they've identified a serial killer. Some guy has been crossing states— Missouri, Kansas, Oklahoma—and helping to kill people. Family men, or older people sometimes, who got trapped with too much debt, credit cards maxed out, subprime mortgages, no way out."

"He kills people because they aren't good with money?" I said, rolling my eyes.

"Nah, nah. They think he's like a Kevorkian for people who have bad credit and good life insurance. They call him the Angel of Debt."

One of the Booth 31 members, a young guy with a jutting mandible and lips that didn't quite cover his teeth, was eavesdropping and eagerly turned to Lyle: "We think we've got the Angel in Iowa last month: a guy with a McMansion and four kids has a picture-perfect snowmobile accident at a really convenient time. That's like one a month the past year. Economy, man."

The kid was about to keep going, wanting to pull us into the booth, with its charts and calendars and news clippings and a messy nut-mix that was scattered all over the table, the men grabbing over-flowing handfuls, pretzels and peanuts bouncing down to their sneakers. I shook my head at Lyle, steered him away for a change. Out in the aisle, I took a breath of unsalted air and looked at my watch.

"Right," said Lyle. "It's a lot to take in. Let's head over. You really will appreciate our group, I think. It's much more serious. Look, there are already people there." He pointed toward a tidy corner booth, where a fat, frizz-haired woman was sipping coffee out of a jug-sized Styrofoam cup, and two trim, middle-aged men were scanning the room, hands on hips, ignoring her. Looked like cops. Behind them, an older, balding guy sat hunched at a card table, scribbling notes on a legal pad, while a tense college-aged kid read over his shoulder. A handful of nondescript men crowded toward the back, flipping through stacks of manila file folders or just loitering.

"See, more women," Lyle said triumphantly, pointing at the frizz-haired female mountain. "You want to go over now, or do you want to wait and make a big entrance?"

"Now's fine."

"This is a sharp group, serious fans. You're going to like them. I bet you'll even learn a few things from them."

I humphed and followed Lyle over. The woman looked up first, narrowed her eyes at me, then widened them. She was holding a homemade folder on which she'd pasted an old junior-high photo of me wearing a gold-heart necklace someone had mailed me. The woman looked like she wanted to hand the folder to me—she was holding it like a theater program. I didn't reach out. I noticed she'd drawn Devil horns on my head.

Lyle put an arm on my shoulder, then took it off. "Hi, everyone. Our special guest has arrived, and she's the star of this year's Kill Convention—Libby Day."

A few eyebrows raised, several heads nodded appreciatively, one of the cop-looking guys said, *holy shit.* He was about to give Lyle a high-five and then thought better: his arm froze in an accidental Nazi salute. The older man darted his eyes away from me and scribbled more notes. I worried for a moment I was supposed to make a speech—instead I mumbled a tart hello and sat down at the table.

There were the usual greetings, questions. Yes, I lived in Kansas City, no, I was sort of between jobs, no, I didn't have any contact with Ben. Yes, he wrote me a few times a year but I tossed the envelopes straight into the trash. No, I wasn't curious what he wrote. Yes, I'd be willing to sell the next one I got.

"Well," Lyle finally interrupted with a grandiose rumble. "You have here in front of you a key figure in the Day case, a so-called eyewitness, so why don't we move on to real questions?"

"I have a real question," said one of the cop-looking guys. He gave a half-twist smile and turned in his chair. "If you don't mind me cutting to the chase."

He actually waited for me to say I didn't mind.

"Why did you testify that Ben killed your family?"

"Because he did," I said. "I was there."

"You were hiding, sweetheart. No way you saw what you say you did, or you'd be dead, too."

"I saw what I saw," I began, the way I always did.

"Bullshit. You saw what they told you to see because you were a good, scared little girl who wanted to help. The prosecution screwed you up royally. They used you to nail the easiest target. Laziest police work I ever seen."

"I was in the house . . ."

"Yeah, how do you explain the gunshots your mom died from?" the guy hammered, leaning forward on his knees. "Ben didn't have any residue on his hands—"

"Guys, guys," the older man interrupted, waving thick, crimped fingers. "And ladies," he added, greasily, nodding at me and the Frizz-Head Woman. "We haven't even presented the facts of the case. We have to have protocol or this might as well be some Internet chat session. When we have a guest like this, we should be particularly sure we're all on the same page."

No one disagreed more than a grumble's worth, so the old guy wet his lips, looked over his bifocals and rearranged some throat phlegm. The man was authoritative, yet somehow unwholesome. I pictured him at home by himself, eating canned peaches at the kitchen counter, smacking at the syrup. He began reciting from his notes.

"Fact: Somewhere around 2 a.m. on January 3, 1985, a person or persons killed three members of the Day family in their farmhouse in Kinnakee, Kansas. The deceased include Michelle Day, age ten; Debby Day, age nine; and the family matriarch, Patty Day, age thirty-two. Michelle Day was strangled; Debby Day died of axe wounds, Patty Day of two shotgun wounds, axe wounds, and deep cuts from a Bowie hunting knife."

I felt the blood rush in my ears, and told myself I wasn't hearing anything new. Nothing to panic about. I never really listened to the details of the murder. I'd let the words run over my brain and out my ears, like a terrified cancer patient hearing all that coded jargon and understanding nothing, except that it was very bad news.

"Fact," the man continued. "Youngest child Libby Day, age seven, was in the house at the time, and escaped the killer or killers through a window in her mother's room.

"Fact: Oldest child Benjamin Day, fifteen, claims he was out sleeping in a neighbor's barn that night after an argument with his mother. He has never produced another alibi, and his demeanor with the police was extremely unhelpful. He was subsequently arrested and convicted, based largely on rumors within the community that he'd become involved in Satan worship—the walls of the house were covered in symbols and words associated with Devil worship. In his mother's blood."

The old man paused for dramatic effect, eyed the group, returned to his notes.

"More damning was the fact his surviving sister, Libby, testified that she *saw* him commit the murders. Despite Libby's confused testimony and young age, Ben Day was convicted. This *despite a startling lack of physical evidence.* We convene to explore other possibilities and to debate the merits of the case. What I think we can agree on is that the killings can be traced to the events of January 2, 1985. It all went wrong in a single day—no pun intended." Murmurs of laughter, guilty looks toward me. "When that family got up that morning, it wasn't like there was a hit on them. Something went really wrong *that day.*"

Part of a crime-scene photo had slid out of the speaker's folder: a plump, bloody leg and part of a lavender nightgown. Debby. The man noticed my gaze and tucked it back in, like it wasn't my business.

"I think the general consensus is that Runner Day did it," the fat woman said, rummaging in her purse, wadded tissues falling out the side of it.

I started at the sound of my dad's name. Runner Day. Miserable man.

"I mean, right?" she continued. "He goes to Patty, tries to bully her for money, as usual, gets nothing, gets pissed, goes haywire. I mean, the guy was crazy, right?"

The woman produced a bottle and popped two aspirin the way people in the movies did, with a sharp, violent throwback of the head. Then she looked at me for confirmation.

"Yeah. I think so. I don't remember him that well. They divorced when I was, like, two. We didn't have much contact after. He came back and lived with us for a summer, the summer before the murders, but—"

"Where's he now?"

"I don't know."

She rolled her eyes at me.

"But what about the big guy's footprint?" said a man in the back.

"The police never explained why a man's dress shoe shows up tracking blood in a house where no men wore dress shoes . . ."

"The police never explained a lot," started the older guy.

"Like the random bloodstain," Lyle added. He turned to me. "There was a bloodstain on Michelle's bedsheets—and it was a different blood type than anyone in the family. Unfortunately the sheets were from Goodwill, so the prosecution claimed the blood could have come from anyone."

"Gently used" sheets. Yes. The Days were big fans of Goodwill: sofa, TV, lamps, jeans, we even got our curtains there.

"Do you know how to find Runner?" the younger kid asked. "Could you ask him some questions for us?"

"And I still think it'd be worthwhile to question some of Ben's friends from the time. Do you still have any connections in Kinnakee?" said the old man.

Several people started arguing about Runner's gambling and Ben's friends and poor police procedure.

"Hey," I snapped. "What about Ben? Ben is just off the table?"

"Please, this is the grossest miscarriage of justice ever," said the fat lady. "And don't pretend you think otherwise. Unless you're protecting your daddy. Or you're too ashamed about what you did."

I glared at her. She had a glop of egg yolk in her hair. *Who ate eggs at midnight?* I thought. *Or had that been there since this morning?*

"Magda here is very involved with the case, very involved in the effort to free your brother," said the old guy, with a patronizing rise of his eyebrows.

"He's a wonderful man," Magda said, pointing her chin at me. "He writes poetry and music and he's just a force of hope. You should get to know him, Libby, you really should."

Magda was running her fingernails across a set of folders on the table before her, one for each Day family member. The thickest folder was covered with photos of my brother: Ben, red-headed and young, somberly holding a toy bomber; Ben, black-haired and scared in his mug shot after the arrest; Ben today, in prison, the red hair returned, studious looking, his mouth partly open, as if caught midsentence. Next to that was Debby's folder, bearing a single photo of her dressed as a gypsy for Halloween: red cheeks, red lips, her brown hair covered by my mom's red bandanna, a hip jutted to the side, pretend-sexy. To her right, you can see my freckled arm, reaching for her. It was a family photo, something I thought had never been released.

"Where'd you get that?" I asked her.

"Around." She covered the folder with a thick hand.

I looked down at the table, resisting the urge to lunge. The photograph of Debby's dead body had slipped out of the old guy's folder again. I could see the bloody leg, a sliced-up belly, an arm nearly off. I leaned across the table and grabbed the man's wrist.

"You put that shit away," I murmured. He tucked the photo away again, then held the folder shield-like, and blinked at me.

The group was all looking at me now, curious, a little concerned, like I was some pet bunny they just realized might be rabid.

"Libby," Lyle said in the soothing tones of a talk-show host. "No one doubts you were in the house. No one doubts you survived an incredibly horrific ordeal no child should ever endure. But did you really see with your own eyes what you say you saw? Or may you have been coached?"

I was picturing Debby, sifting my hair with nimble, pudgy fingers, braiding it in the fishbone style she insisted was more difficult than French braids, huffing warm baloney breath on the back of my neck. Tying a green ribbon on the end, turning me into a present. Helping me balance on the edge of the bathtub so I could hold a handmirror and see the back of my furrowed head in the looking glass over the sink. Debby, who so desperately wanted everything to be pretty.

"There's no proof that anyone but Ben killed my family," I said, pulling back to the land of the living, where I live by myself. "He never even filed an appeal, for Christsakes. He's never tried to get out." I had no experience with convicts, but it seemed to me that they were always launching appeals, that it was a passion for them, even if they had no shot. When I pictured prison, I pictured orange jumpsuits and yellow legal pads. Ben had proved himself guilty by sheer inertia—my testimony was beside the point.

"He had reason enough for eight appeals," Magda pronounced, grandly. I realized she was one of those women who would show up on my doorstep to scream at me. I was glad I'd never given Lyle my address. "Not fighting doesn't mean he's guilty, Libby, it means he's lost hope."

"Well, then good."

Lyle widened his eyes.

"Oh, God. You really think Ben did it." Then he laughed. Once, accidentally, quickly swallowed but entirely genuine. "Excuse me," he murmured.

No one laughs at me. Everything I say or do is taken very, very seriously. No one mocks a victim. I am not a figure of mirth. "Well, you all enjoy your conspiracy theories," I said, and bumped up from the chair.

"Oh don't be like that," said the cop-guy. "Stay. Convince us."

"He never . . . filed . . . an appeal," I said, like a preschool teacher. "That's good enough for me."

"Then you're an idiot."

I flipped him off, a hard gesture like I was digging into cold earth. Then I turned away, someone behind me saying, "She's still a little liar."

I darted back into the crowd, pushing my way under armpits and past groins until I arrived back into the cool of the stairwell, the noise behind me. My only victory of the night was the wad of money in my pocket and the knowledge that these people were as pathetic as I was.

I GOT HOME, turned every light on, and got into bed with a bottle of sticky rum. I lay sideways, studying the intricate folds of Michelle's note, which I'd forgotten to sell.

THE NIGHT FELT tilted. Like the world had once been carefully parceled out between people who believed Ben guilty and people who believed him innocent, and now, those twelve strangers crunched in a booth in a downtown basement had scrambled over to the side of the innocent with bricks in their pockets, and—boom!— that's where all the weight was now. Magda and Ben and poetry and a force of hope. Footprints and bloodstains and Runner going berserk. For the first time since Ben's trial, I had fully subjected myself to people who believed I was wrong about Ben, and it turns out I wasn't entirely up to the challenge. Me of little faith. On another night, I might have shrugged it all off, like I usually did. But those people were so assured, so dismissive, as if they'd discussed me countless times and decided I wasn't worth grilling that hard. I'd gone there assuming they'd be like people used to be: they might want to help me, take care of me, fix my problems. Instead they mocked me. Was I really that easy to unsettle, that flimsy?

No. I saw what I saw that night, I thought, my forever-mantra. Even though that wasn't true. The truth was I didn't see anything. OK? Fine. I technically saw nothing. I only heard. I only heard because I was hiding in a closet while my family died because I was a worthless little coward.

THAT NIGHT, THAT night, that night. I'd woken up in the dark in the room I shared with my sisters, the house so cold that frost was on the inside of the window. Debby had gotten in bed with me at some point—we usually jammed in together for warmth—and her plump behind was pushed into my stomach, pressing me against the chilled wall. I'd been a sleepwalker since I could toddle, so I don't remember pulling myself over Debby, but I do remember seeing Michelle asleep on the floor, her diary in her arms as usual, sucking on a pen in her sleep, the black ink drooling down her chin with her saliva. I hadn't bothered trying to wake her up, get her back in bed. Sleep was viciously defended in our loud, cold, crowded house, and not one of us woke without a fight. I left Debby in my bed and opened the door to hear voices down the hall in Ben's room—urgent whispers that bordered on noise. The sounds of people who think they're being quiet. A light coming from the crack under Ben's door. I decided to go to my mom's room, padded down the hall, pulled back her covers and pressed myself against my mother's back. In the winter, my mom slept in two pairs of sweats and several sweaters—she always felt like a giant stuffed animal. She usually didn't move when we got in bed with her, but that night I remember she turned to me so quickly I thought she was angry. Instead she grabbed me and squeezed me, kissed my forehead. Told me she loved me. She hardly ever told us she loved us. That's why I remember it, or think I do, unless I added that for comfort after the fact. But we'll say she told me she loved me, and that I fell immediately back to sleep.

When I next woke, it could have been minutes or hours later, she was gone. Outside the closed door, where I couldn't see, my mother was wailing and Ben was bellowing at her. There were other voices too; Debby was sobbing, screaming *Mommymommymom-mymichelle* and then there was the sound of an axe. I knew even then what it was. Metal on air—that was the sound—and after the sound of the swing came the sound of a soft thunk and a gurgle and Debby made a grunt and a sound like sucking for air. Ben screaming at my mom: "Why'd you make me do this?" And no sound from Michelle, which was strange, since Michelle was always the loudest, but nothing from her. Mom screaming *Run! Run! Don't Don't.* And a shotgun blast and my mom still yelling but no longer able to make words, just a screeching sound like a bird banging into the walls at the end of the hallway.

Heavy foot treads of boots and Debby's small feet running away, not dead yet, running toward my mom's room and me thinking *no, no, don't come here* and then boots shaking the hallway behind her and dragging and scratching at the floor and more gurgling, gurgling, banging and then a thud and the axe sound and my mom still making horrible cawing sounds, and me standing, frozen, in my mom's bedroom, just listening and the shotgun blasting my ears again and a thunk that rattled the floorboards beneath my feet. Me, coward, hoping everything would go away. Huddling half in and out of the closet, rocking myself. *Go away go away go away.* Doors banging and more footsteps and a wail, Ben whispering to himself, frantic. And then crying, a deep male crying and Ben's voice, I know it was Ben's voice, screaming *Libby! Libby!*

I opened a window in my mom's room and pushed myself through the broken screen, a breech birth onto the snowy ground just a few feet below, my socks immediately soaked, hair tangling in the bushes. I ran.

Libby! Looking back at the house, just a single light in a window, everything else black.

My feet were raw by the time I reached the pond and crouched in the reeds. I was wearing double layers like my mom, longjohns under my nightgown, but I was shaking, the wind ruffling the dress and blasting cold air straight up to my belly.

A flashlight frenetically scanned the tops of the reeds, then a copse of trees not far away, then the ground not far from me. *Libby!* Ben's voice again. Hunting me. *Stay where you are, sweetheart! Stay where you are!* The flashlight getting closer and closer, those boots crunching on the snow and me weeping hard into my sleeve, racking myself until I was almost ready to stand up and get it over with, and then the flashlight just swung back around and the footsteps marched away from me and I was there by myself, left to freeze to death in the dark. The light in the house went out and I stayed where I was.

Hours later, when I was too numb to stand upright, I crawled in the weak dawn light back to the house, my feet like ringing iron, my hands frozen in crow's fists. The door was wide open, and I limped inside. On the floor outside the kitchen was a sad little pile of vomit, peas and carrots. Everything else was red—sprays on the walls, puddles in the carpet, a bloody axe left upright on the arm of the sofa. I found my mom lying on the floor in front of her daughters' room, the top of her head shot off in a triangular slice, axe gashes through her bulky sleeping clothes, one breast exposed. Above her, long strings of red hair were stuck to the walls with blood and brain matter. Debby lay just past her, her eyes wide open and a bloody streak down her cheek. Her arm was nearly cut off; she'd been chopped through the stomach with the axe, her belly lay open, slack like the mouth of a sleeper. I called for Michelle, but I knew she was dead. I tiptoed into our bedroom and found her curled up on her bed with her dolls, her throat black with bruises, one slipper still on, one eye open.

The walls were painted in blood: pentagrams and nasty words. Cunts. Satan. Everything was broken, ripped, destroyed. Jars of food had been smashed against the walls, cereal sprayed around the floor. A single Rice Krispie would be found in my mother's chest wound, the mayhem was so haphazard. One of Michelle's shoes dangled by its laces from the cheap ceiling fan.

I hobbled over to the kitchen phone, pulled it down to the floor, dialed my aunt Diane's number, the only one I knew by heart, and when Diane answered I screamed *They're all dead!* in a voice that hurt my own ears for its keening. Then I jammed myself into the crevice between the refrigerator and the oven and waited for Diane.

At the hospital, they sedated me and removed three frostbitten toes and half of a ring finger. Since then I've been waiting to die.

I SAT UPRIGHT in the yellow electricity. Pulled myself out of our murder house and back to my grown-up bedroom. I wasn't going to die for years, I was hunting-dog healthy, so I needed a plan. My scheming Day brain thankfully, blessedly returned to thoughts of my own welfare. Little Libby Day just discovered her angle. Call it survival instinct, or call it what it was: greed.

Those "Day enthusiasts," those "solvers" would pay for more than just old letters. Hadn't they asked me where Runner was, and which of Ben's friends I might still know? They'd pay for information that only I could get. Those jokers who memorized the floor plans to my house, who packed folders full of crime-scene photos, all had their own theories about who killed the Days. Being freaks, they'd have a tough time getting anyone to talk to them. Being me, I could do that for them. The police would humor poor little me, a lot of the suspects even. I could talk to my dad, if that's what they really wanted, and if I could find him.

Not that it would necessarily lead to anything. At home under my bright hamster-y lights, safe again, I reminded myself that Ben was guilty (had to be *had to be*), mainly because I couldn't handle any other possibility. Not if I was going to function, and for the first time in twenty-four years, I needed to function. I started doing the math in my head: $500, say, to talk to the cops; $400 to talk to some of Ben's friends; $1,000 to track down Runner; $2,000 to talk to Runner. I'm sure the fans had a whole list of people I could cajole into giving Orphan Day some of their time. I could drag this out for months.

I fell asleep, the rum bottle still in my hand, reassuring myself: Ben Day is a killer.

Ben Day

Ben was free-spinning over ice, the wheels of his bike shimmying. The path was for dirtbikes, for summer, and it had iced over, so it was stupid to ride it. It was more stupid what he was doing: pedaling as fast as he could over the bumpy ground, broken corn stalks on both sides like stubble, and him picking at the goddam butterfly sticker one of his sisters had pasted to the speedometer. It'd been there for weeks, buzzing in and out of his vision, pissing him off, but not enough to deal with it. He bet it was Debby who put it there, loll-eyed and mindless: *This looks pretty!* Ben had the sparkly thing halfway off when he hit a patch of dirt, his front wheel turning completely to the left, his rear bucking out from under him. He didn't fly clear. He jerked up, one leg still caught on the bike, and fell sideways, his right arm scraping the corn shards, his right leg bending beneath him. His head smashed the dirt hard, his teeth sang like a bell.

By the time he could breathe again—ten tear-blink seconds—he could feel a warm trickle of blood snake down past his eye. Good. He smeared it with his fingertips down across the side of his cheek, felt a new line of blood immediately stream out of the crack in his forehead.

He wished he'd hit harder. He'd never broken a bone, a fact he admitted only when pressed. *Really, dude? How do you get through life without breaking something? Your mom wrap you in bubble wrap?* Last spring, he'd broken into the town pool with some guys, and stood on the diving board over the big dry hole, staring at the concrete bottom, willing himself to flip in, really smash himself up, be the crazy kid. He'd bounced a few times, taken another swig of whiskey, jiggled up and down some more, and walked back to the guys, who he hardly knew, who'd been watching him only out the sides of their eyes.

A broken bone would be best, but some blood wasn't bad. It was flowing steadily now, down his cheek, under his chin, dripping on the ice. Pure, round red ponds.

Annihilation.

The word came from nowhere—his brain was sticky, phrases and snatches of songs were always wedging themselves in there. Annihilation. He saw flashes of Norse barbarians swinging axes. He wondered for a second, only a second, if he'd been reincarnated, and this was some leftover memory, flittering down like ash. Then he picked up his bike and banished the idea. He wasn't ten.

He started pedaling, his right hip knotted, his arm sizzling with the scrape from the corn. Maybe he'd get a good bruise too. Diondra would like that, she'd brush one soft fingertip over it, circle it once or twice and give it a poke so she could tease him when he jumped. She was a girl who liked big reactions, Diondra—she was a screamer, a weeper, a howler when she laughed. She made her eyes go wide, her brows almost up to her hairline when she wanted to seem surprised. She liked to jump out from behind doors and scare him so he'd pretend to chase her. Diondra, his girl with the name that made him think of princesses or strippers, he wasn't sure which. She was a little of both: rich but sleazy.

Something had rattled loose on his bike, there was a sound like a nail in a tin can coming from somewhere near his pedals. He stopped a second to look, his hands pink and wrinkled in the cold like an old man's, and just as weak, but could see nothing wrong. More blood pooled into his eyes as he willed himself to find the problem. Fuck, he was useless. He'd been too young when his dad left. He never had a chance to learn anything practical. He saw guys working on motorcycles and tractors and cars, the insides of the engines looking like the metal intestines of an animal he'd never seen before. Now animals he did know, and guns. He was a hunter like everyone else in his family, but that didn't stand for much since his mom was a better shot than he was.

He wanted to be a useful man, but he wasn't sure how to make that happen, and it scared him shitless. His dad had come back to live on the farm for a few months this summer, and Ben had been hopeful, figuring the guy would teach him something after all this time, bother to be a father. Instead, Runner just did all the mechanical stuff himself, didn't even invite Ben to watch. Made it clear, in fact, that Ben should stay out of his way. He could tell Runner thought he was a pussy: whenever his mom talked about needing to fix something, Runner would say, "that's men's work," and shoot a smile at Ben, daring Ben to agree. He couldn't ask Runner to show him shit.

Also, he had no money. Correction, he had $4.30 in his pocket, but that was it for him, for this week. His family had no money saved. They had a bank account that was always just short of empty—he'd seen a statement once where the balance was literally $1.10, so at one point his entire family had less in the bank than what he was carrying in his coat right now. His mom couldn't run the farm right—somehow she was screwing it up. She'd take a load of wheat over to the elevator in a borrowed truck and get nothing—less than what it cost to grow it—and whatever money she did get, she owed. *The wolves are at the door,* his mom always said, and when he was younger, he pictured her leaning out the back door, throwing crisp green cash at a pack of hounds, them snapping it up like it was meat. It was never enough.

Was anyone going to take the farm away at some point? Shouldn't someone? The best thing might be to get rid of the farm, start all over fresh, not tied to this big, dead, living thing. But it was his mom's parents' place, and she was sentimental. It was pretty selfish, when you thought about it. Ben worked all week on the farm, and then went back to the school on weekends to work his crap janitor's job. (School and farm and farm and school, that's all his life was before Diondra. Now he had a nice triangle of places to go: school

and farm and Diondra's big house on the edge of town.) He fed cattle and hauled manure at home, and pretty much did the same at
school, cleaning locker rooms and mopping the cafeteria, wiping up
other kids' shit. And still he was expected to turn over half his paycheck to his mom. *Families share.* Yeah? Well, parents take care of
their children, how about that one? How about not squirting out
three more kids when you could barely afford the first one?

The bike clattered along, Ben waiting for the whole thing to go
to pieces like some comedy routine, some cartoon where he ended up
peddling on just a seat and a wheel. He hated that he had to bike
places like Opie going to the fishing hole. He hated that he couldn't
drive. *Nothing sadder than a boy just short of sixteen,* Trey would say,
shaking his head and blowing smoke toward him. He said this every
time Ben showed up to Diondra's on his bike. Trey was mostly cool,
but he was the kind of guy who always had to get a jab in at another
guy. Trey was nineteen, with long hair, black and dull like week-old
tar, Diondra's step-cousin or something weird like that, great-uncle
or family friend or stepson of a family friend. He either changed his
story a few times, or Ben wasn't paying close enough attention.
Which was entirely possible, since whenever he was around Trey,
Ben immediately tensed up, got way conscious of his body. Why was
he standing with his legs at that angle? What should he do with his
hands? On his waist or in his pockets?

Either way felt weird. Either way would lead to jokes. Trey was
the kind of guy that would look for something just slightly but truly
wrong about you that you didn't even notice and point it out to the
whole room. *Nice highwaters* was the first thing Trey ever said to him.
Ben was wearing jeans that were maybe, possibly, half an inch too
short. Maybe an inch. *Nice highwaters.* Diondra had screeched at
that. Ben had waited for her to stop laughing, and Trey to start talking again. He'd waited ten minutes, saying nothing, just trying to sit
at an angle where his socks wouldn't peek out too much. Then he'd
retreated to the bathroom, unlooped his belt a notch, pulled the jeans
down near his hips. When he came back to the room—Diondra's
downstairs rec room, with blue carpet and beanbags everywhere like
mushrooms—the second thing Trey ever said to him was, "Your
belt's down to your dick now, man. Ain't foolin' no one."

Ben rattled down the trail in the cold shade of winter, more flakes of snow floating in the air like dust motes. Even when he turned sixteen, he wouldn't have a car. His mom had a Cavalier that she bought at an auction; it had once been a rental car. They couldn't afford a second one, she'd already told Ben that. They'd have to share, which immediately made Ben not want to use it at all. He already pictured trying to pick up Diondra in a car that smelled of hundreds of other people, a car that smelled completely used—old french fries and other people's sex stains—and on top of that, a car that was now cluttered with girls' schoolbooks and yarn dolls and plastic bracelets. That wouldn't work. Diondra said he could drive her car (she was seventeen, another problem, because wasn't that sort of embarrassing to be two grades below your girlfriend?). But that was a much better vision: the two of them in her red CRX, with its jacked-up rear end, Diondra's menthol cigarettes filling the car with perfumey smoke, Slayer blasting. Yeah, much better.

They'd drive out of this crap town, to Wichita, where her uncle owned a sporting-goods store and might give him a job. Ben had tried out for both the basketball and football teams and been cut early and hard, in a don't-come-back sort of way, so spending his days in a big room filled with basketballs and footballs seemed ironic. Then again, with all that equipment around, he might be able to practice, get good enough to join some men's league or something. Seemed like there must be a plus-side.

Of course, the biggest plus-side was Diondra. He and Diondra in their own apartment in Wichita, eating McDonald's and watching TV and having sex and smoking entire packs of cigarettes in a night. Ben didn't smoke much when Diondra wasn't around—she was the addict, she smoked so much she smelled like tobacco even after a shower, like if she slit her skin, menthol vapor would ooze out. He'd come to like it, it smelled like comfort and home to him, the way warm bread might to someone else. So that's how it would be: He and Diondra, with her brown spiraly curls all crunchy with gel (another smell that was all her—that sharp, grape-y sting of her hair), sitting on the sofa watching the soap operas she taped every day. He'd gotten caught up in the drama: big-shouldered ladies drinking champagne with diamonds flashing from their fingers while they cheated or their husbands cheated or people got amnesia and cheated. He would come home from work, his hands smelling of that dusty basketball leather smell, and she'd have bought his McDonald's or Taco Bell and they'd hang out and joke about the spangly ladies on TV, and Diondra would point out the ones with the nicest nails, she loved her nails, and then she'd insist on painting his, or putting lipstick on him, which she loved to do, she loved to make him pretty, she always said. They'd end up in a tickle fight on the bed, naked with ketchup packets smashed to their backs, and Diondra would monkey-laugh so loud the neighbors would bang on the ceiling.

This image wasn't quite complete. He'd deliberately left out one very frightening detail, just completely erased certain realities. That can't be a good sign. It meant the entire thing was a daydream. He was an idiot kid who couldn't even have something as small as a shitty apartment in Wichita. Not even something as tiny as that could he have. He felt a surge of familiar fury. His life was a long line of denials, just waiting for him.

Annihilation. Again he saw axes, guns, bloody bodies smashed into the ground. Screaming giving way to whimpers and birdsong. He wanted to bleed more.

Libby Day

NOW

When I was a kid, I lived with Runner's second cousin in Holcomb, Kansas, for about five months while poor Aunt Diane recuperated from my particularly furious twelfth year. I don't remember much about those five months except that we took a class trip to Dodge City to learn about Wyatt Earp. We thought we'd see guns, buffalo, whores. Instead, about twenty of us shuffled and elbowed into a series of small file rooms, looking up records, the entire day packed with dust motes and whining. Earp himself made no impression on me, but I adored those Old West villains, with their dripping mustaches and slouchy clothes and eyes that glowed like nickel. An outlaw was always described as "a liar and a thief." And there, in one of those inside-smelling rooms, the file clerk droning on about the art of archiving, I jiggled with the good cheer of meeting a fellow traveler. Because I thought, "That's me."

I am a liar and a thief. Don't let me into your house, and if you do, don't leave me alone. I take things. You can catch me with your string of fine pearls clickering in my greedy little paws, and I'll tell you they reminded me of my mother's and I just had to touch them, just for a second, and I'm so sorry, I don't know what came over me.

My mom never owned any jewelry that didn't turn her skin green, but you won't know that. And I'll still swipe the pearls when you're not looking.

I steal underpants, rings, CDs, books, shoes, iPods, watches. I'll go to a party at someone's house—I don't have friends, but I have people who invite me places—and I'll leave wearing a few shirts under my sweater, with a couple of nice lipsticks in my pocket, and whatever cash is floating inside a purse or two. Sometimes I even take the purse, if the crowd is drunk enough. Just sling it over a shoulder and leave. Prescription pills, perfume, buttons, pens. Food. I have a flask someone's granddad carried back from WWII, I own a Phi Beta Kappa pin earned by some guy's favorite uncle. I have an antique collapsible tin cup that I can't remember stealing, I've had it so long. I pretend it's always been in the family.

The actual stuff my family owned, those boxes under my stairs, I can't quite bear to look at. I like other people's things better. They come with other people's history.

One item in my home I didn't steal is a true-crime novel called *Devil's Harvest: The Satan Sacrifice of Kinnakee Kansas.* It came out in 1986, and was written by a former reporter named Barb Eichel, and that's all I really know. At least three semi-boyfriends have given me a copy of this book, solemnly, wisely, and all three of them were dumped immediately after. If I say I don't want to read the book, I don't want to read the book. It's like my rule about always sleeping with the light on. I tell every man I sleep with that I always keep the lights on, and they always say something like, "I'll take care of you, baby," and then try to switch off the lights. Like that's that. They somehow seem surprised that I actually sleep with the lights on.

I dug out *Devil's Harvest* from a leaning stack of books in the corner—I keep it for the same reason I keep the boxes of my family's papers and crap, because maybe I'll want it someday, and even if I don't, I don't want anyone else to have it.

The opening page read:

> Kinnakee, Kansas, in the heart of America, is a quiet farm-ing community where folks know each other, go to church

with each other, grow old alongside each other. But it is not impervious to the evils of the outside world—and in the early hours of January 3, 1985, those evils destroyed three members of the Day family in a torrent of blood and horror. This is a story not just of murder, but of Devil worship, blood rituals, and the spread of Satanism to every corner of America—even the coziest, seemingly safest places.

My ears started their hum with the sounds of that night: A loud, masculine grunt, a heaving, dry-throat wail. My mother's banshee screams. Darkplace. I looked at the back-page photo of Barb Eichel. She had short, spiky hair, dangling earrings, and a somber smile. The biography said she lived in Topeka, Kansas, but that was twenty-some years ago.

I needed to phone Lyle Wirth with my money-for-info proposal, but I wasn't ready to hear him lecture me again about the murder of my own family. *(You really think Ben's guilty!)* I needed to be able to argue with him instead of sitting there like some ignoramus with nothing useful to say. Which is basically what I was.

I scanned the book some more, lying on my back, propped up on a twice-folded pillow, Buck monitoring me with watchful kitty eyes for any movement toward the kitchen. Barb Eichel described Ben as "a black-clad loner, unpopular and angry" and "obsessed with the most brutal form of heavy metal—called black metal—songs rumored to be little more than coded calls to the Devil himself." I skimmed, naturally, until I found a reference to me: "angelic but strong," "determined and sorrowful" with an "air of independence that one usually doesn't find in children twice her age." Our family had been "happy and bustling, looking forward to a future of clean air and clean living." Mmm-hmm. Still, this was supposedly the definitive book on the murders, and, after all those voices at the Kill Club telling me I was a fool, I was eager to speak with an outsider who also believed that Ben was guilty. Ammo for Lyle. I pictured myself ticking off facts on my fingers: *this, this, and this proves you jackasses are wrong,* and Lyle unpursing his lips, realizing I was right after all.

I'd still be willing to take his cash if he wanted.

Not sure where to start, I called the Topeka directory and, most beautiful bingo ever, got Barb Eichel's number. Still in Topeka, still listed. Easy enough.

She picked up on the second ring, her voice merry and shrill until I told her who I was.

"Oh, Libby. I always wondered if you'd ever get in touch," she said after a making a throat-sound like *eehhhhh*. "Or if I should reach out to you. I didn't know, I didn't know . . ." I could picture her looking around the room, picking at her nails, skittish, one of those women who studied the menu twenty minutes and then still panicked when the waiter came.

"I was hoping I could talk to you about . . . Ben," I started, not sure what my wording should be.

"I know, I know, I've written him several letters of apology over the years, Libby. I just don't know how many times I can say I'm sorry for that damn, damn book."

Unexpected.

BARB EICHEL WAS going to have me over for lunch. She wanted to explain to me in person. She didn't drive anymore (here I caught a whiff of the real story—meds, she had the shiny coating of someone on too many pills), so I'd come out to her and she'd be so grateful. Luckily, Topeka's not far from Kansas City. Not that I was eager to go there—I'd seen enough of it growing up. The town used to have a hell of a psychiatric clinic, seriously, there was even a sign on the highway that said something like, "Welcome to Topeka, psychiatric capital of the world!" The whole town was crawling with nutjobs and therapists, and I used to get trucked there regularly for rare, privileged outpatient counseling. Yay for me. We talked about my nightmares, my panic attacks, my issues with anger. By the teenage years, we talked about my tendency toward physical aggression. As far as I'm concerned, the entire city, the capital of Kansas, smells like crazy-house drool.

I'd read Barb's book before I went to meet her, was armed with facts and questions. But my confidence was flattened somewhere in the three hours it took to make the one-hour drive. Too many wrong turns, me cursing myself for not having the Internet at home, not being able to just download directions. No Internet, no cable. I'm not good at things like that: haircuts or oil changes or dentist visits. When I moved into my bungalow, I spent the first three months swaddled in blankets because I couldn't deal with getting the gas turned on. It's been turned off three times in the past few years, because sometimes I can't quite bring myself to write a check. I have trouble maintaining.

Barb's house, when I finally got there, was dully homey, a decent block of stucco she'd painted pale green. Soothing. Lots of wind chimes. She opened the door and pulled back, like I'd surprised her. She still had the same haircut as her author photo, now a spiky cluster of gray, and was wearing a pair of eyeglasses with a beaded chain, the type that older women describe as "funky." She was somewhere north of fifty, with dark, darting eyes that bulged out of a bony face.

"Ohhh, hi, Libby!" she gasped, and suddenly she was hugging me, some bone of hers poking me hard in my left breast. She smelled like patchouli and wool. "Come in, come in." A small rag-dog came clicking across the tiles toward me, barking happily. A clock chimed the hours.

"Oh, I hope you don't mind dogs, he's a sweetheart," she said, watching him as he bounded up on me. I hate dogs, even small, sweet dogs. I held my hands aloft, actively not petting it. "Come on, Weenie, let our friend get by," she babytalked it. I disliked it even more after I heard its name.

She sat me down in a living room that seemed stuffed: chairs, sofa, rug, pillows, curtains, everything was plump and round and then layered with even more material. She bustled in and out a bit, calling over her shoulder instead of standing still, asking me twice what I wanted to drink. Somehow I knew she'd try to give me dirt-smelling, crystal-happy, earthen mugs of Beebleberry Root Tea or Jasmine Elixir Smoothie, so I just asked for water. I looked for liquor bottles but couldn't spot any. There were definitely some pills being swallowed here though. Everything just plinked off this woman—bing, bang!—like she was shellacked.

She brought sandwiches on trays for us to eat in the living room. My water was all ice cubes. I was done in two swallows.

"So, how is Ben, Libby?" she asked when she finally sat down. She kept her tray to her side though. Allowing for a quick retreat.

"Oh, I don't know. I don't have contact with him."

She didn't really seem to listen; she was tuned to her own inner radio station. Something light jazz.

"Obviously, Libby, I feel a lot of guilt over my part in this, although the book came out after the verdict, it had no bearing on that," she said in a rush. "Still, I was part of that rush to judgment. It was the *time* period. You were so young, I know you don't remember this, but the '80s. I mean, it was called the Satanic Panic."

"What was?" I wondered how many times she'd use my name in conversation. She seemed like one of those.

"The whole psychiatric community, the police, law enforcement, the whole shebang—they thought everyone was a Devil worshiper back then. It was . . . *trendy*." She leaned toward me, her earrings bobbing, her hands kneading. "People really believed there was this vast network of Satanists, that it was a commonplace thing. A teenager starts acting strange: he's a Satan worshiper. A preschooler comes home from school with a weird bruise or an odd comment about her privates: her teachers are Satan worshipers. I mean, remember the McMartin preschool trial? Those poor teachers suffered *years* before the charges were dropped. Satanic panic. It was a good story. I fell for it, Libby. We didn't question enough."

The dog sniffed over to me, and I tensed up, hoping Barb would call it away. She didn't notice, though, her eyes on a dangling stained-glass sunflower casting golden light from the window above me.

"And, I mean, the story just worked," Barb continued. "I will now admit, and it took me a good decade, Libby, that I breezed over a lot of evidence that didn't fit this Ben-Satan theory, I ignored obvious red flags."

"Like what?"

"Um, like the fact that you were clearly coached, that you were in no way a credible witness, that the shrink they had assigned to you, to quote 'draw you out' was just putting words into your head."

"Dr. Brooner?" I remembered Dr. Brooner: A whiskery hippie dude with a big nose and small eyes—he looked like a friendly storybook animal. He was the only person besides my aunt Diane I liked that whole year, and the only person I talked to about that night, since Diane was unwilling. Dr. Brooner.

"Quack," Barb said, and giggled. I was about to protest, feeling defensive—the woman had basically just called me a liar to my face, which was true, but still pissed me off—but she was going again. "And your dad's alibi? That girlfriend of his? No way that should have held. That man had no real alibi, and he owed a lot of people a lot of money."

"My mom didn't have any money."

"She had more than your dad did, believe me." I did. My dad once sent me to a neighbor's house for a free pity lunch, told me to look under their sofa cushions and bring him any change.

"And then there was a footprint of a men's dress shoe *in blood* that no one ever traced. But then again, the entire crime scene was contaminated—that's something else I skipped over in the book. There were people going in and out of that place all day. Your aunt came in and took out whole closets of junk, clothes and stuff for you. It was all against any rules of police procedure. But *no one cared.* People were freaking out. And they had a strange teenage boy that no one in the whole town liked that much, who had no money, who didn't know how to look out for himself, and who happened to like heavy metal. It's just embarrassing." She checked herself. "It's awful. Tragedy."

"Can anything get Ben out?" I asked, my stomach gone eely. The fact that the definitive voice on Ben's guilt had changed her mind was sickening me. As was meeting yet another person who was positive I'd committed perjury.

"Well, you're trying to, right? I think it's almost impossible to undo these things after all these years—his time for an appeal, per se, is up. He'd need to try for habeas corpus and that's . . . you all would need some big new evidence at this point to get the ball rolling. Like some really compelling DNA evidence. Unfortunately, your family was cremated so—"

"Right, well, thank you," I interrupted, needing to get home, right then.

"Again, I wrote the book after the verdict, but if I can do anything to help you, let me know, Libby. I do bear some culpability. I take that responsibility."

"Have you made any statements, told the police you don't think Ben did it?"

"Well, no. It seems like most people concluded a long time ago that Ben didn't do it," Barb said, her voice going shrill. "I assume you've officially recanted your testimony? I'd think that'd be a huge help."

She was waiting for me to say more, to explain why I'd come to her now. To tell her, yeah, sure, Ben was innocent and I was going to fix all this. She sat eyeing me, eating her lunch, chewing each bite with excessive care. I picked up my sandwich—cucumber and hummus—and set it back down, leaving a thumbprint in the damp bread. The room was lined with bookshelves, but they contained only self-help books. *Open the Sunshine!; Go, Go, Girl; Stop Punishing Yourself; Stand up—Stand Tall; Be Your Own Best Friend; Moving On, Moving Up!* They went on, and on, the relentless, cheerful, buck-up titles. The more I read, the more miserable I felt. Herbal remedies, positive thinking, forgiveness of self, living with mistakes. She even had a book for beating tardiness. I don't trust self-helpers. Years ago, I left a bar with a friend of a friend, a nice, cute, crew-necked, normal guy with an apartment nearby. After sex, after he fell asleep, I started nosing around his room, and found that his desk was covered with sticky notes:

> *Don't sweat the small stuff, it's all small stuff.*
> *If only we'd stop trying to be happy we'd have a*
>   *pretty good time.*
> *Enjoy life—no one gets out of here alive.*
> *Don't worry, be happy.*

To me, all that urgent hopefulness was more frightening than if I'd found a pile of skulls with hair still attached. I ran out in full panic, my underwear tucked up a sleeve.

I didn't stay much longer with Barb. I left with promises to call her soon and a blue paperweight in the shape of a heart I stole from her sidetable.

Patty Day

JANUARY 2, 1985
9:42 A.M.

The sink was stained a sludgy purple from where Ben had dyed his hair. Sometime in the night, then, he'd locked himself in the bathroom, sat down on the closed toilet seat, and read through the instructions on the carton of hair color she'd found in the trash. The carton had a photograph of a woman with light pink lips and jet-black hair, worn in a pageboy. She wondered if he'd stolen it. She couldn't imagine Ben, chin-to-chest Ben, setting a dye kit on the checkout counter. So he'd shoplifted it. Then in the middle of the night, her son, all by himself, had measured and combined and lathered. He'd sat with that mudpile of chemicals on his red hair and waited.

The whole idea made her incredibly sad. That in this house of women, her boy had colored his hair in the night by himself. Obviously, it was silly to think he'd have asked her for help, but to do such a thing without an accomplice seemed so lonely. Patty's older sister, Diane, had pierced Patty's ears in this bathroom two decades ago. Patty heated a safety pin with a cheap lighter and Diane sliced a potato in half and stuck its cold, wet face against the back of Patty's ear. They froze her lobe with an ice cube, and Diane—*hold still, hold stillllll*—jabbed that pin into Patty's rubbery flesh. Why did they need the potato? For aim or something. Patty had chickened out after the first ear, had plopped down on the side of the bathtub, the lancet of the pin still sticking out the lobe. Diane, intense and unbudging in a mountainous wool nightgown, closed in on her with another hot pin.

"It'll be over in a second, you can't do just one, P."

Diane, the doer. Jobs were not to be abandoned, not for weather, or laziness, or a throbbing ear, melted ice, and a scaredy kid sister.

Patty twirled her gold studs. The left one was off-center, her fault for squirming at the last minute. Still, there they were, twin markers of teenage brio, and she'd done it with her sister, just like she'd first applied lipstick or hooked elastic clips to sanitary napkins the size of a diaper, circa 1965. Some things were not meant to be done alone.

She poured Comet into the sink and started scrubbing, the water turning an inky green. Diane would be by soon. She always dropped in midweek if she was "in her car," which was her way of making the thirty-mile drive out to the farm seem like just part of a day's errands. Diane would make fun of this latest Ben saga. When Patty was worried about school, teachers, the farm, Ben, her marriage, the kids, the farm (after 1980, it was always, always, always the farm), it was Diane she craved, like a stiff drink. Diane, sitting in a lawn chair in their garage, smoking a series of cigarettes, would pronounce Patty a dope, would tell her to lighten up. Worries find you easily enough without inviting them. With Diane, worries were almost physical beings, leachy creatures with latchhooks for fingers, meant to be vanquished immediately. Diane didn't worry, that was for less hearty women.

But Patty couldn't lighten up. Ben had gone so remote this past year, turned himself into this strange, tense kid who walled himself into his room, kicking around to music that rattled the walls, the belchy, screaming words seeping out from under his door. Alarming words. She'd not bothered to listen at first, the music itself was so ugly, so frantic, but one day she'd come home early from town, Ben thinking no one was home, and she'd stood outside his door and heard the bellows:

I am no more,
I am undone,
the Devil took my soul,
now I'm Satan's son.

The record skipped and again came the coarse chant: I am no more, I am undone, the Devil took my soul, now I'm Satan's son.

And again. And then again. And Patty realized Ben was just standing over his record player, picking up the needle and playing the words over and over, like a prayer.

It was Diane she wanted here. Now. Diane, settled down on the couch like a friendly bear in one of her three old flannel shirts, now chewing a series of nicotine gums, would talk about the time Patty came home in a minidress and their folks actually gasped, as if she were a lost cause. "And you weren't, were you? You were just a kid. So is he." And Diane would snap her fingers like it was that simple.

The girls were hovering outside the bathroom door—they'd be out there when she emerged, waiting. They knew from Patty's scrubbing and mutterings that something further had gone wrong, and they were trying to decide if this was a situation for tears or recrimination. When Patty cried, it invariably set off at least two of her girls, and if someone got in trouble, the house got windy with blame. The Day women were the definition of mob mentality. And here they were on a farm with plenty of pitchforks.

She rinsed her hands, chapped, red and hard, and glanced at herself in the mirror, making sure her eyes weren't wet. She was thirty-two but looked a decade older. Her forehead was creased like a child's paper fan, and crow's feet rayed out from her eyes. Her red hair was shot with white, wiry threads, and she was unattractively thin, all bumps and points, like she'd swallowed a shelf's worth of hardware: hammers and mothballs and a few old bottles. She did not look like the kind of person you'd want to hug, and, in fact, her children never snuggled into her. Michelle liked to brush her hair (impatiently and aggressively, the way Michelle did most things) and Debby leaned into her whenever they were both standing (loosely and distractedly, as was Debby's way). Poor Libby tended not to touch her at all, unless she was really hurt, and that made sense, too.

Patty's body had been so used up that by her mid-twenties even her nipples were knobby; she'd bottle-fed Libby almost immediately.

There was no medicine cabinet in the cramped bathroom (what would she do when the girls hit high school, one bathroom for four women, and where would Ben be? She had a quick, miserable image of him in some motel room, all by himself in a boy-mess of stained towels and spoiled milk), so she kept a small cluster of toiletries stacked along the sink. Ben had shoved all the containers into one corner—aerosol deodorant and hairspray, a midget can of baby powder she didn't remember buying. They were now splattered with the same violet stain that dirtied her sink. She wiped them down like they were china. Patty wasn't ready for another trip to the department store. She'd driven to Salina a month ago in a positive, bright mood to pick up some prettifying items: cream rinse, face lotion, lipstick. She had folded a $20 bill in her front pocket just for the trip. A splurge. But the sheer amount of options in face cream alone—hydrating, wrinkle-fighting, sun-thwarting—had overwhelmed her. You could buy one moisturizer, but then you had to get a matching cleanser, too, and something called toner, and before you were even ready for the night cream, you'd have blown fifty bucks. She'd left the store with nothing, feeling chastened and foolish.

"You've got four kids—no one expects you to look like a daisy," was Diane's response.

But she wanted to look like a daisy every now and then. Months back, Runner had returned, just dropped out of the sky with a tan face and blue eyes and stories of fishing boats in Alaska and the race circuit in Florida. He'd stood on her doorstep, lanky in dirty jeans, with not even a wink about the fact they hadn't heard from him in three years, hadn't gotten any money from him. He asked if he could board with them til he got settled—naturally he was broke, although he handed Debby half a warm Coke he'd been drinking as if it were a wonderful gift. Runner swore he'd fix things up around the farm and keep it all platonic, *if she wanted.* It was summer then, and she let him sleep on the couch, where the girls would run to him in the morning as he lay sprawled and stinky in torn boxers, his balls half out.

He charmed the girls—he called them Baby Doll, Angelface—and even Ben watched him attentively, swooping in and out of interactions like a shark. Runner didn't exactly engage Ben, but he tried to joke with him a little, be friendly. He'd include Ben as a male, which was good, he'd say things like, "That's a man's job," and give Ben a wink. After the third week, Runner rolled up in his truck with an old fold-out sofa he'd found and suggested he camp out in the garage. It seemed OK. He helped her with dishes and he opened doors for her. He'd let Patty catch him looking at her butt, and then pretend to be embarrassed. They exchanged a smoky kiss one night as she was handing him clean bedsheets, and he'd immediately been on her— hands up her shirt, pressing her against the wall, pulling her head back by her hair. She pushed him off, told him she wasn't ready, tried to smile. He sulked and shook his head, looking her up and down with pursed lips. When she undressed for bed, she could smell the nicotine from where he'd grabbed her just below the breasts.

He'd stayed another month, leering around, starting jobs and leaving them half done. When she asked him to leave during break-fast one morning, he called her a bitch, threw a glass at her, left juice stains on the ceiling. After he was gone, she discovered he'd stolen sixty bucks, two bottles of booze, and a jewelry box that he'd soon discover had nothing in it. He moved to a decrepit cabin a mile away—smoke came from the chimney at all times, the only form of heat. Sometimes she could hear gunfire in the distance, the sounds of bullets shot straight up in the air.

That would be her last romance with the man who fathered her children. And now, it was time for more reality. Patty tucked her hair, dry and unwieldy, behind her ears and opened the door. Michelle sat on the floor right in front of her, pretending to study the floorboard. She assessed Patty from behind gray-tinted glasses.

" 's Ben in trouble?" she asked. "Why'd he do that? With his hair?"

"Growing pains, I think," Patty said, and just as Michelle took a deep breath—she always gulped air before she said something, her sentences were tight, fast links of words that just kept coming til she had to breathe again—they heard a car coming up the driveway. The driveway was long, someone would pull onto it and they wouldn't ar-rive for another minute. Somehow Patty knew it wasn't her sister, even though the girls were shrieking *Diane! Diane!* already, running toward the window to look out. There'd be sad little sighs when it wasn't Diane after all. Somehow she knew it was Len, her loan officer. Even his driving had a possessive sound to it. Len the Letchy Lender. She'd been wrangling with him since 1981. Runner had left by then, announcing this kind of life wasn't for him, looking around like it was his place instead of hers, her parents', her grandparents'.

All he'd done was marry her and ruin it. Poor, disappointed Runner, when his dreams had been so high in the '70s, when people actually thought they could get rich from farming. (Ha! She snorted out loud, there in her kitchen, at the thought of it, imagine.) She and Runner had taken over the farm from her parents in '74. It was a big deal, bigger even than her marriage or the birth of her firstborn. Neither of those had thrilled her sweet and quiet parents—Runner stank of trouble even then, but, bless them, they never said a thing against him. When, at age seventeen, she told them that she was knocked up and they were getting married, they just said: *Oh.* Like that. Which said enough.

Patty had a blurry photograph of the day they took on the farm: her parents, stiff and proud, smiling shyly at the camera, and her and Runner, triumphant grins, bountiful hair, incredibly young, holding champagne. Her parents had never had champagne before, but they drove to town and got a bottle for the occasion. They toasted out of old jelly jars.

It went wrong fast, and Patty couldn't entirely blame Runner. Back then, everyone thought the value of land would keep skyrocketing—*they're not making any more of it!*—and why not buy more, and better, all the time? *Plant fencepost to fencepost*—it was a rallying cry. Be aggressive, be brave. Runner with his big dreams and no knowledge had marched her down to the bank—he'd worn a tie the color of lime sherbet, thick as a quilt—and hemmed and hawed to get a loan. They ended up with double what they asked for. They shouldn't have taken it, maybe, but their lender said don't worry—boom times.

They're just giving it away! Runner had howled, and all of a sudden they had a new tractor, and a six-row planter when the four-row was fine. Within the year there was a glinting red Krause Dominator and a new John Deere combine. Vern Evelee, with his respectable five hundred acres down the way, made a point of mentioning each new thing he spotted on their property, always with a little twitch in his eyebrow. Runner bought more land and a fishing boat, and when Patty had asked *was he sure, was he sure?* he'd sulked and barked about how much it hurt that she didn't believe in him. Then everything went to hell at once, it was like a joke. Carter and the Russian grain embargo (fight the Commies, forget the farmers), interest rates to 18 percent, price of fuel creeping up and then leaping up, banks going bust, countries she barely heard of—Argentina—suddenly competing in the market. Competing with *her* back in little Kinnakee, Kansas. A few bad years and Runner was done. He never got over Carter—you heard about Carter all the time with him. Runner'd sit with a beer watching the bad news on the TV and he'd see those big, rabbit teeth flash and his eyes would go glassy, he'd get so hateful it seemed like Runner must actually know the guy.

So Runner blamed Carter, and everyone else in the rotten town blamed her. Vern Evelee made a noise with his tongue whenever he saw her, a for-shame noise. Farmers who weren't going under never had sympathy, they looked at you like you played naked in the snow and then wanted to wipe your snotty nose on them. Just last summer, some farmer down near Ark City had his hopper go screwy. Dumped 4,000 pounds of wheat on him. This six-foot man, he drowned in it. Suffocated before they could get him out, like choking on sand. Everyone in Kinnakee was so mournful—so regretful about this *freak accident*—til they found out the man's farm was going under. Then all of a sudden, it was: *Well, he should have been more careful.* Lectures on taking proper care of equipment, being safe. They turned on him that fast, this poor dead man with lungs full of his own harvest.

Ding-dong and here was Len, just as she dreaded, handing his wool hunting cap to Michelle, his bulky overcoat to Debby, carefully swiping snow from loafers that were too shiny-new. Ben wouldn't approve of those, she thought. Ben spent hours grubbing up his new sneakers, letting the girls take turns walking on them, back when he let the girls near him. Libby glowered at Len from the sofa and turned back to the TV. Libby loved Diane, and this guy wasn't Diane, this guy had tricked her by walking in the door when he should have been Diane.

Len never said hello as a greeting; he said something like a yodel, *He-a-lo!* and Patty had to brace for it each time, she found the sound so ridiculous. Now he yelled it as she walked down the hall, and she had to duck back into the bathroom and curse for just a second, then put her smile back on. Len always hugged her, which she was pretty sure he didn't do with any other farmer that needed his services. So she went to his open arms and let him do his hug thing where he held her just a second too long, his hands on both her elbows. She could feel him making a quick sucking noise, like he was smelling her. He reeked of sausage and Velamints. At some point, Len was going to make a real pass at her, forcing her to make a real decision, and the game was so pathetic it made her want to weep. The hunter and the hunted, but it was like a bad nature show: He was a three-legged, runt coyote and she was a tired, limping bunny. It was not magnificent.

"How's my farm girl?" he said. There was an understanding between them that her running the farm by herself was something of a joke. And, she supposed, it was at this point.

"Oh, hanging in there," she said. Debby and Michelle retreated to their bedroom. Libby snorted from the couch. The last time Len had come all the way to the house, they'd had an auction a few weeks later—the Days peeking out through the windows as their neighbors underpaid and underpaid some more for the very equipment she needed to run a working farm. Michelle and Debby had squirmed, seeing some of their schoolmates, the Boyler girls, tagging along with their folks as if it were a picnic, skipping around the farm. *Why can't we go outside?* they whined, twisting themselves into begging-angry outlines, watching those Boyler girls taking turns on their tire swing—might as well have sold them that, too. Patty had just kept saying: *Those aren't our friends out there.* People who sent her Christmas cards were running their hands over her drills and disc rippers, all those curvy, twisty shapes, grudgingly offering half what anything was worth. Vern Evelee took the planter he once seemed to resent so much, actually driving the auctioneer down from the starting price.

Merciless. She ran into Vern a week later at the feed store. The back of his neck went pink as he turned away from her. She'd followed him and made his *for-shame* noise right in his ear.

"Well, it sure smells good in here," Len said, almost resentfully. "Smells like someone had a good breakfast."

"Pancakes."

She nodded. *Please don't make me ask you why you're here. Please, just once, say why you came.*

"Mind if I sit down?" he said, wedging himself on the sofa next to Libby, his arms rigid. "Which one's this?" he said assessing her. Len had met her girls at least a dozen times, but he could never figure out who was who, or even hazard a name. One time he called Michelle "Susan."

"That's Libby."

"She's got red hair like her mom."

Yes, she did. Patty couldn't bring herself to say the nicety out loud. She was feeling sicker the longer Len delayed, her unease building into dread. The back of her sweater was moist now.

"The red come from Irish? You all Irish?"

"German. My maiden name was Krause."

"Oh, funny. Because Krause means curly-haired, not red-haired. You all don't have curly hair, really. Wavy maybe. I'm German too."

They had had this conversation before, it always went one of two ways. The other way, Len would say that it was funny, her maiden name being Krause, like the farm equipment company, and it was too bad she wasn't related, huh. Either version made her tense.

"So," she finally gave in. "Is there something wrong?"

Len seemed disappointed she was bringing a point to the conversation. He frowned at her as if he found her rude.

"Well, now that you mention it, yes. I'm afraid something's very wrong. I wanted to come out to tell you in person. Do you want to do this somewhere private?" He nodded at Libby, widening his eyes. "You want to go to the bedroom or something?" Len had a paunch. It was perfectly round under his belt, like the start of a pregnancy. She did not want to go into the bedroom with him.

"Libby, would you go see what your sisters are doing? I need to talk to Mr. Werner." Libby sighed and slid off the couch, slowly: feet, then legs, then butt, then back, as if she were made of glue. She hit the floor, rolled over elaborately a few times, crawled a bit, then finally got to her feet and slumped down the hall.

Patty and Len looked at each other, and then he tucked his bottom lip under and nodded.

"They're going to foreclose."

Patty's stomach clenched. She would not sit down in front of this man. She would not cry. "What can we do?"

"*Weeeee,* I'm afraid, are out of options. I've held them off for six months longer than they should've been held off. I really put my job on the line. Farm girl." He smiled at her, his hands clasped on his knees. She wanted to scratch him. The mattresses started screeching in the other room, and Patty knew Debby was jumping on the bed, her favorite game, bouncing from one bed to the next to the next in the girls' room.

"Patty, the only way to fix this is money. Now. If you want to keep this place. I'm talking borrow, beg, or steal. I'm saying time is over for pride. So: How badly do you want this farm?" The mattress springs bounced harder. The eggs in Patty's belly turned. Len kept smiling.

Libby Day

After my mother's head was blown off, her body axed nearly in two, people in Kinnakee wondered whether she'd been a whore. At first they wondered, then they assumed, then it became a loose jingle of fact. Cars had been seen at the house at strange times of night, people said. She looked at men the way a whore would. In these situations, Vern Evelee always remarked that she should have sold her planter in '83, as if that was proof she was prostituting herself.

Blame the victim, naturally. But the rumors turned so substantial: everyone had a friend who had a cousin who had another friend who'd fucked my mom. Everyone had some bit of proof: they told of a mole on the inside of her thigh, a scar on her right buttock. I don't think the stories can be true, but like so much from my childhood, I can't be sure. How much do you remember from when you were seven? Photos of my mother don't reveal a wanton woman. As a teenage girl, hair shooting from her ponytail like fireworks, she was the definition of nice looking, the kind of person who reminds you of a neighbor or an old babysitter you always liked. By her twenties, with one or two or four kids clambering up her, the smile was bigger, but hassled, and she was always leaning away from one of us. I picture her as constantly under siege by her children. The sheer weight of us. By her thirties there weren't many photos of her at all. In the few that exist, she's smiling in an obedient fashion, one of those take-the-dang-photo smiles that will disappear with the camera flash. I haven't looked at the photos in years. I used to paw at them obsessively, studying her clothes, her expression, whatever was in the background. Looking for clues: Whose hand is that on her shoulder? Where is she? What occasion is it? When I was still a teenager, I sealed them away, along with everything else.

Now I stood looking at the boxes as they slouched under my staircase, apologetic. I was gearing up to reacquaint myself with my family. I'd brought Michelle's note to the Kill Club because I couldn't bear to actually open those boxes, instead I'd reached into one cardboard corner where the tape was loose, and that's the first thing I pulled out, a pathetic carnival game. If I was really going to take this on, if I was really going to think about the murders after all these careful years spent doing just the opposite, I needed to be able to look at basic household possessions without panicking: our old metal egg-beater that sounded like sleigh bells when you turned it fast enough, bent knives and forks that had been inside my family's mouths, a coloring book or two with defined crayoned borders if it was Michelle's, bored horizontal scrawls if it was mine. Look at them, let them just be objects.

Then decide what to sell.

To the Kill Creeps, the most desired items from the Day home are unavailable. The 10-gauge shotgun that killed my mom—her goose gun—is snug away in some evidence drawer, along with the axe from our toolshed. (That was another reason Ben got convicted: those weapons were from our house. Outside killers don't arrive at a sleeping home with limp hands, just hoping to find convenient murder weapons.) Sometimes I tried to picture all that stuff—the axe, the gun, the bedsheets Michelle died on. Were all those bloody, smoky, sticky objects all together, conspiring in some big box? Had they been cleaned? If you opened the box, what would the smell be like? I remembered that close, rot-earth smell just hours after the murder—was it worse now, after so many years of decay?

I'd once been to Chicago, seen Lincoln's death artifacts in a museum: thatches of his hair; bullet fragments; the skinny spindle bed he'd died on, the mattress still slouched in the middle like it knew to preserve his last imprint. I ended up running to the bathroom, pressing my face against the cold stall door to keep from swooning. What would the Day death house look like, if we reunited all its relics, and who would come to see it? How many bundles of my mother's blood-stuck hair would be in the display cabinet? What happened to the walls, smeared with those hateful words, when our house was torn down? Could we gather a bouquet of frozen reeds where I'd crouched for so many hours? Or exhibit the end of my frostbitten finger? My three gone toes?

I turned away from the boxes—not up to the challenge—and sat down at a desk that served as my dining room table. The mail had brought me a package of random, crazy-person offerings from Barb Eichel. A videotape, circa 1984, titled *Threat to Innocence: Satanism in America;* a paperclipped packet of newspaper stories about the murders; a few Polaroids of Barb standing outside the courthouse where Ben's trial was being held; a dog-eared manual entitled *Your Prison Family: Get Past the Bars!*

I removed the paperclip from the packet and put it in my paperclip cup in the kitchen (no one should ever buy paperclips, pens—any of those free-range office supplies). Then I popped the videotape into my very old VHS player. Click, whir, groan. Images of pentagrams and goat-men, of screaming rock bands and dead people flashed on the screen. A man with a beautiful, hairsprayed mullet was walking along a graffiti'd wall, explaining that "This video will help you identify Satanists and even watch for signs that those you love most may be flirting with this very real danger." He interviewed preachers, cops, and some "actual Satanists." The two most powerful Satanists had tire-streak eyeliner and black robes and pentagrams around their necks, but they were sitting in their living room, on a cheap velveteen couch, and you could just see into the kitchen on the right, where a yellow refrigerator hummed on a cheery linoleum floor. I could picture them after the interview, rummaging through the fridge for tuna salad and a Coke, their capes getting in the way. I turned off the video right about when the host was warning parents to scour their children's rooms for He-Man action figures and Ouija boards.

The clippings were just as useless, and I had no idea what Barb wanted me to do with the photos of her. I sat defeated. And lazy. I could have gone to the library to look things up properly. I could have set myself up with home Internet access three years ago, when I said I would. Neither seemed like an option right now—I was easily wearied—so I phoned Lyle. He picked up on the first ring.

"Heeyyyy, Libby," he said. "I was going to call you. I really wanted to apologize for last week. You must have felt ganged-up on, and that wasn't what was supposed to happen." Nice speech.

"Yeah, it really sucked."

"I guess I didn't realize that all of us had our own theories, uh, but none of them included Ben being guilty. I didn't think it through. And I didn't realize. I didn't take into account. Just. You know, this is real to you. I mean, I know that, we know that, but we *don't* at the same time. We really just never will. I don't think. Totally get that. You spend so much time discussing and debating it becomes . . . But. Well. I'm sorry."

I didn't want to like Lyle Wirth, as I'd already decided he was a prick. But I appreciate a straightforward apology the way a tone-deaf person enjoys a fine piece of music. I can't do it, but I can applaud it in others.

"Well," I said.

"There are definitely members who'd still like to acquire any, you know, mementos you want to sell. If that's why you're calling."

"Oh, no. I just wondered. I have been thinking a lot about the case." I might as well have said *dot dot dot* aloud.

WE MET AT a bar not far away from me, a place called Sarah's, which always struck me as a weird name for a bar, but it was a mellow enough place, with a good amount of room. I don't like people up on me. Lyle was already seated, but he stood up as I came in, and bent down to hug me, the action causing much twisting and collapsing of his tall body. The side of his glasses poked my cheek. He was wearing another '80s-style jacket—this one denim, covered with slogan buttons. Don't drink and drive, practice random kindness, rock the vote. He jangled as he sat back down. Lyle was about a decade younger than me, I guessed, and I couldn't figure if his look was intentionally ironic-retro or just goofy.

He started to apologize again, but I didn't want any more. I was full up, thanks.

"Look, I'm not even saying I'm sold on the idea that Ben is innocent, or that I made any mistakes in my testimony."

He opened his mouth to say something, then snapped it back shut.

"But if I were to look into it more, is that something the club would be able to help finance? Pay for my time, in a way."

"Wow, Libby, it's great news that you're even interested in looking into this," Lyle said. I hated this kid's tone, like he didn't realize he was talking to someone with seniority. He was the type who, when the class was over and kids were tapping toes and the teacher asked, "Any more questions?" actually had more questions.

"I mean, the thing is, we all have theories about this case, but so many more doors would open for you than for anyone else," Lyle said, his leg jittering under the table. "I mean, people actually *want* to talk to you."

"Right." I pointed at the pitcher of beer Lyle had next to him, and he poured some into a plastic cup for me, mostly foam. Then he actually swiped his finger against his nose and put it in the beer, oil-flattened the foam, and poured more.

"So. What kind of compensation were you thinking?" He handed me the cup, and I set it in front of me, debating whether to drink it.

"I think it would have to be case by case," I said, pretending I was just thinking of this for the first time. "Depending on how hard it was to find the person and what questions you'd want me to ask."

"Well, I think we'd have a long list of people we'd want you to talk to. Do you really have no contact with Runner? It's Runner that would be tops on most lists."

Good old fucked-in-the-head Runner. He'd called me once in the past three years, mumbling crazily into the phone, crying in a *wee-heee!* shudder and asking me to wire him money. Nothing since.

Hell, not much before either. He'd shown up sporadically at Ben's trial, sometimes in an old tie and jacket, mostly in whatever he slept in, so drunk he listed. He was finally asked by Ben's defense to stop coming. It looked bad.

Now it looked even worse, with everyone in the Kill Club saying they believed he was the murderer. He'd been in jail three times I knew of before the killings, but just podunk crap. Still, the guy always had gambling debts—Runner bet on everything—sports, dog races, bingo, the weather. And he owed my mom child support. Killing us all would be a good way to be quit of that obligation.

But I couldn't picture Runner getting away with it, he wasn't smart enough, and definitely not ambitious enough. He couldn't even be a dad to his lone surviving child. He'd slunk around Kinnakee for a few years after the murders, sneaking away for months at a time, sending me duct-taped boxes from Idaho or Alabama or Winner, South Dakota: inside would be truck-stop figurines of little girls with big eyes holding umbrellas or kittens that were always broken by the time they reached me. I'd know he was back in town not because he came to visit me but because he'd light that stinky fire in the cabin up on the ridge. Diane would sing "Poor Judd Is Dead" when she saw him in town, face smudged with smoke. There was something both pitiful and frightening about him.

It was probably a blessing he chose to avoid me. When he'd come back to live with my mom and us, that last summer before the end, all he did was tease me. At first it was leering, *got your nose* sort of stuff—and then it was just mean. He came home from fishing one day, clomping through the house with his big wet waders, banging on the door to the bathroom when I was in the tub, just screwing with me. *Come on, open up, I gotta surprise for you!* He finally flung the door wide, his beer odor busting in with him. He had something bundled in his arms, and then he flung them wide, threw a live, two-foot catfish in the water with me. It was the pointlessness that frightened me. I tried to scrabble out of the tub, the fish's slimy skin sliding over my flesh, its whiskered mouth gaping, prehistoric. I could have put my foot in that mouth and the fish would have slid all the way up, tight like a boot.

I flopped over the side of the tub, panting on the rug, Runner screaming at me to stop my damnbaby crying. *Every single one of my kids is a scared-ass dumbshit.*

We couldn't clean ourselves for three days because Runner was too tired to kill the thing. I guess I get my laziness from him.

"I never know where Runner's at. Last I heard, he was somewhere in Arkansas. But that was a year ago. At least."

"Well, it might be a good idea to try to track him down. Some people would definitely want you to talk to him. Although I don't think Runner did it," Lyle said. "It maybe makes the most sense—debts, history of violence."

"Craziness."

"Craziness." Lyle smiled pertly. "But, he doesn't seem smart enough to pull that off. No offense."

"None taken. So, then, what's your theory?"

"I'm not quite ready to share that yet." He patted a stack of file folders next to him. "I'll let you read through the pertinent facts of the case first."

"Oh for the love of Pete," I said. Realizing, as my lips were pressed into the *P,* that it was my mother's phrase. *For the love of Pete, let's skeedaddle, where are my ding dang keys?*

"So if Ben's really innocent, why doesn't he try to get out?" I asked. My voice went high, urgent on this last part, a child's whinny: but *why* can't I have *dessert?* I realized I was stealthily hoping Ben was innocent, that he'd be returned to me, the Ben I knew, before I was afraid of him. I had allowed myself a dangerous glimpse of him out of prison, striding up to my house, hands in his pockets (another memory that came back, once I let myself start thinking again: Ben with his hands always burrowed deep in his pockets, perpetually abashed). Ben sitting at my dinner table, if I had a dinner table, happy, forgiving, no harm done. If he was innocent.

If ifs and buts were candies and nuts we'd all have a very Merry Christmas, I heard my aunt Diane boom in my head. Those words had been the bane of my childhood, a constant reminder that nothing turned out right, not just for me but for anyone, and that's why someone had invented a saying like that. So we'd all know that we'd never have what we needed.

Because—*remember, remember, remember, Baby Day*—Ben was

home that night. When I got out of bed to go to my mom's room, I saw his closed door with the light under it. Murmuring from inside. He was there.

"Maybe you could go ask him, make that your first stop, go see Ben."

Ben in prison. I'd spent the last twenty-odd years refusing to imagine the place. Now I pictured my brother in there, behind the wire, behind the concrete, down a gray slate hall, inside a cell. Did he have photos of the family anywhere? Would he even be allowed such a thing? I realized again I knew nothing about Ben's life. I didn't even know what a cell looked like aside from what I'd seen in the movies.

"No, not Ben. Not yet."

"Is it a money thing? We'd pay you for that."

"It's a lot-of-things thing," I grumbled.

"Okaaaaaaaay. You want to look into Runner then? Or . . . what?"

We sat silent. Neither of us knew what to do with our hands; we couldn't keep eye contact. As a child, I was constantly being sent on playdates with other kids—the shrinks insisted I interact with co-horts. That's what my meeting with Lyle was like: those first loose, horrible ten minutes, when the grown-ups have left, and neither kid knows what the other one wants, so you stand there, near the TV they've told you to keep off, fiddling with the antenna.

I picked through the complimentary bowl of peanuts in their shells, brittle and airy as beetle husks. I dropped a few in my beer to get the salt. I poked at them. They bobbed. My whole scheme seemed remarkably childish. Was I really going to go talk to people who might have killed my family? Was I really going to try to *solve* something? In any way but wishful thinking could I believe Ben was innocent? And if he was innocent, didn't that make me the biggest bastard in history? I had that overwhelming feeling I get when I'm about to give up on a plan, that big rush of air when I realize that my stroke of genius has flaws, and I don't have the brains or energy to fix them.

It wasn't an option to go back to bed and forget the whole thing. I had rent coming up, and I'd need money for food soon. I could go on welfare, but that would mean figuring out how to go on welfare, and I'd probably sooner starve than deal with the paperwork.

"I'll go talk to Ben," I mumbled. "I should start there. But I'd need $300."

I said it thinking I wouldn't really get it, but Lyle reached into an old nylon wallet, held together with duct tape, and counted out $300. He didn't look unhappy.

"Where you get all this money from, Lyle?"

He beefed up a bit at that, sat up straighter in his chair. "I'm treasurer of the Kill Club; I have a certain amount of discretionary funds. This is the project I choose to use them for." Lyle's tiny ears turned red, like angry embryos.

"You're embezzling." I suddenly liked him more.

Ben Day

I t was an hour bike ride from the farm to Kinnakee proper. At least an hour, at a good pace when the cold wasn't turning your lungs metal-red and blood wasn't dripping down your cheek. Ben planned his work at the school for the times when it was most empty—like, he'd never go there on a Saturday because the wrestling team had the gym on Saturdays. It was just too lame holding a mop when all these blocky, muscled, loud guys were waddling around, spitting chaw on the floor you just cleaned and then looking at you, half guilty, half daring you to say something.

Today was Wednesday, but it was still Christmas break, so the place should be kind of quiet—well, the weight room was always busy, always making that sound like a thumping steel heart. But it was early. Early was always best. He usually went from eight to noon, mopped and straightened and shined like the fucking monkey he was, and got the hell out before anyone saw him. Sometimes Ben felt like a fairy-tale elf who'd creep in and leave everything spotless without anyone noticing. The kids here didn't give a shit about keeping things clean: They'd toss a carton toward a trash can, the milk drooling all over the floor, and just shrug. They'd spill sloppy-joe meat on their cafeteria seat and just leave it there, hardening, for someone else to deal with. Ben did it, too, just because that's what everyone did. He'd actually drop a glob of tuna sandwich on the floor and roll his eyes like it wasn't worth dealing with, when he was the guy who'd be dealing with it in a few days. It was the stupidest thing, he was actually abusing himself.

So it sucked to deal with this shit at any point, and it was even worse to deal with it when other kids were around, trying to avoid seeing him. Today, though, he'd take his chances, go ahead and put in his shift. Diondra was driving into Salina for the morning to shop. The girl had at least twenty pairs of jeans, all of them looking the same to Ben, and she needed more, some special brand. She wore them baggy, rolled the cuffs tight at her ankle with those bulky socks peeking out. He always made sure he complimented the new jeans, and Diondra would then immediately say, *but what about the sooooocks?* It was a joke, but not really. Diondra wore only Ralph Lauren socks—they cost, like, $20 a pair, a fact that turned Ben's stomach. She had an entire dresser filled with socks—argyle and polka-dotted and striped, all with the horseman at the top, midswing. Ben had done the math: must be $400 of socks in that drawer, sitting there like a bin of Florida fruits—worth probably half what his mom made in a month. Well, rich people need stuff to buy, and socks are probably as good as anything. Diondra was a strange one, not really preppy—she was too flashy and wild to fit in that crowd—but not entirely in the metal crowd, either, even though she blared Iron Maiden and loved leather and smoked tons of weed. Diondra wasn't in any clique, she was just the New Girl. Everyone knew her but didn't at the same time. She'd lived all over, a lot of it in Texas, and her standard line whenever she did anything you might want to frown on, was "That's how they do it in Texas." No matter what she did, it was OK, because that's how they did it in Texas.

Before Diondra, Ben had just floated: he'd been a poor, quiet farm boy, who hung out with other farm kids in an unnoticed corner of the school. They weren't dorky enough to be actually reviled; they were never picked on. They were the background noise of high school. To him, that was worse than being humiliated. Well, maybe not, there was this guy with big bifocals, a kid Ben knew since kindergarten who'd always been weird. The kid crapped his pants the first week of high school—the stories varied how: one had him dropping bundles of shit out his shorts while he climbed the rope in gym, another had him losing a load in homeroom, there were third and fourth and fifth versions. The main point was, he was forever branded Shitshorts. He kept his head down between classes, those moon-sized glasses aimed at the floor, and still some jock would slap him in the head, Hey Shitshorts! He'd just keep walking, his face in this grim smile, like he was pretending to be in on the joke. So yeah, there were worse things than being unnoticed, but Ben hadn't liked it, didn't want to be the same Nice, Quiet Red-headed Kid he'd been since first grade. Dickless and boring.

Big fucking thanks then to Diondra for claiming him, at least in private. She'd actually hit him with her car, that's how they met. It was summer—orientation for freshmen and new kids. It was a crummy three hours, and after, as he was walking across the school parking lot, she'd plowed into him. Knocked him right up on her hood. She'd gotten out, screaming at him, *What the fuck is fucking wrong with you?* her breath smelling of wine cooler, the bottles clinking in the footwell of her CRX. When Ben apologized—he *apologized* to her—and Diondra realized he wasn't going to get angry at her, she got real sweet, she offered to give him a ride home and instead they drove to the outside of town and parked and drank more wine coolers. Diondra said her name was Alexis, but after a little bit she told him she'd lied. It was Diondra. Ben told her she should never lie about a cool name like that and it made her happy and after a little bit longer Diondra said, "You know what, you have a really nice face," and then a few seconds later, she said, "You wanna scam or what?" and then they were full-on making out, which wasn't his first time, but was only his second. After an hour, Diondra had to go, but she said he was a great listener, it was really cool how great a listener he was. She didn't have time to drive him home after all. She dropped him off right back where she'd hit him.

So they started dating. Ben didn't really know her friends, and he didn't ever hang out with her at school. Diondra darted in and out of the schoolweek like a hummingbird, sometimes she'd show up, sometimes not. It was enough to see her on the weekends, in their own space where school didn't matter. Being with her had rubbed off on him, he was just more *there*.

By the time Ben pedaled into Kinnakee, a cluster of pickup trucks and beat-up sports cars sat in the school parking lot. So, basketball players as well as wrestlers. He knew who drove each car. He thought about ducking out, but Diondra wouldn't be home for hours, and he didn't have enough money to linger at the hamburger joint—the owner was red-faced crazy about kids hanging out there without buying something. Plus sitting by yourself at a diner during Christmas break was worse than actually working. Fuck his mom for being such a stress case. Diondra's mom and dad didn't care what she did—they were out of town half the time at their place in Texas. Even when Diondra was busted for missing two whole weeks of school last month, her mom had just laughed. *When the cat's away, huh, sweetie? At least try to do some homework.*

The back entrance to the school was chained shut, so he had to go in through the locker rooms. The smell of flesh and footspray hit him as he entered. The overhead thunk of the basketball court and clank of the weight room reassured him that the locker room, at least, would be empty. Outside in the hallway, he heard a single long yell—*Coooooper! Hold uppp!*—echo against the marble floor like a battle cry. Tennis shoes slapped down the hall, a metal door banged open, and then everything was relatively quiet. Just gym and weight-room noise: thunk-thunk, clank, thunk.

The school's athletes had this trust thing, a sign of teamwork, that they never put locks on their lockers. Instead they all tied thick shoestrings through the loops where a lock would go. At least twelve white strings hung on the lockers and Ben wavered as usual about looking inside one. What the hell did these guys need anyway? If you had school lockers for books, what would go in these gym bins? Were there deodorants or lotions, some kind of underclothes that he was missing? Did they all wear the same kind of jockstrap? Thunk-thunk, clank, thunk. One shoelace hung limply, unknotted, just a quick yank and the locker would open. Before he could talk himself out of it, he pulled off the lace and gently, quietly lifted the metal latch. Inside the locker was nothing of interest: some gym shorts crumpled at the bottom, a rolled-up sports magazine, a gym bag hanging loosely from a hook. The bag looked like it contained a few objects, so Ben leaned in and unzipped it.

"Hey!"

He turned around, the bag swaying wildly on the hook and falling to the bottom of the locker. Mr. Gruger, the wrestling coach, was standing with a newspaper in his hand, his rough, splotchy face twisted up.

"What the hell do you think you're doing in that locker?"

"I, uh, it was open."

"What?"

"It was, I saw it was open," Ben said. He shut it as quietly as he could. Please fuckfuckfuck just not let any of the team come back in, Ben thought. He could picture all the angry faces aimed at him, the nicknames to come.

"It was open? Why were you in it?" Gruger let the question hang there, didn't move, didn't give any clue what he was going to do, what level of trouble this was. Ben tried just staring at the floor, waiting to be chastened.

"I said, why were you in that locker?" Gruger smacked the newspaper against his fat hand.

"I don't know."

The old man just kept standing there, Ben thinking all the while, *just yell and get it done with.*

"Were you going to take something?"

"No."

"Then why were you in it?"

"I was just . . ." Ben trailed off again. "I thought I saw something."

"You thought you saw something? What?"

Ben's mind flashed on things forbidden: pets, drugs, titty magazines. He pictured firecrackers and he thought for a second he'd say the locker was on fire, be a hero.

"Uh, matches."

"You thought you saw matches?" The blood in Gruger's face had moved from his cheeks straight up to the flesh beneath his fuzzy crewcut.

"I wanted a cigarette."

"You're the janitor boy, right? Something Day?"

Gruger made the name sound silly, girlish. The coach's eyes examined the cut on Ben's forehead, then marched pointedly up to his hair.

"You dyed your hair."

Ben stood under his thatch of black and felt himself being categorized and discarded, sectioned off into a group of losers, druggies, wimps, fags. He was sure he heard that word snarl into the coach's mind—Gruger's upper lip twitched.

"Get out of here. Go clean somewhere else. Don't come back in here til we're gone. You are not welcome here. You understand?"

Ben nodded.

"Why don't you say it out loud, just so we're clear."

"I'm not welcome here," Ben mumbled.

"Now go." He said it like Ben was a boy, a five-year-old being sent back to his mother. Ben went.

Up the stairwell to the janitor's dank closet, a droplet of sweat dripping down his back. Ben wasn't breathing. He forgot to breathe when he was this angry. He got out the industrial-sized bucket and rattled it into the sink, ran hot water into it, poured in the piss-colored cleaning mixture, ammonia fumes burning his eyes. Then heaved it back into the wheelframe. He'd filled the bucket too heavy, it tipped as he tried to get it over the edge of the sink, sloshing a half-gallon of water down his front. His crotch and leg were nice and soaked. Looked like he wet himself, Janitor Boy Day. The jeans stuck to his thighs, turned rigid. He'd have three hours of shitty grunt work with a wet crotch and jeans like cardboard.

"Fuck you, fucker," he muttered quietly. He kicked the wall with a workboot, spraying plaster, and smashed the wall with a hand. "Fuuuuuck!" he bellowed, his voice going high at the end. He waited in the closet like a coward, worrying that Gruger would track the scream and decide to screw with him some more.

Nothing happened. No one was interested enough to see what was going on in the janitorial closet.

———

HE WAS SUPPOSED to have cleaned a week earlier, but Diondra had whined it was officially Christmas break, leave it. So the cafeteria trash was filled with old soda cans dripping syrup, sandwich wrappers covered in chicken salad, and moldy helpings of 1984's final lunch special, a hamburger casserole with sweet tomato sauce. All of it rotten. He got a little bit of everything on his sweater and jeans, so in addition to ammonia and B.O. he smelled like old food. He couldn't go to Diondra's like this, he was an idiot to have planned it like this in the first place. He'd have to bike home, deal with his mom—that was a thirty-minute lecture right there—shower, and bike back over to her place. If his mom didn't ground him. Screw it, he'd still leave. It was his body, his hair. His fucked-up faggoty black hair.

He mopped the floors, then bagged the trash in all the teachers' rooms—his favorite chore because it sounded big but amounted to gathering bunches of crumpled paper, light as leaves. His final duty was to mop down the hall that connected the high school to the grade school (which had its own embarrassed student-janitor). The hallway was papered with loud notices about football and track and drama club on the high school side, and then slowly disintegrated into children's territory, the walls covered with letters of the alphabet and book reports on George Washington. Bright-blue doors marked the grade-school entrance, but they were ceremonial; they didn't even have locks. He mopped his way from Highschooland to Kiddieville and dropped the mop into the bucket, kicked the whole thing away from him. The bucket rolled smoothly across the concrete floor and hit the wall with a modest splash.

From kindergarten through eighth grade, he'd gone to Kinnakee Grade School; he had more connection with that side of the building than the high school side where he stood now, pieces of its refuse stuck to him.

He thought about opening the door, wandering through the silence on the other side, and then that's what he was doing. Just saying hi to the old place. Ben heard the door shut behind him, and felt more relaxed. The walls here were lemon yellow, with more decorations outside each classroom. Kinnakee was small enough that each grade was just one class. The high school was different, twice as big because other towns funneled their teens in. But the grade school was always nice and cozy. On the wall, he spotted a smiley felt sunshine, Michelle D., Age 10, written along one side. And here was a drawing of a cat in a vest with buckle shoes—or maybe they were high heels—anyway it was smiling and handing a present to a mouse who was holding a birthday cake. Libby D., Grade 1. He looked but saw nothing from Debby, he wasn't sure the kid could draw, come to think of it. She tried to help his mom bake cookies one time, breathing loudly and botching the recipe, then eating more of the dough than she cooked. Debby was not the kind of kid who had anything put up on the wall.

All along the hallway were rows of yellow bins where the students were allowed to keep personal items, each kid's name written on masking tape on their bin. He looked in Libby's and found a peppermint candy, partially sucked, and a paper clip. Debby's had a brown lunchsack that stank of baloney; Michelle's a pack of dried-up markers. He looked in a few others just for kicks, and realized how much more stuff they had. Sixty-four Crayola crayon box sets, battery-operated toy cars and dolls, thick reams of construction paper, key chains and sticker books and bags of candy. Sad. That's what you get when you have more kids than you can take care of, he thought. It was what Diondra always said when he mentioned tight times at home: *Well, your mom shouldn't have had so many babies then.* Diondra was an only child.

Ben started back toward the high school side, and caught himself scanning the fifth grade bins. There she was, the little girl Krissi with the crush on him. She'd written her name in bright green letters and drawn a daisy next to it. Cute. The girl was the definition of cute, like something on a cereal commercial—blond hair, blue eyes, and just well taken care of. Unlike his sisters, her jeans always fit and were clean and ironed; her shirts matched the color of her socks or barrettes or whatever. She didn't have food-breath like Debby or scrapes all over her hands like Libby. Like all of them. Her fingernails were always painted bright pink, you could tell her mom did them for her. He bet her bin was filled with Strawberry Shortcake dolls and other toys that smelled good.

Even her name was right—Krissi Cates was just a naturally cool name. By high school, she'd be a cheerleader, that long blond hair down her back, and she'd probably forget she ever went crazy over this older boy named Ben. He'd be what then, twenty? Maybe drive in with Diondra from Wichita for a game and she'd look over mid-bounce and see him, break into a big white smile, do a little excited wave, and Diondra would do her hee-haw laugh and say, "Isn't it enough that half the women in Wichita are in love with you, you gotta pick on poor little high school girls too?"

Ben might never have met Krissi—she was a grade above Michelle—but he got recruited one day at the beginning of the school year. Mrs. Nagel, who always liked him, grabbed Ben to help monitor the after-school art class. Just for the day. Her usual monitor hadn't shown up. He'd been due back home, but knew his mom couldn't get pissed at him helping with the little ones—she was always on him to help with the little ones at home—and mixing paint was a hell of a lot more inviting than hauling manure. Krissi was one of his kids, but she didn't seem that interested in painting. She just moved the stuff around with her brush until her whole paper turned shit brown.

"You know what that looks like," he'd said.

"Poop," she said and started laughing.

She was flirty, even for a kid, you could tell she was born cute and just assumed people would like her. Well, he did. They talked between long flatlines of silence.

So where do you live?

Pour, slap, swipe. Dip the brush in the water and repeat.

Near Salina.

And you come all the way out here for school?

They haven't finished my school yet. Next year, I'll go near home.

That's a long drive.

Squeak of a seat, slump of a shoulder.

Yup. I hate it. I have to wait hours after school for my dad to get me.

Well, art's good.

I guess. I like ballet more, that's what I do on weekends.

Ballet on weekends said a lot. She probably was one of those kids with a pool in the backyard, or if not a pool a trampoline. He thought about telling her they had cows at his house—see if she liked animals—but felt like he was already too eager with her. She was a kid, she should be the one trying to impress.

He volunteered the rest of that month in art, teasing Krissi about her bad drawings *(what's this supposed to be, a turtle?)* and letting her go on about ballet *(no, you big goof, it's my dad's BMW!)*. One day, gutsy girl, she snuck over to the high school side of the building and was waiting at his locker in jeans with sequin butterflies on the pocket and a pink shirt that poked out in gumdrop lumps where her breasts would be. No one was bothering her, except for one maternal girl who tried to mother her back to the right side of the building.

"I'm OK," she told her, flipping her hair, and turned to Ben. "I just wanted to give you this."

She handed him a note, folded into the shape of a triangle, with his name written in bubble letters on the front. Then she pranced away, half the size of most the kids around her, but not looking like she noticed.

> *Once I was in art class and met a boy named*
> *   Ben.*
> *It was his heart I knew I would win.*
> *He has red hair and really nice skin.*
> *Are you "in"?*

At the bottom was a big *L,* with *-onger -etter -ater* written alongside it. He'd seen friends of friends with notes like these, but hardly ever got them himself. Last February, he got three valentines, one from the teacher because she had to, one from the nice girl who gave everybody one, and one from the urgent fat girl who always seemed on the edge of crying.

Diondra wrote him now sometimes, but the notes weren't cute, they were dirty or angry, stuff she scrawled in detention. No girl had ever done a poem for him, and it was even cuter that she seemed to have no idea he was way too old for her. It was a love poem from a girl who had no idea about sex or making out. (Or did she? When did normal kids start making out?)

The next day she waited for him outside art class and asked him if he'd sit in the stairwell with her, and he said OK but just for a second, and they'd joked around for a whole hour on those shadowy stairs. At one point she grabbed his arm and leaned into him and he knew he should tell her not to, but it felt so sweet and not at all weird and just nice, not like Diondra's sex-crazed scratching and yelling or his sisters' poking and roughhousing, but sweet the way a girl should be. She wore lipgloss that smelled like bubblegum, and since Ben never had enough money for bubblegum—how fucked-up was that—it always made his mouth water.

So they'd gone on like that for the last few months, sitting in the stairwell, waiting for her dad. They never talked on the weekends, and sometimes she even forgot to wait for him, and he'd be standing in the stairwell like a dick holding a packet of warm Skittles he'd found cleaning the cafeteria. Krissi loved sweet things. His sisters were the same way, they scrounged for sugar like beetles; he came home one time to find Libby eating jelly straight out of the jar.

Diondra never knew about the thing with Krissi. When Diondra did come to school, she beat it straight home at 3:16 to watch her soaps and *Donahue*. (She usually did this while eating cake batter straight from the mixing bowl, what was it with girls and sugar?) And even if Diondra did know, there was nothing wrong going on. He was like a guidance counselor in a way. An older guy advising a girl on homework and high school. Maybe he should go into psychology, or be a teacher. His dad was *five* years older than his mom.

The only iffy thing with him and Krissi happened just before Christmas and wouldn't happen again. They were sitting in the stairwell, sucking on green apple Jolly Ranchers and jostling each other and suddenly she was much closer than usual, a small nudge of nipple on his arm. The apple smell was hot on his neck, and she just clung there against him, not saying anything, just breathing, and he could feel her heartbeat like a kitten on his bicep and her fingers squirm up near his armpits and suddenly her lips were right there on his ear, that breath turning his ear wet, his gums twitching from the tartness of the candy, and then the lips were trailing down his cheek, sending chills down his arms and neither of them acknowledging what was going on and then her face was in front of his, and those little lips pushing against his, not really moving, and the two of them just staying there with identical beating hearts, her entire body now fitted between his legs and his hands kept rigidly down by his sides, gone all sweaty, and then a small moving of his lips, just a little opening and her tongue was there, sticky and lapping and them both tasting of green apple and his dick got so hard he thought it might explode in his pants and he put his hands on her waist and held her for a second and moved her off him and ran down the stairwell to the boy's bathroom—yelling, *sorry sorry* behind him—and he made it into a stall just in time to jerk twice and come all over his hands.

Libby Day

NOW

So I was going to meet my brother, all grown up. After my beer with Lyle, I actually went home and looked at Barb Eichel's copy of *Your Prison Family: Get Past the Bars!* After reading a few confusing chapters about the administration of the Florida State Penitentiary system, I flipped back through the foxed pages to the copyright: 1985. How not remotely useful. I worried about receiving more pointless bundles from Barb: pamphlets about defunct Alabama waterslide parks, brochures about smithereened Las Vegas hotels, warnings about the Y2K bug.

I ended up making Lyle handle all the arrangements. I told him I couldn't get through to the right person, was overwhelmed by it all, but the truth was I just didn't want to. I don't have the stamina: press numbers, wait on hold, talk, wait on hold, then be real nice to some pissed-off woman with three kids and annual resolutions to go back to college, some woman just wiggling with the hope you'll give her an excuse to pull the plug on you. She's a bitch all right, but you can't call her that or all of a sudden there you are, chutes-and-laddered back to the beginning. And that's supposed to make you nicer when you phone back. Let Lyle deal with it.

Ben's prison is right outside Kinnakee and was built in 1997 after another round of farm consolidations. Kinnakee is almost in the middle of Kansas, not so far from the Nebraska border, and it once claimed to be the geographic center of the forty-eight contiguous United States. The heart of America. It was a big deal back in the '80s, when we were all patriotic. Other cities in Kansas made a grab for the title, but Kinnakeeans ignored them, stubbornly, proudly. It was the city's only point of interest. The Chamber of Commerce sold posters and T-shirts with the town's name cursived inside a heart. Every year Diane bought all us girls a new shirt, partly because we liked anything heart-shaped, and partly because Kinnakee is an old Indian word, which means Magical Little Woman. Diane always tried to get us to be feminists. My mom joked that she didn't shave much and that was a start. I don't remember her saying it but I remember Diane, broad and angry as she always was after the murders, smoking a cigarette in her trailer, drinking ice tea out of a plastic cup with her name written in log-cabin letters on the side, telling me the story.

Turns out we were wrong after all. Lebanon, Kansas, is the official center of the United States. Kinnakee was working from bad information.

I'D THOUGHT I'D have months before I got permission to see Ben, but it seems the Kinnakee Kansas State Penitentiary is quick with the visitor passes. ("It's our belief that interaction with family and friends is a beneficial activity for inmates, helping them stay socialized and connected.") Paperwork and bullshit and then I spent the few intervening days going over Lyle's files, reading the transcript of Ben's trial, which I'd never mustered enough courage to do.

It made me sweat. My testimony was a zigzag of confusing kid-memories *(I think Ben brought a witch to the house and she killed us,* I said, to which the prosecutor replied only, *Mmmm, now let's talk about what really happened")* and overly coached dialogue *(I saw Ben as I was standing on the edge of my Mom's room, he was threatening my Mom with our shotgun).* As for Ben's defense attorney, he might as well have wrapped me in tissue paper and set me on a feather bed, he was so delicate with me *(Might you be a little confused about what you saw, Libby? Are you positive, positive it was your brother, Libby? Are you maybe telling us what you think we want to hear?* To which I replied *No Yes No.)* By the end of the day, I answered *I guess* to every single question, my way of saying I was done.

Ben's defense attorney had hammered at that bit of blood on Michelle's bedspread, and the mysterious dress shoe that left a print in my family's blood, but couldn't come up with a convincing alternate theory. Maybe someone else had been there, but there were no footprints, no tire treads outside the house to prove it. The morning of January 3 brought a twenty-degree bump in the temperature, melting the snow and all its imprints to a springlike mush.

Besides my testimony, Ben had weighing against him: fingernail scratches across his face he couldn't explain, a story about a bushy-haired man he initially claimed killed everyone—a story he quickly exchanged for the "out all night, don't know nothing" defense—a large chunk of Michelle's hair found on the floor of his room, and his general crazy demeanor that day. He'd dyed his hair black, which everyone deemed suspicious. He'd been spotted "sneaking" around school, several teachers testified. They wondered if he was perhaps trying to retrieve some of the animal remains that he'd kept in his locker (animal remains?) or if he was gathering other students' personal items for a satanic mass. Later in the day he apparently went to some stoner hangout and bragged about his Devil sacrifices.

Ben didn't help himself either: He had no alibi for the murders; he had a key to the house, which had not been broken into; he'd had a fight with my mother that morning. Also he was kind of a shit. As the prosecutors proclaimed that he was a Satan-worshiping killer, Ben responded by enthusiastically discussing the rituals of Devil worship, particular songs he liked that reminded him of the underworld, and the great power of Satanism. *(It encourages you to do what feels good, because we are all basically animals.)* At one point the prosecutor asked Ben to "stop playing with your hair and get serious, do you understand this is serious?"

"I understand you think it's serious," Ben replied.

It didn't even sound like the Ben I remembered, the quiet, bundled brother of mine. Lyle had included a few news photos from the trial: Ben with his black hair in a ponytail (why didn't his lawyers make him cut it?), wedged into a lopsided suit, always either smirking or completely affectless.

So Ben didn't help himself, but the trial transcript made me blush. Then again, the whole thing left me feeling a little better. It wasn't all my fault Ben was in jail (if he was truly innocent, if he truly was). No, it was a little bit of everybody's fault.

A WEEK AFTER agreeing to meet Ben, I was meeting Ben. I was driving back toward my hometown, where I hadn't been in at least twelve years, which had turned itself into a prison town without my permission. The whole thing was too quick, it gave me emotional bends. The only way I could get in the car was to keep reassuring myself I would not go into Kinnakee proper, and I would not go down that long dirt road that would take me home, no I would not. Not that it was my home anymore: Someone had bought the property years ago, razed the house immediately, crushing walls my mother had prettied with cheap flowery posters, smashing windows we'd breathed against while waiting to see who was coming down the drive, splintering the doorframe where my mom had penciled the growth of Ben and my sisters but been too tired to chart me (I had just one entry: Libby 3'2").

I drove three hours into Kansas, rolling up and down the Flint Hills, then hitting the flatlands, signs inviting me to visit the Greyhound Hall of Fame, the Museum of Telephony, the Largest Ball of Twine. Again a burst of loyalty: I should go to them all, if only to smack ironic road-trippers. I finally turned off the highway, heading north and west and north and west on jigsaw back roads, the farm fields dots of green and yellow and brown, pastoral pointillism. I huddled over the wheel, flipping stations between weepy country tunes and Christian rock and fuzz. The struggling March sun managed to warm the car, blazed my grotesque red hairline. The warmth and the color made me think again of blood. In the passenger seat next to me was a single airplane bottle of vodka I planned to swallow when I got to the prison, a self-prescribed dose of numbness. It took an uncharacteristic amount of willpower not to gulp it on the drive, one hand on the wheel, throat tilted back.

Like a magic trick, just as I was thinking *Getting close now,* a tiny sign popped up on the wide, flat horizon. I knew exactly what it would say: *Welcome to Kinnakee: Heart of America!* in 1950s cursive. It did, and I could just make out a spray of bullet holes in the bottom left-hand corner, where Runner blasted it from his pickup truck decades before. Then I got closer and realized I was imagining the bullet holes. This was a tidy new sign, but with the same old script: *Welcome to Kinnakee: Heart of America!* Sticking with the lie, I liked it. Just as I passed the sign, another one arrived: Kinnakee Kansas State Penitentiary, next left. I followed the direction, driving west over land that was once the Evelee farm. *Ha, serves you right, Evelees,* I thought, but I couldn't remember why the Evelees were bad. I just remembered they were.

I slowed to a crawl as I drove down this new road, far on the outer edge of town. Kinnakee had never been a prosperous place—it was mostly struggling farms and optimistic plywood mansions from a preposterously brief oil boom. Now it was worse. The prison business hadn't saved the town. The street was lined with pawn shops and flimsy houses, barely a decade old and already sagging. Stunned children stood in the middle of grubby yards. Trash collected everywhere: food wrappers, drinking straws, cigarette butts. An entire to-go meal—Styrofoam box, plastic fork, Styrofoam cup—sat on a curb, abandoned by the eater. A scatter of ketchupy fries lay in the gutter nearby. Even the trees were miserable: scrawny, stunted, and stubbornly refusing to bud. At the end of the block, a young, dumpy couple sat in the cold on a Dairy Queen bench, staring out at the traffic, like they were watching TV.

On a nearby telephone pole flapped a grainy photocopy of an unsmiling teen, missing since October 2007. Two more blocks, and what I thought was a copy of the same poster turned out to be a new missing girl, vanished in June 2008. Both girls were unkempt, surly, which explained why they weren't getting the Lisette Stephens treatment. I made a mental note to take a smiling, pretty photo of myself in case I ever disappeared.

A few more minutes, and the prison appeared within a big sun-burnt clearing.

It was less imposing than I'd pictured, the few times I'd pictured it. It had a sprawling, suburban look to it, could be mistaken for some regional offices of a refrigeration company, maybe a telecommunications headquarters, except for the razor wire that curlicued around the walls. The looping wire reminded me of the phone cord that Ben and my mom always fought over toward the end, the one we were always tripping on. Debby was cremated with a little starburst scar on her wrist because of that goddang phone cord. I made myself cough loudly, just to hear something.

I rolled into the lot, the poured-tar surface wonderfully smooth after an hour of potholes. I parked and sat staring, my car crinkling from the drive. From just inside the walls came the murmur and shouts of men, taking their rec time. The vodka went down with a medicinal sting. I chewed a piece of hardened spearmint gum once, twice, then spit it into a sandwich wrapper, feeling my ears get booze-warmed. Then I reached under my sweater and undid my bra, feeling my breasts woosh down, big and dog-eared, to the background noise of murderers playing hoops. That's one thing Lyle had advised me on, stuttering and careful with his words: *You only get one chance to get through the metal detector. It's not like at the airport—there's no wand thing. So you should leave everything metal in your car. Um, including, um, with women, uh, the, I think is it underwire? In the bras. That would be, could be a problem.*

Fine, then. I stuck the bra in my glove compartment and let my breasts roam free.

In the interior of the prison, the guards were well mannered, as if they'd seen many instructional videos on courtesy: yes ma'am, right this way ma'am. Their eye contact was without depth, my image bounced right back at me, hot-potato. Searches, questions, yes ma'am, and lots of waiting. Doors opened and shut, opened and shut, as I walked through a series of them, each shifting in size, like a metal Wonderland. The floors stank of bleach and the air smelled beefy and humid. Somewhere nearby must be the lunchroom. I suffered a nauseous wave of nostalgia, picturing us Day kids and our subsidized school meals: the bosomy, steamed women, yelling *Free*

Lunch! toward the cash register as we came through with a dump of stroganoff and some room-temperature milk.

Ben had good timing, I thought: Kansas's disappearing-reappearing death penalty was in moratorium when the murders happened (here I paused at my jarring new mental phrasing, "when the murders happened," as opposed to "when Ben killed everyone"). He was sentenced to prison for life. But at least I didn't get him killed. I now stood outside the smooth, submarine-metal door of the visitation room and then stood longer. "Nothing to it but to do it, nothing to it but to do it." Diane's mantra. I needed to stop thinking family thoughts. The guard with me, a stiff blond man who'd spared me small talk, made an *after-you* overture.

I swung the door open and shoved myself inside. Five booths sat in a row, one occupied by a heavyset Native Indian woman, talking to her inmate son. The woman's black hair speared down her shoulders, violent-looking. She was muttering dully to the young guy, who nodded jerkily, the phone close to his ear, his eyes down.

I sat two booths away, and was just settling in, taking a breath, when Ben shot through the door, like a cat making a break for the outside. He was small, maybe 5'6", and his hair had turned a dark rust. He wore it long, sweeping his shoulders, tucked girlishly behind his ears. With wire-rim glasses and an orange jumpsuit, he looked like a studious mechanic. The room was small, so he got to me in three steps, all the while smiling quietly. Beaming. He sat down, placed a hand on the glass, nodded at me to do the same. I couldn't do it, couldn't press my palm against his, moist against the window like ham. I smiled milkily at him instead and picked up the phone.

On the other side of the glass, he held the phone in his hand, cleared his throat, then looked down, started to say something, then stopped. I was left looking at the crown of his head for almost a minute. When he looked up, he was crying, two tears from both his eyes trickling down his face. He wiped them away with the back of a hand, then smiled, his lips wavering.

"God, you look just like Mom," he said all at once, getting it out, and coughed, wiped more tears. "I didn't know that." His eyes flickered between my face and his hands. "Oh, God, Libby, how are you?"

I cleared my own throat and said, "I guess I'm OK. I just

thought it was time I came and saw you." *I do sort of look like Mom,* I thought. *I do.* And then I thought, *my big brother,* and felt the same chesty pride I'd had as a kid. He looked so much the same, pale face, that Day knob of a nose. He hadn't even grown much since the murders. Like we both got stunted that night. My big brother, and he was happy to see me. *He knows how to play you,* I warned myself. Then I set the thought aside.

"I'm glad, I'm glad," Ben said, still looking at the side of his hand. "I've thought about you a lot over these years, been wondering about you. That's what you do in here . . . think and wonder. Every once in a while someone'll write me about you. But it's not the same."

"No," I agreed. "Are they treating you OK?" I asked, stupidly, my eyes glazed, and suddenly I was crying and all I wanted to say was *sorryI'msorryI'msosorry.* Instead I said nothing, looking only at a constellation of acne scattered around one corner of Ben's lips.

"I'm fine, Libby, Libby, look at me." My eyes to his. "I'm fine. I really am. I got my high school degree in here, which is more than I ever prolly would have done outside, and I'm even partway to a college degree. English. I read fucking Shakespeare." He made the guttural sound that he always tried to pass off for a laugh. "Forsooth, you dirty bugger."

I didn't know what the last part meant, but I smiled because he was waiting for me to smile.

"Man, Libby, I could just drink you in. You don't know how good it is to see you. Shit, I'm sorry. You just look like Mom, do people tell you that all the time?"

"Who would tell me that? There's no one. Runner's gone, don't know where, Diane and I don't talk." I wanted him to feel sorry for me, to float around in my big empty pool of pity. Here we were, the last of the Days. If he felt sorry for me, it would be harder to blame me. The tears kept coming and now I just let them. Two chairs down, the Indian woman was saying her good-byes, her weeping just as deep as her voice.

"Ya'all by yourself, huh? That's no good. They should've took better care of you."

"What are you, born again?" I blurted, my face wet. Ben

frowned, not understanding. "Is that it? You forgiving me? You're not supposed to be nice to me." But I craved it, could feel the need for the relief, like setting down a hot plate.

"Nah, I'm not that nice," he said. "I got a lot of anger for a lot of people, you're just not one."

"But," I said, and gulped down a sob like a kid. "But my testimony. I think, I may, I don't know, I don't know . . ." *It had to have been him,* I warned myself again.

"Oh that." He said, like it was a minor inconvenience, some snag in a summer vacation best forgotten. "You don't read my letters, huh?"

I tried to explain with an inadequate shrug.

"Well, your testimony . . . It only surprised me that people believed you. It didn't surprise me what you said. You were in a totally insane situation. And you always were a little liar." He laughed again and I did too, quick matching laughs like we'd caught the same cough. "No, seriously, the fact that they believed you? They wanted me in here, I was going to be in here, that just proved it. Fucking little seven-year-old. Man, you were so small . . ." His eyes turned up to the right, daydreaming. Then he pulled himself back. "You know what I thought of the other day, I don't know why. I thought of that goddam porcelain bunny, the one Mom made us put on the toilet."

I shook my head, no clue what he was talking about.

"You don't remember that, the little bunny? Because the toilet didn't work right, if we used it twice in an hour it stopped flushing. So if one of us crapped when it wasn't working, we were supposed to close the lid and put the bunny on top, so no one else would open the lid and see a toilet full of crap. Because you guys would scream. I can't believe you don't remember this. It was so stupid, it made me so mad. I was mad I had to share a bathroom with all of you, I was mad I lived in a house with one toilet that didn't even work, I was mad about the bunny. The bunny," he broke into his confined laugh, "I found the bunny, like, it humiliated me or something. Unmanned me. I took it very personally. Like Mom was supposed to find a car figurine or a gun figurine for me to use. Man, I would get so worked up about it. I'd stand there by the toilet and think, 'I will not put that bunny down,' and then I'd get ready to leave and I'd think, 'Goddamit, I gotta put the bunny down or one of them's gonna come in here and all the screaming—you guys were screamers, high, *Eeeeeeaaaahh!*—and I don't want to deal with that so fine here's the goddam bunny on your goddam toilet!' " He laughed again, but the memory had cost him, his face was flushed and his nose was sweaty. "That's the kind of stuff you think of in here. Weird stuff."

I tried to find that bunny in my memory, tried to inventory the bathroom and the things in it, but I came out with nothing, a handful of water.

"Sorry, Libby, that's a strange memory to throw at you."

I put one tip of my finger near the bottom of the glass window and said, "That's fine."

WE SAT IN silence for a bit, pretending to listen to noise that wasn't there. We had just started but the visit was almost over. "Ben, can I ask you something?"

"I think so." His face went blank, preparing.

"Don't you want to get out of here?"

"Sure."

"Why don't you give the police your alibi for that night? There is no way you were sleeping in a barn."

"I just don't have a good alibi, Libby. I just don't. It happens."

"Because it was, like, zero degrees out. I remember." I rubbed my half finger beneath the counter, wiggled my two toes on my right foot.

"I know, I know. You can't imagine." He turned his face away. "You can't imagine how many weeks, *years,* I've spent in here wishing I'd done it all differently. Mom and Michelle and Debby might not be dead if I'd just . . . been a man. Not some dumb kid. Hiding in a barn, angry at Mommy." A tear splashed onto the phone receiver, I thought I could hear it, *bing!* "I'm OK being punished for that night . . . I feel . . . OK."

"But. I don't understand. Why were you so . . . unhelpful with the police?"

Ben shrugged his shoulders, and again the face went death-mask.

"Oh God. I just. I was such an unconfident kid. I mean, I was fifteen, Libby. Fifteen. I didn't know what it was to be a man. I mean,

Runner sure wasn't helpful. I was this kid no one paid much attention to one way or the other, and here all of a sudden, people were
treating me like *I* scared *them*. I mean, presto chango, I was this big
man."

"A big man charged with murdering his family."

"You want to call me a stupid fuck, Libby, please, go ahead. To
me, it was simple: I said I didn't do it, I knew I didn't do it, and—I
don't know, defense mechanism?—I just didn't take it as seriously as
I should have. If I'd reacted the way everyone expected me to, I probably wouldn't be here. At night I bawled into a pillow, but I played it
tough when anyone could see me. It's fucked up, believe me I know
it. But you should never put a fifteen-year-old on a witness stand in a
courtroom filled with a bunch of people he knows and expect a lot of
tears. My thoughts were that of course I'd be acquitted, and then I'd
be admired at school for being such a bad-ass. I mean, I daydreamed
about that shit. I never ever thought I was in danger of . . . ending up
like this." He was crying now, wiped his cheek again. "Clearly, I've
gotten over whether people see me cry."

"We need to fix this," I said, finally.

"It's not going to be fixed, Libby, not unless they find who did it."

"Well, you need some new lawyers, working on the case," I reasoned. "All the stuff they can do with DNA now . . ." DNA to me
was some sort of magical element, some glowing goo that was always
getting people out of prison.

Ben laughed through closed lips, the way he did when we were
kids, not letting you enjoy it.

"You sound like Runner," he said. "About every two years I get a
letter from him: *DNA! We need to get some of that DNA.* Like I have a
lockerful of it and just don't want to share. *D-N-A!*" he said again,
doing Runner's crazy-eyed head nod.

"You know where he is now?"

"Last letter was care of Bert Nolan's Group Home for Men,
somewhere in Oklahoma. He asked me to send him 500 bucks, so he
could continue his research on my behalf. Whoever Bert Nolan is,
he's ruing the day he let goddam Runner into his home for men." He
scratched his arm, raising his sleeve just enough for me to see a tattoo

of a woman's name. It ended in *-olly* or *-ally*. I made sure he saw me notice.

"Ah this? Old flame. We started as penpals. I thought I loved her, thought I'd marry her, but turned out she didn't really want to be stuck with a guy in prison for life. Wish she'd told me before I got the tat."

"Must've hurt."

"It didn't tickle."

"I meant the breakup."

"Oh, that sucked too."

The guard gave us the three-minute signal and Ben rolled his eyes: "Hard to decide what to say in three minutes. Two minutes you just start making plans for another visit. Five minutes you can finish your conversation. Three minutes?" He pushed out his lips, made a raspberry noise. "I really hope you come again, Libby. I forgot how homesick I was. You look just like her."

Patty Day

She'd retreated to the bathroom after Len left, his livery smile still offering something unsavory, some sort of help she knew she didn't want. The girls had flooded out of their bedroom as soon as they heard the door shut, and after a quick, whispery caucus outside the bathroom door, had decided to leave her alone and go back to the TV.

Patty was holding her greasy belly, her sweat turned cold. Her parents' farm, gone. She felt the guilty twist of the stomach that had always made her such a good girl, the constant fear of disappointing her folks, *please, please God, don't let them find out.* They had entrusted this place to her, and she had been found wanting. She pictured them up in the clouds of heaven, her dad's arm around her mom as they looked down on her, shaking their heads, *What in the world possessed you to do such a thing?* Her mom's favorite scold.

They'd have to move to an entirely different town. Kinnakee had no apartments, and they were going to have to cram into an apartment while she got a job in some office, if she could find one. She'd always felt sorry for people who lived in apartments, stuck listening to their neighbors belch and argue. Her legs puddled and suddenly Patty was sitting on the floor. She didn't have enough energy to leave the farm, ever. She'd used the last of it up these past few years. Some mornings she couldn't even get out of bed, physically couldn't make her legs swing out from under the covers, the girls had to drag her, yanking her with dug-in heels, and as she made breakfast and got them somewhat ready for school, she daydreamed about dying. Something quick, an overnight heart attack, or a sudden vehicular clobbering. Mother of four, run down by a bus. And the kids adopted by Diane, who would keep them from lying around in their pajamas all day, and make sure they saw a doctor when they were sick, and snap-snap at them til they finished their chores. Patty was a slip of a woman, wavery and weak, quickly optimistic, but even more easily deflated. It was Diane who should have inherited the farm. But she wanted none of it, had left at eighteen, a joyful, rubberband trajectory that had landed her as a receptionist at a doctor's office thirty mere-but-crucial miles away in Schieberton.

Their parents had taken Diane's leaving stoically, as if it had always been part of the plan. Patty could remember back in high school, them all coming to watch her do her cheerleading thing one wet October night. It was a three-hour drive for them, deep into Kansas, almost Colorado, and it rained lightly but steadily the whole game. When it was over (Kinnakee lost), there on the field were her two gray-haired parents and her sister, three solid ovals, encased in rough wool coats, all rushing to her side, all smiling with such pride and gratitude you'd have thought she'd cured cancer, their eyes crinkled behind three sets of rain-speckled glasses.

Ed and Ann Day were dead now, had died early but not unexpectedly, and Diane was now a manager in the same doctor's office, and lived in a mobile home in a tidy trailer park bordered with flowers.

"It's a good enough life for me," she'd always say. "Can't imagine wanting anything different."

That was Diane. Capable. She was the one who remembered little treats that the girls liked, she never forgot to get them their yearly

Kinnakee T-shirts: Kinnakee, Heart of America! Diane had fibbed to the girls that it meant Magical Little Woman in Indian, and they'd been so gleeful about it that Patty could never bring herself to tell them it just meant rock or crow or something.

DIANE'S CAR HORN intruded on her thoughts with its usual cele-bratory honkhonkhonk!

"Diane!" screeched Debby, and Patty could hear the three girls racing toward the front door, could picture the mass of pigtails and muffin-bottoms, and then imagined them still running, straight out to the car, and Diane driving away with them and leaving her in this house where she would make everything go silent.

She pulled herself off the floor, wiped her face with a mildewy washcloth. Her face was always red, her eyes always pink, so it was impossible to tell if she'd been crying, the only advantage to looking like a skinned rat. When she opened the door, her sister was already unpacking three grocery loads of canned foods and sending the girls out to her car for the rest. Patty had come to associate the smell of brown paper bags with Diane, she'd been bringing them food for so long. That was the perfect example of the fall-short life Patty had made: She lived on a farm but never had enough to eat.

"Got them one of those sticker books, too," Diane said, flapping it out on the table.

"Oh, you're spoiling them, D."

"Well, I only got them one, so they'll have to share. So that's good, right?" She laughed and started making coffee. "You mind?"

"Of course not, I should have put some on." Patty went to the cabinet to find Diane's mug—she favored a heavy cup the size of her head that had been their father's. Patty heard the predictable spitty sound, and turned around, pounded the blasted coffee maker once; it always stalled after its third drool of coffee.

The girls came back in, heaving bags up on the kitchen table, and, with some prompting from Diane, started to unpack them.

"Where's Ben?" Diane asked.

"Mmmm," Patty said, scooping three teaspoons of sugar into Diane's mug. She motioned to the kids, who'd already slowed their cupboarding of cans and were peering up at various angles of pretend nonchalance.

"He's in trouble," Michelle exploded, gleefully. "Again."

"Tell her about his, you know what," Debby nudged her sister.

Diane turned to Patty with a grimace, clearly expecting a tale of genital mishap or mutilation.

"Girls, Aunt D got you a sticker book . . ."

"Go play with it in your room so I can talk to your mother." Diane always spoke more roughly to the girls than Patty did, it was Diane playing the pretend-gruff persona of Ed Day, who'd rumble and grumble at them with such exaggerated fatigue they knew even as kids that he was mostly teasing. Patty added a beseeching look toward Michelle.

"Oh boy, a sticker book!" Michelle announced with only slightly overdone enthusiasm. Michelle was always happy to be complicit in any grown-up scheme. And once Michelle was pretending she wanted something, Libby was all gritted teeth and grabby hands. Libby was a Christmas baby, which meant she never got the right amount of presents. Patty would hold one extra gift aside—and Happy Birthday to Libby!—but they all knew the truth, Libby got ripped off. Libby rarely felt less than ripped off.

She knew these things about her girls, but she was always forgetting. What was wrong with her, that these bits of her children's personalities were always surprising her?

"Wanna go to the garage?" Diane asked, patting the cigarettes in her bosom pocket.

"Oh," was all Patty answered. Diane had quit and returned to smoking at least twice a year every year since she was thirty. Now she was thirty-seven (and she looked much worse than Patty did, the skin on her face diamonded like a snake), and Patty had long learned the best support was just to shut up and make her sit in the garage. Just like their mom had with their dad. Of course, he was dead of lung cancer not long after his fiftieth.

Patty followed her sister, making herself breathe, getting ready to tell Diane the farm was gone, waiting to see if she'd scream about Runner's reckless spending and her allowing Runner's reckless spending or if she'd just go quiet, just do that single nod.

"So what's up with Ben's you-know-what?" Diane said, settling into her creaky lawn chair, two of the criss-crossed straps broken and hanging toward the floor. She lit a cigarette, immediately waving the smoke away from Patty.

"Oh, it's not that, it's not anything weird. I mean weird, but . . . he dyed his hair black. What does that mean?"

She waited for Diane to cackle at her, but Diane sat silent.

"How's Ben doing, Patty? In general, how does he seem?"

"Oh, I don't know. Moody."

"He's always been moody. Even when he was a baby he was like a cat. All snuggly one second and then the next, he'd be looking at you like he had no idea who you were."

It was true, Ben at age two was an astonishing thing. He'd demand love outright, grab at a breast or an arm, but as soon as he had enough affection, and that came quickly, he'd go completely limp, play dead until you let him go. She'd taken him to the doctor, and Ben had sat rigid and tight-lipped, a stoic turtle-necked boy with a disturbing ability to withhold. Even the doctor seemed spooked, proffering a cheap lollipop and telling her to come back in six months if he was the same. He was always the same.

"Well, moody's not a crime," Patty said. "Runner was moody."

"Runner is an asshole, not the same. Ben's always had that re-move to him."

"Well, he is fifteen," Patty started, and trailed off. Her eyes caught a jar of old nails on the shelf, a jar she doubted had been moved since their dad's time. It was labeled *Nails* in his long, upright handwriting on a scrap of masking tape.

The garage had an oily concrete floor that was even colder than the air. In one corner, an old gallon jug of water had turned to ice, busted its plastic seams. Their breath hung thick with Diane's ciga-rette smoke. Still, she was oddly contented here, among all these old tools she could picture in their dad's hands: rakes with bent tines, axes of every length, shelves packed with jars filled with screws and nails and washers. Even an old metal ice chest, its base speckled with rust, where their dad used to keep his beer cold while he listened to ball games on the radio.

It unnerved her that Diane was saying so little, since Diane liked to offer opinions, even when she didn't really have any. It unnerved her more that Diane was staying so motionless, hadn't found a project, something to straighten or rearrange, because Diane was a doer, she never just sat and talked.

"Patty. I got to tell you something I heard. And my first instinct was to not say anything, because of course it's not true. But you're a mom, you should know, and . . . hell, I don't know, you should just know."

"OK."

"Has Ben ever played with the girls in a way that someone might get confused about?"

Patty just stared.

"In a way that people might get the wrong idea about . . . sexually?"

Patty almost choked. "Ben *hates* the girls!" She was surprised at the relief she felt. "He has as little to do with them as possible."

Diane lit another cigarette, gave a taut nod of her head. "Well, OK, good. But there's something more. A friend of mine told me a rumor that there's been a complaint about Ben over at the school, that a few little girls, Michelle's age or so, had talked about kissing him and maybe him touching them or something. Maybe worse. The stuff I heard was worse."

"Ben? You realize that's completely crazy." Patty stood up, couldn't figure out what to do with her arms or legs. She turned to the right and then the left too quickly, like a distracted dog, and sat back down. A strap in her chair broke.

"I do know it's crazy. Or some misunderstanding."

That was the worst word Diane could have said. As soon as she said it, Patty knew she'd been dreading just exactly that. That wedge of possibility—*misunderstanding*—that could turn this into something. A pat on the head might be a caress of the back might be a kiss on the lips might be the roof caving in.

"Misunderstanding? Ben wouldn't misunderstand a kiss. Or touching. Not with a little girl. He's not a pervert. He's an odd kid, but he's not sick. He's not crazy." Patty had spent her life swearing

Ben *wasn't* odd, was just an average kid. But now she'd settle for odd. The realization came suddenly, a wild jolt, like having your hair blown in your face while driving.

"Will you tell them he wouldn't do that?" Patty asked, and the tears came all at once, suddenly her cheeks were soaked.

"I can tell everyone in Kinnakee, everyone in the state of Kansas that he wouldn't do that, and it might not be the end of it. I don't know. I don't know. I just heard yesterday afternoon, but it seems to be getting . . . bigger. I almost came out here. Then I spent the rest of the night convincing myself that it wasn't anything. Then I woke up this morning and realized it was."

Patty knew that feeling, a dream hangover, like when she jumped up from a panicky sleep at 2 in the morning and tried to talk herself into thinking the farm was OK, that this year would pick up, and then felt all the sicker when she woke up to the alarm a few hours later, guilty and duped. It was surprising that you could spend hours in the middle of the night pretending things were OK, and know in thirty seconds of daylight that that simply wasn't so.

"So you came over here with groceries and a sticker book and all along you had this *story* about Ben you were going to tell me."

"Like I said . . ." Diane shrugged sympathetically, splayed her fingers except for the ones holding the cigarette.

"Well, what happens now? Do you know the girls' names? Is someone going to phone me or talk to me, or talk to Ben? I need to find Ben."

"Where is he?"

"I don't know. We had a fight. About his hair. He took off on his bike."

"So what was the story with his hair?"

"I don't know, Diane! What in God's name does it matter now?"

But of course Patty knew it did matter. Everything now would be filtered and sifted for meaning.

"Well, I don't think this is an emergency," Diane said quietly. "I don't think we need to get him home right now unless you want him home right now."

"I want him home right now."

"OK, well let's start calling people then. You can give me a list of his friends and I'll start phoning."

"I don't even know his friends anymore," Patty said. "He was talking to someone this morning, but he wouldn't say who."

"Let's hit redial."

Her sister grunted, stamped out her cigarette with a boot, pulled Patty out of her chair, led her inside. Diane snapped at the girls to stay in their room when the bedroom door cracked, and made her way to the phone, purposefully hit the redial button with one braut-sized finger. Sing-song numeric tones blared out of the receiver—beepBeepBEEPbeepbeepbupBEEP—and before it even rang, Diane hung up.

"My number."

"Oh, yeah. I called after breakfast to see when you'd be over."

The two sisters sat at the table, and Diane poured more mugs of coffee. The snow glared into the kitchen like a strobelight.

"We need to get Ben home," Patty said.

Libby Day

NOW

Moony as a grade-school girl, I drove home thinking about Ben. Since I was seven, I pictured him in the same haunted-house flashes: Ben, black-haired, smooth-faced, with his hands clasped around an axe, charging down the hall at Debby, a humming noise coming from his tight lips. Ben's face speckled in blood, howling, the shotgun going up to his shoulder.

I'd forgotten there was once just Ben, shy and serious, those weird unsettling blasts of humor. Just Ben my brother, who couldn't have done what they said. What I said.

At a stoplight, my blood sizzling, I reached behind my seat and grabbed the envelope from an old bill. Above the plastic window, I wrote: *Suspects.* Then I wrote: *Runner.* Then I stopped. *Someone with a grudge against Runner?* I wrote. *Someone Runner owed money to?* Runnerrunnerrunner. It came back to Runner. That male voice, bellowing in our house that night, that could have been Runner or an enemy of Runner's as easily as it was Ben. I needed this to be true, and provable. I had a gust of panic: I can't live with this, Ben in jail, this open-ended guilt. I needed it finished. I needed to know. Me, me. I was still predictably selfish.

As I passed the turnoff for our farm, I refused to look.

I stopped in a 7-Eleven on the outskirts of Kansas City, filled up with gas, bought a log of Velveeta, some Coke, white bread, and kibble for my old, starving cat. Then I drove home to Over There That Way, pulled up my slope of a hill, got out, and stared at the two old ladies across the street who'd never look at me. They sat on the porch swing as always, despite the chill, their heads rigidly straight, lest I muddy their view. I stood with my hands on my hips, on top of my hill, and waited until one finally caved. Then I waved rather grandly, an Old West corral sort of wave. The wrinkled biddy nodded at me, and I went inside and fed poor Buck, feeling a bubble of triumph.

While I still had the energy, I knifed bright yellow mustard onto my white bread, stacked thick smushy chunks of Velveeta on top, and swallowed the sandwich while negotiating with three different but equally bored phone operators to reach the Bert Nolan Group Home for Men. That's another thing to add to my list of potential occupations for ole Jim Jeffreys: operator. As a kid, that was something little girls wanted to be when they grew up, an operator, but I couldn't remember why.

A thin layer of bread pasted to the roof of my mouth, I finally reached a voice at the Bert Nolan Home, and was surprised to find it was Bert Nolan himself. I'd assumed anyone with a home named after him must be dead. I told him I was trying to find Runner Day, and he paused.

"Well, he's been in and out, mostly out the past month, but I'd be happy to give him a message," Bert Nolan said in a voice like an old car horn. I gave my name—no recognition on his part—and started to give my phone number when Nolan interrupted me.

"Oh, he's not going to be able to phone long distance, I can tell you that right now. The men here tend to be big corresponders. By mail, you know? Less'n fifty cents for a stamp and you don't have to worry about waiting in line for the phone. You want to leave your address?"

I did not. I shivered at the idea of Runner clomping up my steps with his overstacked dress boots, his grimy hands around his little waist, grinning like he'd beaten me at a game.

"If you want, I can take any message you have and you can give me your address privately," Bert Nolan said reasonably. "And once Runner finishes his letter to you, I can mail it for him, and he'll never even know your zip code. A lot of family members do it that way. It's a sad but necessary thing." In the background, a soda machine rattled out a sodapop, someone asked Nolan if he wanted one, and he said *No thanks, trying to cut back* in the kindly voice of a town doctor. "You want to do that, Miss? Otherwise it'll be hard to reach him. Like I said, he's not really one to sit by the phone and wait for you to call back."

"And there's no e-mail?"

Bert Nolan grunted. "No, no e-mail, I'm afraid."

I'd never known Runner to be much of a letter writer, but he always wrote more than he phoned, so I guessed that would be my best shot, short of driving down to Oklahoma and waiting on one of Bert Nolan's cots. "Would you tell him I need to talk about Ben and that night? I can come down to see him if he just gives me a day."

"OK . . . you said, Ben and *that night*?"

"I did."

I KNEW LYLE would be too smug about my turnaround—semi-possible, potential turnaround—on Ben. I could picture him addressing the Kill Club groupies in one of his weird tight jackets, explaining how he convinced me to go see Ben. "She really was refusing at first, I think she was scared of what she might discover about Ben . . . and about herself." And all those faces looking up at him, so happy about what he'd done. It irritated me.

Who I wanted to talk to was Aunt Diane. Diane who'd taken care of me for seven of my eleven years as an underage orphan. She'd been the first to take me in, shuffling me into her mobile home with my suitcase of belongings. Clothes, a favorite book, but no toys. Michelle hoarded all the dolls with her at night, she called it her slumber party, and she peed on them when she was strangled. I still remember a sticker book Diane had given us the day of the murders—flowers and unicorns and kittens—and always wondered if it had been in that ruined pile.

Diane couldn't afford a new place. All the money from my

mom's life insurance went to get Ben a decent lawyer. Diane said my mother would want that, but she said it with a drawn face, like she'd give my mother a good talking to if she could. So no money for us. Being runty, I was able to sleep in a storage closet where the washer/dryer would have gone. Diane even painted it for me. She worked overtime, shuttled me to Topeka for therapy, tried to be affectionate with me, even though I could tell it hurt her to hug me, this pissy reminder of her sister's murder. Her arms encircled me like a hula-hoop, like it was a game to get them around me but touch as little as possible. But every single morning she told me she loved me.

Over the next ten years, I totaled her car twice, broke her nose twice, stole and sold her credit cards, and killed her dog. It was the dog that finally broke her. She'd gotten Gracie, a mop-haired mutt, not long after the murders. It was yappy and the size of Diane's forearm and Diane liked her more than me, or so I felt. For years I was jealous of that dog, watching Diane brush Gracie, her big manly hands wrapped around a pink plastic comb, watching her barrette Gracie's tassled fur, watching her whip out a photo of Gracie from her wallet, instead of me. The dog was obsessed with my foot, the bad one, with only two toes, the second and the pinky, skinny gnarled things. Gracie was always smelling at them, like she knew they were wrong somehow. It did not endear her to me.

I'd been grounded for something, the summer between sophomore and junior year, and while Diane worked, I sat in the hot trailer getting angrier and angrier with that dog, the dog getting feistier and feistier. I refused to walk it, so it had resorted to running in frantic loops from the sofa to the kitchen to the closet, yipping the whole time, nipping at my feet. As I coiled up, nursing my fury, pretending to watch a soap opera but instead letting my brain turn good and red, Gracie paused in one of her loops and bit at the pinky toe on my bad foot, just grabbed onto it with her canines and shook. I remember thinking, *If this dog takes one of my last toes,* and then getting enraged at how ridiculous I was: On my left hand was a stump where a man would never put a wedding ring, and my unsupported right foot gave me a permanent sailor's gait in a land-locked town. The girls at school called my finger a nubbin. That was worse, it sounded both quaint and grotesque at the same time, something to giggle at while

looking quickly away. A physician had recently told me the amputa-
tions probably weren't even necessary, "Just an overambitious country
doctor." I grabbed Gracie around her middle, feeling her ribcage,
that chilly tremble of a little thing. The tremble only made me angrier, and suddenly I was ripping her off my toe—the flesh going
with her—and throwing her as hard as I could toward the kitchen.
She hit the pick-axe edge of the counter and collapsed in a twitching
pile, bleeding all over the linoleum.

I hadn't meant to kill her, but she died, not as quickly as I'd have
liked, but within about ten minutes as I paced around the trailer trying to figure out what to do. When Diane came home, bearing an of-
fertory of fried chicken, Gracie was still lying on the floor, and all I
could say was, "She bit me."

I tried to say more, to explain why it wasn't my fault, but Diane
just held up a single, shaking finger: *Don't.* She'd called her best
friend, Valerie, a woman as delicate and motherly as Diane was bulky
and bluff. Diane stood hunched over the sink, looking out the window as Valerie folded Gracie into a special blanket. Then they huddled behind a closed bedroom door, and emerged, Valerie standing
silently next to Diane, teary and kneading, as Diane told me to pack
my things. In retrospect, I assume Valerie must have been Diane's
girlfriend—every night, Diane would climb in bed and talk to her on
the phone til she fell asleep. They conferred on everything together
and even had the exact same gently feathered wash-n-wear haircut.
At the time I didn't care who she was to Diane.

I lived my last two high school years with a polite couple in Abilene who were twice-removed somethings and whom I only mildly
terrorized. From then on, every few months, Diane would phone. I'd
sit with her on the line, all heavy telephone buzz and Diane's smoky
breathing into the receiver. I'd picture the bottom half of her mouth
hanging there, the peach fuzz on her chin and that mole perched
near her bottom lip, a flesh-colored disc that she once told me, cackling, would grant wishes if I rubbed it. I'd hear a creak-squeak in
the background, and knew Diane was opening the middle cabinet in
the kitchen of her trailer. I knew that place better than I did the
farmhouse. Diane and I would make unnecessary noises, pretend to

sneeze or cough, and then Diane would say, "Hold on, Libby," point-lessly since neither of us had been talking. Valerie would usually be there, and they'd murmur to each other, Valerie's voice coaxing, Diane's a grumble, and then Diane would give me about twenty more seconds of conversation and make an excuse to go.

She stopped taking my calls when *Brand New Day* came out. Her only words: *What possessed you to* do *such a thing?* which was prim for Diane, but filled with more hurt than three dozen fuckyous.

I knew Diane would be at the same number, she was never going to move—the trailer was attached to her like a shell. I spent twenty minutes digging through piles at my house, looking for my old ad-dress book, one I'd had since grade school, with a pig-tailed red-headed girl on the cover that someone must have thought looked like me. Except for the smile. Diane's number was filed under *A* for Aunt Diane, her name inked in purple marker in my balloon-animal cursive.

What tone to take, and what explanation for calling? Partly I just wanted to hear her wheeze into the phone, her football-coach voice bellowing in my ear, *Well, why'd it take you so long to phone back?* Partly I wanted to hear what she really thought about Ben. She'd never railed against Ben to me, she'd always been very careful about how she spoke of him, another thing I owed her retroactive thanks for.

I dialed the number, my shoulders pulling up to my ears, my throat getting tight, holding my breath and not realizing it until the third ring when it went to the answering machine and I was suddenly exhaling.

It was Valerie's voice on the machine asking me to leave a mes-sage for her or Diane.

"Hi, uh, guys. This is Libby. Just wanting to say hi and let you all know I'm still alive and." I hung up. Dialed back. "Please ignore that last message. It's Libby. I called to say I'm sorry, for. Oh, a lot of things. And I'd like to talk . . ." I trailed on in case anyone was screen-ing, then left my number, hung up, and sat on the edge of my bed, poised to get up but having no reason to.

I got up. I'd done more this day than the previous year. While I still held the phone, I made myself call Lyle, hoping for voicemail and, as usual, getting him. Before he could annoy me, I told him the meeting with Ben had gone fine and I was ready to hear who he believed was the killer. I said this all in a very precise tone, like I was doling out information with a measuring spoon.

"I knew you'd like him, I knew you'd come around," he crowed, and once again I pleased myself by not hanging up.

"I didn't say that, Lyle, I said I was ready for another assignment, if you want."

We met again at Tim-Clark's Grille, the place cloudy with grease. Another old waitress, or else the same one with a red wig, hustled around on spongy tennis shoes, her miniskirt flapping around her, looking like an ancient tennis pro. Instead of the fat man admiring his new vase, a table of hipster dudes were passing around '70s-era nudie playing cards and laughing at the big bushes on the women. Lyle was sitting tightly at a table next to them, his chair turned awkwardly away. I sat down with him, poured a beer from his pitcher.

"So was he what you expected? What did he say?" Lyle started, his leg jittering.

I told him, except for the part about the porcelain bunny.

"See what Magda meant, though, about him being hopeless?"

I did. "I think he's made peace with the prison sentence," I said, an insight I shared only because the guy had given me $300 and I wanted more. "He thinks it's penance for not being there to protect us or something. I don't know. I thought when I told him about my testimony, about it being . . . exaggerated, that he'd jump on it, but . . . nothing."

"Legally it's maybe not that helpful after this long," Lyle said. "Magda says if you want to help Ben, we should compile more evidence, and you can recant your testimony when we file for habeas corpus—it'll make more of a splash. It's more political than legal at this point. A lot of people made big careers on that case."

"Magda seems to know a lot."

"She heads up this group called the Free Day Society—all about getting Ben out of prison. I sometimes go, but it seems mostly for, uh, fans. Women."

"You ever hear of Ben with a serious girlfriend? One of those Free Day women whose name is Molly or Sally or Polly? He had a tattoo."

"No Sallys. Polly seems like a pet's name—my cousin had a dog named Polly. One Molly, but she's seventy or so."

A plate of fries appeared in front of him, the waitress definitely different from our previous one, just as old but much friendlier. I like waitresses who call me hon or sweetie, and she did.

Lyle ate fries for a while, squeezing packets of ketchup on the side of the plate, then salting and peppering the ketchup, then dipping each fry individually and placing it in his mouth with girlish care.

"Well, so tell me who you think did it," I finally nudged.

"Who what?"

I rolled my eyes and set my head in my hands, as if it was too much for me, and it almost was.

"Oh, right. I think Lou Cates, Krissi Cates's dad, did it." He leaned back in his chair with satisfaction, as if he'd just won a game of Clue.

Krissi Cates, the name jangled something. I tried to fake Lyle out, but it didn't work.

"You do know who Krissi Cates is, right?" When I didn't say anything, he continued, his voice taking on a sleek, patronizing tone. "Krissi Cates was a fifth-grader at your school, at Ben's school. The day your family was killed, the police were looking to question Ben— she'd accused him of molesting her."

"What?"

"Yeah."

We both stared each other down, with matching you-are-crazy looks.

Lyle shook his head at me. "When you say people don't talk to you about this stuff, you aren't kidding."

"She didn't testify against Ben . . ." I started.

"No, no. It's the one smart thing Ben's defense did, making the case that they weren't legally linked, the molestation and the murders. But the jury was sure poisoned against him. Everyone in the area had heard that Ben had molested this nice little girl from this nice family, and that was probably what led up to his 'satanic murders.' You know how rumors go."

"So, did the Krissi Cates thing ever go to trial?" I asked. "Did they prove Ben did anything wrong with her?"

"It never went forward—the police didn't bring charges," Lyle said. "The Cates family got a quick settlement with the school district and then they moved. But you know what I think? I think Lou Cates went to your home that night to question Ben. I think Lou Cates, who was this powerfully built sort of guy, went to the house to get some answers, and then . . ."

"Flew into such a rage he decided to kill the whole family? That makes no sense at all."

"This guy did three years for manslaughter when he was younger, that's what I found out, he hurled a pool ball full-throttle at a guy, ended up killing him. He had a violent temper. If Lou Cates thought his daughter'd been molested, I can see rage. Then he did the pentagrams and stuff to throw off suspicion."

"Mmmm, it doesn't make sense." I had really wanted it to make sense.

"Your brother doing it doesn't make sense. It's an insane, insane crime, a lot of it isn't going to make sense. That's why people are so obsessed with these murders. If they made any sense, they wouldn't really be mysteries, right?"

I didn't say anything. It was true. I started fidgeting with the salt and pepper shakers, which were surprisingly nice for a dive.

"I mean, don't you think it's at least worth looking into?" Lyle pushed. "This massive, horrible allegation exploding the same day your family is murdered?"

"I guess. You're the boss."

"So, I say until you find Runner, see if you can get someone in the Cates family to talk to you. Five hundred dollars if it's Krissi or Lou. I just want to see if they're still telling the same story about Ben. If they can live with themselves, you know? I mean, it's got to be a lie. Right?"

I was feeling shaky again. My faith did not need to be tested right now. Still, I clung to a weird bit of assurance: Ben had never molested me. If he was a child molester, wouldn't he have started with a little girl right at home?

"Right."

"Right," Lyle repeated.

"But I'm not sure I'll have more luck than you would. I mean, I'm the sister of the guy they say molested her."

"Well, I tried and got nowhere," Lyle shrugged. "I'm not good with that kind of thing."

"What kind of thing?"

"Finessing."

"Oh, well that's definitely my kind of thing."

"Excellent. And if you're able to set up a meeting, I'd like to come along."

I shrugged silently, stood up, planning on leaving him with the bill, but he belted my name before I got three steps.

"Libby, do you know you have the salt and pepper shakers in your pocket?"

I paused for a second, debated acting stunned—*oh my gosh, I am so absentminded.* Instead I just nodded and hustled out the doors. I needed them.

LYLE HAD TRACKED down Krissi Cates's mother in Emporia, Kansas, where she lived with her second husband, with whom she'd had a second daughter almost twenty years after the first. Lyle had left several messages in the past year, but she'd never returned his call. That was as far as he'd gotten.

Never leave a message for someone you really want to reach. No, you keep phoning and phoning until someone picks up—out of anger or curiosity or fear—and then you blurt out whatever words will keep them on the line.

I rang Krissi's mother twelve times before she picked up the phone, then, in a rush, said, "This is Libby Day, Ben Day's little sister, do you remember Ben Day?"

I heard moist lips part with a puckery sound, then a thin voice murmured, "Yes, I remember Ben Day. What is this about, please?" Like I was a telemarketer.

"I'd like to talk to you or someone in your family about the charges your daughter Krissi made against Ben."

"We don't talk about that . . . what was your name, Lizzy? I've remarried, and I have very little contact with my previous family."

"Do you know how I can reach Lou or Krissi Cates?"

She let out a sigh like a single puff of smoke. "Lou would be in some bar, somewhere in the state of Kansas, I'd guess. Krissi? Drive west on I-70, just past Columbia. Take a left into any of those strip clubs. Don't call again."

Ben Day

He took a piece of pink construction paper from Krissi's bin, folded it in two, wrote on it, It's Christmas Break and I'm Thinking of You—Guess Who? With a *B* at the bottom. She'd get a blast out of that. He thought about taking something from Krissi's bin and transferring it to Libby's but decided not to. Libby turning up with something nice would be suspicious. He wondered how big a joke he and his sisters were at school. The three girls shared one-and-a-half wardrobes, Michelle running around in his old sweaters, Debby wearing what she scrounged from Michelle, and Libby in what was left: patched-up boys' blue jeans, soiled old baseball jerseys, cheap knit dresses that Debby's belly had stretched out. That was the difference with Krissi. All her clothes had snap. Diondra, too, with her perfect jeans. If Diondra's jeans were faded, it was because that was the latest style, if they had bleach splatters, it was because she'd bought them with bleach splatters. Diondra had a big allowance, she'd taken him shopping a few times, holding clothes up to him like he was a baby, telling him to smile. Telling him he could work it off, wink wink. He wasn't sure if guys should let girls buy their clothes, wasn't sure if it was cool or not. Mr. O'Malley, his homeroom teacher, always joked about new shirts his wife was making him wear, but Mr. O'Malley was married. Anyway. Diondra liked him in black and he didn't have the money to buy anything. Fucking Diondra would have her way as usual.

That's another reason it was cool to hang out with Krissi: She assumed he was cool because he was fifteen, and to her fifteen seemed extremely mature. She wasn't like Diondra, who laughed at him at weird moments. He'd ask her, "What's so funny?" and she'd just giggle through a closed mouth and sputter, "Nothing. You're cute." The first time they'd tried to have sex, he'd been so clumsy with the condom she'd started laughing and he'd lost his hard-on. The second time she'd grabbed the condom away from him and tossed it across the room, said screw it, and put him inside her.

Now he had a hard-on, just thinking about it. He was dropping the note in Krissi's bin, his dick hard as hell, and in walked Mrs. Darksilver, the teacher for second grade.

"Hey Ben, watchoo doing here?" she smiled. She was in jeans and a sweater, penny loafers, and toddled toward him, carrying a bulletin board and a length of plaid ribbon.

He turned away from her, started toward the door back to the high school.

"Ah nothing, just wanted to drop something off in my sister's bin."

"Well, don't run away, come give me a hug at least. Never see you anymore now that you're the big high school man."

She kept coming toward him, loafers padding on the concrete, that big pink grin on her face, with the bangs cut straight across. He'd had a crush on her as a kid, that sharp fringe of black hair. He turned completely away from her and tried to hobble toward the door, his dick still jammed up against his pant leg. But just as he was turning he could tell she knew what was going on. She dropped that smile and a disgusted, embarrassed grimace came across her whole face. She didn't even say anything else, that's how he knew that she'd seen it. She was looking at the bin he was in front of—Krissi Cates, not his sister.

He felt like an animal limping away, some wounded buck that needed to be put down. Just shoot. He had flashes of guns sometimes, a barrel against his temple. In one of his notebooks, he'd written a quote by Nietzsche that he'd found while flipping through *Bartlett's* one day, waiting for the football players to leave the building so he could clean:

> It is always consoling to think of suicide;
> it's what gets one through many a bad night.

He'd never actually kill himself. He didn't want to be the tragic freak that girls cried over on the news, even though they never talked to him in real life. Somehow that seemed more pathetic than his life already was. Still, at night, when things were really bad and he felt the most trapped and dickless, it was a nice thought, getting into his mother's gun cabinet (combination 5-12-69, his parents' anniversary, now a joke), taking that nice metal weight in his hands, sliding some bullets into the chamber, just as easy as squirting toothpaste, pressing it against his temple, and immediately shooting. You'd have to immediately shoot, gun to temple, finger on trigger, or you might talk yourself out of it. It had to be one motion—and then you just drop to the ground like clothes falling off a hanger. Just . . . swoosh. On the floor, and you were someone else's problem for a change.

He didn't plan on doing any of that, but when he needed some release and he couldn't jerk off, or he'd already jerked off and needed more release, that's usually what he thought of. On the floor, sideways, like his body was just a pile of laundry waiting to be gathered up.

HE BUSTED THROUGH the doors and his dick went down, like just crossing into the high school emasculated him. Grabbed the bucket and rolled it back to the closet, washed his hands with hard Lava soap.

He headed down the stairwell and toward the back door as a pack of upperclassmen brushed past him toward the parking lot, his head feeling hot under the black hair, imagining what they were thinking—*freak,* just like the coach—and they said nothing, didn't even look at him, actually. Thirty seconds behind them, he banged open the doors, the sun against the snow a shocking white. If this was a video, now would be the guitar flare, the whammy bar . . . Bweeeerrrr!

Outside, the guys were piling into a truck and peeling out in loose, showy loops across the parking lot. And he was unchaining his bike, his head throbbing, a drip of blood falling on the handlebar. He smeared it up with a fingertip, swiped the fingertip across the trickle on his forehead and, without thinking, put the finger in his mouth, like it was a stray glob of jelly.

He needed some relief. Beer and maybe a joint, undo himself a little. The only place to try was Trey's. Actually it wasn't Trey's place, Trey never said where he lived, but when Trey wasn't at Diondra's he most likely was at the Compound, down a long dirt road off Highway 41, surrounded by hedgeapples on both sides, and then came a big brush-hogged clearing, with a warehouse made of a hard, tin material. The whole thing rattled in the wind. In the winter, a generator hummed inside, just enough juice to run a bunch of spaceheaters and a TV with sketchy reception. Dozens of carpet samples sat in bright, smelly patches on the dirt floor and a few old ugly couches had been donated. People gathered smoking around the spaceheaters like they were actual bonfires. Everyone had beer—they just kept the cans sitting in the frost outside the door—and everyone had joints. Usually there was a 7-Eleven run at some point, whoever was flush would come back with a few dozen burritos, some microwaved, some still frozen. If they had extra, they jammed the burritos in the snow alongside the beer.

Ben had never been there without Diondra, it was her crowd, but where the fuck else was he going to go? Showing up with a broken forehead was sure to get him a grudging nod and a can of Beast. They might not be friendly—Trey was never exactly friendly—but it wasn't in their code to turn anyone away. Ben was sure to be the youngest, although there'd been younger: once a couple had shown up with a little boy, naked except for a pair of jeans. While everyone got stoned, the kid sat silently sucking his thumb on the sofa, staring at Ben. Mostly though, people were twenty, twenty-one, twenty-two, the age where they'd have gone to college if they hadn't dropped out of high school. He'd stop by, and maybe they'd like him, and Diondra would stop calling him Tag (short for Tagalong) every time she took him there. They'd at least let him sit in the corner and drink a beer for a few hours.

Maybe it'd be smarter to go home, but fuck that.

THE WAREHOUSE WAS rattling when Ben finally pedaled up, the tin sides vibrating with a guitar riff inside. Sometimes guys brought amps with them, worked the whammy bar until everyone's ears shrank to pinholes. Whoever was playing was pretty good—some Venom song, perfect for his mood. RumadumDUMrum! It was the noise of incoming horsemen, looters, and burners. The sound of chaos.

He let his bike fall over in the snow and worked his hands loose, cracked his neck. His head hurt now, a ringing sort of hurt, not as easy to ignore as a headache. He was hungry as shit. He'd ridden up and down the highway, trying to talk himself into making the turn for the warehouse. He needed a good story for the cut on his face, something that wouldn't get him as much shit as *awwww, baby fell off his bike.* Now he daydreamed that Diondra or Trey would pull up just in time, escort him in, no biggie, everyone all smiles and liquor when he walked through the door.

But he'd have to go in alone. He could see for miles across all that flat snow, and no cars were coming. He pushed the flap up with a boot and squeezed in, the guitar peel banging around the walls like a cornered animal. The guy playing the guitar, Ben had seen before. He claimed he was a roadie at one point with Van Halen but he was short on details of how anything really worked on the road. He glanced past Ben but didn't register him, his eyes floating out to an imaginary crowd. Four guys and a girl, all with fried-out kinky hair, all older, passing around a joint, slouched around the carpet squares. They barely looked at him. The ugliest guy had his hands on the girl's hips, she was stretched across him like a cat. Her nose was stunted and her face was red with acne sores and she seemed deeply stoned.

Ben walked across the space—there was a huge gap between the door and the carpet squares—and sat down on one thin green patch about four feet away from the group, kept his eyes sideways on them so he could give a nod. No one was eating, there'd be no food to scrounge. If he'd been Trey, he'd have given them a shake of his head and said, "Set me up with some of that, will ya?" and he'd be smoking with them at least.

The guitar player, Alex, was actually pretty decent. A guitar was another thing Ben wanted, a Floyd Rose Tremolo. He'd fucked around on one in Kansas City when he and Diondra had gone into a guitar store, and it felt OK, like something he could pick up. At least learn enough to play a few really kickass songs, come back here and make the warehouse shake. Everyone he knew had something they were good at, even if it was just being good at spending money, like Diondra. Whenever he told her things he wanted to learn, things he wanted to do, she laughed and said what he needed to do was get a decent paycheck.

"Groceries cost money, electricity costs money, you don't even understand," she'd say. Diondra paid a lot of the bills at her house since her parents were gone so much, that was true, but she paid the bills with her parents' stinking money. Ben wasn't sure being able to write a check was such an amazing thing. He wondered what time it was and wished he'd just gone over to her house and waited. Now he'd have to stay here and hour or so, so they wouldn't think he was leaving because no one was talking to him. His pants were still damp from the bucket spill, and he could smell old tuna on the front of his shirt.

"Hey," said the girl. "Hey kid."

He looked up at her, the black hair falling over an eye.

"Shouldn't you be in school or something?" she said, her words coming in dopey mounds. "Why are you here?"

"It's break."

"He says it's break," she told her boyfriend. The guy, mangy and sunk-cheeked, with an outline of a moustache, peered up at that.

"You know someone here?" the boyfriend asked him.

Ben gestured toward Alex. "I know him."

"Hey Alex, you know this kid?"

Alex stopped the guitar, paused with both legs wide in a rocker pose and looked at Ben, hunched on the floor. Shook his head.

"Nah, man. I don't hang out with middle schoolers."

This was the sort of shit they always gave him. Ben had thought the new black hair would have helped, made him look less young. But guys just liked to fuck with him, or ignore him. It was something about the way he was built, or the way he walked, or something in his blood. He was always picked third to last in any team game—the afterthought boy who was grabbed right before the real shitballs. Guys seemed to know it instantly; they flirted with Diondra in front of him all the time. Like they knew his dick wilted a little bit when he entered a room. Well, fuck them, he was sick of it.

"Suck my dick," Ben muttered.

"Wohhhh! The little guy is pissed!"

"Looks like he's been in a fight," the girl said.

"Dude, dude, you been in a fight?" The music had stopped entirely now. Alex had propped his guitar up against one icy wall and was smoking with the rest, grinning and bobbing his head. Their voices boomed up to the ceiling and echoed out, like fireworks.

Ben nodded.

"Yeah, who'd you fight?"

"No one you know."

"Ah, I know pretty much everyone. Try me. Who was it, your little brother? You get beat up by your little brother?"

"Trey Teepano."

"You lie," Alex said. "Trey'd kick your ass."

"You fought that crazy Indian mother fucker? Isn't Trey part Indian?" said the boyfriend, ignoring Alex now.

"What the fuck that got to do with anything, Mike?" one of their friends asked. He sucked in some weed with a roach clip, the bright pink feather fluttering in the cold. The girl finished it off, cashed the joint, and snapped the roach clip back into her hair. One mousy curl tweaked out crookedly from her head.

"I hear he's into some scary-ass shit," Mike said. "Like serious, conjuring Satan shit."

Trey was a poser, so far as Ben could tell. He talked about special midnight meetings in Wichita where blood was spilled in different rituals. He had shown up at Diondra's one night in October, cranked and shirtless and smeared with blood. Swore he and some friends had killed some cattle outside of Lawrence. Said they'd thought about going into campus, kidnapping some college kid for sacrifice too, but had gotten wasted instead. He may have been telling the truth on that one—it was all over the news the next day, four cows slaughtered with machetes, their entrails gone. Ben had seen the photos: all of them lying on their sides, big mound-bodies and sad knobby legs. It was fucking hard to kill a cow, there was a reason they made good leather. Of course, Trey worked out a few hours a day to metal, pumping and squeezing and cursing, Ben had seen the routine. Trey was a strutting, tan bundle of knots, and he could probably kill a cow with a machete, and he was probably fucking loony enough to do it for kicks. But as for the Satan part? Ben thought the Devil would want something more useful than cow entrails. Gold. Maybe a kid. To prove loyalty, like when gangs make a new guy shoot somebody.

"He is," Ben said. "We are. We get into some dark shit."

"I thought you just said you were fighting him," Mike said, and finally, finally reached behind him into a Styrofoam cooler and handed Ben an Olympia Gold, icy-wet. Ben chugged it, put out his hand for another, and was surprised to actually get a second beer instead of a load of shit.

"We fight. When you do some of the stuff we do, you're going to end up in a fight." This sounded as vague as Alex's roadie stories.

"Were you one of the guys who killed those cows?" the girl asked.

Ben nodded. "We had to. It was an order."

"Weird order, man," said the quiet guy from the corner. "That was my hamburger."

They laughed, everyone did, and Ben tried to look smooth but tough. He shook his hair down in front of his eyes and felt the beer chill him. Two fast, tinny beers on an empty belly and he was buzzing, but he didn't want to come off as a lightweight.

"So why do you kill cows?" the girl asked.

"Feels good, satisfies some requirements. You can't just be in the club, you have to really do stuff."

Ben had hunted lots, his dad taking him out once, and then his mom insisted he go with her. A bonding thing. She didn't realize how embarrassing it was to go hunting with your mom. But it was his mom who'd made him a decent shot, taught him how to handle the recoil, when to pull the trigger, how to wait and be patient for hours in the blind. Ben had shot and killed dozens of animals, from rabbits up to deer.

Now he thought of mice, how his mom's barncat had rooted out a nest, and gobbled down two or three gooey newborn mice before dropping the other half dozen on the back steps. Runner had just left—the second time this was—so it was Ben's job to put them out of their misery. They'd wriggled silently, twisting like pink eels, eyes glued shut, and by the time he'd run back and forth to the barn twice, trying to figure out what to do, the ants were swarming them. He'd taken a shovel, finally, and smashed them into the ground, bits of flesh splattering his arms, getting angrier, each big loose wield of the shovel infuriating him more. *You think I'm such a pussy, Runner, you think I'm such a pussy!* By the time it was over, only a sticky spot on the ground remained. He was sweaty, and when he looked up, his mother was watching him from behind the screen door. She'd been quiet at dinner that night, that worried face turned on him, the sad eyes. He just wanted to turn to her and say, *Sometimes it feels good to fuck with something. Instead of always being fucked with.*

"Like?" the girl nudged.

"Like . . . well, sometimes things have to die. We have to kill them. Just like Jesus requires sacrifice, well, so does Satan."

Satan, he said it, like it was some guy's name. It didn't feel bogus and it didn't feel scary. It felt normal, like he actually knew what he was talking about. Satan. He could almost picture him here, this guy all long-faced and horned, with those split-open goat eyes.

"You seriously believe this shit—what's your name again?"

"Ben. Day."

"Ben-Gay?"

"Yeah, never heard that one." Ben took another beer from the cooler, without asking, he'd bumped over a few feet since they started talking, and as the booze chilled him out, everything he said, all the shit rolling out of his mouth, seemed undeniable. He could become an undeniable guy, he could see it, even with that last crack, how that asshole knew his joke was going to whistle out and flop.

They fired up another joint, the girl pulling her clip out of her hair again, the goofy, friendly flip of hair falling back to its normal place, her not looking as nice without it. Ben breathed in, took a decent amount, but—don't cough, don't cough—not enough so he got seeds in the back of his throat. This was ditchweed stuff, the kind that got you dirty high. It got you paranoid and talky, instead of mellowing you out. Ben had a theory that all the chemical runoff from all the farms rolled into the ground and was sucked up by these mean, greedy plants. It infected them: all that insecticide and bright green fertilizer was settling into the grooves of his lungs and his brain.

The girl was looking at him now, that dazed look Debby got after too much TV, like she needed to say something but was too lazy to move her mouth. He wanted something to eat.

The Devil is never hungry. That's what he thought then, out of nowhere, the words in his brain like a prayer.

Alex was plucking at his guitar again, some Van Halen, some AC/DC, a Beatles song, and then suddenly he was fingering "O Little Town of Bethlehem," the binky chords making Ben's head ache more.

"Hey, no Christmas songs, Ben wouldn't like that," Mike called out.

"Holy shit, he's bleeding!" the girl said.

The cut in his forehead had opened up, and now it was dripping lushly down his face onto his pants. The girl tried to hand him a fast-food napkin, but he waved her off, smeared the blood across his face like warpaint.

Alex had stopped playing the song, and they all just stared at Ben, uneasy smiles and stiff shoulders, leaning slightly away from him. Mike held out the joint like an offering, on the tips of his fingers to avoid contact. Ben didn't want it, but breathed in deep again, the sour smoke burning more lung tissue.

It was then that the door-flap made its wavy warble and Trey walked in. He had his arms folded, feet planted, slouchy stance going, rolling his eyes over the room and then jerking his head back like Ben was a fish gone bad.

"What are you doing here? Diondra here?"

"She's in Salina. Just thought I'd stop by, kill some time. They been entertaining me."

"We heard about your fight," the girl said, all sly smiles, her lips thin crescents. "And other bad stuff."

Trey, his long slick black hair and chiseled face, was unreadable. He looked at the group on the floor, and at Ben squatting with them, and for once seemed unsure of how to play the situation.

"Yeah, what's he been saying?" He kept his eyes on Ben and grabbed a beer from the girl without even looking at her. Ben wondered if they'd slept together, Trey had the same disdain Ben once saw him direct at an ex-girlfriend: *I am not angry or sad or happy to see you. I could not give a shit. You don't even ripple.*

"Some shit about the Devil and what you guys do to . . . help him," she said.

Trey got his grin going then, sat down across from Ben—Ben avoiding eye contact.

"Hey Trey?" Alex said. "You're Indian aren't you?"

"Yeah, you want me to scalp you?"

"You're not full though, right?" the girl blurted.

"My mom's white. I don't date Indian chicks."

"Why not?" she asked, running the roach clip feather in and out of her hair, the metal teeth tangling themselves in the waves.

"Because Satan likes white pussy." He smiled and cocked his head at her, and she started to giggle, but then he kept the same expression and she shut down, her ugly boyfriend putting an arm back on her hip.

They'd liked Ben's patter, but Trey was spookier. He sat there almost cross-legged, eyeing them in a way that seemed friendly on the surface, but was entirely without warmth. And while his body was folded in a casual way, every limb was held at a tense, sharp angle. There was something deeply unkind about him. No one offered to pass the joint again.

They all sat quietly for a few minutes, Trey's mood unnerving everyone. Usually he was the loud, smart-ass, fight-starting beer swigger, but when he got upset it was like he sent out hundreds of invisible, insistent fingers to push everyone down by the shoulders. Sink everyone.

"So you want to go?" he suddenly asked Ben. "I got my truck. I got Diondra's keys. We can go to her place til she gets home, she's got cable. Better'n this freezing cold shithole."

Ben nodded, gave a jittery wave to the crowd, and followed Trey who was already outside, tossing his beer can on the snow. Ben was definitely altered. Words clotted in the back of his throat, and as he climbed into the GMC he tried to stammer some excuse to Trey. Trey who'd just saved his ass, for unclear reasons. Why was he the one with Diondra's keys? Probably because he'd asked for them. Ben didn't think to ask enough.

"I hope you're ready to back that shit up, what you were saying in there," Trey said, putting the stick in reverse. The GMC was a tank, and Trey drove it straight across the farm property, bumping over old cornstalks and irrigation ditches, forcing Ben to grab on to the armrest to keep from biting his tongue off. Trey landed a meaningful glance on Ben's tight grip.

"Yeah, of course."

"Maybe tonight you become a man. Maybe."

Trey flicked on his cassette player. Iron Maiden, midsong, hell yes, the words hissing at Ben: *666 . . . Satan . . . Sacrifice.*

Ben worked the music in his head, his brain sizzling, feeling angry-frantic, the way he always did to metal, the guitar strum never letting up, bundling him tenser and tenser, bumping his head up and down, the drums shooting up his spine, the whole thing this rage-frenzy, not letting him think straight, just keeping him in a tight shake. His whole body felt like a cocked fist, ready for release.

Libby Day

NOW

The stretch of I-70 between Kansas City and St. Louis was hours and hours of pure ugly driving. Flat, dead-yellow, and littered with billboards: a fetus curled up like a kitten (Abortion Stops a Beating Heart); a living room turned red from the glare of ambulance lights (Take Care Crime-Scene Cleanup Specialists); a remarkably plain woman giving fuck-me eyes to passing motorists (Hot Jimmy's Gentlemen's Club). The billboards ominously advising love of Jesus were in direct proportion to those advertising porn liquidators, and the signs for local restaurants consistently misused quotation marks: Herb's Highway Diner—The "Best" Meal in Town; Jolene's Rib House—Come in for Our "Delicious" Baby Back Ribs.

Lyle was in the passenger seat. He'd debated the pros and cons of joining me (maybe I would have more rapport with Krissi alone, us both being women; on the other hand, he did know this part of the case better; but then again, he may get too excited, ask her too many questions, and then blow it, he sometimes got ahead of himself, if he had one flaw it was that he sometimes got ahead of himself; then again, $500 was a lot of money and he felt somewhat entitled, no offense, to come along). Finally I'd snapped into the phone that

I'd swing by Sarah's Pub in thirty minutes, and if he was out front, he could come. Click. Now he was fussing next to me, flicking the door lock up and down, fiddling with the radio, reading each sign out loud, like he was trying to reassure himself of something. We drove past a fireworks warehouse the size of a cathedral, and at least three bundles of fatality markers: small white crosses and plastic flowers gathering dust on the side of the road. Gas stations made themselves known with signs skinnier and taller than the wilting weather vanes of nearby farms.

On one ridge was a billboard with a familiar face: Lisette Stephens, with that joyful grin, a phone number below for information on her disappearance. I wondered how long til they took it down, drained of hope or money.

"Oh God, her," Lyle said, as we passed Lisette. I bristled, but my feelings were similar. After a while it was almost rude to ask you to worry about someone who was clearly dead. Unless it was my family.

"So Lyle, can I ask you, what is it that makes you so obsessed with the . . . this case?" As I said it, the sky got just dark enough to switch the highway lights on, and all in a row, into the horizon, they blinked white, like my question had intrigued them.

Lyle was staring at his leg, listening sideways like he usually did. He had a habit of pushing one ear toward whoever was speaking, and then he'd wait a few seconds, like he was translating whatever was said into another language.

"It's just a classic whodunit. There are a lot of viable theories, so it's interesting to talk about," he said, still not looking at me. "And there's you. And Krissi. Children who . . . caused something. I'm interested in that."

"Children who caused something?"

"Something to happen, something that got bigger than they were, something that had unintentionally major consequences. Ripples. That interests me."

"Why?"

He paused. "Just does."

We were the two unlikeliest people to charm information out of someone. Stunted human beings who got awkward every time we tried to express ourselves. I didn't really care if we got much from

Krissi, though, as the more I thought about Lyle's theory, the more it seemed like bunk.

After another forty minutes of driving, the strip clubs started showing up: dismal, crouched blocks of cement, most without any real name, just neon signs shouting Live Girls! Live Girls! Which I guess is a better selling point than Dead Girls. I imagined Krissi Cates pulling into the gravel parking lot, getting ready to take off her clothes at a strip club that was so entirely generic. There's something disturbing about not even bothering with a name. Whenever I see news stories about children who were killed by their parents, I think: But how could it be? They cared enough to give this kid a name, they had a moment—at least one moment—when they sifted through all the possibilities and picked one specific name for their child, decided what they would call their baby. How could you kill something you cared enough to name?

"This will be my first strip bar," Lyle said, and gave his pert-lipped smile.

I pulled off the highway, to the left, as Krissi's mother had advised—when I'd phoned the only club listed, a greasy man told me he thought Krissi was "around"—and rattled into a pasture-sized parking lot for three strip bars, all in a row. A gas station and trucker park sat at the far, far end: in the bright white glow, I saw the silhouettes of women scuttling like cats between the cabs, doors opening and shutting, bare legs kicking out as they leaned in to line up the next trick. I assumed most of the strippers ended up working the trucker park once the clubs were done with them.

I got out of the car and fumbled with the notes Lyle had given me, a neat, numbered list of questions to ask Krissi, if we found her. (Number One: Do you still maintain that you were molested by Ben Day when you were a child? If so, please explain.) I started to review the rest of the questions when a movement to my right caught my attention. Far down in the trucker park, a small shadow dislodged itself from the side of a cab and started toward me in an intensely straight line, the kind of straight you walk when you're wasted and trying not to look it. I could see the shoulders pushed forward, far out ahead of the body, as if the girl had no choice but to keep moving toward me once she started. And she *was* a girl, I saw when she reached the other side of my car. She had a wide, doll-like face that glowed in the streetlight, light brown hair pulled back in a ponytail from a domed forehead.

"Hey, you got a cigarette I could bum?" she said, her head jittering like a Parkinson's patient.

"You OK?" I asked, trying to get a better look at her, guess her age. Fifteen, sixteen. She was shivering in a thin sweatshirt over a miniskirt and boots that were supposed to look sexy but on her looked childish, a kindergartner playing cowgirl.

"You got a cigarette?" she repeated, brightening, her eyes wet. She gave a quick bounce on her heels, looked from me to Lyle, who was watching the pavement.

I had a pack somewhere in the back of my car, so I leaned in and rummaged through old fast-food wrappers, an assortment of tea bags I'd swiped from a restaurant (another thing no one should ever buy: tea bags), and a pile of cheap metal spoons (ditto). The cigarette pack had three cigs left, one of them broken. I doled out the other two, flicked a lighter, the girl leaning in crookedly, then finally hitting the flame, *Sorry I can't see a thing without my glasses.* I lit my cigarette, let my head do its heat-wave dance after that first rush of nicotine.

"I'm Colleen," she said, sucking on the cigarette. The temperature had dropped quickly with the sun, we stood across from each other bouncing up and down to keep warm.

Colleen. It was too sweet a name for a hooker. Someone had once had different plans for this girl.

"How old are you, Colleen?"

She glanced back toward the truck park and smiled, hunched down in her shoulders. "Oh, don't worry, I'm not working there. I work over there." She pointed to the middle strip club with her middle finger. "I'm legal. I don't need to . . ." She nodded back toward the row of trucks, all of them immobile, despite what was happening inside. "We just try to keep an eye out for some of the girls that do work it. Sisterhood thing. You new?"

I'd worn a low-cut top, assuming it might make Krissi more comfortable when I found her, signal I wasn't a prude. Colleen was looking at my cleavage now with the eyes of a jeweler, trying to match my tits to the correct club.

"Oh, no. We're looking for a friend. Krissi Cates? You know her?"

"She may have a different last name now," Lyle said, then looked away toward the highway.

"I know a Krissi. Older?"

"Mid-thirties or so." Colleen's whole body was humming. I assumed she was on uppers. Or maybe she was just cold.

"Right," she said, finishing her cigarette in one aggressive pull. "She picks up some day shifts at Mike's sometimes." She pointed to the farthest club, where the neon said only G-R-S.

"That doesn't sound good."

"It's not. But you gotta retire sometime, right? Still it sucks for her, because I guess she spent a lot of money on a boob job, but Mike still didn't think she was primetime anymore. But at least the boob job was tax deductible."

Colleen said all this with the perky ruthlessness of a teenager who knew she had decades before such humiliations touched her.

"So should we come back during the day shift?" Lyle asked.

"Mmm. You could wait here," she said in a babyish voice. "She should be done soon." She motioned back toward the line of trucks. "I need to get ready for work, thanks for the cigarette."

She trotted, again with that push of the shoulders, toward the dark middle building, flung the door wide, and disappeared inside.

"I think we should go, this sounds like a dead end," Lyle said. I was about to snap at him for going chickenshit on me, tell him to just wait in the car, when another shadow climbed out of a truck far back in the line, and began heading toward the parking lot. All the women here walked as if they were pushing against a monstrous headwind. My stomach lurched at a lonely image of me trapped here or somewhere like it. It wasn't so unlikely, for a woman with no family, no money and no skills. A woman with a certain unwholesome pragmatism. I'd spread my legs for nice men I knew would be good for a few months of free meals. I'd done it and never felt guilty, so how much would it take to find me here? I felt my throat tighten for a second, and then snapped to. I had money coming now.

The figure was all shadow: I could make out a halo of ruined hair, the jutting edges of short shorts, an oversized purse, and thick, muscular legs. She came out of the dark to reveal a tanned face with eyes that were set slightly close together. Cute but canine. Lyle nudged me, gave me a searching look to see if I recognized her. I didn't but I gave a quick wave just in case and she stopped jerkily. I asked if she was Krissi Cates.

"I am," she said, her vulpine face surprisingly eager, helpful, like she thought something good might be about to happen. It was a strange expression to see, considering the direction she'd come from.

"I was hoping to talk to you."

"OK." She shrugged. "About what?" She couldn't figure me out: not a cop, not a social worker, not a stripper, not her kid's teacher, assuming she had a kid. Lyle she only glanced at, since he was taking turns gaping at her or turning almost entirely away from us. "About working here? You a reporter?"

"Well, to be frank, it's about Ben Day."

"Oh. OK. We can go inside Mike's, you can buy me a drink?"

"Are you married? Is your name still Cates?" Lyle blurted.

Krissi frowned at him, then looked at me for explanation. I widened my eyes, grimaced: the look women give each other when they're embarrassed of the men they're with. "I got married, once," she said. "Last name's Quanto now. Only because I been too lazy to change it back. You know what a pain in the ass that is?"

I smiled as if I did, and then suddenly I was following her across the parking lot, trying to keep out of the way of the giant leather purse that bounced against her hip, giving Lyle a look to pull it together. Just before we got to the door, she ducked against the side of the club, murmuring, *you mind?* and snuffed something from a packet of foil she pulled from her rear pocket. Then she turned her back entirely to me and made a gargling sound that must have hurt.

Krissi turned back, a broad smile on. "Whatever gets you through the night . . ." she sang, waggling the foil packet, but partway through the verse she seemed to forget the tune. She snuffed her nose, which was so compact it reminded me of an outie belly button, the kind pregnant women get. "Mike's a Nazi about this stuff," she said, and flung the door open.

I'd been to strip clubs before—back in the '90s when it was considered brazen, back when women were dumb enough to think it was sexy, standing around pretending to be hot for women because men thought it was hot if you were hot for women. I guess I hadn't been to one this low-rent though. It was small and filmy, the walls and floors seemed to have an extra wax coating. A young girl was dancing gracelessly on a low stage. She marched in place, actually, her waist rolling over a thong two sizes too small, pasties waffling over nipples that pointed outward, walleyed. Every few beats she would turn her back to the men, then bend over and peer at them through her spread legs, her face going quickly red from the flood of blood to her head. In response, the men—there were only three of them, all in flannel, hunched over beers at separate tables—would grunt or nod. A massive bouncer studied himself in the wall mirror, bored. We sat down, three in a row at the bar, me in the middle. Lyle had his arms folded, his hands in his armpits, trying not to touch anything, trying to look like he was looking at the dancer without really looking at her. I turned away from the stage, wrinkled my nose.

"I know, right?" Krissi said. "Goddam armpit of a place. This is on you, right? Because I have no cash." Before I even nodded she was ordering herself a vodka and cranberry, and I just asked for the same. Lyle got carded, and as he was showing the bartender his ID, he started doing some uncomfortable impersonation, his voice going even more ducklike, a weird smile pasted to his face. He made no eye contact, and gave no real signal that he was doing an impersonation. The bartender stared at him, and Lyle said, *The Graduate. You seen it?* And the guy just turned away.

So did I.

"So, what do you want to know?" Krissi smiled, leaned toward me. I debated whether to tell her who I was, but she seemed so disinterested I decided to save myself the trouble. Here was a woman who just wanted company. I kept glancing at her breasts, which were even bigger than mine, tightly packed and well trussed so they poked straight out. I pictured them under there, shiny and globular like cellophaned chicken.

"You like 'em?" Krissi chirped, giving them a bounce. "They're semi-new. Well, I guess they're almost a year now. I should have a birthday party for them. Not that they've helped me here. Fuckin' Mike keeps screwing me on shifts. It's OK though, I always wanted bigger boobs. And now I have them. If I could only get rid of this, is what I need to get rid of." She grabbed at a minimal fat roll, pretending it was much worse than it was. Just beneath it, the white glint of a caesarian scar snaked out.

"So, Ben Day," she continued. "Red-headed bastard. He really fucked my life up."

"So, you maintain you were molested by him?" Lyle said, leaning out from behind me like a squirrel.

I turned around to glare at him, but Krissi didn't seem to care. She had the incuriosity of the drugged. She continued to speak only to me.

"Yeah. Yeah. It was all part of his satanic thing. I think he'd have sacrificed me, I think that was the plan. He'd have killed me if they hadn't caught him for, you know, what he did to his family."

People always wanted their piece of the murders. Just like everyone in Kinnakee knew someone who'd screwed my mom, everyone had suffered some close call with Ben. He'd threatened to kill them, he'd kicked their dog, he'd looked at them really scary-like one day. He'd bled when he heard a Christmas song. He'd shown them the mark of Satan, tucked behind one ear, and asked them to join his cult. Krissi had that eagerness, that intake of air before she started talking.

"So what happened exactly?" I asked.

"You want the PG or R version?" She ordered another round of vodka and cranberry and then called out for three Slippery Nipple shots. The bartender poured them, pre-made, from a plastic jug, raised an eyebrow at me, asked us if we wanted to start a tab.

"It's fine, Kevin, my friend's got it," Krissi said, and then laughed. "What's your name anyway?"

I avoided the question by asking the bartender how much I owed, paid it from a fan of twenties so Krissi knew I had more money. Takes a mooch to catch a mooch.

"You'll love these, like drinking a cookie," she said. "Cheers!" she raised the shot up with a screw-you gesture toward a dark window in the back of the club, where I guessed Mike was sitting. We drank, the shot sitting thick in my throat, Lyle making a *whoo!* noise like it had been whiskey.

After a few beats, Krissi readjusted a boob and then pulled in another big gulp of air. "So, yeah. I was eleven, Ben was fifteen. He started hanging around me after school, just always watching me. I mean, I got that a lot, I always got that. I was always a cute kid, I'm not bragging, I just was. And we had a lot of money. My dad—" here I caught a flicker of pain, a quick wrinkle of her lip that exposed a single tooth—"he was a self-made man. Got into the videotape industry right at the start, he was the biggest videotape wholesaler in the Midwest."

"Like, movies?"

"No, like blank tapes, for people to record stuff on. Remember? Well, you probably were too young."

I wasn't.

"Anyway, so I was kind of an easy target maybe. Not like I was a latchkey kid or anything, but my mom didn't keep the best eye out for me all the time, I guess." This time a more obvious look of bitterness.

"Wait, why are you here again?" she asked.

"I'm researching the case."

Her mouth drooped down at the corners. "Oh. For a second I thought my mom sent you. I know she knows I'm here."

She clicked long, coral nails on the counter and I hid my left hand, with its stumped finger, under my shotglass. I knew I should care something about Krissi's homelife but I didn't. Well, I cared enough not to tell her that her mom was never going to check up on her.

One of the patrons at one of the plastic tables kept peeling off glances at us, looking over his shoulder with a drunk pissiness. I wanted to get out of there, leave Krissi and her issues behind.

"So," Krissi began again. "Ben was really sneaky with me. He'd, like . . . you want some chips? The chips are really good here."

The chips hung in cheap snack packs behind the bar. *The chips are really good here.* I had to like the woman for working me so hard. I nodded a yes and soon Krissi was tearing into a bag, the stench of sour-cream-and-onion making my mouth water in spite of its better judgment. Yellow flavoring stuck to Krissi's bubblegum lipgloss.

"Anyway, so Ben earned my trust and then started molesting me."

"How did he earn your trust?"

"You know, gum, candy, saying nice things to me."

"And how did he molest you?"

"He'd take me into the closet where he kept his janitor stuff, he was a janitor at the school, I remember he always smelled horrible, like dirty bleach. He'd take me in there after school and make me perform oral sex on him and then he'd perform oral sex on me and he'd make me swear allegiance to Satan. I was so so scared. He'd tell me, you know, that he'd hurt my parents if I told."

"How did he make you go into the closet?" Lyle asked. "If it was at school?"

Krissi turtled her neck at that, the same angry gesture I've always made when anyone questioned my testimony about Ben.

"Just, you know, threaten me. He had an altar in there, he'd pull it out, it was an upside-down cross. I think some dead animals too that he'd killed were in there. A sacrifice thing. That's why I think he was working up to killing me. But he got his family instead. The whole family was into it, that's what I heard. That the whole family was worshiping the Devil and stuff." She licked chip shards off her thick plastic fingernails.

"I doubt that," I muttered.

"Well, how do you know?" Krissi snapped. "I lived through this, OK?"

I kept waiting for her to figure out who I was, to let my face— not so different from Ben's face—float into her memory, to notice the wide hairline of red roots springing from my head.

"So how many times did Ben molest you?"

"Countless. Countless." She nodded somberly.

"How did your dad react when you told him what Ben had done to you?" Lyle asked.

"Oh my god he was so protective of me, he freaked, went totally ballistic. He drove around town that day, the day of the murders, looking for Ben. I always think if he'd only found Ben, he'd have killed him, and then Ben's family would still be alive. Isn't that sad?"

My gut clenched at that and then my anger flared back.

"Ben's family—the horrible Devil worshipers?"

"Well, maybe I was exaggerating on that." Krissi cocked her

head, the way grown-ups do when they're trying to placate a child. "I'm sure they were nice Christian people. Just think, if my dad had found Ben though . . ."

Just think if your dad didn't find Ben and instead found my family. Found a gun, found an axe, wiped us out. Almost wiped us out.

"Did your dad come back to your house that night?" Lyle asked. "Did you see him after midnight?"

Krissi lowered her chin again, raised her eyebrows at me, and I added a more reassuring, "I mean, how did you know he never made contact with any of the Days?"

"Because I'm serious, he would have done some serious damage. I was like, the apple of his eye. It killed him, what happened to me. Killed him."

"He live around here?" Lyle was freaking her out, his intensity was laserlike.

"Uh, we've lost touch," she said, already looking around the bar for the next score. "I think it was all too much for him."

"Your family sued the school district, didn't they?" Lyle said, leaning in, getting greedy. I moved my stool so I blocked him off a bit, hoping he'd get the idea.

"Hell yeah. They needed to be sued, letting someone like that work there, letting a little girl get molested right under their noses. I came from a really good family—"

Lyle cut her off. "Do you mind if I ask, with the settlement . . . how did you end up, uh, here?" The customer at the table was now turned around entirely in his chair, watching us, belligerent.

"My family had some business setbacks. The money's been gone a long time. It's not like it's a bad thing, working here. People always think that. It's not, it's empowering, it's fun, it makes people happy. How many people can say all that about their jobs? It's not like I'm a whore."

I frowned before I could help myself, looked in the direction of the truck park.

"That?" Krissi fake-whispered. "I was just getting a hold of a little something for tonight. I wasn't . . . oh God. No. Some girls do, but I don't. There's some poor girl, sixteen years old, works it with her mom. I try to look out for her. Colleen. I keep thinking I should call child services on her or something? Who do you even call for something like that?"

Krissi asked it with all the concern of finding a new gynecologist.

"Can we get your dad's address?" Lyle asked.

Krissi stood up, about twenty minutes after I would have. "I told you, we're not in touch," she said.

Lyle started to say something when I turned to him, poked a finger toward his chest and mouthed, Shut up. He opened his mouth, shut it, looked at the girl onstage, who was now pantomiming fucking the floor, and walked out the door.

It was too late, though, Krissi was already saying she had to go meet someone. As I was settling up with the bartender she asked me if she could borrow twenty dollars.

"I'll buy Colleen some dinner with it," she lied. Then she quickly changed it to fifty. "I just haven't cashed my work check yet. I will totally pay you back." She made an elaborate play out of getting a sheet of paper and a pen for me, told me to write down my address and she'd totally totally mail me the money.

I mentally put the cash on Lyle's tab, forked it over to Krissi, her counting it in front of me like I might shortchange her. She opened the big maw of her purse and a child's sippy cup rolled out onto the floor.

"Leave it," she waved at me when I bent to pick it up, and so I left it.

Then I took the greasy scrap of paper and wrote down my address and my name. Libby Day. My name is Libby Day, you lying whore.

Patty Day

JANUARY 2, 1985
1:50 P.M.

P atty wondered how many hours she and Diane had spent rumbling around in cars together: a thousand? two thousand? Maybe if you added it all up, a sum total of two years, put end to end, the way mattress companies always did: You spend a third of your life asleep, why not do it on a ComfortCush? Eight years standing in lines, they say. Six years peeing. Put like that, life was grim. Two years waiting in the doctor's office, but a total of three hours watching Debby at breakfast laughing until milk started dribbling down her chin. Two weeks eating soppy pancakes her girls made for her, the middle still sour with batter. Only one hour staring in amazement as Ben unconsciously tucked his baseball cap behind his ears in a gesture mirror-perfect to what his grandpa did, his grandpa dead when Ben was just a baby. Six *years* of hauling manure, though, three years of ducking calls from bill collectors. Maybe a month of having sex, maybe a day of having good sex. She'd slept with three men in her life. Her gentle high school boyfriend; Runner, the hotshot who stole her from her gentle high school boyfriend and left her with four (wonderful) children; and a guy she dated for a few months somewhere in the years after Runner left. They'd slept together three times with the kids at home. It always ended awkwardly. Ben, sulky and possessive at age eleven, would park himself in the kitchen so he could glower at them as they left her bedroom in the morning, Patty worrying about the guy's semen on her, that smell so stark and embarrassing with your children still in their pajamas. It was clearly not going to work from the start, and she'd never gotten the courage up to try again. Libby would graduate from high school in eleven years, so maybe then. She'd be forty-three, which was right when women were supposed to peak sexually. Or something. Maybe it was menopause.

"We heading to the school?" Diane asked, and Patty pulled out of her three-second trance to remember their horrible errand, their mission: find her son and, what? Hide him away til this blew over? Drive him to the little girl's house and straighten it all out? In family movies, the mom always caught the son stealing, and she'd march him back over to the drugstore and get him to hand over the candy on a shaky palm, and beg forgiveness. She knew Ben shoplifted some. Before he started locking his door, she'd occasionally find strange, pocket-sized items in his room. A candle, batteries, a plastic packet of toy soldiers. She'd never said anything, which was horrible. Part of her didn't want to deal with it—drive all the way into town, and talk to some kid who got paid minimum wage and didn't care anyway. And the other part (even worse) thought, Why the hell not? The boy had so little, why not keep pretending this was something a friend gave him? Let him have this stolen trifle, a pebble-plunk of a wrongdoing in the grand scheme.

"No, he wouldn't go to the school. He only works Sundays."

"Well, where?"

They came to a stoplight, swaying on a line like laundry. The road dead-ended onto the pasture of a land-rich family that lived in Colorado. Turn right and they were heading to Kinnakee proper—the town, the school. Turn left and they were going deeper into Kansas, all farmland, where Ben's two friends lived, those shy Future Farmers of America who couldn't bear to ask for Ben when she picked up the phone.

"Take a left, we'll go see the Muehlers."

"He still hangs around with them? That's good. No one could think those boys would do anything . . . weird."

"Oh, because Ben would?"

Diane sighed and turned left.

"I'm on your side, P."

The Muehler brothers had dressed as farmers for Halloween every year since birth, their parents driving them into Kinnakee in the same wide-body truck, the boys deposited on Bulhardt Avenue for trick-or-treating in their tiny John Deere baseball caps and overalls while the parents drank coffee at the diner. The Muehler brothers, like their parents, talked only about alfalfa and wheat and weather, and went to church on Sunday, where they prayed for things that were probably crop-related. The Muehlers were good people with no imagination, with personalities so tied to the land, even their skin seemed to take on the ridges and furrows of Kansas.

"I know." Patty reached to put her hand on Diane's just as Diane shifted gears, so her hand hung just above her sister's and then went back to her lap.

"Oh you bleeping jerk!" Diane said to a car ahead of her, rolling along at twenty miles an hour and deliberately going slower as Diane closed in on the bumper. She swerved up to pass them and Patty stared rigidly ahead, even though she could feel the driver's face on her, a murky moon in her peripheral. Who was this person? Had they heard the news? Is that why they were staring, maybe even pointing? *There's the woman who raised that boy.* The Day boy. A hundred phones were rattling this morning, if Diane had heard last night. At home her three girls were probably sitting in front of the TV, turning from cartoons to the blaring telephone, which they'd been told to pick up in case Ben called. They seemed unlikely to follow that instruction: they were strung out with the fear of the morning. If anyone dropped by, they'd find three unattended, teary kids, age ten and under, huddled on the living room floor, cringing at the noise.

"Maybe one of us should have stayed home . . . in case," Patty said.

"You're not going anywhere by yourself while this is going on, and I don't know where to go. This is the right thing. Michelle's a big girl. I watched you when I was younger'n her."

But that was back when people still did that, Patty thought.

Back when people went out for a whole night and left the kids on their own and no one thought anything of it. In the '50s and '60s, out on that quiet old prairie where nothing ever happened. Now little girls weren't supposed to ride bikes alone or go anywhere in groups of less than three. Patty had attended a party thrown by one of Diane's work friends, like a Tupperware party, but with rape whistles and mace instead of wholesome plastic containers. She'd made a joke about what kind of lunatic would drive all the way out to Kinnakee to attack someone. A blond woman she'd just met looked up from her new pepper-spray keychain and said, "A friend of mine was raped once." Patty had bought several cans of mace out of guilt.

"People think I'm a bad mother, that's why this is happening."

"No one thinks you're a bad mother. You're superwoman as far as I'm concerned: you keep the farm going, get four kids to school every day, and don't drink a gallon of bourbon to do it."

Patty immediately thought of the freezing cold morning two weeks ago, when she almost wept with exhaustion. Actually putting on clothes and driving the girls to school seemed an entirely remote possibility. So she let them all stay home and watch ten hours of soap operas and game shows with her. She made poor Ben ride his bike, shooed him out the door with a promise she'd petition again to get the school bus to come to them next year.

"I'm not a *good* mother."

"Hush."

THE MUEHLERS' HOME was on a decent chunk of land, four hundred acres at least. The house was tiny and looked like a buttercup, a swipe of yellow against miles of green winter wheat and snow. It was blowing even harder than before now; the forecast said it would snow through the night, and then would come sudden springlike temperatures. That promise was wedged in her brain: sudden spring-like temperatures.

They drove up the skinny, unwelcoming strip of road leading to the house, past a tiller sitting just inside the barn like an animal. Its hooked blades cast claw shadows on the ground. Diane made a sinus noise she always resorted to when she was uncomfortable, a fake clearing of the throat to fill the silence. Neither of them looked at the other as they got out of the car. Attentive black grackles perched in the trees, cawing continually, ill-natured, noisy birds. One of them flew past, a silvery trail of Christmas tinsel fluttering from its beak. But otherwise the place was immobile, no motors of any kind, no gates clanking shut, no TV within, just the silence of land packed under snow.

"Don't see Ben's bike," was all Diane said as they banged the doorknocker.

"Could be around back."

Ed answered the door. Jim, Ed, and Ben were all in the same grade, but the brothers weren't twins, one of them had flunked at least once, maybe twice. She thought it was Ed. He goggled at her for a second, a short kid of only 5'4" or so, but with a man's athletic build. He shoved his hands in his pockets and looked behind him.

"Well, hi, Mrs. Day."

"Hi, Ed. Sorry to bother you on Christmas break."

"No, no problem."

"I'm looking for Ben—is he here? Have you seen him?"

"Be-en?" He said it in two syllables, like he was tickled at the idea. "Ah, no, we ain't seen Ben in . . . well, I don't think we seen him this whole year. Aside from school. He's been hanging around with a different group now."

"What group?" asked Diane, and Ed looked at her for the first time.

"Uh, we-ell . . ."

She could see Jim's silhouette approaching the door, backlit by the picture window in the kitchen. He lumbered toward them, bigger and wider than his brother.

"Can we help you, Mrs. Day?" He nudged his face in, then his torso, slowly moving his brother to the side. The two of them effectively closed off the doorway. It made Patty want to crane her neck around them and peek inside.

"I was just asking Ed if you two'd seen Ben today, and he said you hadn't been seeing much of him this whole school year."

"Mmm, no. Wish you'd phoned, could have saved you some time."

"We need to find him soon, you have any idea where we can find him, it's sort of a family emergency," Diane interrupted.

"Mmm, no," said Jim again. "Wish we could help."

"You can't give us even a name of who he spends time with? Surely you must know that."

Ed had swung to the background now, so he was calling from the shadow of the living room.

"Tell her to phone 1-800-Devils-R-Us!" he cackled.

"What?"

"Nothing." Jim looked at the door knob in his hand, debating whether to start closing it.

"Jim, can you help us, please?" Patty murmured. "Please?"

The boy frowned, tapped the point of a cowboy boot against the floor like a ballerina, refused to raise his eyes. "He hangs out with, like, the Devil crowd."

"What does that mean?"

"Some older guy heads it, I don't know his name. They do a lot of drugs, peyote or whatever, and kill cows and sh-stuff. That's just what I heard. They don't go to our school, the kids in it. Except for Ben, I guess."

"Well, you must know the name of someone," Patty coaxed.

"I really don't, Mrs. Day. We steer clear of that stuff. I'm sorry, we tried to stay friends with Ben, but. We go to church here, my parents, they run a tight ship. Er . . . I'm real sorry."

He looked at the ground, and stopped talking, and Patty couldn't think of anything else to ask.

"OK, Jim, thanks."

He shut the door and before they could turn around, from inside the house they heard a bellow: *Asshole, why'd you gotta say that!* followed by a heavy bang against the wall.

Libby Day

Back in the car, Lyle said only three words. "What a nightmare." In reply, I said, *mmmm*. Krissi reminded me of me. Grasping and anxious, always bundling things aside for future use. That packet of chips. We scroungers always like little packets of food because people give them up with less hassle.

Lyle and I drove for twenty minutes without saying much, until finally he said, in his summing-up, newscaster voice, "So obviously she's lying about Ben molesting her. I think she lied to her dad too. I think Lou Cates went nuts, killed your family, and then later, he found out she'd lied. He killed an innocent family for nothing. Hence, his own family disintegrates. Lou Cates disappears, starts drinking."

"Hence?" I nipped at him.

"It's a solid theory. Don't you think?"

"I think you should not come on any more of these interviews. It's embarrassing."

"Libby, I'm financing this whole thing."

"Well, you're not helping it."

"*Sorry,*" he said, and then we stopped talking. As the lights of Kansas City turned the sky a sick orange in the distance, Lyle said, without looking at me, "It's a solid theory though, right?"

"Everything's a theory, that's why it's a *mystery!*" I mimicked him. "Just a great mystery, Who Killed The Days?" I proclaimed, brightly. After a few minutes, I said grudgingly. "I think it's an OK theory, I think we should look at Runner too."

"Fine by me. Although I'm still going to track down Lou Cates."

"Be my guest."

I dropped him back outside Sarah's, not offering to take him home, Lyle standing on the curb like a kid baffled that his parents can really bear leaving him at camp. I got home late and cranky and anxious to count my money. I'd made $1,000 so far from the Kill Club, with another $500 that Lyle owed me for Krissi, even though Krissi clearly would have talked to anybody. But even as I thought that, I knew it wasn't true. None of those Kill Club misfits could have made that work with Krissi, I thought. She talked to me because we had the same chemicals in our blood: shame, anger, greed. Unjustified nostalgia.

I'd earned my money, I thought, resentful for no reason. Lyle seemed completely fine with paying me. That's what I did, though— I had angry, defensive conversations in my head, got mad at things that hadn't even happened yet. Yet.

I'd earned my money (now I felt calmer), and if I heard from Runner, if I talked to Runner, I'd earn a lot more money and be set for a good four months. If I lived very still.

Make that five months: by the time I got home, Lyle had already left a message saying some local Kill Creeps wanted to have a swap meet, buy some of my family's "memorabilia." Magda would host, if I was interested. Magda the cave troll who'd drawn Devil horns on my photo. *Yes, Magda, I would love to be a guest in your home, where do you keep your silver again?*

I clicked off the answering machine, which I'd stolen from a roommate two moves ago. I thought of Krissi and knew her house was probably filled with other people's crap too. I had a stolen answering machine, a nearly full set of pocketed restaurant silverware, and a half-dozen salt-and-pepper shakers, including the new pair, from Tim-Clark's that I couldn't manage to transfer from the hall table to the kitchen. In one corner of my living room, by my old TV set, is a box with more than a hundred small bottles of lotion I've swiped. I keep them because I like to look at the lotions all together, pink and purple and green. I know this would look crazy to anyone who came to my home, but no one does, and I like them too much to get rid of them. My mom's hands were always rough and dry, she was constantly oiling them, to no avail. It was one of our favorite ways to tease her: "Oh mom don't touch, you're like an alligator!" The church we fitfully attended kept lotion in the women's room that she said smelled like roses: we'd all take turns squirting and sniffing our hands, complimenting each other on our ladylike scent.

No phone call from Diane. She'd have gotten my message by now, and she hadn't called. That seemed strange. Diane always made it easy for me to apologize. Even after this latest round of silent treatment—six years. Guess I should have autographed my book for her.

I turned around to the other set of boxes, the under-the-stairs boxes that had grown more ominous the more I let myself think about the murders. It's just stuff, I told myself. It cannot hurt you.

When I was fourteen, I thought a lot about killing myself—it's a hobby today, but at age fourteen it was a vocation. On a September morning, just after school started, I'd gotten Diane's .44 Magnum and held it, babylike, in my lap for hours. What an indulgence it would be, to just blow off my head, all my mean spirits disappearing with a gun blast, like blowing a seedy dandelion apart. But I thought about Diane, and her coming home to my small torso and a red wall, and I couldn't do it. It's probably why I was so hateful to her, she kept me from what I wanted the most. I just couldn't do it to her, though, so I made a bargain with myself: If I still feel this bad on February 1, I will kill myself. And it was just as bad on February 1, but again I made the bargain: If it's this bad May 1, I'll do it. And so on. I'm still here.

I looked at the boxes and made a quieter kind of bargain: If I can't stand doing this anymore in twenty minutes, I'll burn the whole lot.

The first box came apart easily, one side collapsing as soon as I pulled off the tape. Inside, at the top of the pile, was a concert T-shirt for The Police that was my mom's, food-stained and extremely soft.

Eighteen minutes.

Below that was a rubberbanded bunch of notebooks, all Debby's. I flipped through random pages:

> *Harry S Truman was the 33rd American*
> *president and from Missouri.*
> *The heart is the pump of the body it keeps blood*
> *going all over the body.*

Under that was a pile of notes, from Michelle to me, from me to Debby, from Debby to Michelle. Sifting through these, I plucked out a birthday card with an ice-cream sundae on the front, its cherry made with red sequins.

> *Dear Debby,* wrote my mom in her cramped handwriting. *We are so lucky to have such a sweet, kind, helpful girl in our family. You are my cherry on top! Mom*

She never wrote Mommy, I thought, we never called her that even as kids. *I want my mommy,* I thought. We never said that. *I want my mom.* I felt something loosen in me, that shouldn't have loosened. A stitch come undone.

Fourteen minutes.

I rummaged through more notes, putting the boring, inane ones aside for the Kill Club, missing my sisters, laughing at some of them, the strange worries we had, the coded messages, the primitive drawings, the lists of people we liked and didn't like. I'd forgotten we were tight, the Day girls. I wouldn't have said we were, but now, studying our writings like a spinster anthropologist, I realized it was true.

Eleven minutes. Here were Michelle's diaries, all rubberbanded together in a faux-leathery bundle. Every year she got two for Christmas—she needed twice as many as a normal girl. She'd always start the new one right there while we were still under the tree, chronicling every gift each of us got, keeping score.

I flipped open one from 1983 and remembered what a rotten busybody Michelle was, even at age nine. The day's entry talked about how she heard her favorite teacher, Miss Berdall, saying dirty things to a man on the phone in the teachers' lounge—and Miss Berdall wasn't even married. Michelle wondered if she confronted her, maybe Miss Berdall would bring her something nice for lunch. (Apparently Miss Berdall had once given Michelle half her jelly donut, which had left Michelle permanently fixated on Miss Berdall and her brown paper bags. Teachers were usually reliable for half a sandwich or a piece of fruit if you stared at them long enough. You just couldn't do it too much or you'd get a note sent home and Mom would cry.) Michelle's diaries were filled with drama and innuendo of a very grade-school level: At recess, Mr. McNany smoked just outside the boys' locker room, and then used breath spray (breath spray underlined several times) so no one would know. Mrs. Joekep from church was drinking in her car . . . and when Michelle asked Mrs. Joekep if she had the flu, since why was she drinking from that bottle, Mrs. Joekep laughed and gave her $20 for Girl Scout cookies, even though Michelle wasn't a Girl Scout.

Hell, she even wrote things about me: she knew, for instance, I lied to Mom about punching Jessica O'Donnell. This was true, I gave the poor girl a black eye but swore to my mom she fell off a swing. *Libby told me the Devil made her do it,* Michelle wrote. *Think I should tell Mom?*

I closed the book on 1983, browsed through 1982 and 1984. The diary for the second half of 1984 I read carefully, in case Michelle said anything noteworthy about Ben. Not much, except repeated claims that he was a big jerk and no one liked him. I wondered if the cops had had the same idea. I pictured some poor rookie, eating Chinese food at midnight while reading about how Michelle's best friend got her period.

Nine minutes. More birthday cards and letters, and then I dug up a note that was folded more expertly than the rest, origami'd so it looked almost phallic, which, I supposed, was the intention, as the word STUD was written at the top. I opened it up, and read the rounded girlish writing:

11/5/84
Dear Stud,
    I'm in biology and I'm fingering myself under the desk I

am so hot for you. Can you picture my pussy? It's still nice and red from you. Come over to my house after school today, K? I want to jump your bones!!! I'm so horny, even now. I wish you'd just live with me whenever my parents are gone. Your mom won't know, she's so spacy! Why would you stay at home when you could be with me?! Get some balls and tell your mom to go to hell. I'd hate for you to come for a visit one day and find me getting some action somewhere else. JK! Oh I want to cum so much. Meet me at my car after school, I'll park over on Passel St.

See ya soon,
Diondra

Ben had not had a girlfriend, he hadn't. Not a single person, including Ben, had ever said so. The name didn't even sound familiar. At the bottom of the box was a stack of our school yearbooks, from 1975, when Ben started school, to 1990, when Diane sent me away the first time.

I opened the yearbook for 1984–1985, and scanned Ben's class. No Diondra, but a photo of Ben that hurt: sloped shoulders, a loose half-mullet, and an Oxford shirt that he always wore on special occasions. I pictured him, back home, putting it on for Picture Day, practicing in the mirror how he'd smile. In September 1984 he was still wearing shirts my mom bought him, and by January he was an angry, black-haired kid accused of murder. I skimmed through the class above Ben's, jerking occasionally as I hit Dianes and Dinas, but no Diondra. Then to the class above that, about to give up, when there she was, Diondra Wertzner. Worst name ever, and I pulled my finger over the row, expecting to find a lunchlady in the making, someone coarse and mustached, and instead found a pretty, plump-cheeked girl with a fountain of dark spiral curls. She had small features, which she overplayed with heavy makeup, but even in the photo she popped off the page. Something in the deep-set eyes, a daring, with her lips parted so you could see pointy puppy-teeth.

I pulled out the yearbook for the previous year, and she was gone. I pulled out the yearbook for the following year, and she was gone.

Ben Day

Trey's truck smelled like weed, sweat socks, and sweet wine cooler that Diondra had probably spilled. Diondra tended to pass out while still holding a bottle in her hand, it was her preferred way to drink, to do it til it knocked her out, that last sip nearby just in case. The truck was littered with old fast-food wrappers, fish hooks, a *Penthouse,* and, on the fuzzy mat at Ben's feet, a crate of cartons labeled Mexican Jumping Beans, each box featuring a little bean wearing a sombrero, swooshes at its feet to make it look like it was bouncing.

"Try one," Trey said, motioning at it.

"Nah, isn't that supposed to be bugs or something?"

"Yeah, they're like beetle larvae," Trey said, and gave his jackhammer laugh.

"Great, thanks, that's cool."

"Oh shit, man, I'm just fucking with you, lighten up."

They pulled into a 7-Eleven, Trey waving to the Mexican guy behind the counter—*now there's a bean for you*—loading Ben up with a case of Beast, some microwave nachos that Diondra always whined for, and a fistful of beef jerky, which Trey held in his hand like a bouquet.

The guy smiled at Trey, made an ululating Indian war sound. Trey crossed his arms in front of his chest and pretended to do a hat dance. "Just ring me up, José." The guy didn't say anything else, and Trey left him the change, which was a good three bucks. Ben kept thinking about that on the drive to Diondra's. That most of this world was filled with people like Trey, who'd just leave behind three dollars without even thinking of it. Like Diondra. A few months back, at the very hot end of September, Diondra ended up having to babysit two of her cousins or step-half-cousins or something, and she and Ben had driven them to a water park near the Nebraska border. She'd been driving her mom's Mustang for a month (she was bored with her own car) and the backseat was filled with things they'd brought, things it would never occur to Ben to own: three different kinds of sunscreen, beach towels, squirt bottles, rafts, inflatable rings, beach balls, pails. The kids were small, like six or seven years old, and they were jammed back there with all that crap, the inflatable rafts making a whoogee-whoogee sound every time they moved, and somewhere near Lebanon, the kids rolled down the window, giggling, the rafts making more and more noise, like they were climaxing in some air mattress mating ritual, and Ben realized what the kids were giggling about. They were scraping all the change Diondra left in the backseat, on the floor, in the crevices—she just tossed any change she had back there—and the kids were throwing it by the handful out the window so they could watch it scatter like sparks. And not just pennies, a lot of it was quarters.

Ben thought that was how you could tell the difference between most people. It wasn't *I'm a dog person* and *I'm a cat person* or *I'm a Chiefs fan* and *I'm a Broncos guy*. It was whether you cared about quarters. To him, four quarters was a dollar. A stack of quarters was lunch. The amount of quarters those little shits threw out the window that day could have bought him half a pair of jeans. He kept asking the kids to stop, telling them it was dangerous, illegal, they could get a ticket, they needed to sit down and face forward. The kids laughed and Diondra howled—*Ben won't get his allowance this week if you keep taking his change*—and he realized he'd been found out. He hadn't been as quick-wristed as he'd thought: Diondra knew he scraped after her leftover coins. He felt like a girl whose dress just shot up in the wind. And he wondered what that said about her, see-ing her boyfriend scrape around for change and saying nothing, did that make her nice? Or mean.

Trey rolled up full speed to Diondra's house, a giant beige box surrounded by a chainlink fence to keep Diondra's pit bulls from killing the mailman. She had three pits, one a white sack of muscles with giant balls and crazy eyes that Ben disliked even more than the other two. She let them in the house when her parents were gone, and they jumped on tables and crapped all over the floor. Diondra didn't clean it up, just sprayed bathroom air freshener on all the shit-entwined carpet threads. That nice blue rug in the rec room—a dusty violet, Diondra called it—was now a land mine of ground-in dumps. Ben tried not to care. It wasn't his business, as Diondra was happy to remind him.

The back door was open, even though it was freezing, and the pit bulls were running in and out, like some sort of magic act—no pit bull, one pit bull, two pit bulls in the yard! Three! Three pit bulls in the yard, prancing around in rough circles, then shooting back inside. They looked like birds in flight, teasing and nipping at each other in formation.

"I hate those fucking dogs," Trey groaned, pulled to a stop.

"She spoils them."

The dogs launched into a round of attack-barking as Ben and Trey walked toward the front of the house, the animals trailing them obsessively along the fence, snouts and paws poking through the gaps, barking barking barking.

The front door was open, too, the heat pouring out. They passed through the pink-papered entryway—Ben unable to resist shutting the door behind him, save some energy—and downstairs, which was Diondra's floor. Diondra was in the rec room, dancing, half naked in oversized hot pink socks, no pants and a sweater built for two, with giant cables that reminded Ben of something a fisherman would wear, not a girl. Then again, all the girls at school wore their shirts big. They called them boyfriend shirts or daddy sweaters. Diondra, of course, had to wear them super big and layered with stuff under-neath: a T-shirt hanging down, then some sort of tank top, and a bright striped collar-shirt. Ben had once offered Diondra one of his

big black sweaters to be a boyfriend sweater, him being her boyfriend, but she'd wrinkled her nose and proclaimed, "That's not the
right kind. And there's a hole in it." Like a hole in a shirt was worse
than dog shit all over your carpet. Ben was never sure if Diondra
knew all sorts of secret rules, private protocols, or if she just made
shit up to make him feel like a tool.

She was bouncing around to Highway to Hell, the fireplace
shooting flames behind her, her cigarette held far away from her new
clothes. She had about twelve items all in plastic wraps or on hangers
or in shiny bags with tissue paper sparking out the top like fire. Also,
a couple of shoe boxes and the tiny packets he knew meant jewelry.
When she looked up and saw his black hair, she gave him a giant
happy smile and a thumbs-up. "Awesome." And Ben felt a little better, not as stupid. "I told you it'd look good, Benji." And that was it.

"What'd you buy, Dio?" Trey asked, rummaging in the bags. He
took a drag from her cigarette while she was still holding it, while she
was without pants. She caught Ben's look, flipped up the sweater to
reveal boxers that weren't his.

"It's OK, nerd-o." She came over and kissed him, her smell of
grape hairspray and cigarettes hitting him, calming him. He held her
gently, the way he did now, loose-armed, and when he felt her tongue
hit his, he twitched.

"Oh God, please get over this 'Diondra's untouchable' phase,"
she snapped. "Unless I'm too old for you."

Ben laughed. "You're seventeen."

"If you could hear what I hear," Diondra sang to a silver-bell
tune, sounding angry, sounding downright pissed.

"What's that mean?"

"Mean's seventeen may just be too old for your taste."

Ben didn't know what to say. To pursue something with Diondra
when she was in this peekaboo mood only encouraged endless
rounds of, "No it's nothing," and "I'll tell you later," or "Don't worry,
I can handle it." She pulled her crunchy hair back and danced around
for them, a drink now appearing from behind a shoe box. Her neck
was lined with purple hickeys he'd given her on Sunday, him Dracul-
ing into her neck, her demanding more, "Harder, harder, it won't
leave a mark if you keep doing it that way, don't tighten your lips, no

tongue, no harder . . . Do! It! Harder! How can you not even know how to give a hickey?" and with a furious tight face, she'd grabbed him by the head, turned him sideways, and worked at his neck like a dying fish, the flesh going inoutinout in frantic rhythm. Then she pulled away, "There!" and made him look in the mirror. "Now do me, like that."

The result was a march of leeches down her throat, brown and blue and embarrassing to Ben until he caught Trey staring at them.

"Oh no, baby, you're all busted up." Diondra simpered, finally noticing his cracked head. She licked a finger and started wiping at the blood. "Someone get to you?"

"Baby fell off his bike," Trey grinned. Ben hadn't told him he fell off his bike, and he felt a billow of rage at Trey for trying to make fun of him and actually just telling the truth.

"Fuck off, Trey."

"Heyyyy," said Trey, his hands shooting up, his eyes going slate.

"Someone push you off the bike, baby? Someone try to hurt you?" Diondra petted at him.

"You buy anything for Benny-boy, so he doesn't have to wear those shitty work jeans for another month?" Trey asked.

"Of course I did." She grinned, forgetting Ben's injury, which he'd imagined would take up much more time. She skipped across to a giant red bag and pulled out a pair of black leather pants, thick as cow hide, a striped T-shirt, and a black denim jacket with studs gleaming off it.

"Whoa, leather pants, you think you're dating David Lee Roth?" Trey cackled.

"He'll look good. Go try 'em on." She scrunched her nose up at him as he tried to pull her to him. "You ever heard of a shower, Ben? You smell like the cafeteria." She pushed the clothes into Ben's hands and shuffled him off to the bedroom. "It's a gift, Ben," she yelled after him. "You might want to say thank you at some point."

"Thank you!" he called back.

"Take a shower before you put them on, for Christsakes." So she was actually serious, he stunk. He knew he stunk, but hoped no one else could smell him. He walked into the bathroom across from Diondra's bedroom—she had her own dang bathroom, and her parents had their own giant one with two sinks—and dropped his stained clothes into a ball on the bright pink carpet. His crotch was still wet from the bucket spill at his school, his dick shriveled and clammy. The shower felt good, felt relaxing. He and Diondra had had sex a lot in this shower, all sudsy and warm. The soap was always there, you didn't have to wash yourself with baby shampoo because your mom couldn't ever fucking get to a store.

He dried off, put his boxers back on. He was wearing boxers Diondra had also bought him. The first time they got naked, she'd laughed at his tightie-whities til she actually choked on her own spit. He tried to jam the boxers into the taut leather—all snaps and zippers and hooks, and him squirming to haul them up over his ass, which Diondra said was his best feature. The problem was the boxers, they bunched up around his waist when he got the pants on, leaving bulbs in all the wrong places. He yanked the pants back off and kicked his boxers onto the pile of his old clothes, his hackles going up as Trey and Diondra whispered and giggled in the other room. He got back into the pants with nothing underneath, and they clung like a leathery scuba suit. Hot. His ass was already sweating.

"Come model for us, stud," Diondra called.

He pulled on the T-shirt, walked into her bedroom to check the mirror. The metalhead rockers Diondra loved stared at him from posters on the walls, even on the ceiling over her bed, giant pointy hair and bodies tightly packed in leather with buckles and belts like alien robot knobs. He didn't think he looked bad. He looked pretty on target. When he walked back into the living room, Diondra squealed and ran to him, jumped into his arms.

"I knew it. I knew it. You are a stud." She flipped his hair back, which was at an awkward bushy chin-length. "You need to keep growing this out, but otherwise, you are a stud."

Ben looked at Trey, who shrugged. "I'm not the one going to fuck you tonight, don't look at me."

On the floor was a pile of garbage, long, fingerlike wrappers from the Slim Jims, and a plastic square with a few streaks of cheese and some nacho crumbs.

"You already ate everything?" Ben asked.

"Now your turn, Teep-beep," Diondra gushed, taking her hand from Ben's hair.

Trey held up a metal-studded shirt that Diondra had bought for him (and why does Trey get something, Ben thought), and slunk back toward the bedroom for his portion of the fashion show. From the hallway came silence, then the pop of a beer, and then laughter, teary, fall-on-the-floor laughter.

"Diondra, come here!"

Diondra was already laughing as she ran back to Trey, Ben left standing, sweating in his new tight pants. Soon she was howling too, and they emerged, faces folded in pure joy, Trey shirtless, holding Ben's boxers.

"Dude, you wearing those ballhuggers naked?" Trey said between laughs, his eyes crazy-big. "Do you know how many dudes have jammed their shit into those pants before you got 'em? Right now you got eight different guys' ballsweat on you. Your asshole is pressed right against some other guy's asshole." They laughed again, Diondra making her poor-Ben sound: *Ooohhhaaa*.

"I think these got some shit stains in them too, Diondra," Trey said, peeking inside the boxers. "You better take care of this, little woman."

Diondra plucked them by two fingers, walked across the living room, and tossed them in the fire, where they sizzled but didn't catch.

"Even fire can't destroy those things," Trey wheezed. "What are they, Ben, polyester?" They plopped down on the couch, Diondra huddling on her side to finish laughing, Trey's head on her haunches. She laughed with her face squeezed shut, then, still reclining, blinked one bright blue eye open, and assessed him. He was about to walk back to the bathroom to change into his jeans, when Diondra leapt up and grabbed him by the hand.

"Oh, sweetie, don't be mad. You look great. You really do. Ignore us."

"They are cool, dude. And stewing in another guy's juices might be just what you need to grow a pair, right?" He started laughing again, but when Diondra didn't join, he went to the fridge and got another beer. Trey still hadn't put on the new shirt, he seemed to like walking around shirtless, sprigs of black chest hair and dark nipples the size of fifty-cent pieces, muscles lumping everywhere, a treasure trail down his belly Ben would never get. Ben, pale and small-boned and red-headed, would never look like that, not five years, not ten years from now. He glanced at Trey, wanting to take a long look but knowing that was a bad idea.

"Come on, Ben, let's not fight," Diondra said, pulling him down on the sofa. "After all the shit I heard today about you, I should be the one who's mad."

"See? Now what does that even mean?" Ben said. "It's like you're talking in code or something. I've had a shit day and I'm not in the goddam mood!"

This is what Diondra did, she baited you, nips and bites here and there til you were half crazy, and then she was all, "Why are you so upset?"

"Awwww," she whispered into his ear. "Let's not fight. We're together, let's not fight with each other. Come to my room and we'll make up." She had beer breath and her long fingernails rested on his crotch. She pulled him up.

"Trey's here."

"Trey won't care," she said, and then louder. "Watch some cable for a little bit, Trey."

Trey made an *mmmm* sound, didn't even look at them, and flopped headlong on the sofa, his beer spraying like a fountain.

Ben was pissed off now, which was always how Diondra seemed to like him. He wanted to ram it into her, make her whine. So as soon as they closed the door, that plywood door Trey could surely hear through—good—Ben reached to grab her and Diondra turned around and scratched his face, hard, drawing blood.

"Diondra, what the hell?" He now had another scrape on his face, and he didn't mind it. Scar up these big baby cheeks, do it. Diondra stepped back for a second, opened her mouth, then just pulled him toward her til they fell on her bed, stuffed animals bouncing to lemming deaths on either side. She scratched him again on his neck and he really wanted to fuck her good then, he was literally seeing red, like they say in cartoons, and she helped him get the pants back off, peeling down like a sunburn, and his dick bouncing right up, hard as it ever had been. She pulled off her sweater, her tits huge, milk-blue and soft, and he ripped down her boxers. When he stared at her belly, she turned her back to him and guided him in from behind, her yelling, *Is that it? Is that all you got for me? You can do me harder than that* and him pounding away 'til his balls ached and his eyes went blind and then it was over and he was on his back, wondering if he was having a heart attack. He was heaving for air, fighting off that depression that always came to smother him after they had sex, the *that's-all* blues.

Ben had had sex twenty-two times now, he was keeping track, all with Diondra, and he'd seen enough TV to know that men were supposed to fall peacefully asleep right afterward. He never did. He got more agitated, actually, like he'd had too much caffeine, snappy and mean. He thought sex was supposed to chill you out—and the during part was good, the coming part was great. But afterward, for about ten minutes he felt like crying. He felt like, Is this it? The greatest thing in life, the thing men kill for and this is it, over in a few minutes, leaving you all gutted and depressed. He could never tell if Diondra liked it or not, came or not. She grunted and screamed but she never seemed happy afterward. She lay next to him now, her belly up, not touching him, barely breathing.

"So I saw some girls at the mall today," Diondra said next to him. "They say you're fucking little girls at school. Like ten-year-olds."

"What are you talking about?" Ben said, still dazed.

"Do you know a little girl named Krissi Cates?"

Ben tried to keep himself from bolting up. He crossed an arm behind his head, put it back down by his side, crossed it over his chest.

"Uh, yeah, I guess. She's in that art class I been helping out after school."

"Never told me about no art class," Diondra said.

"Nothing to tell, I just did it a few times."

"Just did what a few times?"

"The art class," Ben said. "Just helping kids. One of my old teachers asked me to."

"They say the police want to talk to you. That you did some

wrong stuff with some of those girls, girls who are, like, your sisters' age. Touched them funny. Everyone's calling you a perv."

He sat upright, a vision of the basketball team mocking his dark hair, his perviness, trapped in the locker room while they fucked with him til they were bored, drove off in their bigass trucks. "You think I'm a perv?"

"I don't know."

"You don't know? Why'd you just have sex with me if you think I might be a perv?"

"I wanted to see if you could still get it up with me. If you would still come a lot." She turned away from him again, her legs pulled up to her chest.

"Well, that's pretty fucked up, Diondra." She said nothing. "So do you want to hear me say it: I didn't do anything with any girls. I haven't done anything with anyone but you since we started going out. I love you. I don't want to have sex with any little girls. OK?" Silence. "OK?"

Diondra turned part of her face toward him, that single blue eye fixed on him with no emotion: "Shhh. The baby's kicking."

Libby Day

NOW

Lyle was stiff and silent as we drove toward Magda's for our meeting. I wondered if he was judging me, me and my packet of notes I was going to sell. Nothing I'd decided to part with was particularly interesting: I had five birthday cards my mom had given Michelle and Debby over the years, cheerful quick notes scrawled at the bottom, and I had a birthday card she'd written to Ben I thought might bring decent money. I felt guilty about all of it, not good at all, but I feared having no money, really feared being broke, and that came before being nice. The note to Ben, on the inside of a card for his twelfth birthday, read: *You are growing up before my eyes, before I know it you'll be driving!* When I read it, I had to turn it facedown and back away, because my mom would be dead before Ben would ever learn how to drive. And Ben would be in prison, would never learn how to drive anyway.

Anyway.

We drove across the Missouri River, the water not even bothering to glisten in the afternoon sun. What I didn't want was to watch these people read the notes, there was something too intimate about that. Maybe I could leave while they looked at them, assessed them like old candlesticks at a yard sale.

Lyle guided me to Magda's, through middle-middle-class neighborhoods where every few houses waved a St. Patrick's Day flag—all bright clovers and leprechauns just a few days stale. I could feel Lyle fiddling beside me, twitchy as usual, and then he turned toward me, his knees almost punching my stickshift out of gear.

"So," he said.

"So."

"This meeting, as is often the case with Magda, has turned into something a little different than planned."

"What's that mean?"

"Well, you know she's in that group—the Free Day Society. To get Ben out of prison. And so she's invited a few of those . . . women."

"Oh. No." I said. I pulled the car over to the curb.

"Listen, listen, you said you wanted to look into Runner. Well, this is it. They will pay us—you—to find him, ask him some questions, father to daughter."

"Daughter to father?"

"Right. See, I'm running out of money. So this is where the next funding will come from."

"So I have to sit here and let them be rude to me? Like last time?"

"No, no, they can fill you in on the investigation into Runner. Bring you up to speed. I mean, you think Ben is innocent now, right?"

I had a flash of Ben watching TV, my mom rustling his hair with one hand as she walked past with a load of laundry on her hip, and him smiling but not turning around. Waiting til she left the room before he combed his hair back into place.

"I haven't gotten that far."

My keys dangled from the ignition, turning in time to a Billy Joel song on the radio. I switched stations.

"Fine, let's go," I said.

I drove another few blocks. Magda's neighborhood was as cheap as mine, but nicer. Every house had been built shabby, but the owners still found enough pride to slap on a coat of paint now and then, hang a flag, plant some flowers. The houses reminded me of hopeful homely girls on a Friday night, hopping bars in spangly tops, packs of them where you assumed at least one might be pretty, but none were, and never would be. And here was Magda's house, the ugliest girl with the most accessories, frantically piled on. The front yard was spiked with lawn ornaments: gnomes bouncing on wire legs, flamingos on springs, and ducks with plastic wings that circled when the wind blew. A forgotten cardboard Christmas reindeer sat soggy in the front garden, which was mostly mud, baby-fuzz patches of grass poking through intermittently. I turned off the car, and we both stared into the yard, with its jittering denizens.

Lyle turned to me, fingers outstretched like a coach giving advice on a difficult play: "So, don't worry. I guess the only thing to remember is to be careful how you talk about Ben. These people can get pretty riled when it comes to him."

"What's pretty riled?"

"Like, do you go to church at all?"

"When I was a kid."

"So it would be kind of like someone coming into your church and saying they hate God."

IT DID FEEL like a church. Or maybe a wake. Lots of coffee, dozens of people murmuring in dark wool clothes, regretful smiles. The air was blue with cigarette smoke, and I thought how rarely I saw that anymore, after growing up in Diane's foggy trailer. I took a deep breath of it.

We'd knocked several times on the open door, and when no one heard, we just walked in. Lyle and I stood there, American Gothic style, for a good five seconds as the conversation trailed off and people started staring. An older woman with Brillo-wire hair in barrettes blinked at me with the force of someone giving a secret code, a smile frozen large on her face. A brunette in her early twenties, startlingly pretty, looked up from dishing peaches into a baby's mouth and she too offered an expectant smile. One glaring old broad with a snow-man's build tightened her lips and fingered the crucifix on her neck, but everyone else in the room was clearly following orders: Be nice.

They were all women, more than a dozen, and they were all white. Most looked care-worn, but a handful had the bright, full-hour-in-front-of-the-mirror look of the upper class. That's how you pick 'em, not by the clothes or the cars, but by the extra touches: an antique brooch (rich women always have antique brooches) or lip-liner that was blended just the right amount. Probably drove in from Mission Hills, feeling magnanimous about setting foot north of the river.

Not a single man there, it was what Diane would call a hen party (and then make that disapproving sinus sound). I wondered how they'd all found Ben, stuck in prison as he was, and what attraction he had for them. Did they sit in their tousled beds at night with their gelatined husbands snoring next to them and daydream about a life with Ben once they freed him? Or did they think of him as a poor kid in need of their altruism, a cause to be nurtured between tennis matches?

Out of the kitchen stomped Magda, six foot tall, her frizzy hair almost as wide. I wouldn't have been able to place her from the Kill Club meeting, where everyone's face was smeared from my memory, a Polaroid yanked out too early. Magda wore a denim jumper dress over a turtleneck, and an incongruous amount of jewelry: dangly gold earrings, a thick gold chain, and rings on almost every finger but her wedding finger. All those rings unsettled me, like barnacles growing where they shouldn't be. I shook Magda's outstretched hand anyway. Warm and dry. She made a sound like *mmmaaahhhh!* and pulled me in for a hug, her big breasts parting and closing on me like a wave. I stiffened, then pulled away, but Magda held on to my hands.

"Bygones be bygones. Welcome to my home," she said.

"Welcome," called the women behind her, too close to unison.

"You are welcome here," Magda reasserted.

Well, obviously, since I'd been invited, I wanted to say.

"This, everyone, is Libby Day, Ben's youngest sister."

"Ben's only sister," I added.

The women nodded solemnly.

"And that's part of the reason we're here today," Magda addressed the room. "To help bring some peace to that situation. And help. Bring. Ben. Home!"

I glanced at Lyle, who wrinkled his nose minutely. Beyond the living room, a boy of about fifteen, chubby in a less authoritative way than his mother, came down the carpeted stairs. He'd put on khakis and a button-down for the occasion, and he looked out into the room without making any eye contact, one thumb fiddling with the top of his belt.

Magda sighted the kid but didn't introduce him. Instead she said, "Ned, go in the kitchen and make more coffee." The boy walked through the circle of women without moving his shoulders, staring at a spot on the wall no one else could see.

Magda pulled me into the room, me pretending to cough so I could free my hand. She set me down in the middle of the sofa, one woman on each side of me. I don't like sitting in the middle, where arms brush lightly against mine and knees graze my pant leg. I balanced on one buttock and then the other, trying not to sink into the cushion, but I'm so small I still ended up looking like a cartoon kid in an overstuffed chair.

"Libby, I'm Katryn. I'm so sorry for your loss," said one of the rich ladies next to me, looking down into my face, her perfume widening my nostrils.

"Hi, Katherine." I wondered when the time limit lapsed on expressing sadness for a stranger's dead. I guess never.

"It's Kate-ryn," she said with sugar, her gold flower brooch bobbling on its clasp. There's another way to pick rich women: They immediately correct how their names are said. A-lee-see-a, not Al-eesh-a, Deb-or-ah, not Debra. I said nothing in response. Lyle was talking tightly with an older woman across the room, giving her his profile. I pictured her hot breath tunneling into his tiny snail ear. Everyone kept talking and looking at me, whispering and looking at me.

"Well, wanna get the show going?" I said and clapped once. It was rude, but I didn't need the suspense.

"Well, Libby . . . Ned, will you get that coffee out here?" Magda started. "We're here to talk with you about your father, as the prime suspect in the murders your brother has been wrongfully convicted of."

"Right. The murders of my family."

Magda pulled in an impatient breath, annoyed I would assert my rights to my family.

"But before we work on that," Magda continued, "we want to share with you some of our stories about your brother, who we all love."

A slender fifty-something woman with administrative hair stood up. "My name is Gladys, I met Ben three years ago, through my charity work," she said. "He changed my life. I write to a lot of prisoners"—here I physically scoffed, and the woman noted it—"I write to prisoners because to me it's the ultimate Christian act, loving the usually unlovable. I'm sure everyone here's seen *Dead Man Walking*. But I began writing Ben, and the purity of him just shined through his letters. He is true grace under fire, and I love that he's able to make me laugh—make *me* laugh, when I'm supposed to be helping *him*—about the horrible conditions he endures each day."

Everyone added a note then: *he's so funny . . . that's so true . . . he's amazing that way.* Ned appeared with a coffeepot and started refilling a dozen outstretched plastic mugs, the ladies hand-signaling to stop pouring without even looking at him.

A younger woman stood up, about Lyle's age, trembling. "I'm Alison. I met Ben through my mom, who couldn't be here today . . ."

"Chemo, ovarian cancer," whispered Katryn.

". . . but we both feel the same, which is her work on this earth is not done until Ben is a free man." There were scattered claps at this. "And it's just, it's just," here the girl's trembles turned to tears, "he's so good! And it's all so wrong. And I just can't believe we live in a world where someone as good as Ben is . . . is in a cage, for no good reason!"

I set my jaw then. I could feel this going south.

"I just think you need to set this all right," spat the crucifixed snow-woman who looked the least friendly. She didn't bother to stand up, just leaned around a few people. "You need to right your wrongs, just like anybody else. And I'm real sorry for the loss of your family, and I'm real sorry for what you've gone through, but now you need to be a grown-up and fix it."

I couldn't spot anyone nodding at that little speech, but the room was full of an agreement so strong it seemed to have a sound, an *mmm-hmm* sound I couldn't trace. Like the hum of a railroad track when the train is still miles away but churning toward you. I glanced at Lyle, and he rolled his eyes discreetly.

Magda moved to the center of the entryway, swelling like a red-nosed orator on the hustings. "Libby, we have forgiven you for your part in this fiasco. We believe your father committed this horrible crime. We have motive, we have opportunity, we have . . . many important facts," she said, unable to pull up more legal jargon. "Motive: Two weeks before the murders your mother, Patricia Day, filed a complaint against your father concerning child support. For the first time, Ronald "Runner" Day was going to be legally on the hook to his family. He also was in hock several thousand dollars for gambling debts. Removing your family from this situation would help his finances tremendously—he was assuming he was still in your mother's will when he went there that night. As it turned out, Ben was not at home when he arrived, and you escaped. He killed the others."

I pictured Runner breathing heavily, striding through the house with that shotgun, his grimy Stetson tilted back as he sighted my mother with the 10-gauge. I heard the bellowing in my head that I always heard when I remembered that night, and tried to make it come out of Runner's mouth.

"Fibers from your home were found in Runner's cabin, although this has been continually dismissed because he'd been in and out of your home that summer, but it's still a viable fact. None of the victims' blood or tissue was found on Ben, although the prosecution made a lot of the fact that Ben's blood was found in the house."

"Hell-ooo? Like you aren't allowed to cut yourself shaving?" the angry crucifixed woman said.

The women laughed on cue, primed.

"Finally, the part that I'm most excited for, Libby, is the opportunity portion. As you know, your father was vouched for by a girlfriend of his at the time, a Ms. Peggy Bannion. Just so you know there's no shame in righting a wrong, Peggy is currently in the process of recanting that alibi. Even though she could be sentenced up to five years."

"Well, she won't be," cheered Katryn. "We won't let that happen."

The others applauded as a spindly woman in elasticized jeans stood up. She wore her hair short, the top part permed and frosted, and her eyes were small and bland as dimes that had been in someone's pocketbook too long. She looked at me, then away. She fiddled with the oversized blue stone she wore on a chain, which matched a blue stripe on her sweatshirt. I pictured her at home in front of a water-stained mirror, enjoying the slight bit of good fortune of matching her necklace to the sweatshirt.

I stared at my dad's girlfriend—this special guest of Magda's—and willed myself not to blink.

"I just want to thank you all for your support these past months," she began, her voice reedy. "Runner Day used me like he used everyone. I'm sure you know." It took a few seconds before I realized she was talking to me. I nodded, then wished I hadn't.

"Share your story with us, will you, Peggy," Magda said. I could tell Magda watched a lot of *Oprah*. She had the cadence but not the warmth.

"The truth of the story is this. On the evening of January 2, I cooked dinner for Runner at his cabin. It was chop suey with rice, and of course with Runner, a lot of beer. He drank these beers called Mickey's Big Mouths, you had to pull the tab off, but the tabs came off at these sharp angles, looked like crab claws and he was always all cut up by them. Do you remember that, Libby? He was always bleeding with those."

"What happened after dinner?" Lyle interrupted. I waited for him to look over at me for an appreciative smile, but he didn't.

"We, uh, had relations. Then Runner was out of beer, so he left to get more beer. I think this was about 8 p.m. because I watched *The Fall Guy*, although I remember it was a repeat and that was discouraging."

"She watched *The Fall Guy*," Magda piped in. "Isn't that ironic?"

Peggy looked at her blankly.

"Anyway, Runner left and he didn't come back, and, you know, it's winter time, so I fell asleep early. I woke up to him coming home, but he didn't have a clock, so I don't know what time it was. But it was definitely middle of the night, definitely late, because I kept waking up, and I finally got up to pee and the sun was starting to come up and that couldn't have been more than a few hours later."

When this woman was peeing, and looking for toilet paper and probably not finding toilet paper, then wending her way back to bed through the motors and blades and TV intestines that Runner always pretended to be working on, maybe stubbing a toe, feeling sulky, I was crawling through snow toward my blood-soaked house, my family dead. I held it against her.

"Lord help me, the police came by in the morning, asking Runner where he was between 12 and 5 a.m., asking *me* where he was. The whole time, he was so insistent: *I was home early, I was home way before midnight*. And I don't think he was, but I went along with it. I just went along."

"Well, you're done with that, girl!" said the brunette with the baby.

"I haven't even heard from him in a year."

"Well, that's more than me," I said, and regretted it. I wondered if this woman would have kept her secret if Runner had just stayed in touch a bit more. Phoned every three months instead of every eight. "And, like I said," Peggy continued, "he had these scratches on him, all over his hands, but I can't be sure that it wasn't from those beer tabs. I just don't remember if he scratched himself before he left that night, or if maybe someone scratched him."

"Only one victim, Michelle Day, was found to have any skin under her nails, which makes sense, since she was strangled, so she was physically closest to the killer," Lyle said. We all sat quietly for a second, the baby's coos fluttering higher, heading toward squeals. "Unfortunately, that piece of skin was lost somewhere before it reached the laboratory."

I pictured Runner, with that leery, wide-eyed look of his, bearing down on Michelle, the weight of him pushing her into the mattress, and Michelle scrambling to breathe, trying to rip his hands away, getting one good scratch in, a scrawl over the back of his small, oil-stained hands, wrapping themselves more tightly around her neck . . .

"And that's my story," Peggy said with an open-handed shrug, a comedian's whatcha-gonna-do? gesture.

"Ned, we're ready for the dessert!" Magda hollered toward the kitchen, and Ned hustled in, shoulders up near his ears, crumbs on his lower lip as he bore a depleted plate of dry cookies with hard-jelly centers.

"Jesus, Ned, stop eating my stuff!" Magda snapped, glowering over the tray.

"I just had two."

"Bullshit you had two." Magda lit a cigarette from a limp pack. "Go to the store, I need cigarettes. And more cookies."

"Jenna's got the car."

"Walk, then, it'll be good for you."

The women were clearly planning on making a night of it, but I wasn't going to stay. I parked myself near the door, eyeing a cloisonné candy dish that seemed too nice for Magda. I slipped it into my pocket as I watched Lyle work out the deal, Magda saying *She'll do it? She's got him? Does she actually believe?* as she flapped her checkbook. Each time I blinked, Peggy was edging closer to me, some grotesque chess game. Before I could make a break for the bathroom, she was there at my elbow.

"You don't look like Runner at all," she said, squinting. "Maybe the nose."

"I look like my mother."

Peggy seemed stricken.

"You with him a long time?" I offered.

"Off and on, I guess. Yeah. I mean I'd have boyfriends in between. But he had a way of coming back and making you feel like it was part of the plan. Like, almost like you'd discussed it that he'd disappear but come back and it would be the same as it was before. I don't know. I wished I'd met an accountant or something like that. I never know where to go to meet nice men. In my whole life. I mean, where do you go?"

She seemed to be asking for a geographic place, like there was a special town where all the accountants and actuaries were kept.

"You still in Kinnakee?"

She nodded.

"I'd leave there, for a start."

Patty Day

JANUARY 2, 1985
3:10 P.M.

Patty flew into the driver's seat of Diane's car—her eyes on the keys dangling from the ignition, *get out of here, now, get out.* Diane hopped into the passenger side as Patty turned over the engine. She actually made a burned-rubber noise as she squealed away from the Muehlers' house, the rear end of the car flailing behind her. All the crap in Diane's trunk—baseballs and garden tools and the girls' dolls—rolled and banged like passengers in a turnover wreck. She and Diane bumped along the gravel road, dust flying, skidding toward the trees on the left and then veering toward a ditch on the right. Finally Diane's strong hand appeared and landed gently on the wheel.

"Easy."

Patty rumbled along until she got off the Muehler property, swung a wide left, pulled to the side of the road and cried, fingers grasped around the wheel, her head on the center causing an aborted honk.

"What the hell is going on!" she shrieked. It was a child's tear-scream, wet, enraged and baffled.

"Some strange stuff," Diane said, patting her back. "Let's get you home."

"I don't want to go home. I need to find my son."

The word *son* started her weeping again and she let it rip: gulping sobs and thoughts jabbing her like needles. He'd need a lawyer. They didn't have money for a lawyer. He'd get some bored county guy appointed to him. They'd lose. He'd go to jail. What would she tell the girls? How long did someone go away for something like that? Five years? Ten? She could see a big prison parking lot, the gates opening, and her Ben gingerly walking out, twenty-five years old, frightened of the open space, eyes narrowed against the light. He comes near her, her arms open, and he spits on her for not saving him. How do you live with not being able to save your son? Could she send him away, on the run, fugitive? How much money could she even give him? In December, numb from exhaustion, she'd sold her dad's army 45 Auto to Linda Boyler. She could picture Dave Boyler, who she'd never liked, opening it up Christmas morning, this gun he didn't earn. So Patty, right now, had almost three hundred bucks squirreled away in the house. It was all owed to others, she'd planned on making her first-of-the-month rounds later today, but that wouldn't happen now—plus $300 would only keep Ben going a few months.

"Ben will come home when he finishes blowing off steam," Diane reasoned. "How far can he get on a bike in January?"

"What if *they* find him first?"

"Sweetheart, there's no mob after him. You heard, the Muehler boys didn't even know about the . . . accusation. They were talking about other bullshit rumors. We need to talk to Ben to straighten this out, but for all we know he could be home right now."

"Who's the family that's saying he did this?"

"No one said."

"You can find out though. They can't just say things like that and expect us to lie down and take it, right? You can find out. We have a right to know who's saying this. Ben has a right to confront his accuser. *I* have a right."

"Fine, let's go back to the house, check in on the girls, and I'll make some calls. Now will you let me drive?"

———

THEY WALKED INTO pure din. Michelle was trying to fry salami strips on the skillet, screaming at Debby to go away. Libby had a splatter of bright pink burns up one arm and a cheek where the grease had hit her, and was sitting on the floor, mouth wide, crying the way Patty had just been crying in the car: as if there was absolutely no hope, and even if there was, she wasn't up to the challenge.

Patty and Diane moved like they were choreographed, one of those German clocks with the fancy men and women dancing in and out. Diane strode to the kitchen in three big steps and yanked Michelle away from the stove, dragging her by the one arm, doll-like, to the living room, depositing her on the sofa with a swat on her tush. Patty crisscrossed them, swooped up Libby, who monkey-wrapped herself around her mother and continued crying into her neck.

Patty turned on Michelle, who was loosing fat silent tears. "I told you: You may only use the stove to heat soup. You could have set this whole place on fire."

Michelle glanced around the shabby kitchen and living room as if wondering whether that would be a loss.

"We were hungry," Michelle mumbled. "You've been gone forever."

"And that means you need a fried salami sandwich your mom told you not to make?" snapped Diane, finishing up the frying, slapping the meat on a plate. "She needs you to be good girls right now."

"She always needs us to be good girls," Debby mumbled. She was nuzzling a pink stuffed panda that Ben had won years ago at the Cloud County fair. He'd knocked down a bunch of milk bottles, just as his pre-teen muscles were coming in. The girls had celebrated as if he'd won a Medal of Honor. The Days never won anything. They always said that, marveling, whenever they had a tiny piece of good luck: *We never win anything!* It was the family motto.

"And is it really so hard to be good?" Diane gave Debby a soft chuck under her chin and Debby lowered her gaze even more as she started to smile.

"I guess not."

Diane said she'd make the calls, grabbing the kitchen phone and pulling it all the way down the hall as far as it could go. As she walked away, she told Patty to feed her dang children—the words riling Patty, as if she was so negligent she often forgot meals. Make tomato soup from ketchup and milk from a powder, yes. Toast some stale bread, add a squirt of mustard and call it a sandwich, yes. On the worst days, yes. But she never forgot. The kids were on the free-lunch program at school, so they always got something there at least. Even as she thought this, she felt worse. Because Patty went to the same school as a kid, and she never had to do Half-Lunch or Free-Lunch, and now her stomach knotted as she remembered the Free-Lunch kids and her patronizing smiles toward them as they presented their dog-eared cards, and the steamy cafeteria ladies would call it out: Free Lunch! And the boy next to her, buzz-haired and confident, would whisper inanely: *There's no such thing as a free lunch.* And she'd feel sorry for the kids, but not in a way that made her want to help, just in a way that made her not want to look at them anymore.

Libby was still heaving and crying in her arms; Patty's neck was sweaty from the girl's hot breaths. After twice asking Libby to look at her, the girl finally blinked and turned her face up to her mother's.

"I, got, buuurrrned." Then she started crying again.

"Baby, baby, it's just a few ouchies. It won't be permanent, is that what you're worried about? They're just some little pink ouchies—you won't even remember next week."

"Something bad's gonna happen!"

Libby was her worrier; she came out of the womb wary and stayed that way. She was the nightmare girl, the fretter. She was an outta-nowhere pregnancy; neither Patty nor Runner were happy. They didn't even bother with a baby shower; their families were so sick of them procreating that the entire pregnancy was an embarrassment. Libby must have marinated in anxious stomach acid for nine months, soaking up all that worry. Potty training her was surreal—she screamed when she saw what came out of her, ran away naked and frantic. Dropping her off at school had always been an act of utter abandonment, her daughter with the giant, wet eyes, face pressed against the glass, as a kindergarten teacher restrained her.

This past summer she refused to eat for a week, turned white and haunted, then finally (finally, finally) revealed to Patty a pod of warts that had sprouted on one knee. Eyes down, in slow sentences that Patty extracted from her over the course of an hour, Libby explained that she thought the warts might be like poison ivy, that they'd eventually cover her and (sob!) no one would be able to see her face anymore. And when Patty had asked why, why in the world hadn't Libby told her these worries before, Libby just looked at her like she was crazy.

Whenever possible, Libby prophesized doom. Patty knew that, but the words still made her clench. Something bad had already happened. But it would get worse.

She sat with Libby on the couch, smoothing her hair, patting her back. Debby and Michelle hovered near, fetching tissues for Libby and fussing over her the way they should have done a good hour ago. Debby tried to make the panda pretend-talk to Libby, telling her she was OK, but Libby shoved it away and turned her head. Michelle asked if she could cook everyone soup. They ate soup all through the winter, Patty keeping giant vats of it in the freezer-locker in the garage. They usually ran out right around the end of February. February was the worst month.

Michelle was dumping a big frozen square of beef and vegetables into a stew pot, cracking off the ice, ignoring the plate of salami, when Diane returned with her mouth tugged into a grimace. She lit a cigarette—*trust me, I need it*—and sat down on the sofa, her weight bumping up Patty and Libby like a seesaw. She sent the girls into the kitchen with Michelle, the kids not saying anything, obedient in their nervousness.

"OK. So it's this family named Cates that started it—they live halfway between here and Salina, send their kid to Kinnakee because the public school's not finished in their suburb. So it started because Ben was doing after-school volunteering with the Cates girl. Did you know he was volunteering?"

Patty shook her head.

"Volunteering?"

Diane pushed her lips out: didn't jive with her either.

"Well, for whatever reason, he was volunteering with these

young kids in the elementary school, and this girl's parents say something wrong went on between them. And so do some others. The Hinkels, the Putches, and the Cahills."

"What?"

"They're all comparing notes, they've all talked to the school. From what I hear, the police are now involved, and you should expect someone, a cop, to come by today to talk to you and Ben. It's reached that stage. Not everyone at school knows—we're lucky this happened on Christmas break—but I guess after today that won't be the case. I guess any kid who Ben helped after school, the school is talking to the parents. So, like, ten families."

"What should I do?" Patty put her head between her knees. She felt laughter in her stomach, it was all so ludicrous. *I wonder if I'm having a breakdown,* she thought. *Maybe I could have a breakdown and then I won't have to talk to anyone.* A safe white room, and Patty being ushered like a child from breakfast to lunch to dinner, maneuvered by people with gentle whispers, Patty shuffling like someone who's dying.

"I guess everyone's over at the Cates place, talking right now," Diane said. "I got the address."

Patty just stared.

"I think we should go over there," Diane said.

"Go over there? I thought you said someone would come here."

"The phone's been ringing off the hook," Michelle said, Michelle who'd been in the kitchen and shouldn't have heard any of this.

Patty and Diane both turned to the phone, waiting for it to go off.

"Well, why didn't you answer it like we asked, Michelle?" Diane said.

Michelle shrugged. "I forgot if we were supposed to or not."

"Maybe we should wait here," Patty said.

"Patty, those families are over there talking . . . *shit* about your son. Now who knows what kernel of truth may be in there or not, but don't you want to go speak for him? Don't you want to hear what they're saying, make them say it to our face?"

No, she didn't. She wanted the stories to go away, nice and quiet, creep backward into oblivion. She didn't want to hear what people in her town—Maggie Hinkel went to high school with her, for Pete's sake—were saying about Ben. And she was afraid she'd crumble with all those furious faces on her. She'd weep, beg for forgiveness. Already, all she wanted was forgiveness, and they hadn't even done anything wrong.

"Let me put on some better clothes."

SHE FOUND A sweater without rips in the armpits and a pair of khaki slacks. She ran a comb through her hair, and exchanged her gold studs for a pair of imitation pearl earrings and matching necklace. You really couldn't tell they were fake, they even felt heavy.

As she and Diane went toward the front door—further admonishments about using the stove, a request to turn off the TV and do chores at some point—Libby began wailing again, running toward them with her arms flapping. Michelle crossed her arms over her stained sweatshirt and stomped a foot.

"I can't deal with her when she's like this," she said, a perfect imitation of Patty. "She's too much. It's too much for me."

Patty took a breath in, thought about reasoning with Michelle, thought about bullying Michelle, but Libby was bawling louder, a howling animal, screaming iwanttogowithyouiwanttogowithyou, Michelle arching an eyebrow. Patty pictured a cop showing up here while she was away, a burnt-faced, weeping child lying inconsolable on the floor. Should she take all three then? But someone should be here to answer the phone, to be here, and it was probably better to have both Michelle and Debby here than . . .

"Libby, go put on your boots," Diane ordered. "Michelle, you are in charge. Answer the phone, don't answer the door. If it's Ben he'll have a key, if it's someone else, we don't want you two worrying about it. Michelle?"

"What's going on?"

"Michelle, I'm not messing with you. Michelle?"

"OK."

"OK," Diane said, and that, literally was the final word.

Patty stood in the hallway, useless, watching Libby put on her boots and a pair of dirt-caked mittens. Patty grabbed one woolly hand and walked her toward the car. It might be good, anyway, if people were reminded Ben had little sisters who loved him.

Libby wasn't a big talker—Michelle and Debby seemed to hog all her words. She made pronouncements: I like ponies. I hate spaghetti. I hate you. Like her mother, she had no poker face. No poker mood. It was all right there. When she wasn't angry or sad, she just didn't say much. Now, seat belted in back, taken along for the ride, she sat silently, her pink-blotched face aimed out the window, a finger against the glass, tracing the tops of trees outside.

Neither Patty nor Diane spoke either, and the radio stayed off. Patty tried to picture the visit (visit? Could you really call something this repulsive a visit?), but all she could see was her screaming "Leave my son alone!" She and Maggie Hinkel had never been friends, but they'd always exchanged conversation at the grocery store, and the Putches she knew from church. These weren't unkind people, they wouldn't be unkind to her. As for the parents of the first girl, Krissi Cates, Patty had no idea. She pictured the Cateses as brightly blond and preppy, with everything matching and the house pristine and smelling of potpourri. She wondered if Mrs. Cates would spot the fake pearls.

Diane guided her off the highway, and into the neighborhood, past a big blue sign boasting of model units in Elkwood Park. So far it was just blocks and blocks of wooden skeletons, each one an outline of a house, each one allowing you to see the outline of the one next to it, and the outline of the one next to that. A teenage girl sat smoking on the second floor of one skeleton house, she looked like Wonder Woman in her invisible plane, sitting in the outlines of a bedroom. When she tapped her cigarette, the ashes fluttered down into the dining room.

All the pre-houses unnerved Patty. They were recognizable but totally foreign, an everyday word you suddenly couldn't remember to save your life.

"Pretty, huh?" Diane said, wagging a finger at the neighborhood.

Two more turns and they were there, a block of tidy houses, real houses, a cluster of cars in front of one.

"Looks like a party," Diane sniffed. She rolled down the window and spat outside.

The car was silent for a few seconds, except for Diane's throat-noises.

"Solidarity," Diane said. "Don't worry, worst they can do is yell."

"Maybe you should stay here with Libby," Patty said. "I don't want yelling in front of her."

"Nah," Diane said. "No one stays in the car. We can do this. Yeah, Libby? You're a tough little girl, right?" Diane turned her bulk to Libby in the backseat, her parka rustling, and then back to Patty. "It'll be good for them to see her, know he's got a little sister around who loves him." Patty had a shot of confidence that she'd thought the same thing.

Diane was out of the car then, on the other side, rousting Libby, and opening the door wide for her to get out. The three of them walked up the sidewalk, Patty immediately feeling ill. Her ulcers had been quiet for a bit, but now her belly burned. She had to unclench her jaw and work it loose. They stood on the doorstep, Patty and Diane in front, with Libby just behind her mother, glancing out backward. Patty imagined a stranger driving past, thinking they were friends joining the festivities. The door still had a Christmas wreath on it. Patty thought, *They had a nice happy Christmas and now they are frightened and angry and I bet they keep thinking, but we just had such a nice happy Christmas.* The house was like something from a catalog, and there were two BMWs in the driveway and these were not people who were used to bad things happening.

"I don't want to do this, I don't think we should do this," she blurted.

Diane rang the doorbell and gave her a look straight from their dad, the calm, unmoved look he gave whiners. Then she said exactly what Dad always said when he gave the look: "Nothing to it but to do it."

Mrs. Cates answered the door, blond and prairie-faced. Her eyes were red from crying and she was still holding a tissue.

"Hello, may I help you?"

"I. Are you . . . Krissi Cates's mother?" Patty started, and began crying.

"I am," the woman said, fingers on her own pearls, her eyes shifting back and forth to Patty and Diane, and then down to Libby. "Oh, was your little girl . . . did he hurt your little girl too?"

"No," Patty said. "I'm Ben's mother. I'm *Ben Day's* mother." She wiped the tears with the back of her hand, then with the sleeve of her sweater.

"Oh God, Oh God, Oh, *Louuuu* come here. Hurry." Mrs. Cates's voice grew loud and quivery, the sound of an airplane going down. Several faces Patty didn't recognize peered around the corner of the living room. A man walked past from the kitchen holding a tray of sodas. One girl lingered in the hallway, a pretty blond girl wearing flowered jeans.

"Who's that?" the girl chirped.

"Go get your father." Mrs. Cates moved to fill up the doorway, almost physically pushing them from the doorstep. "Louuuu . . ." she called back into the house. A man appeared behind her, slab-like, 6'5" at least, solid, with a way of keeping his chin up that reminded Patty of people who got what they wanted.

"This is her, this is Ben Day's mother," the woman said with such disgust Patty could feel her womb flinch.

"You'd better come inside," the man said, and when Patty and Diane glanced at each other, he snapped, "Come, come," like they were bad pets.

They stepped into the home, into a sunken den, and peered out on a scene that looked like a children's birthday party. Four girls were in various states of play. They wore foil stars on their faces and hands, the kind of stickers teachers use to mark good grades. Several were sitting with their parents, eating cake, the girls looking greedy, the moms and dads looking panicked behind brave faces. Krissi Cates had plopped herself in the middle of the floor and was playing dolls with a large, dark-haired young man who sat cross-legged in front of her, ingratiating himself. They were those spongy, unpretty dolls Patty had seen in Movies of the Week—with Meredith Baxter Birney or Patty Duke Astin as determined mothers or lawyers. They were the dolls that kids used to show how they were abused. Krissi had stripped the clothes off both dolls and was placing the boy doll on top of the girl doll. She bumped it up and down, and chanted nonsense words. A brunette girl watched from her mother's lap while eating icing from under her fingernails. She seemed too old to be in her mother's lap.

"Like that," Krissi concluded, bored or angry, and tossed the doll aside. The young man—a therapist, a social worker, someone who wore Shetland sweaters with plaid shirts underneath, someone who went to college—picked the doll back up and tried to get Krissi's attention.

"Krissi, let's . . ." he said, holding the boy doll carefully off one knee, the doll's penis drooping toward the floor.

"Who *is* that?" Krissi said, pointing at Patty.

Patty strode across the room, ignoring all the parents, who began standing, wavering like strummed wires.

"Krissi?" she said, crouching down on the floor. "My name is Patty, I'm Ben Day's mom."

Krissi's eyes widened, her lips quivered, and she scooted away from Patty. There was a second of silence, like a slow-motion crash, where she and Patty stared at each other. Then Krissi tilted her head back and yelled: "I don't want her here!" Her voice echoed off the skylight. "I don't want her here! You said! You said I wouldn't have to!"

She threw herself on the floor and began ripping at her hair. The brunette girl ran over and wrapped herself over Krissi, wailing, "I don't feel safe!"

Patty stood up, spinning around the room, saw parents with frightened, revolted faces, saw Diane hustling Libby behind her, toward the door.

"We've heard about you," Krissi Cates's mother said, her sweet, drained face twisted into a ball. She motioned back to Maggie Hinkel, Patty's old classmate, who blushed at Patty. "You've got four kids at home," she continued, her voice tight, her eyes wet. "You can't afford a one of them. Their daddy's a drunk. You're on welfare. You leave your little girls alone with that . . . jackal. You let your son prey on girls. Jesus Christ, you've let your son *do* this! God knows what happens out there!"

The Putch girl stood and screamed then, tears rolling past the bright stars on her cheeks. She joined the pack in the middle, where the young man was murmuring soothing words, trying to maintain eye contact with them. "I don't want them here!" Krissi yelled again.

"Where's Ben, Patty?" Maggie Hinkel said, her spade-faced daughter sitting beside her, expressionless. "The police really need to talk to Ben. I hope you're not hiding him."

"Me? I've been trying to find him. I'm trying to straighten this out. Please." *Please help me, please forgive me, please stop screaming.*

Maggie Hinkel's daughter remained quiet, then tugged at her mother's sleeve. "Mom, I want to leave." The other girls continued to howl, watching each other. Patty stood, looking down at Krissi and the therapist, who was still cradling the naked doll-boy that was supposed to be Ben. Her stomach seized, flushed her throat with acid.

"I think you should leave," snapped Mrs. Cates, picking up her daughter like a toddler, the girl's legs dangling almost to the floor, Mrs. Cates wobbling with the weight.

The young therapist stood up, inserting himself between Patty and Mrs. Cates. He almost put a hand on Patty, then moved it to Mrs. Cates instead. Diane was calling from the door, calling Patty's name, or Patty wouldn't have known to move. She was waiting for them to close in on her, scratch her eyes out.

"I'm sorry, I'm sorry," Patty was yelling into the room, frantic and dizzy. "It's a mistake, I'm so sorry."

Then Lou Cates was in front of her, grabbing her by the arm, as if he hadn't just invited her in, and walking her toward the door, the keening of four girls behind her. Mothers and dads were everywhere, grown-ups taking care of their children, and Patty felt stupid. Not foolish, not embarrassed. Unforgivably stupid. She could hear the parents cooing things to their daughters: *good girl, it's ok–it's ok, she's leaving now, you're safe, we'll make this all better, hush, hush, baby.*

Just before Lou Cates propelled her from the room, Patty turned around to see Krissi Cates in her mother's arms, her blond hair over one eye. The girl looked at her and said simply, "Ben is going to hell."

Libby Day

I'd been commissioned to find Runner, but all my feverish, ambitious action of the past week was slopped on the floor next to my bed, like a soiled nightgown. I couldn't get up, even when I heard the kids make their sleepy duckwalk past my house. I pictured them in big rubber rainboots, clomping along, leaving rounded footprints in the March muck, and I still couldn't move.

I'd woken up from a miserable dream, the kind you keep telling yourself doesn't mean anything, shouldn't bother you because it's just a dream, just a dream. It started back at the farm, but it wasn't the farm really, it was far too bright, too tidy to be the farm, but it was and in the distance, against an orange horizon, Runner was galloping toward the farm, hooting like an Old West cowboy. As he got closer—down our hill, through the gate—I saw that his gallop was actually a rickety, bumpalong motion because his horse had wheels. Its top half was flesh, but the bottom was metal, spindly, like a hospital gurney. The horse whinnied at me in panic, its muscled neck trying to separate from the metal below. Runner leapt down, the creature rolling away, one wheel busted, an irritating grocery cart of an animal. It came to a stop near a tree stump, its eyes going white, still struggling to pull itself apart.

"Don't worry about that." Runner grinned at the horse. "I paid for it."

"You got a bad deal," I said.

Runner's jaw tightened and he stood too close to me.

"Your mom says it's fine," he muttered.

That's right! I thought, *My mom is alive.* The idea felt solid, like a pebble in my pocket. My mom was alive, and how foolish I'd been, all these years thinking otherwise.

"You'd better fix your hand first," Runner said, pointing at my stumped ring finger. "I brought you these. Hope you like them better than the horse." He held up a flimsy velvet bag, the kind used for Scrabble, and shook it.

"Oh, I love the horse," I said, batting away my ill will. The horse had torn its hindquarters from the metal and was bleeding a meaty red oil onto the ground.

From his bag, Runner poured eight or nine fingers. Every time I picked one that looked like mine, I realized it was a pinky finger, a man's finger, a finger of the wrong color or size.

Runner was pursing his lips at me. "Just take one, OK? It's not a big deal."

I picked one that was vaguely similar to my lost one, and Runner sewed it to my hand, the ripped horse screaming now behind us, a woman's scream, terrified and angry. Runner threw a shovel at it, and it broke in two, pulsing on the ground, unable to move.

"There," Runner said with a lip smack. "Good as new."

Between my two girlish fingers, a bulbous big toe squatted, tied on with lazy, thick stitches, and suddenly Runner's girlfriend Peggy was there and said, "Honey, her momma's not here, remember? We killed her."

And Runner smacked his head like a man who'd forgotten to bring home milk and said, "That's right. That's right. I got all them girls, except Libby." We three stood blinking at each other, the air turning nasty. Then Runner went back to the horse, and picked up the shovel, which had become an axe.

I flung myself awake, one arm cracking my bedside lamp to the floor. It was barely dawn when I turned and watched the glowing lamp on its side, wondered if the lightbulb would burn a hole in the carpet. Now it was morning and still I couldn't move.

But the light was on in Ben's room. My first real thought: that night the light was on in Ben's room and someone was talking. I wanted to stop thinking about it but I always came back to it. Why would a crazed killer go into Ben's room, close the door, turn on the light and chat?

The light was on in Ben's room. Forget the other stuff: a vengeful Lou Cates, a debt-crazed Runner, a pack of goons who wanted to teach Runner a lesson by murdering his family. Forget the bellowing voice I heard, which—fine, I guess—may not have been Ben's. But he wasn't home when we went to bed, and when I woke up the light was on. I remember a flush of relief because Ben was home because his light was on and the fight was over between him and my mom at least for today because the light was on and he was talking behind the door, maybe on his new phone, or to himself, but the light was on.

And who was Diondra?

I prepared to get out of bed, tossing the covers aside, the sheets dank-smelling, gray from my body. I wondered how long it had been since I'd changed them. And then I wondered how often you were supposed to change them. These were the kinds of things you didn't learn. I changed the bedclothes after sex, now, finally, and that I only learned a few years ago from a movie on TV: Glenn Close, some thriller, and she's just had sex and is changing the sheets and I can't remember the rest, because all I was thinking was: Oh, I guess people change sheets after they have sex. It made sense, but I'd never thought of it. I was raised feral, and I mostly stayed that way.

I got out of bed, finally returning the lamp to my bedtable, and walked roundabout to the living room, sneaking up on the answering machine, not letting it know I cared if it had a message. I might as well have whistled, my feet kicking out ahead of me—*nothing unusual here, just out for a walk.* No Diane. Four days and no Diane.

Well, no problem, I had other family.

———

BEN WAS WAITING for me this time when I came, sliding into view before I was prepared. He sat rigid in the seat behind glass, his eyes unfocused, a jumpsuited mannequin. I wanted to tell him not to do that to me, it gave me the creeps, but I didn't say anything because why would he give me the creeps unless I still didn't entirely believe he was innocent.

Which I didn't, I guess.

I sat down, the chair still humid from someone else, the warmth of the plastic feeling grossly intimate in this place. I mushed my buttocks back and forth, making it mine, trying not to look repulsed, but when I picked up the phone it was still sweaty from the previous user, and whatever look I gave made Ben frown.

"You OK?" he asked, and I nodded once. Yes, sure, absolutely fine.

"So, you came back," he said. He fixed on a smile now. Cautious, the way Ben always was. At a family party, on the last day of school, he looked the same, a kid who lived permanently in the library— waiting to be shushed.

"I came back."

He had a nice face, not handsome but nice, the face of a good guy. Catching me assessing him, his eyes darted to his hands. They were big now, bigger than his small frame, piano hands even though we never played piano. They were scarred, nothing impressive, dark pink confetti strips of nips and cuts. He caught me looking, held one hand up, pointed a finger at one deep gash: "Polo accident."

I laughed because I could tell he was already regretting the joke.

"Nah, actually you know what this is?" Ben said. "This is from that bull, Yellow 5, remember that little bastard?"

We had only a small operation, but we still never named our cattle, that was not a good idea, even as a kid I had no interest in getting attached to Bossy or Hank or Sweet Belle because they'd be sent to slaughter as soon as they were big enough. Sixteen months, that rang out in my head. Once they were a year old, you started tiptoeing around them, you started looking at them sideways with disgust and embarrassment like a guest in your home who just farted. So instead we color-tagged them during calving each year, matching cows with their calves: Green 1, Red 3, Blue 2, sliding out from their mothers, onto the dirt floor of the barn, those feet kicking right away, always trying to get a purchase in the slop. People think of cattle as docile, dumb, but calves? They're kitty-curious, playful, and for that reason I was never allowed in the lot with them, just eyed them through the slats, but I remember Ben, his rubber boots on, trying to sneak, moving slow and deliberate as an astronaut, and then he got near and he might as well have been trying to grab fish. I remember Yellow 5, at least the name, the famous bull calf who'd refused to be castrated—poor Ben and my mom, day after day trying to get ahold of Yellow 5 so they could slit his sack and cut off his nuts, and each day coming to the dinner table as failures, Yellow 5 having outplayed them. It was a joke to be told over a ground round the first night, everyone talking to the steak, pretending it was Yellow 5: You'll be sorry, Yellow 5. By the second night it was cause for chagrined laughter, and by the fifth it was grim mouths and silence, a reminder to both Ben and my mom that they weren't good enough: weak, small, slow, lacking.

I'd have never thought of Yellow 5 again without Ben reminding me. I wanted to tell him to make a list of things to recall, memories I couldn't pluck out of my brain on my own.

"What happened? He bit you?"

"Nah, nothing that dramatic, he pushed me into the fence right when I thought I'd gotten ahold of him, just haunched me to one side, and I fell full on, jammed the back of my hand right onto a nail. It was on a rail Mom had already asked me to fix, a good five times. So, you know, my fault."

I was trying to think of what to say—something clever, commiserative, I still had no grip on what reactions Ben wanted—and Ben interrupted. "No, screw that, it was goddam Yellow 5's fault." He broke into a quick smile, then let his shoulders slump down again. "I remember Debby, she dressed it all up, my cut, put a Band-Aid on it and then put one of her stickers, those shiny stickers with like hearts or whatever, on top of it."

"She loved stickers," I said.

"She put 'em everywhere, that's for sure."

I took a breath, debated flitting over to some other harmless subject, the weather or something, then didn't.

"Hey, Ben, can I ask you a question?"

He went shark-eyed, tight, and I saw the convict again, a guy used to being on the receiving end, taking question after question and getting attitude when he asked his own. I realized what a decadence it was, to refuse to answer a question. *No thanks, don't want to talk about that* and the worst you get is someone thinks you're rude.

"You know that night?"

He widened his eyes. Of course he knew the night.

"I remember, I may have been confused, about exactly what happened . . ."

He was leaning forward now, his arms stiff, huddled over the phone like it was a late-night emergency call.

"But, one thing I do remember, like stake-my-life-on-it remember . . . your light was on. In your bedroom. I saw it under the crack in the door. And there was talking. In the room."

I trailed off, hoping he'd save me. He let me float, that freefall few seconds when your feet go loose on ice and you have just enough time to think, *Oh. I am going to fall.*

"That's a new one," he finally said.

"What's that?"

"A new question. I didn't think there'd be new questions anymore. Congratulations." I caught us both sitting in the same posture, one palm on the edge of the table like we were about to push back from a meal of leftovers. Runner's posture, I remember it from the last time I saw him, me twenty-five or twenty-six, and him wanting money, asking all flirty and sweet at first—*do you think maybe you can help your old man out, Libbydear?*—and me telling him no, straight off, a bat cracking a line drive, shocking, humbling. *Well, why not?* he'd snapped, and his shoulders shot back, his arms flipped up, hands on my table, me thinking: *why'd I let him sit down,* already calculating the time I'd waste getting him back up.

"I snuck out that night," Ben said. "I came home, me and mom got in another fight."

"About Krissi Cates?"

He started at that, then let it slide over him.

"About Krissi Cates. But she believed me, she was completely on my side, that was the great thing about Mom, even when she was pissed as hell at you, she was on your side, you knew that. In your bones. She believed me. But she was angry, and just, scared. I'd kept her waiting for, I don't know, sixteen hours with no word—I didn't even know what was going on, you know, no cell phones back then, you'd go a whole day and not talk, not like today. I hear."

"So, but—"

"Right, we just got in a fight, I don't even remember if it was exactly Krissi Cates or that's where it started and went from there, I wish to God I could remember, but anyway, she kinda grounds me, sends me to my room, and I go there and after an hour I'm pissed off again, and I leave the house, leave the radio on and the lights on so if she peeks out she thinks I'm still there. I mean, you know the way she slept, wasn't like she was going to walk all the way to my room to look in on me. Once she was asleep, she was pretty much asleep."

Ben made it sound like an unbelievable journey, those thirty-some steps, but it was true, my mom was useless once she was asleep. She barely even moved. I remember holding tense vigils over her body, convincing myself she was dead, staring til my eyes watered, trying to make out breathing, trying to get even a moan. Nudge her, and she'd flop back into the same position. We all had stories of encountering her on coincidental overlapping visits to the bathroom in the night—turn the corner to find her peeing on the toilet, robe between her legs, looking through us like we were made of glass. *I just don't know about the sorghum* she'd say, or *That seed come in yet?* And then she'd shuffle past us back to her room.

"Did you tell the police that?"

"Aw, Libby, come on. Come on. This is not how I want this to go."

"Did you?"

"No, I didn't. What difference would it have made? They already knew we had a fight. I tell them we had two? That's . . . there's no point. I was there maybe an hour, nothing happened besides that, it was inconsequential. Entirely."

We eyed each other.

"Who's Diondra?" I asked. I could see him try to go even more still. I could see him thinking. The sneaking out may have been true, may not, but I could tell now he was about to lie. The name Diondra chimed him, I could picture his bones humming. He tilted his head to the right just a little bit, a *funny you ask that* tilt and caught himself.

"Diondra?" He was stalling, trying to figure out exactly what I knew. I gave him a face of slab.

"Uh, Diondra was a girl at school. Where'd you come up with Diondra?"

"I found a note she wrote you, sounds like she was more than 'a girl at school.'"

"Huh. Well, she was a crazy girl, I do remember that. She was always writing notes that, you know, she was a girl who wanted people to think she was, wild."

"I thought you didn't have a girlfriend."

"I didn't. Jeez, Libby how do you go from a note to a girlfriend?"

"From the note." I tensed up, knowing I was about to be disappointed.

"Well, I don't know what to tell you. I wish I could say she was my girlfriend. She was, just totally out of my league. I don't even remember getting a note from her. Are you sure it had my name on it? And how'd you even get a note?"

"Never mind," I said, removing the phone from my ear so he knew I was leaving.

"Libby, hold on, hold on."

"No, if you're going to work me like some . . . convict, I don't see the point."

"Libby, hold the hell up. I'm sorry I can't give you the answer I guess you want."

"I just want the truth."

"And I just want to tell you the truth, but you seem to want . . . a story. I just, I mean Christ, here comes my little sister after all these years and I think, well, here might be one good thing. One good thing. She sure as hell wasn't helpful twenty-four goddam years ago, but, hey, I'm over that, I'm so over that the first time I see her, all I am is happy. I mean there I was in my fucking animal pen, waiting to see you, so nervous like I was going on a date, and I see you and, jeez, it's like, maybe this one thing will be OK. Maybe I can have one person from my family still in my life and I won't be so fucking lonely, because—and I mean, I know you talked to Magda, believe me I heard all about that, and so yeah I have people who visit me and care about me, but they're not you, they're not anyone who knows me except as the guy with the . . . and I was just thinking it'd be so goddam nice to be able to talk with my sister, who knows me, who knows our family, and knows that we were just, like, normal, and we can laugh about goddam cows. That's it, you know, that's all I'm asking for at this point. Just something as tiny as that. And so I wish I could tell you something that won't make you . . . hate me again." He dropped his eyes, looking at the reflection of his chest in the glass. "But I can't."

Ben Day

JANUARY 2, 1985
5:58 P.M.

Diondra had a little belly, it freaked Ben out, and for weeks now she'd been talking about the "quickening." The quickening had happened, the baby was moving, it was a very special, important moment and so Ben had to put his hand on her stomach all the time and feel the baby kick. He was proud of making the belly, proud of making the baby, the idea of it at least, but he didn't like to actually touch that area or look at it. The flesh was weird, hard but globby at the same time, like ham gone bad, and touching it was just embarrassing. For weeks, she'd been grabbing his hand and pressing it there, watching his face for a reaction, and then she'd yell at him when he couldn't feel anything. For a while, actually, he'd thought maybe the pregnancy was just one of Diondra's jokes to make him feel dumb—he'd sit there with his hand sweating on that gross mound of skin, and think, maybe that rumble, was that it, was that the baby or was that just indigestion? He worried. He worried that if he didn't feel anything—and he hadn't those first weeks after the quickening—that Diondra would yell at him, *It's right there, it's like a cannon going off in my womb, how can you not feel it?* And he worried that if he finally said he did, that Diondra would blast him with her laugh, that laugh that bowed her at the midsection like she'd been shot, the knee-grabbing laugh that made her gelled hair shake like a tree after an ice storm, because of course she wasn't really pregnant, she was just fucking with him, didn't he know anything?

He had, in fact, looked for signs she may be lying: those big, bloody maxipads that his mom always rolled up in the trash and that always ended up unfurled within a day. Otherwise he hadn't been sure what to look for, and he wasn't sure if he should ask if it was his. She talked like it was, and that was probably as sure as he'd get.

Anyway, in the past month, it was clear she was definitely pregnant, at least if you saw her naked. She still went to school, dressed in those giant baggy sweaters, and she left her jeans unbuttoned and partly unzipped, and the mound got bigger, Diondra holding it and rubbing it in her hands like it was some sort of crystal ball of their fucked-up future, and one day, she grabbed his hand and he felt it, no doubt—that thing was kicking and all of a sudden he saw the swipe of a little foot move under the surface of Diondra's skin, smooth and fast.

What the hell's wrong with you? You birth cows out there at the farm don't you? It's just a baby was Diondra's reaction when he snatched his hand away. She pulled it back and held it there, held his palm on that twitching thing inside her, and he thought, *calving is damn different than your own real baby,* and then he thought, *let me go let me go let me go* as if the thing were going to grab him like some late-night slasher movie and pull him inside her. That's how he pictured it, a thing. Not a baby.

Maybe it would have helped if they talked about it more. After the quickening, she wouldn't speak to him at all for a few days, and it turned out he was supposed to give her something for the quickening, that you gave pregnant ladies presents to celebrate the quickening, and that her parents had given her a gold bracelet when she got her first period and that this was like that. So in place of a present he made him go down on her ten times, that was the deal, which he thought she probably picked because he didn't really like to do it, the smell made him queasy, especially now, when that whole area seemed used. She didn't seem to like it either, that's why it felt like punishment, her yelling at him about fingers and pressure and higher, it's higher up, go higher and finally sighing and grabbing his head hard, by the ears and pulling him to the spot she wanted and him thinking *you fucking bitch* and wiping her off his mouth when he was done. Eight more to go, you fucking bitch, *you want a glass of water sweetheart?* And she'd said *No but you do, you smell like pussy* and laughed.

Pregnant women were moody. He knew this. But otherwise, Diondra didn't act pregnant. She still smoked and drank, which you weren't supposed to do if you were pregnant but she said only health nuts gave up all that stuff. Another thing she didn't do: plan. Diondra didn't even talk much about what they'd do when it was born—when *she* was born. Diondra had never been to a doctor, but she was sure it was a girl because girls made you sicker and she'd been sick the first month so bad. But she really didn't say more, reality-wise, than to talk about it as a girl, as an actual girl that would come out of her. He'd wondered at first if she was going to get an abortion. He'd said *if you have the baby* instead of *when,* and she'd completely freaked, and Diondra completely freaking was something he never wanted to see again. She was a handful enough at her most calm, this was like watching a natural disaster, the nails the crying the hitting, and her yelling that that was the worst thing anyone had ever said to her, and it's your flesh too, what the hell is wrong with you, you asshole piece of shit?

But otherwise, they didn't plan or couldn't plan, since Diondra's dad would literally kill her if he ever found out she was pregnant outside of marriage. If he ever found out she even did it outside of marriage, he'd kill her. Diondra's parents had only one rule, only one single rule, and that was that she must never, ever let a boy touch her there unless he was her husband. When she turned sixteen, Diondra's dad had given her a promise ring, a gold ring with a big red stone that looked like a wedding ring and she wore it on that finger, and it meant a promise to him and to herself that she would remain a virgin til marriage. The whole thing grossed Ben out—doesn't that seem like you're married to your dad? Diondra said it was a control thing, mostly. This was the one thing her dad had decided to get hung up about, it was the one thing he asked of her, and goddamit, she'd better do it. She said it made him feel better leaving her alone, unsupervised, unprotected, except for the dogs, for months at a time. It was his one parental thing: my daughter may drink or do drugs but she is a virgin and therefore I can't be as fucked up as I seem.

This, she said, with tears in her eyes. This she said while near her pass-out part of a drunk. She said her dad told her if he ever found out she'd broken the promise, he'd take her out of the house and shoot her in the head. Her dad had been in Vietnam, and he talked like that, and Diondra took it seriously, so she didn't do any planning about the baby. Ben made lists of things they might need, and he bought some hand-me-down baby clothes at a Delphos flea market right near Christmastime. He'd been embarrassed, so he just bought the whole bunch from the woman for $8. It turned out to be undershirts and underwear, for a bunch of different ages, lots of ruffly undies—the woman kept calling them bloomers—which is fine, kids need underwear for sure. Ben stored them under his bed, which made him more glad he had the lock, he could picture the girls finding them and stealing whatever fit. So true, he didn't think enough about the kid, and what would happen, but Diondra seemed to think even less.

"I THINK WE should leave town," Diondra said now, a surprise, the hair still over half her face, Ben's hand still clamped to her belly, the baby scuttering around inside like it had dug tunnels. Diondra turned slightly toward him, one lazy boob lolling on Ben's arm. "I can't hide this much longer. My mom and dad will be home any day now. You sure Michelle doesn't know?"

Ben had saved a note from Diondra, it talked about how horny she was and how much sex she wanted from him *even now*, and nosy-ass Michelle had found it going through his jacket pockets. The little bitch had blackmailed him—$10 not to tell Mom—and when Ben complained to Diondra, she went ballistic. *Your little fucking sister could tell on us at any moment, you think that's OK? This is on you, Ben. You fucked up.* Diondra was paranoid that somehow Michelle would figure out she was pregnant from those two words—"even now"—and they'd be undone *by a fucking ten-year-old, how perfect.*

"No, she hasn't mentioned it again."

That was a lie, just yesterday Michelle caught his eye, shook her hips, and said in a teasy voice, "Hey Beee-ennn, how's your seeeex life?" She was such a shitty kid. She'd blackmailed him on other things—chores he'd left undone, extra food he'd eaten from the fridge. Little stuff. It was always little crappy stuff, like she was there just to remind Ben how cramped his life was. She'd spend the money on jelly donuts.

Trey made a loud loogie noise in the other room, and then a *thweeewp!* spit sound. Ben could picture the yellow phlegm dripping down the sliding glass door, the dogs licking at it. That was something Trey and Diondra did: they hocked loogies at things. Sometimes Trey shot it straight into the air, and the dogs would catch it in their drooly mouths. ("It's just body stuff going into another body," Diondra would say. "You've thrown some of your body stuff into my body and it doesn't seem to bother you none.")

As the TV got even louder in the den—*wrap it up you two, I'm goddam bored*—Ben tried to think of the right thing to say. He sometimes thought he never said anything to Diondra that was just pure talking, it was all verbal elbows and arms, trying to fend off her constant annoyance, say what she wanted to hear. But he loved her, he did love her, and that's what men did for their women, they told them what they wanted to hear and shut up. He'd knocked Diondra up and now she owned him, and he had to do right by her. He'd have to drop out of school and get a full-time job, which would be fine, some kid he knew quit last year and worked over near Abilene at the brick factory, got $12,000 dollars a year, Ben couldn't even begin to think how to spend it all. So he'd drop out of school, which was just as well, considering whatever the hell Diondra thought she'd heard about Krissi Cates.

It was weird, at first that made him really nervous, that those rumors were going around, and then part of him got kind of proud. Even though she was a kid, she was one of the cool younger kids. Even some of the high schoolers knew her, the older girls took an interest in her, that pretty, well-bred girl, so it was sort of cool that she had a crush on him, even though she was a kid, and he was sure whatever Diondra had just told him was her usual exaggeration. Hysterical, she sometimes got.

"Hey, hello? Try to stay with me. I said I think we have to leave town."

"Then we'll leave town." He tried to kiss her and she pushed him away.

"Really, that easy? Where d'we go, how will you support us? I won't have my allowance anymore, you know. You'll have to get a job."

"I'll get a job then. What about your uncle or cousin or whoever in Wichita?"

She looked at him like he was crazy.

"With the sporting-goods store?" he pushed.

"You can't work there, you're fifteen. You can't drive. In fact, I don't even think you can get a real job without your mom's permission. When do you turn sixteen again?"

"July thirteenth," he said, feeling like he'd just told her he wet himself.

She started crying then. "Oh my God, Oh my God, what are we going to do?"

"Your cousin can't help?"

"My *uncle* will tell my parents, how will that help?"

She got up, walking naked, her stomach bulge looking dangerously unsupported, Ben wanting to go stick a hand under there, and thinking how much bigger she'd get. She didn't put on any clothes to walk across the hall to the shower, even though Trey could see right down the hallway if he was still sitting on the couch. He heard the guttural sound of the shower twisting on. Conversation over. He wiped himself off with a moldy towel near Diondra's hamper, then squeezed back into his leather pants and striped T-shirt and sat on the edge of the bed, trying to guess what smart-ass comment Trey was going to make when they went back out to the den.

In a few minutes, Diondra breezed into the bedroom, wearing a red towel, her hair wet, not looking at him, and sat in front of her dresser with the mirror in it. She squirted her mousse into her palm, a giant dogshit of a pile, and scrunched it into her hair, aiming the blowdryer at each section—squirt, scrunch, woosh, squirt, scrunch, woosh.

He wasn't sure whether he was supposed to leave or not, so he stayed, sitting on the bed still, trying to catch her eye. She poured dark foundation into her palm, the way an artist might pour paint, and swirled it onto her face. Some girls had called her a base face, he heard them, but he liked the way it looked, tan and smooth, even though her neck sometimes seemed whiter, like the vanilla ice cream under the caramel dip. She put on three coats of mascara—she always said it took three, one to darken, one to thicken and one for drama. Then she started with the lipstick: undercoat, overcoat, gloss. She caught him looking and stopped, dabbing her lips on little foamy triangles, leaving sticky purple kiss marks on them.

"You need to ask Runner for money," she said, looking at him in the mirror.

"My dad?"

"Yeah, he's got money right? Trey always buys weed from him." She dropped the towel, went over to her underwear drawer, a thicket of bright lace and satin, and dug around til she pulled out underwear and a bra, hot pink, with black lace edges, the kind girls wore in the saloons in westerns.

"Are you sure we're talking about the same guy?" he said. "My dad does, you know, handyman stuff. Labor. He works on farms and stuff."

Diondra rolled her eyes at him, tugging at the back of her bra, her tits overflowing everywhere—over the cups, under the clasps, unwrangleable and eggy. She let the bra go finally, threw it across the room—*fuck, I need a goddam fucking bra that fits!* She stood glaring at him, and then her underpants started rolling under themselves, edging away from her stomach, up in her ass crack. None of those sexy underclothes fit. Ben thought first: chubby, and then corrected: pregnant.

"Are you serious? You don't know your own dad deals? He sold to me and Trey last week." She tossed away the underpants, then put on a different bra, an ugly plain bra, and new jeans, pouting about her size.

Ben had never bought drugs himself before. He smoked a lot with Trey and Diondra and whoever had pot in that crowd, and sometimes he chipped in a buck or two, but when he pictured a dealer, he pictured someone with slick hair and jewelry, not his dad in the old Royals baseball cap and the cowboy boots with the big heels and the shirts that looked like they were wilting. Not his dad, definitely not his dad. And weren't dealers supposed to have money? His dad definitely did not have money, so the whole argument was stupid. And if he was a dealer, and he did have money, he wouldn't give any to Ben. He'd make fun of Ben for asking, maybe hold a twenty just out of Ben's reach the way a bully would grab a nerd's notebook, and then he'd laugh and shove it right back in his pants pocket. Runner never had a wallet, he just carried mangled bills in the front of his jeans, and wasn't that enough of a sign he had no cash?

"Trey!" Diondra yelled down the hall. She threw on a new sweater with patterns that looked like a geometry experiment. Ripped off the tags and tossed them to the floor, then rumbled out of the room. Ben was left staring at the rock posters and the astrology posters (Diondra was a Scorpio, she took it very seriously) and crystals and books on numerology. All around her mirror were stapled decrepit, dried corsages from dances Ben had not taken her to, they were mostly from this senior back in Hiawatha named Gary that even Trey said was a prick. Trey, of course, knew him.

The corsages unsettled Ben, they looked like organs, with their folds and their twists, their pink-and-purpleness. They reminded Ben of the stinking globs of meat sitting in his locker right now, a horrible gift Diondra had left him—surprise!—the girl parts of some animal, Diondra refusing to say where it came from. She hinted it was from a blood sacrifice she did with Trey; Ben assumed it was just leftover pieces from a Biology experiment. She liked to freak him out. When her class did baby-pig dissections, she brought him a curlicue tail, thought it was hilarious. It wasn't, it was just nasty. He got up and went to the living room.

"You sorry sack of shit," Trey called from the sofa, where he'd just lit a joint, not taking his eyes off the music video. "You don't know about your dad? The fuck, dude." Trey's bare stomach was almost concave, but rippled, perfect, tan. The opposite of Ben's soft white mouse-belly. Trey had balled the shirt Diondra gave him under his head as a pillow.

"Here, you broke-dick dog." He handed Ben the joint, and Ben took a big pull off it, feeling the back of his head go numb. "Hey, Ben, how many babies does it take to paint a house?"

Annihilation.

There it was back, that word. Ben pictured barbarian hordes busting through the big stone fireplace, and swiping Trey's head off with an axe, right in the middle of one of his fucking dead-baby jokes, the head rolling over across the dogshit and stopping next to one of Diondra's black buckle shoes. And then maybe Diondra dies next. Fuck it all. Ben took another drag, his brain feeling minty, and gave it back to Trey. Diondra's biggest dog, the white one, glided over to him and stared with no forgiveness in its eyes.

"Depends on how hard you throw them," Trey said. "Why do you put a baby in a blender feet first?"

"I'm serious, Trey," Diondra said, continuing a conversation Ben wasn't privy to. "He thinks his dad doesn't deal."

"So you can see its reaction. Hey, Ben? You're smoking your dad's stuff, buddy," Trey said, finally turning to look at him. "It's crap. Potent, but crap. That's why we know your dad has money. He over-charges, but no one else has any right now. Think he said he got it in Texas. He been to Texas lately?"

Runner had disappeared from Ben's life after Patty gave him the boot. For all Ben knew he might have gone to Texas for a while. Hell, you can drive to Texas and back in a day if you drive hard, so why not?

"This is cashed," Trey said, in a toke-choke voice. "Anyway, he owes me money, like everyone in this town. They love to make the bet, they never want to pay it off."

"Hey, I didn't even get any," Diondra pouted. She turned away and started sifting through the cabinets—the basement den had a minikitchen, too, imagine that, needing a separate room for all your junk food—and then cracked open the fridge, got herself a beer, didn't ask Ben if he wanted one. Ben saw the inside of that fridge, which had been packed with food the month before, and now just had beer and a big jar with one single pickle floating in it like a turd.

"You grab me a beer, Diondra?" he said, pissy.

She cocked her head at him, then handed him hers, went back to the fridge for another.

"So let's go find Runner, and we'll get some pot and get some money," Diondra said, draping herself next to him on the chair. "And then we can get the hell out of Dodge."

Ben looked at that blue eye, that bright blue eye—it seemed like Diondra was always looking at him sideways, he never saw both eyes at the same time—and for the first time he felt really bone scared. He couldn't even drop out of school without his mom's permission before he turned sixteen. Much less get a job at the brick plant or anything that made enough money for Diondra to not hate him, not sigh when he came home at night, and now that's what he saw, not even that little apartment in Wichita, but some factory near the border, near Oklahoma, where the really cheap work was, where you worked sixteen hours a day, worked weekends, and Diondra would be with the baby and she'd hate it. She had no mothering instinct, she'd sleep right through the baby crying, she'd forget to feed it, she'd go out drinking with some guys she met—she always was meeting guys, at the mall or the gas station or the movies—and leave the kid there. *What can happen to it, it's a baby, it ain't going nowhere!* He could already hear it, him being the bad guy. The poor, idiot bad guy who can't provide.

"Fine," he said, thinking once they left the house, they'd lose track of the idea. He almost had. His brain was bundling itself up, getting woolly. He wanted to go home.

Trey immediately shot up, jingling his truck keys—*I know where to find him*—and suddenly they were out in the cold, tromping through the snow and ice, Diondra demanding Ben's arm so she wouldn't fall, Ben thinking, but what if she fell? What if she fell and died, or lost the baby? He'd heard girls at school saying if you ate a lemon a day you'd have a miscarriage, and had thought about sneaking lemon into Diondra's diet Cokes and then realized that was wrong, to do it without her knowing, but what if she fell? But she didn't, they were in Trey's truck with the heater wushing on them, and Ben was in the backseat as always—it was half a backseat, really, only a kid could fit on it, so his knees were smashed sideways to his chest—and when he saw a shriveled pinky of a fry on the seat next to him he popped it in his mouth and instead of looking to see if anyone saw, he just looked for more, which meant he was very stoned and very hungry.

Libby Day

NOW

Back in grade school, my shrinks tried to channel my vicious-ness into a constructive outlet, so I cut things with scissors. Heavy, cheap fabrics Diane bought by the bolt. I sliced through them with old metal shears going up and down: *hateyouhateyouhateyou*. The soft growl of the fabric as I sliced it apart, and that perfect last moment, when your thumb is getting sore and your shoulders hurt from hunching and cut, cut, cut . . . free, the fabric now swaying in two pieces in your hands, a curtain parted. And then what? That's how I felt now, like I'd been sawing away at something and come to the end and here I was by myself again, in my small house with no job, no family, and I was holding two ends of fabric and didn't know what to do next.

Ben was lying. I didn't want this to be true but it was undeniable. Why lie about a silly high school girlfriend? My thoughts chased themselves like birds trapped in an attic. Maybe Ben was telling the truth, and the note from Diondra really wasn't to him, it was just part of the haphazard flotsam that went with a houseful of school kids. Hell, Michelle could have pulled it out of the trash after some senior boy tossed it, a useful bit of garbage for her ongoing petty blackmail.

Or maybe Ben knew Diondra, loved Diondra, and was trying to keep it a secret because Diondra was dead.

He'd killed her the same night he killed our family, part of his satanic sacrifices, buried her somewhere out there in that big, flat Kansas farm country. The Ben that frightened me was back in my head: I could picture a campfire, liquor sloshing in a bottle, Diondra-from-the-yearbook, with her spiral curls bouncing as she laughed, eyes closed, or sang, her face orange in the fire and Ben standing behind her, gently raising a shovel, eyes on the crown of her head . . .

Where were the other cult kids, the rest of the pack of Satan worshipers? If there was a ring of pale, sloe-eyed teens who'd recruited Ben, where were they? By now I'd read every scrap of information from the trial. The police had never found anyone involved in Satan worship with Ben. All the wild-haired, pot-smoking Devil kids of Kinnakee morphed back to peachy country boys in the days after Ben's arrest. How convenient for them. Two "habitual drug users" in their early twenties testified that Ben had shown up at some abandoned warehouse, a hangout place, on the day of the murders. They said he screeched like a demon when someone played a Christmas song. They claimed he told them he was going to make a sacrifice. They said he left with a guy named Trey Teepano, who supposedly mutilated cattle and worshiped the Devil. Teepano testified he only vaguely knew Ben. He had an alibi for the time of the killings: his dad, Greg Teepano, testified Trey was at home with him in Wamego, more than sixty miles away.

So maybe Ben was crazy all by his lonesome. Or maybe he was innocent. Again the birds in the attic battered around. Crash thunk shatter. I had probably sat for hours on the couch, wondering what to do, being shiftless, when I heard the heavy footsteps of my mailman thump up my stairs. My mom always had us bake Christmas cookies for our mailman. But my mailman, or lady, changed every few weeks. No cookies.

I had three envelopes offering me credit cards, one bill that belonged to someone named Matt who lived on a street nowhere near me, and one envelope that looked like dirty laundry, it was so soft and wrinkled. Used. Someone else's name and address had been blacked out with a magic marker, and mine written in the cramped space left below it. Mrs. Libby Day.

It was from Runner.

I went upstairs to read the letter, sitting on the edge of my bed. Then, as I always do when I get nervy, I smushed myself into a small space, in this case the spot between my bed and the bedside table, sitting on the floor with my back to the wall. I opened the dirty envelope and pulled out an unwholesome piece of women's stationery, bordered with roses. My father's handwriting swarmed across it: tiny, frenetic, pointy, like a hundred spiders had been splattered across the page.

> *Dear Libby,*
>
> *Well, Libby, we sure find ourselves in a strange place after all these years. At leest I do. Never thought I'd be this old, and tired, and by myself. Got cancer. They say only a few months. All rite by me, Iv'e been here longer than I deserve any way. So I was exited to here from you. Look, I know I was never close with you. I was very young when we had you, and I was'nt the greatest dad, altho I tried to provide for you and be close with you when I was able. Your mother made it difficult. I was imature and she was even more. And then the murders were very hard on me. So there you go. I need to let you know—and please do'nt lechure me I shoold have done this before. I know I shoold have done this before. But between my gambling problems and I am an alcaholic, I have had truble facing my demons. I know the real killer of that night, and I know it was'nt Ben. I will tell the truth before I die. If you can send me some money, I woold be happy to visit you and tell you more. Five hundred bucks shoold work.*
>
> *I look forward to hering from you.*
>
> > *Runner "Dad" Day*
> > *12 Donneran Rd.*
> > *Bert Nolan Home for Men*
> > *Lidgerwood, OK*
>
> *PS Ask somone what the zip code is, I dont know.*

I grabbed the thin neck of my table lamp and hurled the whole thing across the room, the lamp soaring three feet until its electrical cord stopped it short and it fell to the floor. I charged at it, yanked it from its socket, and threw it again. It hit the wall, the lampshade bumping off and rolling drunkenly across the floor, the cracked lightbulb jutting out the top like a broken tooth.

"Fuck. You." I screamed. It was directed toward me as much as my dad. That, at this stage of my life, I was expecting Runner to act correctly was stupid to the point of outrageousness. The letter was just a big long palm stretching out over the miles, asking for a hand-out, working me as a mark. I'd pay that five hundred and never see Runner again, until I wanted more help or answers, and then he'd work me over another time. His daughter.

I was going down to Oklahoma. I kicked the wall twice, rattling the windows, and was going for a good third windup when the doorbell went off downstairs. I looked outside automatically, but from the second floor saw only the top of a sycamore tree and the dusky sky. I stood frozen, waiting for the visitor to go away, but the doorbell went again, five times in a row, the person on my porch knowing I was home, thanks to my tantrum.

I was dressed like my mom in the winter: big, formless sweatshirt, baggy cheap longjohns, thick itchy socks. I turned to the closet for a second and then decided I didn't care as the doorbell went again.

My door has no window in it, so I couldn't get a glimpse of the person. I put the chain on and opened the door a crack to see the back of a head, a mat of tangled tawny hair, and then Krissi Cates turned around to face me.

"Those old women over there are kinda rude," she said, and then gave a showboaty wave, the kind I'd given them the week before, the broad, fuck-you wave. "I mean, *hello?* anyone ever tell them it's not polite to stare?"

I kept looking at her through the chain, feeling like a little old lady myself.

"I got your address from the—when you were at the club," she said, bending down to reach my eye level. "I don't actually have that money for you yet. Uh, but I was hoping to talk to you. I can't believe

I didn't recognize you that night. I drink way, way too much." She said it without embarrassment, the way someone would say they have a wheat allergy. "Your place is really hard to find. And I actually haven't been drinking. But I've just never been good at directions. Like, if I reach a fork in the road, and I can take a right or a left, I will choose whichever is wrong. Like, I should just listen to my gut and then do the opposite. But I don't. I don't know why that is."

She kept talking like that, adding a sentence and then another, without asking to be let in, and that was probably why I decided to let her in.

She walked in respectfully, hands clasped, the way a well-brought up girl would, trying to find something to compliment in my run-down place, her eyes finally alighting on the box of lotions by the TV set.

"Oh, I'm a total lotion fiend too—I have a great pear-scented one I'm really into now, but have you tried udder cream? It's what they used to put on dairy cows? Like on their udders? And it's so smooth, you can get it at a drugstore."

I shook my head loosely, and offered her coffee, even though I had only a few granules of instant left.

"Mmmmm, I hate to say it, but you have anything to drink? Long drive."

We both pretended it was the long drive, like two hours in a car would make anyone need some liquor. I went to the kitchen and hoped a can of Sprite would appear in the back of the fridge.

"I have gin, but nothing to mix it with," I called out.

"Oh, that's OK," she said, "Straight is good."

I had no ice cubes either—I have trouble making myself fill the trays—so I poured us two glasses of room-temperature gin and returned to find her loitering near my lotion box. I bet she had a few of the mini-bottles jammed in her pockets right now. She was wearing a black pantsuit with a pale pink turtleneck underneath, a painfully aspirational look for a stripper. Let her keep the lotion.

I handed her the glass and noticed she'd painted her nails to match her turtleneck and then noticed her noticing my missing finger.

"Is that from . . . ?" she began, the first time I'd known her to trail off. I nodded.

"So?" I said, as nicely as I could. She took a breath and then settled herself down on the sofa, her gestures tea-party delicate. I sat down next to her, twining my legs around each other and then forcing them to untwine.

"I don't even know how to say this," she started, swallowing some gin.

"Just say it."

"It's just that, when I realized who you were . . . I mean, you came to my *house* that day."

"I've never been to your house," I said, confused. "I don't even know where you live," I said.

"No, not now, back then. The day your family was killed—you and your mom came to my house."

"Mmmm," I said, squinting my eyes, trying to think. That day hadn't really been that big a deal—I knew Ben was in trouble, but not why or how deeply. My mom had protected us all from her growing panic. But that day. I could remember going with my mom and Diane to look for Ben. Ben was in trouble and so we went looking for Ben and I was sitting in the backseat alone, uncrowded and pleased with myself. I remember my face on fire from the salami Michelle fried. I remember visiting bustling houses, a birthday party my mom thought Ben might be at. Or something. I remember eating a donut. We never found Ben.

"Never mind," Krissi interrupted. "I just—with everything that's happened, I forgot. About you. Could I have a refill?" she held her glass out to me, briskly, as if a long time had lapsed with it empty. I filled it to the brim so she could keep her story going.

She took a sip, shivered. "Should we go somewhere?" she said.

"No, no, tell me what's going on."

"I lied to you," she blurted.

"Which part?"

"Ben never molested me."

"I didn't think so," I said, again trying to make it gentle.

"And he definitely didn't molest any of the other girls."

"No, everyone dropped their story but you."

She shifted on the sofa, her eyes rolling back toward the right, and I could see her remembering her house, her life, way back when.

"The other stuff was true," she said. "I was a pretty girl, and we had money and I was good in school, good at ballet . . . I always just think, just think if I hadn't told that one stupid lie. That one goddam lie, if it just hadn't come out of my mouth the first time, my life would be totally different. I'd be like a housewife, and have my own ballet studio or something." She pulled a finger across her belly, where I knew her caesarian scar was.

"You have kids though, right?" I said.

"Sorta," she replied and rolled her eyes. I didn't follow up.

"So what happened? How did it start?" I asked. I couldn't figure out the significance of Krissi's lie, what it had done to us that day. But it felt big, relevant—ripply, to quote Lyle. If the police wanted to talk to Ben that day, because of what Krissi had said, that had meaning. It had to.

"Well, I mean, I had a crush. A big crush. And I know Ben liked me too. We hung out, in a way—and I'm totally serious here—that wasn't probably right. I mean, I know he was a kid too, but he was old enough to . . . not have encouraged me. We kissed one day, and it changed everything . . ."

"You kissed him."

"We kissed."

"Like?"

"Inappropriately, grown-up. In a way I definitely wouldn't want my fifth-grade daughter to be kissed by a teenage boy."

I didn't believe her.

"Go on," I said.

"About a week after, I went to a slumber party over Christmas break, and I told the girls about my high school boyfriend. All proud. I made up things we did, sex things. And one of them told her mom, and her mom called my mom. I still remember it, the phone call. I remember my mom talking on the phone, and me just waiting in my room for her to come and yell at me. She was always pissed off about something. And she came to my room, and she was, like, nice. *Sweetheart* and *Honey,* and holding my hand, you know, 'You can trust me, we'll work this out together,' and asking me if Ben had touched me wrong."

"And you said, what?"

"Well, I started out with the kiss, and that was all I was going to say. Just the truth. And I told her and she, she seemed to move away, like 'OK, not that big a deal. No problem.' I remember her saying, *Is that all? Is that all that happened?* Like she was disappointed almost, and all of a sudden, I remember, she was already standing up, and I blurted it out, 'He touched me here. He made me do things.' And then she was back.' "

"And then what?"

"It just kept getting bigger. My mom told my dad when he got home, and he was all, *my baby, my poor little girl,* and they called the school and the school sent over a, like, child psychologist. And I remember he was this college guy, and he made it impossible to tell the truth. He wanted to believe I was molested."

I frowned at her.

"I'm serious. Because I remember, I was going to tell him the truth and have him tell my parents, but . . . he'd ask if Ben had made me do things, sexually, and I said no, and, he'd, like, be mean about it. *You seem like a smart, brave girl, I'm relying on you to tell me what happened. Oh, nothing happened? Gosh I thought you were braver than that. I was really hoping you'd be brave enough to help me out on this. Maybe you can tell me if at least you remember this sort of touching or Ben saying this? Do you remember playing a game like this, can you tell me if you at least remember that? Oh that's good. I knew you could do it, what a smart, good girl.* And I don't know, you're at that age, if a bunch of grown-ups are telling you something or encouraging you, it just . . . it started to feel real. That Ben had molested me, because otherwise, why were all these adults trying to get me to say he had? And my parents would be all stern: *It's OK to tell the truth. It's OK to tell the truth.* And so you told the lie that they thought was the truth."

I was remembering my own shrink, after the murders. Dr. Brooner, who always wore blue, my favorite color, for our sessions, and who gave me treats when I told him what he wanted to hear. *Tell me about seeing Ben with that shotgun, shooting your mother. I know this is so hard for you Libby, but if you say it, say it aloud, you will help your mom and sisters and you will help yourself start to heal. Don't bottle it up, Libby, don't bottle up the truth. You can help us make sure Ben is punished for what he did to your family.* I would be a brave little girl and say that

I saw Ben chop up my sister and I saw Ben kill my mother. And then I'd get the peanut butter with apricot jelly, my favorite, that Dr. Brooner always brought for me. I think he really believed he was helping.

"They were trying to make you comfortable, they thought the harder they believed in you, the easier it'd be for you," I said. "They were trying to help you, and you were trying to help them." Dr. Brooner gave me a star-shaped pin with the words SuperSmart SuperStar printed on it after I nailed Ben with my testimony.

"Yeah!" Krissi said, her eyes going big. "This therapist, he helped me, like visualize, like entire scenes. We'd act it all out with dolls. And then he started talking to the other girls, girls who never even kissed Ben, and, I mean, it was just a few days, that we had made up this entire imaginary world where Ben was a Devil worshiper, doing things like killing rabbits and making us eat the insides while he molested us. I mean, it was insane. But it was . . . fun. I know that's horrible, but we girls would get together, one night we had another slumber party, and we were up in the bedroom, sitting in a circle, egging each other on, making up stories, bigger and juicier, and . . . have you ever played with a Ouija board?"

"When I was a kid."

"Right! And you know, you all want it to be real, so someone moves the heart-thingie a little and you know someone's moving it, but part of you thinks maybe it's real, it's really a ghost, and no one has to say anything, you just all kind of know you've agreed to believe."

"But you've never told the truth."

"I told it to my parents. That day, the day you came over, the police had been called in, all the girls were at my house—they gave us cake, I mean, jeez, how screwed up is that? My parents said they'd buy me a dang puppy so I would feel better. And then the police left and the girls left and the therapist left, and I went up to my room and I just started crying, and it's like, only then did I realize. Only then did I think."

"But you said your dad was out searching for Ben."

"Nah, that's just a little fantasy." She said it, and stared across the room again. "When I told him? My dad shook me so hard I thought my head would come off. And after those murders, all the girls panicked, everyone told the truth. We all felt like we'd really summoned the Devil. Like we made up this bad story about Ben and some part of it became true."

"But your family got a big settlement from the school."

"It wasn't that big." She eyed the bottom of her glass.

"But your parents went ahead with it, after you'd told them the truth."

"My dad was a businessman. He thought we could get some sort of, compensation."

"But your dad definitely knew, that day, that Ben had not molested you."

"Yeah, he did," she said, giving that chickeny neck jerk toward me, defensive. Buck came and rubbed against her pant leg, and she seemed calm, ran her long fingernails through his fur. "We moved that year. My dad said the place was tainted. But the money didn't really help. I remember he bought me a dog, but every time I tried to talk about the dog, he sort of held his hand up, like it was too much. My mom, she just never forgave me. I'd come home and tell her about something that happened at school and—and she'd just say, *Really?* Like I was lying, no matter what I said. I could have told her I ate mashed potatoes for lunch and she'd just go, *Really?* And then she just stopped talking, she'd look at me when I came in the door from school, and then she'd walk over to the kitchen and open a bottle of wine, and she'd just keep refilling, wandering around the house, not talking. Always shaking her head. I remember one time I told her I wish I hadn't made her so sad, and she said, she said, *Well, you did.*"

Krissi was crying now, petting the cat rhythmically.

"And that was it. By the end of the year my mom was gone. I came home from school one day, and her room was cleared out." She let her head drop to her lap then, a childish, dramatic gesture, her hair flung over her head. I knew I was supposed to pet her, soothe her, but instead I just waited and eventually she peered up at me.

"No one ever forgives me for anything," she whimpered, her chin shaking. I wanted to tell her I did, but I didn't. Instead I poured her another drink.

Patty Day

JANUARY 2, 1985
6:11 P.M.

P atty was still muttering sorrys as Lou Cates hustled her toward the door, and suddenly, she was out on the step, in the freezing air, her eyes blinking rapidly. Between blinks, before she could get her mouth to move, to form any sort of word, the door opened again, and out stepped a man in his fifties. He shut the door behind him, and then there they all were, on the small front porch: Patty, Diane, Libby, and the man, basset-hound bags beneath watery eyes, his graying hair brushed straight back. He ran a hand through the pomade while he assessed Patty, his Irish Claddagh ring flashing.

"Mrs. Patty Day?" His coffee breath lingered in the cold air, vaguely discolored.

"I'm Patty Day. Ben Day's mother."

"We came by to find out what's going on with these stories," Diane interrupted. "We've been hearing a lot of rumors, and no one's bothered to talk to us directly."

The man cocked his hands on his hips, looked down at Libby, looked quickly away. "I'm Detective Jim Collins. I'm in charge of this investigation. I had to come by here today to talk to these folks and then of course I was going to get in touch with you. You saved me a drive. Do you want to talk somewhere else? It's a little cold here."

They went to a Dunkin' Donuts just off the highway, separate cars, Diane muttering a joke about cops and donuts, then cursing Mrs. Cates—*wouldn't even give us the time of damn day. Bitch.* Normally Patty would have said something in Mrs. Cates's defense: Diane and Patty's roles, straight-talker and apologist, were grooved deep. But the Cates family was in no need of defense.

Det. Collins was waiting for them with three paper cups of coffee and a carton of milk for Libby.

"Didn't know if you'd want her to have sweets," he said, and Patty wondered if he'd think she was a bad mother if she bought Libby a donut. Especially if he knew they'd had pancakes that morning. *This will be my life from now on,* she thought, *always having to think about what people will think.* Libby was smearing her face against the pastry glass already, though, hopping from one foot to another, and so Patty fished around in her pocket for some change and got a pink frosted donut, gave it to Libby on a napkin. She could not deal with Libby feeling denied, staring mournfully at all those pastel shades of sugar while they tried to have a conversation about whether her son was a Devil-worshiping child-molester. Again she almost laughed. She settled Libby at a table behind them and told her to sit still and eat while the grown-ups talked.

"You all redheads?" Collins said. "Where's the red come from, you Irish?"

Patty thought immediately of her always-conversation with Len about their red hair, and then she thought, *The farm's going away. How did I forget that the farm's going away?*

"German," she said for the second time that day.

"You have another few little ones, don't you?" Collins said.

"Yes. I have four children."

"Same daddy?"

Diane rustled in the seat next to her. "Of course, same daddy!"

"But you are a single mother, correct?" Collins asked.

"We're divorced, yes," Patty said, trying to sound as prim as a churchwife.

"What's this got to do with what's happening with Ben?" Diane snapped, leaning across the table. "I'm Patty's sister by the way. I take care of these kids almost as much as she does."

Patty winced, Det. Collins watched her wince.

"Let's try to start this civilly," Collins said. "Because we've got a long way to go together before this is cleared up. The charges leveled against your son, Mrs. Day, are of a very serious, and very concerning nature. At this point, we've got four little girls who say that Ben touched them in their private areas, that he made them touch him. That he took them out to some farm area and performed certain . . . acts that are associated with ritualistic Devil worship." He said those words—*ritualistic Devil worship*—the way people who don't know cars repeat what the mechanic said: *It's a broken fuel pump.*

"Ben doesn't even have a car," Patty said in a barely audible voice.

"Now the age difference between an eleven-year-old and a fifteen-year-old is only four years, but those are very crucial years," continued Collins. "We would consider him a danger and a predator if these accusations turn out to be true. And, frankly, we'll need to talk not only to Ben, but to your little girls too."

"Ben is a good boy," Patty said, and hated how limp and weak her voice was. "Everyone likes him."

"How is he regarded at school?" Collins asked.

"Pardon?"

"Is he considered a popular kid?"

"He has a lot of friends," Patty mumbled.

"I don't think he does, ma'am," Collins said. "From what we understand, he doesn't have very many friends, he's a bit of a loner."

"So what does that prove?" Diane snapped.

"It proves absolutely nothing, Miss . . . ?"

"Krause."

"It proves absolutely nothing, Miss Krause. But that fact, combined with the fact that he doesn't have a strong father figure around, would lead me to believe he may be more vulnerable to, say, a negative influence. Drugs, alcohol, people who are maybe a bit rougher, a bit troubled."

"He doesn't associate with delinquents, if that's what you're worried about," Patty said.

"Name summa his friends for me then," Collins said. "Name the kids he hangs out with. Name who he was with last weekend."

Patty sat, tongue thick in her mouth, and then shook her head, folded her hands near a smear of someone else's chocolate icing. It was late coming. But now finally, she was being revealed for what she was: a woman who couldn't quite keep it together, who lived from emergency to emergency, borrowing money, scrambling for sleep, sliding by when she should have been tending to Ben, encouraging him to pick up a hobby or join a club, not secretly grateful when he locked himself in his room or disappeared for an evening, knowing it was one less kid to deal with.

"There are some parenting gaps then," Collins sighed, like he already knew the end to the story.

"We want a lawyer before anything else happens, before you talk to any of the kids," Diane interrupted.

"Frankly, Mrs. Day," Collins said, not even glancing at Diane, "with three little girls at home, if I were you, I'd want the truth out more than anyone. This kind of behavior doesn't go away. In fact, if this is true, and to be frank, I think it is, your daughters were probably his first victims."

Patty looked behind at Libby, who sat licking the frosting off her donut. She thought of how much Libby used to hang on Ben. She thought of all the chores the kids did on their own. Sometimes after a day working in the barn with Ben, the girls would come back to the house, irritated, weepy. But . . . what? They were little girls, they got tired out and cranky. She wanted to throw her coffee in Collins's face.

"May I speak plainly?" Collins said, his voice kneading her. "I can't imagine how . . . horrible it must be to hear these things as a mother. But I can tell you something, and this is straight from our psychologist, who's been working one-on-one with these girls, and I can tell you what he tells me. That's that these girls, they're telling us things a fifth-grader wouldn't know about, sexually, unless they'd actually happened. He says they are classic abuse scenarios. You know about the McMartin case, of course."

Patty vaguely remembered. A preschool in California, and all the teachers were on trial for being Devil worshipers, molesting the kids. She could remember the evening newscast: a pretty sunny California house and then black words stamped across it: Daycare Nightmare.

"Satanic worship is not uncommon, I'm afraid," Collins was saying. "It's made its way into all areas of the community, and Devil worshipers tend to target young men, get them in the fold. And part of Devil worship is the . . . the degradation of children."

"Do you have any evidence?" Diane bellowed at Collins. "Any witnesses besides some eleven-year-old girls? Do you even have kids yourself? Do you know how easily they imagine things—their whole lives are make-believe. So do you have anyone to vouch for these lies but a bunch of little girls and some Harvard know-it-all psychiatrist who impresses you all?"

"Well, as far as evidence. The girls all said he took their underpants as some sick souvenir or something," Collins said to Patty. "If you'd let us look around your home, we could start to clear that up."

"We need to talk to a lawyer before that," Diane grumbled to Patty.

Collins swallowed his coffee and stifled a belch, banged his chest with a fist, and smiled mournfully over Patty's shoulder at Libby. He had the red nose of a drinker.

"Right now we just need to be calm. We will talk to everyone involved," Collins said, still ignoring Diane. "We interviewed several faculty members from his high school and the grade school this afternoon, and what we hear doesn't make us feel any better, Mrs. Day. A teacher, Mrs. Darksilver?"

He looked at Patty for her to confirm the name, and Patty nodded. Mrs. Darksilver had always loved Ben, he'd been an especial favorite of hers.

"Just this morning she saw your son nosing around Krissi Cates's locker. In the grade school. During Christmas break. This disturbs me, and," he looked at Patty from the bottom of his eyes, aiming the pink rims at her, "Mrs. Darksilver says, he was apparently aroused."

"What does that mean?" snapped Diane.

"He had an erection. When we looked inside Krissi's bin, we

found a note of a provocative nature. Mrs. Day, in our interviews, your son was repeatedly characterized as an outcast, a misfit. Odd. He's considered a bit of a timebomb. Some of the teachers are actually frightened of him."

"Frightened?" Patty repeated. "How can they be frightened of a fifteen-year-old boy?"

"You don't know what we found in his locker."

WHAT THEY FOUND in his locker. Patty thought Collins would say drugs or girlie magazines, or, in a merciful world, a bunch of outlaw firecrackers. That's what she wanted Ben to be in trouble for: a dozen Roman candles sitting like kindling in his backpack. That she could take.

Even when Collins did his greasy lead-up—*this is very disturbing, Mrs. Day, I want you to prepare yourself*—Patty had figured, maybe a gun. Ben loved guns, always had, it was like his airplane phase and his cement-truck phase, except this one just kept going. It was something they did together—*had* done together—hunting, shooting. Maybe he brought one to school just to show it off. The Colt Peacemaker. His favorite. He was not supposed to go into the cabinet without her permission, but if he had, they'd deal with it. So let it be a gun.

Collins had cleared his throat then, and said, in a voice that made them lean in, "We found some . . . remains . . . in your son's locker. Organs. At first we thought they might be part of a baby, but it seems they're animal. Female reproductive parts in a plastic container, from maybe a dog or a cat. You missing a dog or a cat?"

Patty was still woozy from the revelation they actually thought Ben might have part of a baby in his locker. That they thought he was so disturbed that infanticide was actually their first guess. It was right then, staring down at a scattering of pastel donut sprinkles, that she decided her son was going to prison. If that's how twisted they believed her son to be, he had no chance.

"No, we're not missing any pets."

"Our family is hunters. Farmers," Diane said. "We're around animals, dressing animals all the time. It's not so strange that he might have something from them."

"Really, do you keep parts of dead animals in your home?" For the first time Collins looked straight at Diane, a hard stare he cut off after just a few seconds.

"Is there a law against it?" Diane barked back.

"One of the rituals that Devil worshipers engage in is the sacrifice of animals, Mrs. Day," Collins said. "I'm sure you heard about them cattle axed up over near Lawrence. We think that and the involvement with the little girls all ties together."

Patty's face was cold. It was done, it was all done. "What do you want me to do?" she asked.

"I'll follow you to your place, so we can talk to your son, OK?" Collins said, turning paternal on that last note, his voice going high, almost flitting into babytalk. Patty could feel Diane's hands clench next to her.

"He's not at home. We've been trying to find him."

"We absolutely need to talk to your son, Mrs. Day. Where do you think we can find him?"

"We don't know where he is," Diane interrupted. "We're in the same boat as you."

"Are you going to arrest him?" Patty asked.

"We can't do anything until we talk to him, and the sooner we do, the sooner we'll get this cleared up."

"That's not an answer," Diane said.

"Only one I got, ma'am."

"That means yes," Diane said, and for the first time she lowered her eyes.

Collins stood up and walked over toward Libby during the last exchange, now he was kneeling down next to her, giving her a *Hi sweetie.*

Diane grabbed his arm. "No. Leave her alone."

Collins frowned down on her. "I'm just trying to help. Don't you want to know if Libby is OK?"

"We know Libby is OK."

"Why don't you let her tell me that. Or we could have Child Services—"

"Screw off," Diane said, getting in front of him. Patty sat in her place, willing herself to disconnect. She heard Diane and Collins snapping behind her, but she just sat and watched the woman behind the counter make another pot of coffee, trying to focus all her interest on the coffee. It worked for just a second before Diane was pulling Patty and Libby, her mouth grimy with donut, out of the restaurant.

PATTY FELT LIKE crying some more on the way home, but wanted to wait until Diane was gone. Diane made Patty drive, said it would be good for her to focus. The whole way home, Diane had to tell her which gears to switch to, she was so distracted. *Why don't you try third, P? I think we need to go down to 2, now.* Libby sat in the back-seat, saying nothing, bundling herself up, knees to chin.

"Is something bad going to happen?" Libby finally asked.

"No, honey."

"It seems like something bad's going to happen."

Patty had another panic-flash then: what the hell was wrong with her, taking a seven-year-old into this kind of situation. Her mother would not have done this. Then again, her mother wouldn't have raised Ben the way Patty had—slipshod and fingers-crossed—so it wouldn't have been an issue.

Right now, she had an almost obsessive need to get home, nest up, feel safe. The plan was, Patty would wait for Ben to get back—he had to be back soon, now—and Diane would go out and assess the gossip. Who knew what, whose side people were taking, and who in God's name Ben was hanging around with.

They rattled up to the house and saw Patty's Cavalier and another car, some bucket-seated sportscar that looked about ten years old, spattered with mud.

"Who's that?" Diane asked.

"No idea." She said it tragically. Already Patty knew whoever it was, it would be depressing news.

They opened the front door and felt the heat roll out. The thermostat had to be past eighty. The first thing they saw was an open box of microwave cocoa, the kind with fake marshmallows, on the dining room table, a trail of the cocoa mix leading to the kitchen. Then Patty heard that wheezy laugh and knew. Runner was sitting on the floor, sipping hot chocolate with her daughters leaning on him. Some nature show was on the TV, the girls squealing and grabbing his arms as an alligator boomed out of the water and snapped something with horns.

He looked up lazily, as if she were a delivery person. "Heya, Patty, long time, no seeya."

"We got some family stuff going on," Diane injected. "You should go on home."

During those stretchy weeks that Runner had returned to stay with them, he and Diane had scrapped several times—her bellowing and him blowing her off. *You're not the husband, Diane.* He'd go to the garage, get drunk, throw an old baseball against the wall for hours. Diane was not going to be the one to get Runner to go home.

"It's OK, D. You go on. Call me in an hour or so, let me know what's going on, OK?"

Diane glared at Runner, grumbled something into her chest and stalked out, the door shutting firmly behind her.

Michelle said "Jeez! What's with her?" and made a funny face for her dad, the little traitor. Her brown hair was wild from static where Runner had done his Indian rub. Runner had always been weird with the kids, roughly affectionate, but not in a grown-up way. He liked to pinch and flick them to get their attention. They'd be watching TV, and he'd suddenly lean across and get a good snap on their skin. Whichever of the girls he'd just stung would look over at him in a teary, outraged pout, and he'd laugh and go, "Whaaaat?" or "I's just saying hi. Hi!" And when he went with them anywhere, he trailed a few steps behind instead of walking beside them, eyes sideways on them. It always reminded her of an old coyote, trotting at the heels of its prey, just teasing for a few miles before it attacked.

"Daddy made us macaroni," Debby said. "He's going to stay for dinner."

"You know you aren't supposed to let anyone in the house while I'm away," Patty said, wiping up the powder with a rag that already smelled.

Michelle rolled her eyes, leaned into Runner's shoulder. "Jeez, Mom, it's Daaaaad."

It would have been easier if Runner was just dead. He had so little interaction with his children, was of so little help to them, that if he'd pass on, things would only improve. As it was, he lived on in the vast Out There Somewhere, occasionally swooping in with ideas and schemes and orders that the kids tended to follow. Because Dad said so.

She'd love to tell off Runner right now. Tell him about his son and the disturbing collection in his locker. The idea of Ben cutting and holding on to animal parts made her throat close. The Cates girl and her friends, that was a misunderstanding that may or may not end well. The assortment of body parts she couldn't think of an excuse for, and she was good at thinking up excuses. She didn't worry about what Collins said, that Ben may have molested his sisters. She had examined that thought on the ride home, turned it over, peered in its mouth and inspected its teeth, been excruciatingly thorough. And there was not a doubt in her: Ben would never do that.

But she knew her son did have a taste for hurt. There was that moment with the mice: that robotic shovel pounding, his mouth pulled away from his teeth, his face trickling sweat. He'd gotten some pleasure from that, she knew. He roughhoused with his sisters, hard. Sometimes giggles turned into screams and she'd come round the corner and see him holding Michelle's arm behind her back, just slowly, slowly pulling up. Or grabbing hold of Debby's arm, vise-like, for an Indian rub and what starts as a joke gets more and more frantic, him rubbing until he draws speckles of blood, his teeth grinding. She could see him getting that same look Runner got when he was around the kids: jacked up and tense.

"Dad needs to leave."

"Geez, Patty, not even a hi before you toss me out? Come on, let's talk, I got a business proposition for you."

"I'm in no position to make a business deal, Runner," she said. "I'm broke."

"You're never as broke as you say," he said with a leer, and twisted his baseball cap backward on stringy hair. He'd meant it to sound jokey, but it came out menacing, as if she'd better not be broke if she knew what was good for her.

He dumped the girls off him and walked over to her, standing too close as always, beer sweat sticking his longjohn shirt to his chest.

"Didn't you just sell the tiller, Patty? Vern Evelee told me you just sold the tiller."

"And all that money's gone, Runner. It's always gone as quick as I get it." She tried to pretend to sort through mail. He stayed right on top of her.

"I need you to help me. I just need enough cash to get to Texas."

Of course Runner would want to go where it was warm for the winter, traveling child-free like a gypsy from season to season as he did, an insult to her and her farm and her attachment to this single place on the ground. He picked up work and spent the money on stupid things: golf clubs because he pictured himself golfing some-day, a stereo system he'd never hook up. Now he was planning to hightail it to Texas. She and Diane had driven to the Gulf when Patty was in high school. The only time Patty'd been anywhere. It was the saltiness in the air that stuck with her, the way you could suck on a strand of hair and make your mouth start watering. Some-how Runner would find some cash, and he'd spend the rest of winter in some honkytonk alongside the ocean, sipping a beer while his son went to jail. She couldn't afford a lawyer for Ben. She kept thinking that.

"Well, I can't help you, Runner. I'm sorry."

She tried to aim him toward the door, and instead he pushed her farther into the kitchen, his stale-sweet breath making her turn her head away.

"Come on, Patty, why you going to make me beg? I'm in a real jam here. It's life or death stuff. I got to get the hell out of Dodge. You know I wouldn't be asking otherwise. Like, I might be killed tonight if I can't scrape up some money. Just give me $800."

The figure actually made her laugh. Did the guy really think that was her pocket change? Could he not look around and see how poor they were, the kids in shirtsleeves in the middle of winter, the kitchen freezer stacked with piles of cheap meat, each one marked with a long-gone year? That's what they were: a home past the expiration date.

"I don't have anything, Runner."

He looked at her with fixed eyes, his arm leaning across the doorway so she couldn't leave.

"You got jewelry, right? You got the ring I gave you."

"Runner, please, Ben's in trouble, bad trouble, I got a lot of bad stuff going on right now. Just come back another time, OK?"

"What the hell has Ben done?"

"There's been some trouble at school, some trouble in town, it's bad, I think he might need a lawyer, so I need any money I have for him and . . ."

"So you do have money."

"Runner, I don't."

"Give me the ring at least."

"I don't have it."

The girls were pretending to watch TV, but their rising voices made Michelle, nosy Michelle, turn her head and openly stare at them.

"Give me the ring, Patty." He held out his hand like she might actually be wearing it, that chintzy fake-gold engagement ring that she knew was embarrassing, flimsy, even at seventeen. He'd given it to her three months after he proposed. It took him three months to get off his ass, go down to a five-and-dime, and buy the little bit of tinsel he gave her while on his third beer. *I love you forever, baby,* he'd said. She knew immediately then that he'd leave, that he was not a man to depend on, that he wasn't even a man she liked very much. And still she'd gotten pregnant three more times, because he didn't like to wear condoms and it was too much trouble to nag.

"Runner, do you not remember that ring? That ring is not going to get you any money. It cost about ten dollars."

"Now you're going to be a bitch about the ring? Now?"

"Believe me if it had been worth anything, I'd have pawned it already."

They stood facing each other, Runner breathing like an angry donkey, his hands shaking. He put them on her arms, then removed them with exaggerated effort. Even his mustache was shaking.

"You are really going to be sorry about this, Patty."

"I already am, Runner. Been sorry a long time."

He turned, and his jacket brushed a cocoa packet on to the floor, scattering more brown powder at his feet. "Bye girls, your mom's . . . a BITCH!" He kicked one of the tall kitchen chairs over and it cartwheeled into the living room. They all froze like forest creatures, as Runner paced in tight circles, Patty wondering if she should make a run for a rifle, or grab a kitchen knife, all the while, mind-pleading that he just leave.

"Thanks for FUCKING NOTHING!" he tramped to the front door, swung the door open so hard it cracked the wall behind it and bounced back. He kicked it open again, grabbed it, banged it into the wall, his head bowed low against it, all his strength slamming it again and again.

Then he left, his car screeching down away from the house, and Patty fetched the shotgun, loaded it, and set it atop the mantelpiece with a scattering of shells. Just in case.

Libby Day

NOW

Krissi ended up sleeping on my couch. I'd walked her to the door and realized she wasn't OK to drive, she was slip-slopping in her shoes, a web of mascara down one cheek. As she swayed out onto my porch, she turned around suddenly and asked about her mother, if I knew where her mother was or how to find her, and it was then that I pulled Krissi back inside, made her a Velveeta sandwich, parked her on the sofa, and wrapped a blanket over her. As she rolled into sleep, setting the last quarter of the sandwich carefully on the floor beside her, three of my lotion bottles fell out of her jacket. Once she passed out I tucked them back in.

She was gone when I woke up, the blanket folded with a note scrawled on the back of an envelope: *Thanks. Sorry.*

So Lou Cates didn't kill my family, if Krissi was to be believed. I believed her. On that count at least.

I decided to drive down to see Runner, ignore the two messages from Lyle and the zero messages from Diane. Drive down to see Runner, get some answers. I didn't think he had anything to do with the murders, whatever his girlfriend might say, but I wondered if he knew something, with his debts and his drinking and his gutter-friends. If he knew something or heard something, or if maybe his debts had triggered some horrible vengeance. Maybe I could believe in Ben again, which is what I wanted to do. I knew now why I'd never gone to visit him. It was too tempting, too easy to ignore the prison walls, and just see my brother, hear the Ben-specific cadence of his voice, that downward slope at the end of every sentence, like it might be the last thing he was ever going to say. Just seeing him, I remembered things, nice things, or not even nice. Just regular things. I could get a whiff of home. Way back when everyone was alive. Man, I wanted that.

I stopped at the 7-Eleven on the way out of town, bought a map and some cheese-flavored crackers that I discovered were diet when I bit into them. I ate them anyway, heading south, the orange powder floating through the car. I should have stopped for a meal on the way to Oklahoma. The air on the highway was thick with tempting smell-pockets: french fries, fast-food fish, fried chicken. But I was in an unnatural panic, worried for no good reason I would miss Runner if I stopped, and so I ate the diet crackers and a mealy apple I'd found on the corner of my kitchen counter.

Why was the note, that dirty note that wasn't addressed to Ben, mixed up in a box of Michelle's stuff? If Michelle had found out Ben had a girlfriend, she'd have lorded it over him, all the more if he tried to keep it a secret. Ben hated Michelle. Ben had tolerated me, had dismissed Debby, but he'd hated Michelle actively. I remembered him pulling her out of his room by an arm, her whole body almost sideways, Michelle up on tiptoes, moving with him to keep from being dragged. He tossed her out and she fell against the wall, and he told her if she ever came in his room again, he'd kill her. His teeth flared whenever he talked to her. He screamed at her for always being underfoot—she'd hover outside his door day and night, listening. Michelle always knew everyone's secrets, she never had a conversation that didn't have an angle. I remembered that more vividly since discovering her bizarre notes. If you don't have money, gossip isn't bad leverage. Even inside one's own family.

"Ben talks to himself a lot," Michelle announced at breakfast one morning, and Ben reached across the table, knocking her plate into her lap, and grabbed her by the shirt collar.

"Leave me the fuck alone," he screamed. And then my mom calmed him down, got him to go back to his room, lectured us, as always. Later we found bits of egg that had catapulted up onto the plastic chandelier over the table, the chandelier that looked like it came from a pizza parlor.

So what did that mean? Ben wouldn't kill his family because his little sister found out he had a girlfriend.

I passed a field of cows, standing immobile, and thought about growing up, all the rumors of cattle mutilation, and people swearing it was Devil worshipers. The Devil lurked nearby in our Kansas town, an evil that was as natural and physical as a hillside. Our church hadn't been too brimstoney, but the preacher had certainly nurtured the idea: The Devil, goat-eyed and bloody, could take over your heart just as easily as Jesus, if you weren't careful. In every town I lived in, there were always the "Devil kids," and the "Devil houses," just like there was always a killer clown driving around in a white van. Everyone knew of some old, vacant warehouse on the edge of town where a stained mattress sat on the floor, bloody from sacrifice. Everyone had a friend of a cousin who had actually seen a sacrifice but was too scared to give details.

I was ten minutes into Oklahoma, a good three hours to go, and I started smelling something overpoweringly sweet but rotten. It stang my eyes, made them water. I had a ridiculous quiver of fear that my Devil-think had summoned the beast. Then in the distance, the churning sky turned the color of a bruise, I saw it. Paper plant.

I turned the radio on scan—station 1, station 2, station 3— blasts of unpleasant noise, static, and ads for cars and more static, so I flipped it right back off.

Just past a sign with a picture of a cowboy—*Welcome to Lidgerwood, Oklahoma, Pardner!*—I pulled off the ramp and headed into the town, which turned out to be a busted-down tourist trap of a city. It had once fashioned itself as an Old West locale: The main street was all frosted glass and faux-saloons and shoppes. One storefront called itself The Olde Photo Stoppe, a place where families could commission sepia photos of themselves in frontier garb. In the window hung a poster-sized print: the father holding a lasso, trying to look menacing under a hat too big for him; the little girl in a calico dress and bonnet, too young to get the joke; the mother, dressed as a whore, giving an uncomfortable smile, her arms crossed in front of her thighs where her petticoat was slit. Next to the photo hung a For Sale sign. Another matching sign next door at Daphne's Daffy Taffy, more For Sales at Buffalo Bill's Amazing Arcade and a storefront with the ridiculous stretch of a name, Wyatt Earp's Slurpies. The whole place seemed dusty. Even the defunct waterslide loop-de-looping in the distance was plugged with dirt.

Bert Nolan's Group Home for Men was just three blocks off the downtown drag, a square, low building with a tiny front yard infested with foxtail weeds. I'd always liked foxtail as a kid, it appealed to my literal brain, because it looked like it sounded: a long, thin stem with a length of fuzz at the top, just like a fox's tail, but green. They grew all over our farm—entire meadows were given over to the stuff. Michelle and Debby and I would break off the tops and tickle each other under our wrists. My mom taught us the colloquial names for everything: lamb's ear, coxcomb, all those plants that lived up to their titles. A lamb's ear is as soft as a lamb's ear. Coxcomb actually looks like a rooster's red comb. I got out of the car and fluttered my hands across the tops of the foxtail. Maybe I'd grow a garden of weeds. Windmillgrass actually fans out at the top like windmill blades. Queen Ann's lace is white and frilly. Witchgrass would be appropriate for me. Some devil's claw.

The door to Bert Nolan's Group Home was made of metal, painted dark gray like a submarine. It reminded me of the doors in Ben's prison. I rang the bell and waited. Across the street two teenage boys rode their bikes in lazy, wide circles, interested. I rang the bell again and gave the metal a bang that failed to reverberate inside. I debated asking the guys across the way if anyone was home, just to break the silence. As they were looping closer to me—*watcha doing there, lady?*—the door opened onto a pixie-sized man in bright white sneakers, ironed jeans, a Western shirt. He jiggled the toothpick in his mouth, not looking at me, flipping through a copy of *Cat Fancy* magazine.

"Don't open for the night til . . ." he trailed off when he saw me. "Oh, sorry honey. We're a men's hostel, you have to be a man and over eighteen."

"I'm looking for my dad," I said, leaning into my drawl. "Runner Day. Are you the manager?"

"Ha! Manager, accountant, priest, cleaning boy," he said opening the door. "Recovering alcoholic. Recovering gambler. Recovering deadbeat. Bert Nolan. This is my place. Come in, sweetheart, n're-mind me of your name."

He opened the door onto a room full of cots, the strong odor of bleach rising up from the floor. The elfin Bert led me through the rows of thin beds, each one still indented from the night, to an office just his size, just my size, which held one small desk, a file cabinet, and two foldout chairs we sat down on. The fluorescent light was not flattering to his face, which was pocked with dark, dimpled pores.

"I'm not a weirdo, by the way," he said, flapping the *Cat Fancy* at me. "I just got a cat, never had one before. Don't really like her much so far. She was supposed to be good for morale, but so far she just pisses in the beds."

"I have a cat," I volunteered, surprising myself with my sudden, intense fondness for Buck. "If they go outside their litter box, it's usually because they're angry."

"That right?"

"Yeah, otherwise, they're pretty easy pets."

"Huh," Bert Nolan said. "Huh. So you're looking for your daddy? Yeah I remember, we spoke. Day. He's like most men here—should be happy someone's looking for them, after the crap they've pulled at home. Usually money stuff. Or lack-of-money stuff. No money, too much booze. Does not bring out the best. Runner. Huh."

"He wrote me a letter, said he was back here."

"You want to take him home, take care of him?" Bert said. His eyes were black and shiny, like he'd told himself a joke.

"Well, I'm not sure about that. I just want to check in."

"Ha, good. That was a trick question—people who say they want to find one of my men to take care of them, never do." Nolan smelled his fingertips. "I don't smoke anymore, but sometimes my damn fingers still smell like tobacco."

"Is he here?"

"He's not. He's gone again. I don't allow drinkers here. He just had his third strike."

"He say where he went?"

"Ah sweetheart, I just don't give out addresses. Just don't. Found that was the smartest way to handle all inquiries. But I'll tell you what, because you seem like a nice lady . . ."

"Berrrrrt!" came a howl from outside the building.

"Ah, ignore that, just one of my men trying to get in early. That's another thing you learn to never do: never let anyone in early, ever. And never let anyone in late."

He had lost his train of thought, he stared at me expectantly.

"So you said you'd tell me what?" I prompted.

"What?"

"How you might help me find my dad?"

"Oh, right. You can leave a letter here with me."

"Mr. Nolan, I've already done that. That's why I'm here. I really, really need to find him." I caught myself in the Runner stance, palms on the edge of the table, ready to vault myself up if I got mad.

Nolan picked up a plaster figurine of an old, balding man throwing his arms out in some expression of exasperation, but I couldn't read the words on the base. Bert seemed to find some consolation in the thing. He let out a sharp sigh between barely parted lips.

"Well, sweetheart, I'll tell you what, he may not be here, but I know he's still in Lidgerwood. One of my men saw him just last night outside-a Cooney's. He's laying low somewhere, but he's around. Just prepare yourself for some disappointment."

"Disappointment about what?"

"Oh, you name it."

WHEN BERT NOLAN got up to lead me out of his office, he turned his back to me, and I immediately made a grab for his little figurine. But I made myself set it back down, and took his bag of CornNuts and a pencil instead. Progress. They sat in the car seat next to me as I drove to the nearest bar. Cooney's.

Cooney's had not given in to the Old West theme. Cooney's was proudly crappy in the present day. Three wrinkled faces glared at me as I opened the door. This included the bartender. I ordered a beer, the man snapping that he'd need to see my driver's license, holding it up to the light and then down near his belly, giving a hmmph, when he couldn't prove it was fake. I sipped and sat, letting them get used to me being there. Then I spoke. As soon as I hit the word Runner, the place lit up.

"That jackass stole three cases of beer from me," the bartender said. "Went around back in broad daylight and just took them off the truck. And I'd stood him for a lot of drinks, believe me."

The middle-aged man two stools down grabbed my arm too hard and said, "Your goddam daddy owes me two hundred bucks. And I want my lawn mower back. You tell him I'm looking for him."

"I know where you can find him," said an old guy with a Hemingway beard and the build of a girl.

"Where?" everyone else said at once.

"Bet anything he's living with the rest of them squatters, camped out over at the Superfund site. You should see it," he added more to the bartender than me, "it's like a old-time Hooverville, bonfires and shanties."

"Why the hell would anyone live at the Superfund site?" the bartender snapped.

"Well, you know no one from the government will show up."

They all laughed angrily.

"Is it even safe to go there?" I asked. I pictured toxic waste barrels and lime-green sludge.

"Sure, if you don't drink the well water and you're not a grasshopper."

I raised my eyebrows.

"That's what it's from: the whole site is soaked with arsenic. It's an old dumping spot for grasshopper bait."

"And shitheads," said the bartender.

Ben Day

JANUARY 2, 1985
8:38 P.M.

They drove toward town, snow starting to fall, Ben just remembering he left his bike back at the warehouse and now that was probably gone. "Hey," he yelled up front—Trey and Diondra were talking, but he couldn't hear them over the music screeching on the radio, like ripped sheets of metal, *Weeeeeeeer-weer-weer-weer.* "Could we stop by the Compound real quick so I can grab my bike?"

Trey and Diondra exchanged looks.

"No," Diondra busted out a grin, and they started laughing. Ben sat back for a second, then leaned back up. "I'm serious, I need it."

"Forget it, dude. It's gone," Trey said. "You can't leave shit at the Compound."

They drove onto Bulhardt Avenue, the main strip in town, where nothing was happening, as usual. The hamburger joint was a bright yellow diorama featuring a few jocks and their dates, all draped over each other. The stores were black, and even the bar looked barely open—only a vague light could be seen in the single rectangle of window in the front. The door itself had been painted navy and revealed nothing.

They parked right out front, Diondra still finishing her beer, Trey grabbing it from her and drinking the rest—*the baby won't mind.* On the sidewalk, some old guy, his face a confusion of wrinkles, his nose and mouth looking like they were molded out of a twist of clay, scowled at them once and walked into the bar.

"Let's do it," Trey said, and started to get out of the truck. And then when he saw Ben hesitate, still sitting in back, his hands on his knees, Trey stuck his head back in the car and smiled that businesslike smile: "Don't worry, dude, you're with me. I do a lot of drinking in there. And—heh!—you're pretty much visiting your dad at the office."

Diondra fingered the edges of her crunchy curls, her version of running her fingers through it, and they both followed Trey inside, Diondra with her lips pouty and her eyes sexy-sleepy, the way she looked in most photos, like you woke her up from a dream about you. Next to her, Ben feeling gangly and droopy as usual, literally dragging his feet.

The bar was so smoky Ben choked as soon as he entered, Diondra already with a cigarette lit, slouching next to him as if that made her look older. A nervous guy, his hair in patches like a molting bird, scurried up to Trey immediately, his head lowered, and muttered something in Trey's ear, Trey nodding, sucking his lips in against his teeth, looking concerned and serious. Ben thought maybe the guy was a manager, was kicking them out, because maybe Diondra passed for older with the extra makeup but Ben didn't. But Trey just patted the guy on the back, saying something like, "Don't make me chase, man," and the nervous guy got a big grin and laughed and said "No no no, don't worry about that, don't worry about that at all, not at all" and Trey just said, "Sunday" and walked past the guy to the bar, ordered three beers and a shot of SoCo, which he swallowed straight off.

The bartender was another old, gray-haired fat guy. It seemed like a joke, how much all these dudes looked alike, like living was so hard it just erased your features, rubbed out anything distinctive. The bartender gave Ben and Diondra a wise-guy look, a just-so-you-know, I-know look, but slid them two beers anyway. Ben turned away from the bar to drink his, one foot against a stool, in a way that felt casual, like he'd done it before, because he could feel Trey's eyes on him, looking for something to make fun of.

"I see him, I see Runner," Diondra said, and before Ben could ask her why she sounded so easy saying his name, Trey was calling it out, "Hey Runner, c'mere!" and Runner got the same nervous, weasel look the first guy had.

He came loping over, that seesaw walk of his, his hands jammed in his pockets, his eyes big and yellow.

"I just don't have it, man, I just don't. Tried to scrape it up earlier, but I just, I was going to come try to find you, I just got here myself, I can give you the last of my weed in the meantime—"

"You want to say hi to Diondra?" Trey interrupted.

Runner started, then smiled. "Oh, hey Diondra, hehheh, wow I must be drunk, oblivious!" He pretended to close one eye so he could see better, made a little jump on the tips of his toes. "Heh, yeah drinking myself cross-eyed because I'm so freaked out about this situation."

"Runner, you want to look at who's next to Diondra?" Ben had barely turned to face him, he was trying to think of something to say besides, *Hey Dad,* but he couldn't so he just stood there, waiting for the inevitable shittiness to happen.

Runner peered through the dimness of the bar and didn't recognize Ben.

"Hi . . . there," he said, and then to Trey, "That your cousin? I can't see too well, night vision, I need contacts but—"

"Oh my God," Trey said leaning back to pretend to laugh but looking enraged. "Take another look, asshole." Ben wasn't sure if he was supposed to display himself better, like some girl hoping to scam. Instead he stood rigid, staring at his dark flop of hair in an old Schlitz mirror on the far wall, as he watched Runner sidle up to him, reaching a hand out toward him fairy-tale-like, as if Runner were a troll and Ben some awful treasure. He kept getting closer, stumbling on Ben's foot, and then they made eye contact and Runner yelped, "Ohhhh!" and seemed even more nervous. "Hair's not red."

"You remember your son, right, this is your son, isn't it, Runner?"

"It is, my son! Hey Ben. No one can blame me for that one, hair's not red. I didn't even know you knew Trey."

Ben shrugged, watching Runner's reflection back away from him in the mirror. He wondered how much Runner owed to Trey, why Ben felt like some ransom victim, not that Runner would actually care if he was up for ransom. He wondered too, how accidental this visit was. It had seemed like spur of the moment, but Ben was guessing now that they were always going to end up here tonight.

"I don't get it, Runner," Trey continued, talking one notch above the country music. "You say you don't have any money, Ben here says you don't have any money, and yet, you had that giant stash of weed just a few weeks ago."

"Wun't good weed though." He turned his shoulder toward Trey, cutting Ben out of the conversation, shooting backward glances at him, trying to push Trey toward the center of the room by standing closer and closer to him, Trey not moving, finally saying, "Get off me, man," and Runner settling back on his heels.

"Nah, nah man you're right, it wasn't good stuff," Trey continued. "But you were charging like it was."

"I never charged you nothing, you know."

"You didn't charge me because you owe me, dipshit. But I know for a fact you were charging $20 for a dimebag, now where the fuck is the money, you give it to your wife to hold?"

"Ex! Ex-wife," Runner yelled. And then: "I was trying to *get* money from her, not give it. I know she's got money there, even when we were married, she'd hide money, rolls of it, hundreds, from the harvest sales, and stick it in funny places. Found $200 in the foot of her pantyhose one time. Maybe I should go back." He looked over at Ben, who was listening but trying to pretend he was teasing Diondra, his finger twirling Diondra's hair, Diondra only partly playing along.

"Can I talk to you about the situation over there in private?" Runner pointed over to a corner where three tugboat-sized men were playing pool. The tallest, a pale, white-haired old guy with a Marine tattoo, propped his pool cue up and puffed his chest out at them.

"Right," Trey said.

"You can talk in front of me," Ben said, trying to sound like he didn't care.

"Your son needs money from you, just like I do," Trey said. "Maybe worse than I do."

Runner turned from a shriveled position under Trey's black-lamp eyes, and headed back over to Ben, raising himself to full height. Somewhere since summer Ben had grown. He was just a little bigger than Runner now, 5'5", 5'6".

"You owe Trey money? Your mom said you'uz in trouble. You owe Trey?" he blasted at Ben, his breath yellow—beer and tobacco and maybe a mustardy tuna salad. Ben's stomach grumbled.

"No! No!" He was aware his voice sounded nervous, cowed. Diondra shifted her weight next to him. "I don't owe anyone."

"Then why am I supposed to be giving you money I work my damn tail off for, huh?" Runner said, his voice bitter. "That's what I never understand, this idea of handouts: alimony and child support and the government with its hands in my pockets. I barely can support myself, I don't know why people think I need to take three extra jobs to give money to my wife, who has her own *farm*. Her own *house* on the farm. And four kids to help her out with it. I mean, I sure as hell didn't grow up thinking my daddy owed me a living, my daddy oughta give me money for Nikes and college and dress shirts and . . ."

"Food," Ben said, looking down at his broken boots with sloppy-joe stains on them.

"What's that? What's that you say to me?" Runner was in his face now, those blue irises rolling around in the yellow orbs like fish on the surface of a bad lake.

"Nothing," Ben mumbled.

"You want money for your hair dye, that it? Want money for the beauty parlor?"

"He wants money for his girl . . ." Trey started, but Diondra was giving him quick axes across her throat, no no no.

"Well, I'm definitely not in charge of buying things for his girl-friend," Runner said. "You his girlfriend now, Diondra? Small world. But definitely ain't my business."

The men at the pooltable had stopped playing altogether, sneering at the scene, and then the white-haired guy limped over, put a firm hand on Trey's shoulder.

"Problem, Trey? Runner here, he's good for it. Give him another twenty-four hours, OK? On me. Understand?" The man had a wish-boned stance, like gravity was pulling him toward the ground by both legs, but his hands were muscled, sinewy, and they pressed into Trey's shoulder.

Runner smiled, wiggled his eyebrows up and down at Ben, signaling they should both be pleased. "Don't worry, buddy, it's OK," he told Ben. "It's OK now."

Trey tightened his shoulder under the man's hand, seemed about to shrug it off, then stared into the middle distance.

"Sure, twenty-four OK, Whitey. On you."

"Appreciate it, Injun," the man said. He winked, made a cheerful, creaky noise with his mouth like he was calling a horse, and rejoined his friends, a rustle of laughter going up from the group just before the pool ball clacked.

"Piece of shit pussy," Trey said to Runner. "Tomorrow night, here. Or so help me, Runner, I will hurt you."

Runner's victory rictus, that Halloween smile, faded, and he nodded twice, and as he was turning to the bar, snapped, "Fine, but then stay out of my business."

"Man, I cannot wait to stay out of your business."

As they started to leave, Ben waited for Runner to say something to him—sorry, see ya, something. But Runner was already trying to talk the bartender into giving him one on the house, or maybe on Whitey, Whitey would stand him a round, and he'd already forgotten about Ben. So had Trey and Diondra, they were busting through the doors, and Ben stood with his hands in the front pockets of his pants, caught sight of himself in the mirror, looking so different, and he watched himself in the mirror as he turned around to Runner.

"Hey, uh, Dad," he said, and Runner looked up, annoyed he was still there. It was that feeling of pestiness that made Ben want to make Runner respect him. He'd felt the tiniest jingle of camaraderie before—that word, *buddy*—he wanted it back. He had pictured, just a quick flash, him and his dad at the bar, having a few beers together. That's all he really wanted from the guy, just a beer together every so often. "I just wanted to tell you something. It might make you feel, I don't know, good," and Ben started grinning, couldn't help himself.

Runner just sat there, sleepy eyes, not giving any expression.

"I uh, Diondra's pregnant. I, uh, we, Diondra and I are having a baby." And then his smile split wide for the first time, for the first time really feeling good, saying it out loud like that. Going to be a dad. A dad, with some little one depending on him, thinking he was *it*.

Runner tilted his head to the side, lifted his beer sloppily, and said, "Just be sure it's yours. I doubt it's yours." Then he turned his back on Ben.

OUTSIDE, TREY KICKED the side of his truck, screamed between closed lips. "I tell you what, that old crew better die off soon, because I'm sick to fucking death of them protecting their own—you're telling me it's honor, it's not, it's old white guys trying to hold on to the last bit of business before they start shitting themselves and need name tags attached to them so they know who they are. Fucking Whitey!" He pointed a finger at Ben, the snow everywhere, floating down Ben's shirt and melting on his neck. "And your old man is a piece of crap if he thinks I'm believing his line of bullshit. I hope you're not too attached to him because I'd like to flush him like a piece of shit."

"Let's just go, Trey," Diondra said, opening the door, ushering Ben into the backseat. "My dad is going to come home next week, and I'll be dead anyway."

Ben felt like hitting himself. The one thing he wasn't supposed to tell, and he'd wasted it on Runner. Ben was so angry as soon as he got in the backseat, he began punching it blindly, spittle shooting from his mouth, fuckerfuckerfucker, kicking at the cushion, banging his knuckles on the roof of the car, hitting his head on the window glass over and over until his forehead was bleeding again, Diondra yelling, *baby, baby what?*

"I swear to God, I swear to fucking God, Diondra, fuck."

Annihilation.

He could never tell Diondra he'd told.

"Someone should fucking die," Ben spat. He put his head in his hands, could feel Trey and Diondra consulting each other, silently, Trey finally saying, "Your dad's a fucking douchebag, dude." He threw the car into reverse and squealed out into the street, knocking Ben against the window. Diondra snaked a hand back and stroked

Ben's hair until he sat upright, barely, a pile. Diondra's face was green under the lamplight, and suddenly Ben could see what she'd look like in twenty years, flabby and pimply like she described her mom, her skin hard and wrinkled, but with that electric glow from the tanning booths.

"There's stuff in the glove compartment," Trey said, and Diondra popped it open and began rifling through it. She pulled out an oversized pipe crammed with leaves, the pot spilling everywhere, Trey saying *easy now*, and then she lit it and toked in, passed it to Trey. Ben reached up a hand—he was almost sick now, so shaky from lack of food, dizzy from the streetlights fluttering—but he wasn't going to be left out. Trey kept it from him. "Don't know if you want this, buddy. This is me and Diondra's thing. Hard-ass weed. I'm serious, Diondra, it may be tonight, I need the power in me, I haven't felt it in too long. It may have to happen."

Diondra kept looking up ahead, the snow dizzying.

"Ben might need it too," Trey pushed.

"Fine, let's do it then. Take a left up here," Diondra said.

And when Ben asked what was going on, they both just smiled.

Libby Day

NOW

The sky was an unnatural purple when I left the Lidgerwood bar, bouncing on backroads toward the Superfund site. I wondered what it said about me, that my own father was living at a toxic waste dump and until now I'd neither known nor cared. Grasshopper bait. Bran and molasses and arsenic to help end the grasshopper plague back in the '30s, and when folks didn't need it anymore, they just buried it, bags and bags, open-grave-style. Then people got sick.

I wished I had someone with me. Lyle fidgeting in the seat next to me in one of his shrunken jackets. I should have phoned him. In my nervous rush to get down here, I hadn't told anyone where I was, hadn't used a credit card since filling up in Kansas City. If anything went wrong, no one would miss me for days. Those guys at the bar would have the only clue to where I'd be, and they didn't seem like good citizens.

This is ridiculous, I said out loud so I knew it. I shivered when I thought of the reason I was looking for Runner: a goodly amount of people believed he killed the Days. But I still couldn't make it work in my head, even without the alibi. I had trouble picturing Runner using the axe, in truth. I could see him grabbing a shotgun in a temper—

raise, cock, pow—but the axe didn't fit. Too much work. Plus, he was found at home, asleep and still wasted, the next morning. Runner would have gotten drunk after killing his family, yes. But he wouldn't have had the discipline to stay put. He'd have gone on the lam, accidentally announcing his guilt to everyone.

The dump site was marked off by cheap metal fencing, jagged holes cut into it. Waist-high weeds grew everywhere like prairie grass, and tiny bonfires flashed in the distance. I drove along the perimeter of the fence, the weeds and loose gravel rattling against the undercarriage of my car more and more insistently until I came to a stop. I closed the car door with a quiet tamp, my eyes on those distant flames. It'd be about a ten-minute tromp to reach the camp. I slipped easily through a wire-snipped hole in the fence to my right, started walking, foxtail swatting my legs. The sky was draining quickly now, the horizon just a cuticle of pink. I realized I was humming "Uncle John's Band" to myself for no good reason.

Scraggly trees stood in the distance, but for the first few hundred yards it was all rolling, waist-high weeds. Again I was reminded of my childhood, the safe feeling of all that grass grazing your ears and wrists and the insides of your calves, like the plants were trying to soothe you. I took a few loose strides and jammed the point of my boot into a woman's ribs, actually feeling the bones part as the leather tip slid between them. She had been curled on the ground in a puddle of piss, her arms wrapped around a label-less bottle of liquor. She sat halfway up, groggy, the side of her face and hair caked with mud. She hissed at me with a withered face and beautiful teeth. "Get off me, get off me!"

"What the hell?" I yelled back, taking a scurry of steps away from her, my arms up in the air like I was worried about touching her. I walked briskly on, trying to pretend it hadn't happened, hoping the woman would pass out again, but she kept yelling after me, between gulps off the bottle: *Getoffmegetoffmegetoffme,* the screams turning into song turning into weeping.

The woman's cries aroused the interest of three men, whose faces appeared from behind the crooked copse of trees I was walking toward. Two of them glared at me, belligerent, and the youngest one, a skeletal man maybe in his forties, shot out, running toward me full bore bearing a stick he'd lit on fire. I took two steps back and planted myself.

"Who is it? Who is it?" he yelled. The thin flame of his torch weakened in a gust of wind and blew out as he neared me. The man trotted the last few steps, then stood in front of me, staring limply at the ember and smoke, his machismo turned to sulking with the loss of the fire. "What do you want, you shouldn't be here, you have to have permission to be here, it's not OK." The man was goggle-eyed, smudged everywhere, but his hair was glowing yellow, like a cap, as if it was the one thing he took care of. "It's not OK," he said again, more toward the trees than me. I wished then that I'd brought my Colt and wondered when I'd stop being so goddam stupid.

"I'm trying to find a guy by the name of Runner Day." I didn't know if my dad had bothered with an alias, but I assumed even if he had, he'd have forgotten by his third or eighth beer. I was right.

"Runner? What do you want with Runner? He steal something from you? What'd he take? He took my watch and he won't give it back." The man slouched into himself like a child, picked at a loose button at the bottom of his shirt.

Just off the path, about forty feet away, I saw an irritation of movement. It was a couple rutting, all legs and hair and faces bunched up in anger or distaste. Their jeans were both bundled around their ankles, the man's pink ass going like a jackhammer. The yellow-haired man looked at them, giggled and said something under his breath, like *fun*.

"I'm not upset with him, with Runner," I added, pulling his attention back from the couple. "I'm just his family."

"Runnerrrrr!" the man abruptly screamed over his other shoulder. Then he looked back at me. "Runner lives in that farthest house, out on the edge of camp. You got any food?"

I started walking without a reply, the couple climaxing loudly behind me. The bonfires got brighter and closer together as I hit the main drag—a scorched bit of ground, dotted with tents that sagged like storm-ruined umbrellas. A big firepit blazed in the center of camp, a woman with deep jowls and a distant stare was tending the flames, ignoring the cans of beans and soup that were turning black from the heat, their innards sizzling over. A younger couple with scabby arms watched her from half inside their tent. The woman wore a child's winter hat partway on her head, her pale face peeking out, fishbelly ugly. Just past them, two old men with dandelions woven into their matted hair sat greedily eating food out of a can with their fingers, the thick stew steaming in the air.

"Come on, Beverly!" the scabby man snapped at the fire-tender. "I think it's damn done."

As I walked into the campsite, they all got quiet. They'd heard the screaming of Runner's name. One old man pointed a dirty finger farther west—*he's over there*—and I left the heat of the fires and walked into the cool brambles. The hills rolled more now, like fat ocean waves, just four or five feet high, row after row, and about nine hills away I could see it: a steady glimmer, like a sunrise.

Up and down, floating along, I reached the top of the final ridge and discovered the light source. Runner's home, it turned out, was an industrial-sized mixing vat, which looked like an above-ground pool. Light poured out of it, and for a second I worried it was radioactive. Did grasshopper arsenic glow?

As I started toward the tank, I could hear the amplified echoes of Runner's movements, like a beetle walking across a steel-drum. He was whispering to himself in a schoolteachery, chastising voice—*well, I guess you should have thought of that before, Mister Smarty*—and the tank was broadcasting the noise out into the sky, which was now the violet of a mourning dress. *Yeah, I guess you really did it this time, Runnerman,* he was saying. The tank was about ten feet tall, with a ladder up one side, and I began hauling myself up it, calling out my dad's name.

"Runner, it's Libby. Your daughter," I bellowed, the rust of the ladder making my hands itch. Gargling throat sounds came from within. I climbed a few more rungs, and peered inside the tank. Runner was bent at the waist, retching onto the tank floor, and suddenly he expelled a purple globular mess, like an athlete might spit chaw. Then he lay down on a soiled beach towel, adjusting a baseball cap on his head sideways, nodding as if some job, somewhere, had been well done. A half dozen flashlights glowed around him like candles, illuminating his craggy, tan face and a pile of junk: knobless toaster ovens, a tin pot, a pile of watches and gold chains and a mini-fridge that wasn't plugged into anything. He lay on his back with the loose pose of a sunbather, one leg crossed over the other, a beer to his lips, a saggy twelve-pack carton at his side. I hollered his name again and he focused his eyes, pushed his nose at me when he saw me, like a mean hound-dog. It was one of my gestures.

"Whatdaya want?" Runner snapped up at me, his fingers tightening around his beer can. "I told everyone, no trade tonight."

"Runner, it's Libby. Libby, your daughter."

He raised himself on his elbows then, twisted his hat toward the back. Then he swiped a hand across the lace of dried saliva on his chin. He got part of it off.

"Libby?" he broke into a grin then. "Little, little Libbbby! Well, come on down, sweetheart! Come say hi to your old man." He struggled to an upright position, standing in the center of the tank, his voice sounding deep and melodic bouncing off the walls, the flashlights giving him a crazy campfire radiance. I hesitated on the ladder, which curled over the top of the tank and then ended.

"Come on in, Libby, this is your old man's new home!" He held his arms up to me. The drop into the tank wasn't dangerous, but it wasn't a gimme.

"Come on! Jesus Christ on a crutch, how far you come to see me, and now you're gonna be a scaredy-scared," Runner barked. At that, I swung my legs over the edge and sat on the rim like a nervous swimmer. After another *Ah jesus!* from Runner, I started awkwardly lowering myself. Runner had always been quick to brand his children as crybabies, cowards. I only really knew the guy for one summer, but it had been a hell of a summer. His mockery always worked on me: I'd end up swinging from the tree branch, jumping off the hayloft, throwing myself into the creek even though I couldn't swim. Never feeling triumphant afterward, just pissed. Now I was lowering myself into a rusted tank, and as my arms started to shake, my legs flail, Runner came up and grabbed me by the waist, dislodged me from the wall, and started twirling me around in tight, manic circles. My short legs spun out around me like I was seven again, and I began struggling to stick them on the ground, which only made Runner grip me harder, his arms sliding up beneath my breasts, me floating like a ragdoll.

"Stop it, Runner, set me down, stop it." We knocked over two flashlights, which went cartwheeling, their rays bouncing everywhere. Like those flashlights that hunted me on that night.

"Say uncle," Runner giggled.

"Put me down." He spun harder. My breasts were smashed up to my neck, my armpits aching from the strain of Runner's grip.

"Say uncle."

"Uncle!" I screamed, my eyes squeezed in fury.

Runner released me. Like being thrown from a swing, I was suddenly weightless in the air, soaring forward. I landed on my feet and took three big steps til I hit the side of the tank. A big metallic thunder boomed up. I rubbed my shoulder.

"Man, my kids always were the biggest babies!" Runner panted, both his hands on his knees. He leaned back and cracked his neck loudly. "Pass me one of them beers, sweetheart."

That's how Runner had always been—crazy, then not, and expecting you to pretend whatever indignity he'd just inflicted on you never happened. I stood with my arms crossed, made no move for the beer.

"Goddamit, Debby, er Libby, what you're women's lib now? Help your old man out."

"Do you know why I'm here, Runner?" I asked.

"Nah." He walked over and grabbed himself a beer, shot me an eyebrow-y look that made his entire forehead disappear into folds. I had assumed he'd be more shocked to see me, but Runner had long ago pickled the part of his brain capable of surprise. His days were so baggy and pointless, anything could happen in them, so why not a visit from a daughter after half a decade?

"How long it's been since I seen you, little girl? You get that flamingo ashtray I sent you?" The flamingo ashtray I got more than two decades ago, when I was a nonsmoking ten-year-old.

"Do you remember the letter you wrote me, Runner?" I asked. "About Ben? About how you know he wasn't the one who . . . did it."

"Ben? Why would I write to that jagoff? He's a bad-un. You know, that wasn't me that raised him, that was all his mom. He was born weird and he stayed weird. If he'd been an animal, he'd of been the runt of the litter and we'd of put him down."

"Do you remember the letter you wrote *me,* just a few days ago. You said you were dying and you wanted to tell the truth about what happened that night."

"I sometimes wonder if he was even mine, like if he was even my kid. I always felt kinda like a sucker, raising him. Like people were probably laughing about it when I wasn't around. Because thaint nothing about him that reminds me of me. He was 100 percent your mother's boy. Momma's boy."

"In the letter—remember the letter, Runner, just a few days ago—you said you knew it wasn't Ben that did it. Did you know, even, that Peggy is taking back your alibi? Your old girlfriend, Peggy?"

Runner took a deep pull off the beer, winced. He looped one thumb over the pocket of his jeans and gave an angry laugh.

"Yeah I wrote you a letter. Forgot about that. Yeah, I'm dying, got scoli . . . what's it with the liver when it goes bad?"

"Cirrhosis?"

"Right, got that. Plus something wrong with my lungs. They say I'll be dead within the year. Knew I should have married someone with health insurance. Peggy had some, she was always going to get her teeth cleaned, get *prescriptions.*" He said it like she was dining on caviar, *prescriptions.*

"You should always get health insurance, Libby. Very important. You ain't shit without it." He studied the back of his hand, then blinked. "So I wrote you a letter. A few things need to be put to rest. Lot of shit went down that day of the murders, Libby. I've thought about it a lot, it's tormented me. That was a bad damn day. Like, a cursed day. A cursed Day," he added, pointing at his chest. "But man, there was so much fingerpointing going on then—they'd put anyone in jail. I couldn't come forward like I wish I could have. Just wouldn't have been smart."

He said it like it was a simple business decision, then he burped quietly. I pictured grabbing the tin pot and smashing it across his face.

"Well, you can talk now. What happened, Runner? Tell me what happened. Ben's been in prison now for decades, so if you know something, say it now."

"What, and then I go to jail?" He gave an indignant grunt and sat down on his beach towel, blowing his nose on one corner. "It's not like your brother was some babe in the woods. Your brother was into witchcraft, Devil shit. You hang around with the Devil, sooner or later you're gonna have to fuck . . . shoulda known it when I saw him with Trey Teepano, that fucking . . . fucker."

Trey Teepano, the name that kept coming up but went nowhere. "What did Trey Teepano do?"

Runner broke into a grin, one cracked tooth leering over his bottom lip. "Boy, people do not know shit about what went on that night. It's hilarious."

"It's not hilarious. My mom is dead, my brother is in prison. Your kids are dead, Runner."

He cocked his head at that, stared up at a moon as curvy as a wrench.

"You're not dead," he said.

"Michelle and Debby are dead. Patty is dead."

"But why aren't you, don't you ever wonder?" he spat out a jelly of blood. "Seems weird."

"What's Trey Teepano got to do with it?" I repeated.

"Do I get some reward money or something if I talk?"

"I'm sure, yeah."

"I'm not innocent, not entirely, but neither's your brother, neither's Trey."

"What did you do, Runner?"

"Who ended up with all the money? Wasn't me."

"What money, we had no money."

"Your mom had money. Your queen bitch mom had money, believe me."

He was standing now, glaring at me, his oversized pupils eclipsing his irises, making his blue eyes look like solar flares. He tilted his head again, in a twitchy, beastlike way and started walking toward me. He held his palms outward, as if to show he wasn't going to hurt me, which just made me feel like he would.

"Where'd all that money go, Libby, from Patty's life insurance? That's another mystery for you to think on. Because I sure as shit don't have it."

"No one got money, Runner, it all went to defend Ben."

Runner was standing right on top of me now, trying to scare me the way he did when I was little. He was a small man, but still had a good six inches on me, and he breathed on me hard, his breath all warm, tinny beer.

"What happened, Runner?"

"Your mom, always keeping money to herself, never ever helping me, and I put years in on that farm, never seen a dime. Well, the chickens came home to roost. And your goddam mom brought it on herself. If she'd given me that money . . ."

"You were asking her for money that day?"

"All my life, I owed people money," he said. "All my life, never able to get ahead, always owing. You got any money, Libby? Hell yeah you do, you wrote that book, didn'tcha? So you're not really innocent either. Give me some money, Libby. Give your old man a little cash. I'll buy me a liver on the black market, then I'll testify to whatever you want. Whatever baby wants." He poked me with two fingers in the middle of my chest, and I began slowly trying to back up.

"If you were any part of that night, that will be found out, Runner."

"Well, nothing was found out back then, why should anything be found out now. You think the cops, the lawyers, everyone involved in that case, everyone who got famous from that case"—he pointed at me now, his lower lip jutting out—"You think they're just gonna, what, ooops, our mistake, here you go, Benny boy, go ahead and enjoy your life. Nah. Whatever happened, he's in there the rest of his life."

"Not if you tell the truth."

"You're just like your mother, you know, so . . . cunt. Never go with the flow, always do things the hard way. If she'd just helped me once, in all those years, but she was such a bitch. I'm not saying she deserved to die . . ." he laughed, bit a hangnail . . . "but man, was she a hard woman. And she raised a goddam child molester. Sick fuck. Never, ever was that kid a man. Oh, and you tell Peggy she can suck my dick too."

I turned to go at that, and realized I couldn't get back up without Runner's help. I faced him again.

"Little baby Ben, you really think he did those killings by hisself? Ben?"

"So who was there, Runner? What are you trying to say?"

"I'm saying Trey, he needed money, he was a bookie who needed to be paid."

"By you?"

"I'm not going to cast inpersions right now, but he was a bookie. And that night he was with Ben. How do you think he got into that shit-ass house?"

"If that's what you think happened, if you think Trey Teepano killed our family, you need to testify to that," I interrupted. "If that's the truth."

"Wow, you know nothing." He grabbed me by the arm. "You expect everything, want everything for free, one big handout, me risking my neck for . . . I told you to bring money. I told you."

I slipped his grasp, grabbed the mini-fridge and began dragging it over below the ladder, the thing rattling loud enough to drown out Runner. I climbed up on it, and my fingers were still several inches short of the top of the tank.

"Give me fifty bucks and I'll get you up," Runner said, assessing me lazily. I stretched to grab the edge, up on my tiptoes, straining, and then I could feel the fridge tilt beneath me, and I fell to the ground fast, hitting my jaw, biting the side of my tongue, my eyes watering from the pain. Runner laughed. "Jesus, what a mess," he said looking down at me. "You scared a' me, little girl?"

I skittered behind the fridge, keeping my eyes on him as I looked for things to pile on it, climb out.

"I don't kill girls," he said, out of nowhere. "I wouldn't kill little girls." And then his eyes brightened up. "Hey, did they ever find Dierdre?"

I knew the name, knew what he was trying to say.

"Diondra?"

"Yeah, Di-on-dra!"

"What do you know about Diondra?"

"I always wondered if they killed her that night, you never saw her after that night."

"Ben's . . . girlfriend," I prompted.

"Yeah, right, I guess. Last time I saw her, it was with Ben and Trey and I sort of hope she just run away. I like the idea of being a granddaddy sometimes."

"What are you talking about?"

"Ben'd got her pregnant. Or that's what he said. Made a big deal out of it, like it's hard to do. So I saw her that night and then she never showed up again. I worried she might be dead. In't that's what they do, Devil worshipers—kill pregnant ladies and their babies? She sure did disappear."

"And you didn't say anything to the police?"

"Well, how's that my business?"

Patty Day

The house had gone silent for a few beats after Runner sped away, finding someone else to bully for money. Peggy Bannion, she was his girlfriend now, Patty'd heard—why doesn't he go harass her? Probably already had.

One beat, two beats, three beats. Then the girls had turned into a mess of questions and worries and small hands everywhere on her, as if they were trying to get warm by a really weak campfire. Runner was scary this time. He'd always had a bit of menace to him, he'd always been temperful when he didn't get his own way, but this was the closest he'd come to attacking her. For the most part. When they'd been married, there'd been tussles, little slaps upside the head, designed more to infuriate, to remind you of your helplessness, than to really hurt. *Why is there no food in the fridge?* Smack. *Why is this place such a shithole?* Smack. *Where does all the money go, Patty?* Smack, smack, smack. *You listening to me, girl? What the hell you do with all the money?* The man was obsessed with cash. Even in a rare fatherly moment, grudgingly playing Monopoly with the kids, he'd spend most of his time sneaking money out from the Bank, clutching the bright orange and purple bills in his lap. *You calling me a cheat?* Smack. *You saying your old man's a cheat, Ben?* Smack, smack, smack. *You think you're smarter'n me?* Smack.

Now nearly an hour after Runner had left, the girls were still huddled on her, near her, behind her, all over the sofa asking her what was wrong, what was wrong with Ben, why was Dad so mad. Why'd she make Dad mad? Libby sat the farthest from her, tucked in a bundle, sucking a finger, her worried brain stuck on the visit to the Cates's house, the cop. She looked feverish, and when Patty reached out to touch her cheek, she flinched.

"It's OK, Libby."

"No it's not," she said, unblinking eyes fixed on Patty. "I want Ben back."

"He'll come back," Patty said.

"How do you knoooooww?" Libby whimpered.

Debby hopped on that. "Do you know where he is? Why can't we find him? Is he in trouble because of his hair?"

"I know why he's in trouble," Michelle said in her most wheedling voice. "Because of sex."

Patty turned on her, furious at that simpering, gossipy rhythm. A hair-in-curlers, whisper-in-the-supermarket tone. People were using that tone to discuss her family all over Kinnakee right now. She grabbed Michelle by the arm, harder than she meant to.

"What do you mean, Michelle, what do you think you know?"

"Nothing, Mom, nothing," Michelle blurted. "I was just saying, I don't know." She started to blubber, as Michelle did when she got in trouble and knew she'd done wrong.

"Ben is your brother, you don't talk hateful about your brother. Not inside this family and definitely not out of it. That means, church, school, whatever."

"But Mom . . ." started Michelle, still crying. "I don't like Ben."

"Don't say that."

"He's bad, he does bad things, everyone at school knows . . ."

"Knows what, Michelle?" She felt her forehead start burning, wished Diane were there. "I don't understand what you're saying. Has Ben, are you saying Ben has done anything . . . bad . . . to you?"

She had promised herself she would never ask this question, that it was a betrayal of Ben to even think it. When Ben had been younger, seven or eight, he'd taken to sliding into her bed at night, and she'd wake up with him running fingers through her hair, cupping a breast. Innocent but disturbing moments in which she woke up feeling sensual, excited, and then darted from the bed, pulling robes and nightgowns around her like a horrified maiden. *No, no, no you don't touch Mom like that.* But she never suspected—until now— that Ben might have done anything to his sisters. So she let the question hang, while Michelle got more and more agitated, pushing her big glasses up and down her pointy nose, crying.

"Michelle, I'm sorry I yelled at you. Ben is in trouble. Now, has he done anything to you I need to know about?" Her nerves were jagged: she had moments of pure panic, followed by moods of complete remoteness. She could feel the fear rising now, that propulsion, like taking off in an airplane.

"Done what to me?"

"Has he touched you in a strange way. A not brotherly way?" A free-floating gap now, like the engines shutting off.

"The only time he touches me is when he's pushing me or pulling my hair or shoving me," Michelle droned, her usual litany.

Relief, oh, relief.

"So what do people say about him at school?"

"He's a freak, it's embarrassing. No one likes him. I mean, just look in his room, Mom. He's got all sorts of weird stuff."

She was about to lecture Michelle on not going into Ben's room without his permission, and wanted to slap herself. She thought about what Det. Collins had said, the organs of animals, in Tupperware containers. She imagined them. Some dried in tight, wooden balls, others fresh and assaulting when you opened the lid, let the smell hit you.

Patty stood up. "What's in his room?"

She started walking down the hall, Ben's goddang phone cord tripping her up, as always. She marched past his padlocked door, down the hall, turned the corner left, past the girls' room and into her own. Socks and shoes and jeans lay everywhere, each day's flotsam abandoned in piles.

She opened her bedside table and found an envelope, In Case of Emergency scrawled on the front in Diane's elongated cursive that looked just like their mother's. Inside was $520, cash. She had no idea when Diane had sneaked that in her room, and she was glad she hadn't known, because Runner would have sensed her holding out. She lifted the money to her nose and smelled it. Then she tucked the envelope back inside and pulled out a bolt-cutter she'd bought weeks ago, just to have on hand, just if she ever needed to get into Ben's lair. She'd been ashamed. She started back down the hallway, the girls' room looking like a flophouse, beds against each wall except the doorway. She could picture the police wrinkling their noses—*they all sleep in here?*—and then the aroma of urine hit her and she realized one of them must have wet the bed last night. Or the night before?

She debated switching out the sheets right then, but made herself walk straight back to Ben's, stood eye-level with an old Fender Guitar sticker he'd partly scraped off. She had a quick moment of nausea when she almost decided she couldn't look. What if she found incriminating photos, sickening Polaroids?

Snap. The lock fell to the carpet. She yelled at the girls, peeking out from the living room like startled deer, to go watch TV. She had to say it three times—*gowatchTVgowatchTVgowatchTV*—before Michelle finally went away.

Ben's bed was unmade, rumpled under a pile of jackets and jeans and sweaters, but the rest of the room wasn't a pit. His desk was piled with notebooks and cassette tapes and an outdated globe that had been Diane's. Patty spun it, her finger leaving a mark in the dust near Rhodesia, then began flipping through the notebooks. They were covered in band logos: AC/DC with the lightning slash, Venom, Iron Maiden. On the notebook paper, Ben had drawn pentagrams and poems about murder and Satan.

> *The child is mine*
> *But really not*
> *Cuz Satan has a darker plot*
> *Kill the baby and its mother*
> *Then look for more*
> *And kill another*

She felt a ripple of illness, as if a vein running from her throat to her pelvis had gone sour. She riffled through more notebooks, and as she shook the last one, it flipped naturally to the middle. For pages and pages, Ben had drawn ballpoint pictures of vaginas with hands going into them, uteruses with creatures inside, grinning demonically, pregnant ladies sliced in two, their babies half falling out.

Patty sat down on Ben's chair, feeling giddy, but she kept flipping until she came to a page with several girls' names written in pancake-stack rows: Heather, Amanda, Brianne, Danielle, Nicole, and then over and over, in progressively embellished gothic cursive: Krissi, Chrissy, Krissi, Krissie, Krissi, Krissi Day, Krissi Day, Krissi Dee Day Krissi D. Day, Krissi D-Day!

Krissi Day inside a heart.

Patty rested her head on the cool desktop. Krissi Day. Like he was going to marry little Krissi Cates. Ben and Krissi Day. Is that what he thought? Did that make what he did to her seem OK? Did he picture himself bringing that little girl home for dinner, letting Mom meet his girlfriend? And Heather. That was the name of the Hinkel girl who was at the Cates's. Were the rest of these names even more girls he'd hurt?

Patty's head was heavy, she willed herself not to move. She would just keep her head right here, on the desk, until someone told her what to do. She was good at this, she sometimes sat for hours without leaving a chair, her head bobbing like a nursing-home inmate, thinking about her childhood, when her parents had their list of chores for her, and told her when to go to bed and when to get up and what to do during the day, and no one ever asked her to decide things. But as she was staring at the rumpled sheets on Ben's bed, with the airplane pattern, and remembering him asking for new sheets—*plain* sheets—about a year ago, she notice a wadded plastic bag jutting out from underneath the bed frame.

She got down on her hands and knees, pulled out an old plastic shopping bag. It had a weight to it, swung out like a pendulum. She peered in and saw only clothing, and then she realized she was looking at girly patterns: flowers and hearts, mushrooms and rainbows. She dumped them out in a pile on the floor, afraid even as she was doing it that that those Polaroids she feared would tumble out with them. But it was just clothes: underwear, undershirts, bloomers. They were all different sizes, from Krissi's age to toddler. They were used. As in, they had been worn by little girls. Just like the detective had said. Patty put them back in the bag.

Her son. Her son. He would go to prison. The farm would be gone, Ben would be in jail, and the girls . . . She realized, as she too often did, that she didn't know how to function properly. Ben needed a good lawyer, and she didn't know how to do that.

She walked into the living room, thinking about a trial and how she couldn't bear it. She scattered the girls back to their bedroom in a fierce voice, them staring back at her with open mouths, hurt and scared, and she thought about how she made things even worse for Ben, a single mother who was incompetent, overwhelmed, how much worse it made him look, and she put some kindling and newspapers in the fireplace, and just a few logs on top, and she set fire to the clothes. A pair of underpants with daisies on them was just catching at the waistband when the phone rang.

IT WAS LEN the Lender. She started to make her excuses, explain that there was too much going on to talk about the foreclosure. There was a problem with her son—

"That's why I phoned," he interrupted. "I heard about Ben. I hadn't been going to phone. Before. But. I think I can help. I don't know if you'll want it. But I have an option."

"An option for Ben?"

"A way to help Ben. With legal costs. What you're facing, you're going to need a bundle."

"I thought we were out of options," Patty said.

"Not entirely."

LEN WOULDN'T COME out to the farm, he wouldn't meet her in town. He got all clandestine on her, insisting she drive out to the Rural Route 5 picnic station and park. They haggled and bickered, Len finally breathing a big huff into the phone that made her lips twist. "If you want some help, come out there, now. Don't bring no one else. Don't tell no one. I'm doing this because I think I can trust you, Patty, and I like you. I really want to help you." A pause came on, so deep Patty looked at the phone receiver, and whispered *Len?* into the phone, already thinking he was gone, that she was about to hang up.

"Patty, I really don't know how to help you but this. I think, well, you'll see. I'm praying for you."

She turned back to the fireplace, sifted through the flames, saw only half the clothes were burned. No logs left, so she hurried into the garage, grabbed her dad's old axe with its heavy head and razor-sharp blade—back when they made tools right—and chopped up a bundle of wood, carried it all back in.

She was feeding it to the fire when she felt Michelle's swaying presence at her side. "Mom!"

"What, Michelle."

She looked up and Michelle was in her nightgown pointing at the fire. "You were about to throw the axe in with the wood." Michelle smiled. "Scatterbrain." There was the axe laid across Patty's arms like kindling. Michelle took it from her, holding the blade away from her, as she'd been taught, and set it beside the door.

She watched Michelle walk hesitantly back to her room, as if she were picking through grass, and Patty followed in her daughter's footsteps. The girls were all piled on the floor, murmuring to their dolls. There was that joke people told, that they loved their children most when they were sleeping, hah-hah, and Patty felt a small stab. She really did like them best when they were sleeping, not asking any questions, not needing food or amusement, and she liked them second best when they were like this: tired, calm, disinterested in their mother. She put Michelle in charge and left them there, too worn out to do anything but take direction from Len the Lender.

Don't hope for too much, she told herself. Don't hope.

It was a half-hour drive through bright snow, the flakes turning to stars in her headlights. It was a "good snow," as Patty's mom, the winter lover, would say, and Patty thought how the girls would be playing in it all day tomorrow and then thought: Would they? What happens tomorrow? Where will Ben be?

Where is Ben?

She pulled up to the abandoned picnic area, the shelter a big slab of concrete and metal built in the '70s with communal tables and a roof that was angled like some failed attempt at origami. Two swingsets sat beneath four inches of snow, their old black-rubber seats not swaying at all, as Patty thought they should. There was a breeze, why were they so still?

Len's car wasn't there. In fact, no car was there, and she started to fidget with the zipper of her coat, running a fingernail on each metal tooth so it made a clicking noise. What might happen: She would go up to the picnic bench and find Len had left her an envelope with a stack of money, a gentlemanly gesture she would repay. Or maybe Len had organized a bunch of folks who felt pity on her, and they were about to arrive and Wonderful Life her with cash handouts, Patty realizing everyone did love her after all.

A rap came on her window, bright pink knuckles and a man's thick torso. It wasn't Len. She rolled her window partway down and peered out, ready for him to tell her to move along, lady. It was that kind of rap.

"Come on," he said instead. He didn't lean down, she still couldn't see his face. "Come on, we'll talk up on the benches."

She shut off the car, and pulled herself out, the man already walking up ahead, bundled under a thick ranch coat and a Stetson. She was wearing a wool hat that had never fit right, her ears always popped out, so she was already rubbing at the tips when she reached the man.

He seemed nice, was what she thought. She needed him to be nice. He had dark eyes and a handlebar mustache, the tips drooping off his chin. He was probably forty, looked like he might come from around here. He looked nice, she thought again. They settled down on the picnic benches, pretending they weren't covered in snow. Maybe he was a lawyer? she thought. A lawyer Len had talked into representing Ben. But then why would they be meeting out—

"Hear you got yourself some trouble," he said in a rumbly voice that matched his eyes. Patty just nodded.

"About to foreclose on your farm, and your boy's about to be arrested."

"The police just want to talk to him about an incident that—"

"Your son is about to be arrested, and I know what for. In this next year, you will need money to fend off your creditors, so you can keep your children at home—in their own goddam home—and you will need money for a lawyer for your son, because you do not want your son to go to prison labeled a child molester."

"Of course not but Ben—"

"No, I mean: You do not want *your* son to go *to prison* labeled a *child molester.* There is nothing worse you can be in prison than a child molester. I seen it. What they do to those men, a nightmare. So you need a very good lawyer, which costs a lot of money. You need one right now, not weeks from now, not days from now. Right now. These things get out of control fast."

Patty nodded, waiting. The man's speech reminded her of being with a car salesman: you had to do it now, and this model and at this price. She always lost these conversations, always took what the salesman insisted she take.

The man pressed his Stetson down, breathed out like a bull.

"Now I myself was once a farmer, and my daddy before me and his daddy before him. Eight hundred acres, cattle, corn, wheat, out-side Robnett, Missouri. Fair amount, like your operation."

"We never had eight hundred acres."

"But you had a family farm, you had your goddam land. It's your goddam land. We been swindled, farmers. They say 'plant fencepost to fencepost!' and we goddam well did. Buy more land—they say—cause they ain't making more of it! Then whoops, sorry, we gave you some bad advice. We'll just take your farm, this place been in your family for generations, we'll just take this, no hard feelings. You're the jackass believed us, not really our fault."

Patty had heard this before, thought it before. It was a raw deal. Let's get back to my son. She leaned on one haunch and shivered, tried to seem patient.

"Now I'm no businessman, I'm no accountant, I'm no politician. But I can help, if you're interested."

"Yes, yes I'd like that," she said. "Please."

And in her head she told herself, Don't hope, don't hope for too much.

Libby Day

I drove back home through sickly forests. Somewhere down one of those long stringy roads was a landfill. I never saw the dump itself, but I drove through a good twenty miles of float-away trash. To my right and left, the ground flickered with a thousand plastic grocery bags, fluttering and hovering just above the grass. Looking like the ghosts of little things.

Rain started splattering, then got thicker, freezing. Everything outside my car looked warped. Whenever I saw a lonely place—a dimple in the landscape, a copse of whiskery trees—I pictured Diondra buried beneath, a collection of unclaimed bones and bits of plastic: a watch, the sole of a shoe, maybe the red dangly earrings she wore in the yearbook photo.

Who gives a tinker's damn about Diondra? I thought, Diane's phrases again popping into my head. Who cares if Ben killed her, because he killed your family, and it all ends there anyway.

I'd wanted so badly for Runner to give something up, make me believe he did it. But seeing him only reminded me how impossible it was that he killed them all, how dumb he was. *Dumb,* it was a word you used as a kid, but it was the best way to describe Runner. Wily and dumb at the same time. Magda and the Kill Club would be disappointed, although I'd be happy to give them his address if they wanted to continue the conversation. Me, I hoped he'd die soon.

I passed a thick, flat brown-earth field, a teenage boy leaning against a fence in the rain, in the dark, sulky or bored, staring out at the highway. My brain returned to Ben. Diondra and Ben. Pregnant. Everything else Ben told me about that night felt right, believable, but the lie, the insistent lie about Diondra. That seemed like something to worry about.

I sped home, feeling contaminated. I went straight to the shower and scrubbed myself, Silkwood-style with a hard nail brush, my skin looking like I'd been attacked by a pack of cats when I was done. I got into bed still feeling infected, fussed around in the sheets for an hour, then got up and showered again. Around 2 a.m., I fell into a sweaty, heavy sleep filled with leering old men I thought were my father until I got close enough to see their faces melt. More potent nightmares followed: Michelle was cooking pancakes, and grasshoppers were floating in the batter, their twig legs snapping off as Michelle stirred. They got cooked into the pancakes, and my mom made us eat them anyway, good protein, crunch, crackle. Then we all started dying— choking, slobbering, eyes floating back in our heads—because the grasshoppers were poisoned. I swallowed one of the big insects and felt it fight its way back up my throat, its sticky body surfacing in my mouth, squirting my tongue with tobacco, pushing its head against my teeth to escape.

The morning dawned an unimpressive gray. I showered again— my skin still feeling suspicious—and then drove to the downtown public library, a white pillared building that used to be a bank. I sat next to a pungent man with a matted beard and a stained army jacket, the guy I always end up next to in public places, and finally got on the Internet. I found the massive, sad Missing Persons database and entered her name.

The screen made its churning, thinking sound and I sweated while hoping a No Data screen would come up. No such luck. The photo was different from the yearbook but not too: Diondra with the mousse-hard curls and the cresting bangs, charcoal eyeliner and pink lipgloss. She was smiling just the tiniest bit, pouting her lips out.

DIONDRA SUE WERTZNER
BORN: OCTOBER 28, 1967
REPORTED MISSING: JANUARY 21, 1985

BEN WAS WAITING for me again, this time with his arms crossed, leaned back in the chair, belligerent. He'd given me the silent treatment a week before granting my request to see him. Now he shook his head at me when I sat down.

It threw me off.

"You know, Libby, I've been thinking since we talked last," he finally said. "I've been thinking I don't need this, this pain. I mean, I'm already in here, I don't really need my little sister to show up, believe in me, don't believe in me. Ask me weird questions, put me on the guard after goddam twenty-four years. I don't need the tension. So if you're coming here, trying to 'get to the bottom of things,'" he made angry air quotes, "you know, go somewhere else. Because I just don't need it."

"I found Runner."

He didn't stand up, he stayed solid in his chair. Then he gave a sigh, a might-as-well sigh.

"Wow, Libby, you missed your calling as a detective. What'd Runner have to say? He still in Oklahoma?"

I felt an inappropriate twitch of a smile. "He's at a Superfund dump on the edge of Lidgerwood, got turned out from the group home."

Ben grinned at that. "He's living in a toxic waste dump. Ha."

"He says Diondra Wertzner was your girlfriend, that you got her pregnant. That she was pregnant and you two were together, the night of the murders."

Ben put a hand over his face, his fingers splayed. I could see his eyes blink through them. He talked with his face still covered, and I couldn't hear what he said. He tried twice, me asking each time what he was saying, and on the third try he pulled his head up, chewing on the inside of his cheek, and leaned in.

"I said, what the fuck is your obsession with Diondra? You got a goddam bee in your bonnet about this, and you know what's going to happen, you're going to fuck all this up. You had a chance to believe in me, to do the right thing and finally believe in your brother. Who you *know*. Don't say you don't because that's a lie. I mean, don't you get it, Libby? It's the last chance for us. The world can believe I'm guilty, believe I'm innocent, we both know I'm not going anywhere. There's no DNA going to release me—there's no goddam *house* anymore. So. I'm not getting out. So. The only person I care, to say they know I couldn't have *murdered* my *family*, is you."

"You can't blame me for wondering whether—"

"Of course I can. Of course I can. I can blame you for not believing in me. Now, I can forgive you for your lie, for getting confused, as a kid. I can forgive that. But goddamit, Libby, what about now? You're what, thirty-some years old, and still believe your own blood could do something like that?"

"Oh I totally believe my own blood could do that," I said, my anger surging up, bumping against my ribs. "I totally believe our blood is bad. I feel it in me. I've beaten the shit out of people, Ben. Me. I've busted in doors and windows and . . . I've killed things. Half the time I look down, my hands are in fists."

"You believe we're that bad?"

"I do."

"Even with Mom's blood?"

"Even with."

"Well, I'm sad for you, little girl."

"Where is Diondra?"

"Let it go, Libby."

"What'd you do with the baby?"

I felt queasy, fevered. If the baby had lived, it'd be (he'd be, she'd be), what, twenty-four years old. The baby wasn't a baby anymore. I tried to picture an adult, but my brain kept bouncing back an image of a blanket-swaddled infant. But hell, I could barely picture *me* as an adult. My next birthday I'll be thirty-two, my mom's age when she was killed. She'd seemed so grown up. More grown up than I'd ever be.

So if it was alive, the baby was twenty-four. I had one of my awful visions. A might-have-been vision. Us, if everyone had lived, at home in Kinnakee. There's Michelle in the living room, still fiddling with her oversized glasses, bossing around a bundle of kids who roll their eyes at her but do what they're told. Debby, chubby and chattery with a big, blond farmer-husband and a special room in her own farmhouse for crafts, packed with sewing ribbons and quilting patches and glue guns. My mom, ripe-fifties and sunbaggy, her hair mostly white, still bickering pleasantly with Diane. And into the room comes Ben's kid, a daughter, a redhead, a girl in her twenties, thin and assured, bangly bracelets on delicate wrists, a college graduate who doesn't take any of us seriously. A Day girl.

I choked on my own spit, started coughing, my windpipe shut down. The visitor two booths down from me leaned out to look and then, deciding I wasn't going to die, went back to her son.

"What happened that night, Ben? I need to know. I just need to know."

"Libby, you can't win this game. I tell you I'm innocent, that means you're guilty, you ruined my life. I tell you I'm guilty . . . I don't think that makes you feel much better, does it?"

He was right. It was one reason I'd stayed immobile for so many years. I threw something else out: "And what about Trey Teepano?"

"Trey Teepano."

"I know he was a bookie, and that he was into Devil shit, and that he was a friend of yours, and he was with you that night. With Diondra. That all seems pretty fucked up."

"Where'd you get all that?" Ben looked me in the eye, then raised his gaze up, gave a long stare at my red roots that were to my ears now.

"Dad told me. He said he owed Trey Teepano money and—"

"Dad? He's *Dad* now?"

"Runner said—"

"Runner said fuck-all. You need to grow up, Libby. You need to pick a side. You can spend the rest of your life trying to figure out what happened, trying to reason. Or you can just trust yourself. Pick a side. Be on mine. It's better."

Ben Day

They drove out past the edge of town, the road going from ce-ment to dirt, Ben rattling around in the backseat, hands pressed up against the top of the truck, trying to stay in place. He was stoned, real stoned, and his teeth and head rattled. *You got a screw loose?* He had two or three loose. He wanted to sleep. Eat first, then sleep. He watched the lights of Kinnakee fade away and then it was miles of glowing blue snow, a patch of grass here, a jagged scar of fence there, but mostly snow like the surface of the moon. Like he really was in outer space, on another planet, and he wasn't going home, ever.

They turned down some road, trees sucking them in, tunnel-like on all sides and he realized he had no idea where they were. He just hoped whatever was about to happen was over soon. He wanted a hamburger. His mom made crazy hamburgers, called them kitchen-sinkers, fattened up cheap ground meat with onions and macaroni and whatever else crap was about to go bad. One time he swore he found part of a banana, glopped over with ketchup—his mom thought ketchup made everything OK. It didn't, her cooking sucked, but he'd eat one of those hamburgers right now. He was thinking *I'm so hungry I could eat a cow.* And then, as if his food-prayer worked, he refocused his eyes from a gritty stain on the backseat to the outside and there were ten or twenty Herefords standing in the snow for no reason. There was a barn nearby but no sign of a house, and the cows were too dumb to walk back into the barn, so they stood like a bunch of fat assholes, blowing steam from their nostrils. Herefords were the ugliest cows around, giant, rusty, with white crinkled faces and pink-rimmed eyes. Jersey cows were sort of sweet looking, they had those big deer faces, but Herefords looked prehistoric, belligerent, mean. The things had furry thick waddles and curvy-sharp horns and when Trey pulled to a stop, Ben felt a flurry of nerves. Something bad was going to happen.

"We're here," Trey said as they sat in the car, the heater turned off, the cold creeping in. "All out." Trey reached over Diondra into the glove compartment—here grazing Diondra's baby belly, them both giving weird smiles again—grabbed a cassette and popped it in the deck. The frenetic, zigzag music started scribbling on Ben's brain.

"Come on, Ben," Trey said, crunching down on the snow. He pulled up the driver's seat to let Ben out, and Ben stumbled to the ground, missing the step, Trey grabbing hold of him. "Time for you to get some understanding, feel some power. You're a dad soon, dude." Trey shook him by both shoulders. "A dad!" His voice sounded friendly enough but he didn't smile. He just stared with his lips tight and his eyes red-rimmed, almost bloody. Deciding. He had a deciding look. Then Trey let go, cuffed his jean jacket, and went around to the back of the truck. Ben tried to see across the hood, catch Diondra's eyes, flash her a whatthefuck look, but she was leaning down into the cab, pulling another baggie out from under her seat, groaning with one hand on her belly, like it was really hard to bend down half a foot. She came back up, hand crooked on her back now and began digging around in the baggie. It was filled with foil gum wrappers and she pulled three out.

"Give it," Trey said, stuck two in his pocket and unwrapped the third. "You and Ben can share."

"I don't want to share," Diondra whined. "I feel like shit, I need a whole one."

Trey gave a frustrated sigh, then shot one packet out at her, muttering *Jesus Christ*.

"What is that stuff?" Ben finally asked. He could feel that warm trickle on his head, knew he was bleeding again. His headache was worse too, throbbing behind his left eye, down his neck and into his shoulder, like an infection moving through his system. He rubbed at his neck, it felt like someone had tied a garden hose in knots and planted it under his skin.

"It's Devil rush, dude, ever had it?" Trey poured the powdery stuff into one palm and leaned into it like a horse to sugar, then made a shotgun of a snort, threw his head back, stumbled a few steps backward, then looked at them like they had no business being there. A ring of deep orange covered his nose and mouth.

"The fuck you looking at, Ben Day?"

Trey's pupils jittered back and forth like he was following an invisible hummingbird. Diondra sucked up hers in the same greedy, animal snort, then fell straight to her knees laughing. It was a laugh of joy for three seconds, and then it turned into a wet, choking laugh, the kind you give when you just can't believe your shitty luck, that kind of laugh. She was crying and cackling, lowering herself onto the snow, laughing on her hands and knees and then she was throwing up, nacho cheese and thick strings of spaghetti that almost smelled good in their sweet vomit sauce. Diondra still had a string of spaghetti hanging out of her mouth when she looked up. The strand hung there for a second, before she realized, then she pulled it out, Ben picturing the noodle still half down her throat, tickling its way up. She flung it to the ground still crying on all fours—and as she looked at it, she started in on that scrunched-face baby-bawl his sisters did when they got hurt. The end-of-the-world cry.

"Diondra, you OK, ba-?" he started.

She lurched forward and threw the rest up near Ben's feet. He got out of the way of the spatter and stood, watching Diondra on all fours, weeping.

"My daddy's going to kill me!" she wailed again, sweat wetting the roots of her hair. Her face twisted as she glared down at her belly. "He will *kill* me."

Trey was only looking at Ben, tuning Diondra out entirely, and he made a gesture with a single finger, a flick that meant Ben should stop stalling and take the Devil rush. He put his nose down near it and smelled old erasers and baking soda.

"What is it, like cocaine?"

"Like battery acid for your brain. Pour it in."

"Man I already feel like crap, I don't know if I need this stuff. I'm fucking hungry, man."

"For what's about to happen, you need it. Do it."

Diondra was giggling again, her face white under the beige foundation. A nacho crumble was floating toward Ben's foot on a runny pink stream. He moved. Then turned away from them, toward the watching cows, poured the powder into his palm and let it start to float off on the wind. When it was down to a pile the size of a quarter, he sniffed it, loud and fake as they had, and still only took part of it up his nose.

Which was good, because it shot straight into his brain, harsh as chlorine but with even more sting, and he could picture it crackling out like tree branches, burning the veins in his head. It felt like his whole bloodstream had turned to hot tin, even his wrist bones started to ache. His bowels shifted like a snake waking up, and for a second he thought he might crap himself, but instead he sneezed up some beer, lost his sight and tumbled onto the ground, his head throbbing open, the blood pulsing down his face with each squeeze. He felt like he could run eighty miles an hour, and that he should, that if he stayed where he was, his chest would crack open and some demon would bust out, shake Ben's blood off its wings, crook its head at the idea of being stuck in this world, and fly into the sky, trying to get back to hell. And then as soon as he thought he needed a gun, shoot himself and end this, came a big air bubble of relief that spread through him, soothed his veins, and he realized he'd been holding his breath and started gulping air, and then felt fucking good. Fucking smart to breathe air, that's what it was. He felt he was expanding, turning big, undeniable. Like no matter what he did, it was the right choice, yes sir, sure thing, like he could line up all the skyful of choices he'd need to make in the coming months and he could shoot them down like carnival animals and win something big. Huge. Hurray for Ben, up on everyone's shoulders so the world can fucking cheer.

"What the hell is this stuff?" he asked. His voice sounded solid, like a heavy door with a good swing to it.

Trey ignored him, glanced at Diondra, pulling herself up from the ground, her fingers red from where she'd buried them in the ice. He seemed to sneer at her without realizing it. Then he fished around in the back of his pickup, swung back around with an axe, glowing as blue as the snow. He handed it out toward Ben, blade first, and Ben let his arms go tight to his sides, *nononno can't make me take it,* like he was a kid being asked to hold a crying newborn, *nononono.*

"Take it."

Ben gripped it, cold in his hands, rusty stains on the point. "Is this blood?"

Trey gave one of his lazy side glances, didn't bother answering.

"Oh, I want the axe!" Diondra squealed. She made a skip over to the truck, Ben wondering if they were fucking with him as usual.

"Too heavy for you, take the hunting knife."

Diondra twisted back and forth in her coat, the fur-trim of the hood bouncing up and down.

"I don't want the knife, too small, give Ben the knife, he hunts."

"Then Ben gets this too," Trey said, and handed him a 10-gauge shotgun.

"Let me have the gun, then, I'll take that," Diondra said.

Trey took her hand, opened it, folded the Bowie inside of it.

"It's sharp so don't fuck around."

But wasn't that just what they were doing, fucking around?

"BenGay, wipe your face, you're dripping blood everywhere."

Axe in one hand, shotgun in the other, Ben wiped his face on his sleeve and came away woozy. More blood kept coming, it was in his hair now, and smeared over one eye. He was freezing and remembered that's what happened when you bled to death, you got cold, and then he realized it would be crazy not to be cold, him in his thin little Diondra jacket, his entire torso prickly with goosepimples.

Trey pulled out a massive pick-axe last, its blade so sharp it looked like an icicle sliver. He slung it over his shoulder, a man going to work. Diondra was still pouting at the knife, and Trey snapped at her.

"You want to say it?" he said. "You want to do it?"

She pulled out of the sulk, nodded briskly, set her knife in the middle of the accidental circle they were standing in. But no, not accidental, because then Trey put his pick-axe next to the Bowie, and motioned for Ben to do the same, gave him this impatient gesture like a parent whose kid has forgotten to say grace. So Ben did, piled the shotgun and the axe on top, that pile of glinting, sharp metal making Ben's heart pound.

Suddenly Diondra and Trey were grabbing his hands, Trey's grip tight and hot, Diondra's limp, sticky, as they stood in a circle around their weapons. The moonlight was making everything glow. Diondra's face looked like a mask, all hollows and hills, and when she thrust her chin up toward the moon, between her open mouth and the pile of metal Ben got a hard-on and didn't care. His brain was sizzling somewhere in the back of his consciousness, his brain was literally frying, and then Diondra was chanting.

"To Satan we bring you sacrifice, we bring you pain, and blood, and fear, and rage, the basis of human life. We honor you, Dark One. In your power, we become more powerful, in your exaltation, we become exalted."

Ben didn't know what the words meant. Diondra prayed all the time. She prayed in church, like normal people, but she also prayed to goddesses, and geodes and crystals and shit. She was always looking for help.

"We're going to make your baby a fucking warrior tonight, Dio," Trey said.

They disbanded then, everyone picking up their weapons, silently marching into the field, the snow making a rubbery sound as they stomped through it, breaking its top crust. Ben's feet felt literally frozen, separate things, unnaturally attached to him. But it didn't really matter, not this, not much of anything mattered, they were in a bubble tonight, nothing had any consequence, and as long as he could stay in the bubble, everything would be OK.

"Which one, Diondra?" Trey said, as they came to a stop. Four

Herefords stood nearby, unmoving in the snow, finding the humans unworrying. Limited imaginations.

Diondra paused, pointed a finger around—a silent eeny-meeny-miny-mo—and then rested on the largest one, a bull with a grotesque, furry dribble of cock slung down toward the snow. Diondra pulled her mouth back in a vampire smile, her canine teeth bared, and Ben waited for a fight-cry, a charge, but instead she just strode. Three long, snow-clumsy strides up to the bull, who took only one step away before she jammed the hunting knife through its throat.

It's happening, Ben thought. Here it is, happening. A sacrifice to Satan.

The bull was leaking blood like oil, dark and thick—glug, glug, and then all of a sudden it twitched, the vein shifted or something, and blood sprayed out, an angry mist, coating them in specks of red, their faces, their clothes, their hair. Diondra was screaming now, finally, as if this first part had been underwater and she burst through suddenly, her cries echoing off the ice. She stabbed at the bull's face, chopped its left eye into a mess, the eye rolling back into its head, slick and blood-black. The bull stumbled in the snow, clumsy and confused, sounding like a sleeper awakened to an emergency— frightened but dull. Blood spatters all over its white curly fur. Trey raised his blade toward the moon, made a whooping cry, slung his chopper hard underhand and buried it in the animal's gut. The thing's hindquarters gave out for a second, then it bucked up, started to trot drunkenly. The other cows had widened the circle around it, like kids at a fight, watching and lowing.

"Get him," Diondra yelled. Trey took big loping hops through the snow, his legs kicked high as if he were dancing, his axe circling through the air. He was singing to Satan, and then mid-lyric, he brought the axe down on the animal's back, breaking its spinal cord, dropping it to the snow. Ben didn't move. To move meant he could partake and he didn't want to, he didn't want to feel that bull's flesh breaking open under him, not because it was wrong but because it might feel too good to him, like the weed, where the first time he took a drag he knew he'd never quit it. Like the smoke found a place inside him that had been left hollow just for the smoke, and had curled up in there. There might be a space too, for this. The feel of killing, there might be an empty spot just waiting to be filled.

"Come on, Ben, don't puss out on us now," Trey called, heaving gulps of air after a third, a fourth, a fifth axe chop.

The bull was on its side, moaning now, a mournful, otherworldy mewing, the way a dinosaur in a tar pit might have sounded—dreadful, dying, stunned.

"Come on, Ben, get your kill. You can't come and just stand," Diondra yelled, making standing sound like the most worthless thing in the world. The bull looked up at her from the ground, and she started stabbing it in the jowls, a quick, efficient jab, her teeth gritted, screaming, "Fucker!" as she stabbed it again and again, one hand on the knife, the other covering her belly.

"Hold off, D," Trey said, and leaned against his axe. "Do it, Ben. Do it or I'll fucking hurt you, man." His eyes still had the druggy glow, and Ben wished he'd taken more of the Devil rush, wished he wasn't jammed in this between state, where he had some logic but no fear.

"This is your chance, dude. Be a man. You got the mother of your child here watching, she's been doing her share. Don't be a scared, dickless boy all your life, letting people push you around, letting people bring up the fear in you. I used to be like you, man, and I don't ever want to go back there again. Shit on. Look how your own dad treated you. Like a limp dick. But you get what you deserve, you know? I think you know that."

Ben breathed frozen air into his lungs, the words seeping under his skin, getting him angrier and angrier. He wasn't a coward.

"Come on, Ben, do it, just go," Diondra needled at him.

The bull was only panting now, blood pouring out of dozens of wounds, a red pond in the snow.

"You need to let the rage out, man, it's the key to power, you're so scared, man, aren't you tired of being scared?"

The bull on the ground was so pathetic now, so quickly undone, that Ben found it disgusting. His hands clenched tighter and tighter around the axe, the thing needing to be killed, put out of its misery, and then he raised the blade over his head, high and heavy, and brought it down on the bull's skull, a shocking crack, a final cry from the animal, and shards of brain and bone shattered outward and then his muscles felt so good stretching and working in his shoulders—man's work—that he brought the axe down again, the skull breaking in half, the bull finally dead now, a last jitter of its two front legs, and then he moved his attention to the midsection, where he could really do damage, up and down, Ben sending bone flying, and bubbly bits of entrails. "Fuck you fuck you fuck you," he was screaming, his shoulders impossibly tight, like they were rubberbanded back, his jaw buzzing, his fists shaking, his cock hard and straining, like his whole body might pop in an orgasm. Swing, batter!

He was about to go for the shotgun when his arms gave out, he was done, the anger leaking from his body, and he didn't feel power at all. He felt embarrassed, the way he felt after he jacked off to a dirty magazine, limp and wrong and foolish.

Diondra busted out laughing. "He's pretty tough when the thing's practically dead," she said.

"I killed it, didn't I?"

They were all panting, spent, their faces covered in blood except where they'd each wiped at their eyes, leaving them peering out, raccoon-style. "You sure this is the guy that got you pregnant, Diondra?" Trey said. "You sure he can get it up? No wonder he's better with little girls."

Ben dropped the axe, started walking toward the car, thinking it was time to go home now, thinking this was his mom's fault, her being such a bitch this morning. If she hadn't freaked out about his hair, he'd be at home tonight, clean and warm under his blanket, the sound of his sisters just outside his door, the TV humming down the hall, his mom dumping out some stew for dinner. Instead he was here, being mocked as usual, having done his best to prove himself and coming up short, as always, the truth finally out. This night would always be here to point at, the night Ben couldn't get his kill.

But now he knew how the violence felt, and he wanted more. In a few days, he'd be thinking about it, the bell rung, can't unring it, and so he'd be thinking about it, obsessing about it, the killing, but he doubted Trey and Diondra would take him out again, and he would be too pitiful, too scared, as always, to do it alone.

He stood with his back to them, then raised the shotgun to his shoulder, swung back around, cocking the hammer, his finger on the trigger. Bam! He imagined the air ringing, the shotgun butting against his shoulder like a friend with a punch, saying good job! And him cracking the gun, popping another shell in, walking deeper into the field, swing that gun back up, and bam!

He pictured his ears ringing and the air smelling smoky, and Trey and Diondra for once saying nothing as he stood in a field of corpses.

Libby Day

Lyle had left nine messages in the days I'd gone Oklahoma-incommunicado, their tone wildly varying: He'd started with some sort of impression of an anxious dowager, I think, talking through a pinched nose, inquiring about my welfare, some comedy bit, then he'd moved on to annoyed, stern, urgent and panicked, before swinging back to goofy on the last message. "If you don't call me back, I'm coming . . . and *hell's* coming with me!" he screamed, then added: "I don't know if you've ever seen *Tombstone*."

I have, but it was a bad Kurt Russell.

I phoned him, gave him my address (an unusual choice for me) told him he could come over if he wanted. In the background I could hear a woman's voice asking who it was, telling Lyle to ask me something—*just ask her, don't be silly, justaskher*—and Lyle trying to scramble off the phone. Maybe Magda, wanting a report on Runner? I'd give it. I wanted to talk, in fact, or I would get in bed and not get out for another ten years.

While I waited, I prepped my hair. I'd bought a dye kit at the grocery store on the way home from seeing Ben. I had planned on grabbing my usual blonde—Platinum Pizazz—but in the end I left with Scarlet Sass, a redhead smiling saucily at me on the box. Less upkeep, yes, I always preferred less upkeep. And I'd been thinking about changing back since Ben remarked how much I looked like my mother, the idea irresistible to me, me somehow thinking I'd show up outside Diane's trailer, looking like Patty Day resurrected, and maybe that would be enough to get me inside. Goddam Diane, not phoning me back.

I packed a crimson glob of chemicals on my head, the smell like something gently burning. Fourteen minutes more to go when the doorbell rang. Lyle. Of course he was early. He rushed in, talking about how relieved he was to hear from me, then pulled back.

"What is that, a perm?"

"I'm going back to red."

"Oh. Good. I mean, it's nice. The natural."

In the thirteen minutes I had left, I told Lyle about Runner, and about Diondra.

"OK," Lyle said, looking to his left, aiming his ear at me, his listening-thinking stance. "So according to Ben, Ben had gone back home, that night, briefly, got in a fight with your mom, and then left again, and he knows nothing after that."

"According to Ben." I nodded.

"And according to Runner, what? Either Trey killed your family because Runner owed him, or Ben and Trey killed your family *and* Diondra in some sort of Devil worship ritual. What'd Runner say about his girlfriend recanting his alibi?"

"He said she could suck his dick. I gotta rinse."

He trailed me to the bathroom, filling the doorway, hands on each side of the frame, thinking.

"Can I say something specific about that night, Libby?"

I was bent over the tub, water dribbling out of the attachable nozzle—no showers in Over There That Way—but I paused.

"I mean, doesn't it seem like it could have been two people? Somehow? Michelle's murder was just—Your mom and Debby were like, uh, hunted down almost. But Michelle dies in her bed, covers pulled up. They have different feels to them. I think."

I gave a small, stiff shrug, the Darkplace images swirling, and stuck my head under the spray, where I couldn't hear anymore. The water started running toward the drain, burgundy. While I was still upside down, I could feel Lyle grab the attachment from me and pat at the back of my head. Clumsy, unromantic, just getting the job done.

"You still had some guck," he yelled over the water, then handed the hose back to me. I rose up, and he reached toward me, grabbed an earlobe and swiped. "Some red stuff on your earlobe too. That probably wouldn't go with earrings."

"My ears aren't pierced," I said, combing out my hair, trying to figure out if the color was right. Trying very hard not to think about my family's corpses, to concentrate just on hair.

"Really? I thought every girl had pierced ears."

"Never had anyone to do them for me."

He watched me brush, a sad-sack smile on his face.

"How's the hair?" he asked.

"We'll find out when it dries."

We sat back down on the soggy living-room couch, each of us at opposite ends, listening to the rain get going again.

"Trey Teepano had an alibi," he finally said.

"Well, Runner had an alibi too. Apparently they're easy to come by."

"Maybe you should go ahead and officially recant your testimony?"

"I'm not recanting anything until I'm sure," I said. "I'm just not."

The rain got harder, made me crave a fireplace.

"You know that the farm went into foreclosure the day of the murders, right?" Lyle said.

I nodded. It was one of forty-thousand new facts I had in my brain, thanks to Lyle and all his files.

"Doesn't that seem like something?" he said. "Doesn't this all seem too weird, like we're missing something obvious? A girl tells a lie, a farm goes under, a gambler's bets are called in by a, jeez, by a Devil-worshiping bookie. All on the same day."

"And every single person in this case lies, is lying, did lie."

"What should we do now?" he asked.

"Watch some TV," I said. I flipped on the TV, plomped back

down, pulling out a strand of half-dry hair to check the color. It looked pure shocking red, but then, that was the color of my hair.

"You know, Libby, I'm proud of you, with all this," Lyle said stiffly.

"Ah don't say that, it sounds so fucking patronizing, it drives me crazy when you do that."

"I wasn't being patronizing," he said, his voice going high.

"Just crazy."

"I wasn't. I mean, it's cool to get to know you."

"Yeah what a thrill. I'm so worthwhile."

"You *are.*"

"Lyle, just don't, OK?" I folded a knee up under my chin and we both sat pretending to watch a cooking show, the host's voice too bright.

"Libby?"

I rolled my eyes over at him slowly, as if it pained me.

"Can I tell you something?"

"What."

"You ever hear about those wildfires near San Bernardino, back in 1999, they destroyed, like eighty homes and about ninety thousand acres?"

I shrugged. Seemed like California was always on fire.

"I was the kid who set that fire. Not on purpose. Or at least, I didn't mean for it to get out of control."

"What?"

"I was only a kid, twelve years old, and I wasn't a firebug or anything, but I'd ended up with a lighter, a cigarette lighter, I can't even remember why I had it, but I liked flicking it, you know, and I was hiking back in the hills behind my development, bored, and the trail was just, covered, with old grasses and stuff. And I was walking along, flicking the lighter, just seeing if I could get the tops of the weeds to catch, they had these fuzzy tips—

"Foxtail."

"And I turned around, and . . . and they'd all caught on fire. There were about twenty mini-fires behind me, like torches. And it was during the Santa Anas, so the tops started blowing away, and they'd land and catch another patch on fire, and then blow another hundred feet. And then it wasn't just small fires here and there. It was a big fire."

"That fast?"

"Yeah, in just those seconds, it was a *fire*. I still remember that feeling, like maybe for one moment I might have been able to undo it, but no. Now it was, like, it was all beyond me. And, and it was going to be bad. I just remember thinking I was in the middle of something that I'd never get over. And I haven't. It's hard to be that young and realize something like that."

I was supposed to say something now.

"You didn't mean for it to happen, Lyle. You were a kid with some horrible, weird luck."

"Well, I know, but that's why I, you know, identify with you. Not so long ago, I started learning about your story and I thought, *She might be like me*. She might know that feeling, of something getting completely beyond your control. You know, with your testimony, and what happened after—"

"I know."

"I've never told anyone that story. I mean, voluntarily. I just figured you—"

"I know. Thanks."

If I were a better person, I'd have put my hand on Lyle's then, given him a warm squeeze, let him know I understood, I empathized. But I wasn't, the thanks was hard enough. Buck hopped up on the sofa between us, willing me to feed him.

"So, uh, what are you doing this weekend?" Lyle said, picking at the edge of the sofa, the same spot where Krissi had put her face in her hands and wept.

"Nothing."

"Uh, so my mom wanted me to see if you wanted to come to this birthday party she's having for me," he said. "Just, like dinner or something, just friends."

People had birthday parties, grown-ups did, but the way Lyle said it made me think of clowns and balloons and maybe a pony ride.

"Oh, you probably want to just enjoy that time with your friends," I said, looking around the room for the remote control.

"Right. That's why I invited you."

"Oh. OK then."

I was trying not to smile, that would be too awful, and I was try-ing to figure out what to say, ask him how old he'd be—twelve years old in 1999 means, good God, twenty-two?—but a news bulletin blared in. Lisette Stephens was found murdered this morning, her body at the bottom of a ravine. She'd been dead for months.

Patty Day

Broke-down Kinnakee. She really wouldn't miss this town, especially in winter, when the roads got pitted and the mere act of driving rearranged your skeleton. By the time Patty got home, the girls were full-down-out-asleep, Debby and Michelle splayed out on the floor as always, Debby using a stuffed animal as a pillow, Michelle still sucking her pen on the floor, diary under an arm, looking comfortable despite a leg bent beneath her. Libby was in bed, in her tight little ball, fists up at her chin, grinding her teeth. Patty thought about tucking each one in properly, but didn't want to risk waking them. Instead she blew a kiss and shut the door, the smell of urine hitting her, Patty realizing she'd forgotten to change the sheets after all.

The bag of clothing was completely burned, there were only the tiniest scraps floating at the bottom of the fireplace. One white cotton square with a purple star sat in the ashes, defiant. Patty put on another log just to make sure, tossed the scrap right on the fire. Then she phoned Diane and asked her to come over extra early tomorrow, dawn, so they could look for Ben again.

"I can come over now, if you want the company."

"No, I'm about to climb in bed," Patty said. "Thanks for the envelope. The money."

"I'm already phoning around about lawyers, should have a good list by tomorrow. Don't worry, Ben will come home. He's probably panicked. Staying overnight at someone's. He'll show up."

"I love him so much, Diane . . ." Patty started and caught herself. "Have a good sleep."

"I'll bring some cereal when I come, I forgot to bring cereal today."

Cereal. It was so normal it felt like a gut punch.

Patty headed to her room. She wanted to sit and think, to ponder, get deep. The urge was intense, but she fought it. It was like trying to fight a sneeze. She finally poured herself two fingers of bourbon and put on her thick layers of sleeping clothes. Thinking time was over. Might as well try and relax.

She thought she'd cry—the relief of it all—but she didn't. She got into bed and looked at the cracked ceiling and thought, "I don't need to worry about the roof caving in anymore." She wouldn't have to look at that broken screen window near her bed, thinking year after year she should fix it. She wouldn't need to worry about the morning when she'd wake up and need coffee and find that the coffeemaker finally croaked. She didn't have to worry about commodity prices or operating costs or interest rates or the credit card Runner had taken in her name and overcharged on so she could never pay it off. She'd never see the Cates family again, at least not for a long time. She didn't have to worry about Runner and his peacock strut, or the trial or the fancy, slick-haired lawyer with the thick gold watch, who'd say soothing things and judge her. She didn't have to stay up at night worrying about what the lawyer was telling his wife, lying in their goosedown bed, him telling her stories about "the Day mother" and her dirty brood. She didn't have to worry about Ben going to prison. She didn't have to worry about not being able to take care of him. Or any of them. Things were going to change.

For the first time in a decade, she wasn't worrying, and so she didn't cry. Somewhere after one, Libby banged the door open and sleepwalked into bed with her, and Patty turned over and kissed her goodnight, and said I love you, was happy she could say that aloud to one of her kids, and Libby was asleep so fast Patty wondered if she even heard.

Libby Day

NOW

I woke up feeling like I dreamt about my mom. I was craving her weird hamburgers we always made fun of, filled with carrots and turnip bits and sometimes old fruit. Which was strange since I don't eat meat. But I wanted one of those burgers.

I was considering how one actually cooks hamburgers when Lyle phoned with his pitch. Just one more. That's what Lyle kept saying: just one more person I should talk to, and if nothing came of it, I could give up. Trey Teepano. I should look up Trey Teepano. When I said it'd be too hard to track him down, Lyle recited his address. "It was easy, he has his own business. Teepano Feed," Lyle said. I wanted to say "nice work" back to him—how easy would that have been?—but I didn't. Lyle said Magda's women would give me $500 dollars to talk to Trey. I'd have done it for free, but I took the money anyway.

I knew I would keep going like this, actually, that I couldn't stop until I found some sort of answer. Ben knew, I was sure of that now, Ben knew something. But he wasn't saying. So keep going. I remember watching a very sensible love expert on TV once. The advice: "Don't be discouraged—every relationship you have is a failure, until you find the right one." That's how I felt about this miserable quest: every person I talked to would let me down until I found the one person who could help me figure out that night.

Lyle was coming with me to Teepano Feed, partly because he wanted to see what Trey Teepano was like, and partly, I think, because he was nervous about the guy. ("I don't really trust Devil worshipers.") Teepano Feed was just east of Manhattan, Kansas, somewhere in a squat of farmland wedged between several new suburbs. The developments were blank and clean. They looked as fake as the Western souvenir shops back in Lidgerwood, a place where people only pretended to live. To my left, the boxy houses eventually gave way to an emerald lagoon of grass. A golf course. Brand new and small. In the cold morning rain, a few men remained on the fairway, twisted and tilted as they swung their clubs, looking like flags of yellow and pink against the green. Then just as quickly as the fake houses and the fake grass and the pastel-shirted men appeared, they were gone, and I was looking at a field of pretty brown Jersey cows, staring at me, expectant. I stared back—cows are the few animals that really seem to see you. I stared so hard I missed the big old brick building labeled Teepano Feed and Farm Supply, Lyle tapping my shoulder, LibbyLibbyLibby. I hit the brakes on my car and hydroplaned a good fifty feet, that soaring feeling reminding me of Runner letting me loose after spinning me. I backed up wildly and swerved into the gravel parking lot.

Only one other car was parked in front of the store, the whole place looking worn. The cement grooves between the bricks were filled with muck, and a kids' merry-go-round near the front door—quarter a ride—was missing its seats. As I walked up the wide wooden steps that spanned the front, the neon lights in the windows blinked on. "We Got Llamas!" Odd words to see in neon. A tin sign reading Sevin 5% Dust dangled from one of the building posts. "What's Pharoah quail?" Lyle said as we hit the top step. A bell on the door jangled as I opened it, and we walked into a room colder than the outside—the air conditioner was blasting, as was a soundsystem, playing cacophonous jazz, the soundtrack to a brain seizure.

Behind a long counter, rifles were locked in a glimmering cabinet, the glass enticing as a pond surface. Rows and rows of fertilizer and pellets, pick-axes, soil, and saddles stretched to the back of the store. Against the far wall was a wire cage holding a pack of unblinking bunnies. World's dumbest pet, I thought. Who would want an animal that sat, quivered, and shat everywhere? They say you can litter-box train them, but they lie.

"Don't . . . you know," I started saying to Lyle, who was snapping his head around, shifting into his oblivious inquisitor mode, "You know, don't—"

"I won't."

The crazy-making jazz continued as Lyle called out a hello. I could not see a single employee, nor customer for that matter, but then it was midmorning on a rainy Tuesday. Between the music and the sun-baked lighting from the ruthless fluorescent lamps, I felt stoned. Then I could make out movement, someone in the far back, bending and stooping in one of the aisles, and I started walking toward the figure. The man was dark, muscled, with thick black hair in a ponytail. He reared up when he saw us.

"Oh, dang!" he said flinching. He stared at us, then at the door, as if he'd forgotten he was open for business. "I didn't hear you all come in."

"Probably because of the music," Lyle yelled, pointing up at the ceiling.

"Too loud for you? Probably right. Hold on." He disappeared toward a back office and suddenly the music was gone.

"Better? Now what can I help you with?" He leaned against a seed bag, gave us a look that said we'd better be worth his turning down the music.

"I'm looking for Trey Teepano," I said. "Is he the guy who owns this store?"

"I am. I do. I'm Trey. What can I do you for?" He had a tense energy, bounced on the balls of his feet, tucked his lips into his teeth. He was intensely good-looking with a face that blinked young-old, depending on the angle.

"Well." Well, I didn't know. His name floated in my head like an incantation, but what to do next: ask him if he'd been a bookie, if he knew Diondra? Accuse him of murder?

"Um, it's about my brother."

"Ben."

"Yeah," I said, surprised.

Trey Teepano smiled a cold crocodile smile. "Yeah, took me a second, but I recognized you. The red hair, I guess, and the same face. You're the one who lived, right? Debby?"

"Libby."

"Right. And who're you?"

"I'm just her friend," Lyle offered. I could feel him willing himself to stop talking, not pull a repeat of the Krissi Cates interview.

Trey began straightening the shelves, readjusting bottles of Deer-Off, poorly pretending to be occupied, like reading a book upside down.

"You knew my dad too?"

"Runner? Everyone knew Runner."

"Runner mentioned your name the last time I saw him."

He swung back his ponytail. "Yeah, did he pass on?"

"No, he, he lives down in Oklahoma. He seems to think you were somehow . . . involved that night, that maybe you could shed some light on what happened. With the murders."

"Right. That old man is crazy, always has been."

"He said you were, like, a bookie or something back then."

"Yup."

"And you were into Devil worship."

"Yup."

He said these things with the faded blue-jean tone of a reformed addict, that vibe of broken-in peace.

"So that's true?" Lyle said. Then looked at me guiltily.

"Yeah, and Runner owed me money. Lot of money. Still does, I guess. But it doesn't mean I know what happened in your house that night. I been through all this back ten years ago."

"More like twenty-five."

Trey needled his eyebrows.

"Wow, I guess so," he said, still seeming unconvinced, his face twisted as he added up the years.

"Did you know Ben?" I persisted.

"A little, not really."

"Your name just keeps coming up a lot."

"I got a catchy name," he shrugged. "Look, back then, Kinnakee was racist as hell. Indians they did not like. I got blamed for a lot of shit I didn't do. This was before *Dances with Wolves,* you know what I'm saying? It was just BTI all the time out in BFE."

"What?"

"BTI, Blame the Indian. I admit it, I was a shit. I was not a good guy. But after that night, what happened to your family, it was, like it freaked me out, I got clean. Well, not right after, but a year or so later. Stopped drugs, stopped believing in the Devil. It was harder to stop believing in the Devil."

"You really believed in the Devil?" Lyle said.

He shrugged: "Sure. You gotta believe in something, right? Everyone has their thing."

I don't, I thought.

"It's like, you believe you have the power of Satan in you, so you have the power of Satan in you," Trey said. "But that was a long time ago."

"What about Diondra Wertzner?" I said.

He paused, turned away from us, walked over to the bunnies, started stroking one through the wire with his index finger.

"Where you going with this, Deb, uh, Libby?"

"I'm trying to track down Diondra Wertzner. I heard she was pregnant with Ben's baby at the time of the murders, and that she disappeared after. Some people say she was last seen with you and Ben."

"Ah shit, Diondra. I always knew that girl would bite me in the ass sooner or later." He grinned wide this time. "Man, Diondra. I have no clue where Diondra is, she was always running off, though, always making up drama. She'd run away, her parents would make a big deal, she'd come home, they'd all play house for a little, then her parents would be assholes—they neglected the shit out of her—and she'd need the drama, start some shit, run away, whatever. Total soap opera. I guess she finally ran away, decided it wasn't worth coming home. I mean, you try the white pages?"

"She's listed as a missing person," Lyle said, looked at me again to see if I minded the interruption. I didn't.

"Oh, she's fine," Trey said. "My guess is she's living somewhere under one of her crazy-ass names."

"Crazy names?" I said, put a hand on Lyle's arm to keep him quiet.

"Oh, nothing, she was just one of those girls, always trying to be different. One day she'd talk in an English accent, next day it was Southern. She never gave anyone her real name. Like she'd go to the beauty parlor and give a wrong name, go order a pizza and give the wrong name. She just liked screwing with people, you know, just playing. 'I'm Desiree from Dallas, I'm Alexis from London.' She was always giving, uh, using her porn name, you know?"

"She did porn?" I said.

"No, like that game. What's the name of your childhood pet?" I stared at him.

"What's the name of your childhood pet," he prompted.

I used Diane's dead dog: "Gracie."

"And what was the name of the street you grew up on?"

"Rural Route 2."

He laughed. "Well, that one didn't work. It's supposed to sound slutty, like Bambi Evergreen or something. Diondra's was . . . Polly something . . . Palm. Polly Palm, how great is that?"

"You don't think she's dead?"

He shrugged.

"You think Ben was really guilty?" I asked.

"I got no opinion on that. Probably."

Lyle was suddenly tense, bobbing up and down, pushing his pointy finger against my back, trying to steer me toward the door.

"So thanks for your time," Lyle blurted, and I frowned at him and he frowned back at me. A fluorescent above us thrummed on and off suddenly, flashing sick light on us, the bunnies scampering around in the straw. Trey scowled up at the light and it stopped, as if scolded.

"Well, can I give you my number, in case you think of anything?" I said.

Trey smiled, shook his head. "No thanks."

Trey turned away then. As we walked toward the door, the music got loud again. I turned around as the storm started to crackle, one side of the sky black, the other yellow. Trey was coming back out of the office, watching us with his hands on his sides, the rabbits behind him doing a sudden scuffle.

"Hey Trey, so what's BFE then?" I called.

"Butt Fucked Egypt, Libby. That's our hometown."

LYLE WAS GALLOPING ahead of me, leaping off the steps. He reached the car in three big strides, jiggling the handle to be let in, *comeoncomeoncomeon*. I dropped in next to him, pre-annoyed. "What?" I said. Thunder crackled. A gust of air kicked up a wet gravel smell.

"Just drive first, let's get out of here, hurry."

"Yessir."

I swung out of the parking lot, back toward Kansas City, the rain turning frantic. I'd driven about five minutes when Lyle told me to pull over, aimed himself at me, and said, "Oh my God."

Ben Day

T hey pulled up outside Diondra's, the dogs barking frantically as usual, as if they'd never seen a truck, or a person, or Diondra even. They all three went through the back gate, then Diondra told Ben and Trey to stand in front of the sliding door and to take their clothes off so they wouldn't drip blood everywhere. *Just peel 'em off, put 'em all in a pile, and we'll burn them.*

The dogs were frightened of Trey. They barked but they didn't come near him—he'd beaten the shit out of the white one once, and they all walked carefully around him ever since. Trey pulled his shirt off from the back, the way guys in movies did, the hard way, and then he unbuttoned his jeans, his eyes on Diondra, as if they were about to screw. Like this was some crazy foreplay. Ben pulled his shirt off the same way, and unpeeled his pants, those leather pants he'd sweat through already, and then the dogs were on him, sniffing at his crotch, licking at his arms, like they might devour him. He pushed one away, his palm on its snout, pushing hard, and it just came right back, slobbery, aggressive.

"It wants to suck your dick, man." Trey laughed. "Get it where you can, right?"

"He ain't getting any from me, so he might as well," Diondra snapped, doing her pissy, loop-de-loop head twist. She stepped out of her jeans, tan lines marking where her panties should have been, where no panties were, just white flesh and black fur, sticking up like a wet cat. Then she took off her sweater and stood there in just her bra, her breasts swollen, white stretch marks trailing along the tops of them.

"What?" she said at Ben.

"Nothing, you should go inside."

"Thanks, genius." She kicked her clothes over to a pile and told Trey—somehow she made it clear that it was just Trey—that she'd go get some lighter fluid.

Trey kicked his jeans into the center, stood in blue boxers, told Ben that he'd failed to prove himself.

"I don't see it that way," Ben muttered, but when Trey said *what?* he just shook his head. One dog was fully on him now, his paws on Ben's thighs, trying to lick around his stomach, where the blood had pooled. *"Get off me,"* Ben snapped, and when the dog just leapt right back up, he backhanded it. The dog snarled, then so did the second, the third barking, its teeth bared. Ben shimmied naked back toward the house yelling, "Go'way," to the dogs, the dogs backing off only when Diondra returned.

"Dogs respect strength," Trey said, a slightly upturned lip aimed at Ben's nakedness. "Nice fire bush."

Trey grabbed the lighter fluid from Diondra, still nude from her big stomach on down, her belly button poking out like a thumb. Trey sprayed it over the clothes, holding the can near his dick like he was pissing. He flicked his lighter to one side, and WHOOMP! the clothes fired up, making Trey stumble back two big steps, almost fall. It was the first time Ben had seen him look foolish. Diondra turned away, not wanting to embarrass Trey by seeing it. That made Ben more sad than anything else tonight: the woman he wanted to be his wife, the woman who'd have his child, she'd give this bit of grace to another man, but never, ever to Ben.

He needed to make her respect him.

———

HE WAS STUCK there, at Diondra's, watching them smoke more dope. He couldn't get home without his bike—it was just too cold, dead man's cold, snowing hard again, the wind blowing down the chimney. If it turned into a blizzard, the rest of those cows would freeze to death by morning, if the lazy-ass farmer didn't do something. Good. Teach him a lesson. Ben felt the anger in him coming up again, tight.

Teach everyone a fucking lesson. All those fuckers who never seemed to have any trouble, who seemed to just glide by—hell, even Runner, shitty drunk that he was, seemed to get less hassle than Ben. There were a lot of people who deserved a lesson, deserved to really understand, like Ben did, that nothing came easy, that most things were going to go sour.

Diondra accidentally burned his jeans along with the leather pants. So he was wearing a pair of Diondra's purple sweats, a big sweatshirt, and thick white Polo socks she had already mentioned twice she wanted returned. They were at that aimless time of night, the big event over, Ben still wondering what it meant, if he really did pray to the Devil, if he really would start feeling power. Or if it was all some hoax, or one of those things you talked yourself into believing—like a Ouija board or a killer clown in a white van. Were they all three agreeing silently to believe that they'd really sacrificed for Satan, or was it just an excuse to get really high and fuck stuff up?

They should have stopped early on with the drugs. It was cheap stuff, he could tell by how much it all hurt, even the weed went down fighting, like it was out to damage. It was the cheap stuff that made people mean.

Trey passed out, slowly, watching TV, his eyes blinking first, then his head looping around, up then down, then back up. Then he slumped to his side and was gone.

Diondra said she had to pee, and so Ben just sat there in the living room, wishing he were home. He was picturing his flannel sheets, picturing himself in bed, talking to Diondra on the phone. She never phoned from home, and he wasn't allowed to call her because her parents were so crazy. So she got cigarettes and sat in a phone booth near the gas station or in the mall. It was the one thing she did for him, made him feel good, her making that effort, he really liked it. Maybe he liked the idea of talking to Diondra better than he liked actually talking to her, lately she was so fucking mean to him when they were together. He was thinking again about the bleeding bull and wishing he had the gun back, that's what he wanted, and then Diondra was yelling his name from her bedroom.

He turned the corner and she was standing by her glittery red answering machine, with her head cocked to the side, and she just said, "You're fucked," and hit the button.

"Hey Dio, it's Megan. I'm *to*tally freaked *out* about Ben Day, did you hear about it, that he mol*est*ed all these girls? My sister is in *sixth* grade. She's fine, thank God, but god what a *sicko*. I guess the cops have arrested him. Anyway, call me."

And then a click and a whir and another girl's voice deep and nasal: "Hey Diondra, it's Jenny. I *told* you Ben Day was a Devil-dude, did you hear about this shit? I guess he's, like, on the *run* from the cops. I guess there's going to be some big conference about it at school tomorrow. I don't know, I wanted to see if you want to go."

Diondra was standing over the machine like she wanted to crush it, like it was an animal she could do something to. She turned to Ben and screamed, "What the fuck?" turning pink and spitty and Ben immediately said the wrong thing: "I better go home."

"You better go home? What the fuck is this Ben, what is going on?"

"I don't know, that's why I should go home."

"No no no no no, momma's boy. You fucking *worthless* fucking *momma's* boy. What, you going to go *home*, wait for the police and leave me here while you go to jail? Leave me just sitting here waiting for my fucking *dad* to get home? With your fucking *baby* I can't get rid of?"

"What do you want me to do, Diondra?" Home. That's what he kept thinking.

"We're leaving town tonight. I have about $200 cash left over from my parents. How much can you get at your place?" When Ben didn't say right away, his brain on Krissi Cates and whether the kiss was something to be arrested for and how much was true and whether the cops were really after him, Diondra walked over to him and slapped his face, hard. "How much do you have at your place?"

"I don't know. I have some money I've been saving, and my mom usually has a hundred bucks, two hundred, hidden around. But I don't know where."

Diondra swayed, closed one eye and looked at her alarm clock. "Does your mom stay up late, would she be awake?"

"If the police are there, yeah." If they weren't, she was asleep, even if she was scared out of her mind. It was the big joke in the family that his mom had never celebrated New Year's Eve, she was always asleep before midnight.

"We'll go there, and if we don't see a cop car, we'll go in. You can get money, pack some clothes, and then we'll get the fuck out of here."

"And then what?"

Diondra crossed over to him, petted him where his cheek still stung. Her eye makeup was halfway down her cheek, but he still felt a surge of, what, love? Power? Something. A surge, a feeling, something good.

"Ben baby, I am the mother of your child, right?" He nodded, just a bit. "OK, so get me out of town. Get us all out of town. I can't do this without you. We need to go. Head west. We can camp out somewhere, sleep in the car, whatever. Otherwise you're in jail, and I'm dead from my daddy. He'd make me have the baby and then kill me. And you don't want our kid to be an orphan, right? Not when we can help it? So let's go."

"I didn't do what they said, with those girls, I didn't," Ben finally whispered, Diondra leaning on his shoulder, wisps of her hair curling up, vining into his mouth.

"Who cares if you did?" she said into his chest.

Libby Day

Lyle was bouncing in his seat. "Libby, did you notice? Holy crud, did you notice?"

"What?"

"Diondra's porn name, the one she used all the time, did you notice?"

"Polly Palm, what?"

Lyle was grinning, his long teeth glowing brighter than the rest of him in the dark car.

"Libby, what was the name your brother had tattooed on his arm? Remember the names we went through? Molly, Sally, and the one I said sounded like a dog's name?"

"Oh God."

"Polly, right?"

"Oh God," I said again.

"I mean, that's not a coincidence, right?"

Of course it wasn't. Everyone who keeps a secret itches to tell it. This was Ben's way of telling. His homage to his secret girlfriend. But he couldn't use her real name on the tattoo, Miss Disappearing

Diondra. So he used the name she used when she was playing. I pictured him running his fingers over the swollen lines, his skin still stinging, proud. Polly. Maybe a romantic gesture. Maybe a memoriam.

"I wonder how old the tattoo is," Lyle said.

"It actually didn't look that old," I said. "It was still, I don't know, bright, not faded at all."

Lyle whipped out his laptop, balanced it on tight knees.

"Come on, come on, gimme a signal."

"What are you doing?"

"I don't think Diondra's dead. I think she's in exile. And if you were going into exile, and you had to pick a name, wouldn't you be tempted to use a name you'd used before, one that only a few friends knew, a joke for yourself, and a bit of . . . home? Something your boyfriend could tattoo on his arm and it would mean something to him, something permanent he could look at. Come *on*," he snapped at the laptop.

We drove another twenty minutes, trolling the highways until Lyle got a signal, and began tap-tap-typing in time to the rain, me trying to get a look at the screen without killing us.

He finally looked up, a crazy beam-smile on his face: "Libby," he said, "you might want to pull over again."

I swerved onto the side of the road, just short of Kansas City, a semi blaring its horn at my recklessness, shuddering my car as it sped past.

Her name sat there on the screen: Polly Fucking Palm in Kearney, Missouri. Address and phone number, right there, the only Polly Palm listing in the whole country, except for a nail boutique in Shreveport.

"I really need to get the Internet," I said.

"You think it's her?" Lyle said, staring at the name as if it might disappear. "It's gotta be her right?"

"Let's see." I pulled out my cell.

She answered on the fourth ring, just as I was taking a big gulp of air to leave her a message.

"Is this Polly Palm?"

"Yes." The voice was lovely, all cigarettes and milk.

"Is this Diondra Wertzner?"

Pause. Click.

"Would you find me some directions to that house, Lyle?"

LYLE WANTED TO come, wanted to come, really, really thought he should come, but I just couldn't see it working, and I just didn't want him there, so I dropped him off at Sarah's Pub, him trying not to look sulky as I pulled away, me promising to phone the second I left Diondra's.

"I'm serious, don't forget," he called after me. "Seriously!" I gave him a honk and drove off. He was still yelling something after me as I turned the corner.

My fingers were tight from gripping the steering wheel; Kearney was a good forty-five minutes northeast of Kansas City, and Diondra's address, according to Lyle's very specific directions, was another fifteen minutes from the town proper. I knew I was close when I started hitting all the signs for the Jesse James Farm and Jesse James' Grave. I wondered why Diondra had chosen to live in the hometown of an outlaw. Seems like something I would do. I drove past the turnoff for the James farm—been there in grade school, a tiny, cold place where, during a surprise attack, Jesse's little half brother was killed—and I remember thinking, "Just like our house." I went farther on a looping, skinny road, up and down hills and then out back into country, where dusty clapboard houses sat on big, flat lots, dogs barking on chains in each yard. Not a single person appeared; the area seemed entirely vacant. Just dogs and a few horses, and farther away, a lush line of forest that had been allowed to remain between the homes and the highway.

Diondra's house came another ten minutes later. It was ugly, it had an attitude, leaning to one side like a pissed-off, hip-jutted woman. It needed the attitude, because it didn't have much else going for it. It was set far back from the street, looked like the share-croppers' quarters for a larger farmhouse, but there was no other house, just a few acres of mud on all sides, rolling and bumpy like the ground had acne. That sad remainder of woods in the distance.

I drove up the long dirt road leading to the house, already worrying my car might get stuck and what would happen if my car got stuck.

From behind the storm clouds, the late afternoon sun arrived just in time to blind me as I slammed the door shut and walked toward the house, my gut cold. As I neared the front steps, a big momma possum shot out from under the porch, hissing at me. The thing unnerved me, that pointy white face and those black eyes looking like something that should already be dead. Plus momma possums are nasty bitches. It ran to the bushes, and I kicked the steps to make sure there weren't more, then climbed them. My lopsided right foot swished around in my boot. A dreamcatcher hung near the door, dangling carved animal teeth and feathers.

Just as the rain brings out the concrete smells of the city, it had summoned up the smell of soil and manure here. It smelled like home, which wasn't right.

A long, loose pause followed my knock on the door, and then quiet feet approached. Diondra opened the door, decidedly undead. She didn't even look that different from the photos I'd seen. She'd ditched the spiral perm, but still wore her hair in loose dark waves, still wore thick black eyeliner that made her eyes look Easter-blue, like pieces of candy. Her mascara was double-coated, spidery, and left flecks of black on the pads of flesh beneath her eyes. Her lips were plump as labias. Her whole face and body was a series of gentle curves: pink cheeks with a hint of jowl, breasts that slightly overflowed her bra, a ring of skin bordering the top of her jeans.

"Oh," she said as she opened the door, a flood of heat coming out. "Libby?"

"Yes."

She took my face in her hands. "Holy crap, Libby. I always thought some day you'd find me. Smart girl." She hugged me, then held me out a bit. "Hi. Come in."

I walked into a kitchen with a den to the side, the setup reminding me too much of my own lost home. We walked down a short hallway. To my right, a basement door hung open, leaking gusts of cold air. Negligent. We entered a low-ceilinged living room, cigarette smoke blooming from an ashtray on the floor, the walls yellowed, all the furniture looking drained. A massive TV sat like a loveseat against one wall.

"Would you mind taking off your shoes, please, sweetheart?" she said, motioning toward the living room carpet, which was gummy and soiled. The whole house was crooked, beaten-up, stained. A miniature dog turd sat in a lump near the stairs, Diondra stepping deftly around it.

She led me toward the sofa, trailing at least three different scents: a grape-y hair spray, a flowery lotion, and maybe . . . insect spray? She was wearing a low-cut blouse and tight jeans, with the junk jewelry of a teenager. She was one of those middle-aged women who thought they were fooling people.

I followed her, missing the extra inches my bootheels gave me, feeling childish. Diondra turned her profile to me, marking me from the corner of her eye, and I could see a pointy canine poke out from beneath her upper lip.

She cocked her head to one side and said, "Come on in, sit down. Jeez you're definitely a Day, huh? That fire-red hair, always loved it."

As soon as we sat down three squat-leg poodles came running in, collars jangling like sleigh bells, and clambered up on her lap. I tensed.

"Oh crap, you are *definitely* a Day," she cackled. "Ben was always all jumpy around dogs too. Course the ones I used to have were bigger than these babies." She let the dogs lick at her fingers, pink tongues flashing in and out. "So, *Libby*," she began, like my name, my existence was an inside joke, "did Ben tell you where to find me? Tell me the truth."

"I found you from something Trey Teepano said."

"Trey? Jesus. How'd you get to Trey Teepano?"

"He has a feed store, in the yellow pages."

"A feed store. Wouldn't have called that one. How's he look by the way?"

I nodded enthusiastically—he looks good—before I caught myself. Then said: "You were with Ben that night."

"Mmmm-hmmm. I was." She searched my face, wary but interested.

"I want to know what happened."

"Why?" she asked.

"Why?"

"Sorry, Miss Libby, this is all so out of the blue. Ben say something to you? I mean, why'd you come looking for me now? Why now?"

"I need to know for sure what happened."

"Oh, Libby. Ohhh." She gave me a sympathetic look. "Ben is OK taking the time for what happened that night. He wants to take the time. Let him."

"Did he kill my family?"

"That's why you're here?"

"Did Ben kill my family?"

She just smiled at me, those ridgeless lips staying rigid.

"I need some peace, Diondra, please. Just tell me."

"Libby, this is about peace, then? You think you know the answer, you're going to find peace? Like knowing is somehow going to fix you? You think after what happened there's any peace for you, sweetheart? How about this. Instead of asking yourself what happened, just accept that it happened. Grant me the serenity to accept the things I cannot change, the Serenity Prayer. It's helped me a lot."

"Just say it, Diondra, just tell me. Then I'll try to accept."

The sun was setting, hitting us through the rear window now, making me blink with the brightness. She leaned toward me, took both my hands.

"Libby, I'm so sorry. I just don't know. I was with Ben that night. We were going to leave town. I was pregnant with his baby. We were going to run away. He was going to his house, to get some money. An hour goes by, two hours, three hours. I'm thinking he's lost his nerve. I finally cried myself to sleep. The next morning, I heard what happened. At first I thought he was killed too. Then I hear, no, he's in custody and police think he's part of some coven—a satanic, Charles Manson–type clan they're looking for. I'm waiting for a knock at *my* door. But nothing happens. Days go by, and I hear Ben has no alibi, he hasn't mentioned me at all. He's protecting me."

"All these years."

"All these years, yes. The cops were never satisfied it was just

Ben. They wanted more. Looks better. But Ben never said a word. He's my goddam hero."

"So no one knows what happened that night. I'm never, ever going to find out." I felt a strange relief, saying it aloud. I could quit now, maybe. If I could never, ever know, then maybe I could quit.

"I do think you could find some peace, if you accept that. I mean, Libby, I don't think Ben did it. I think he's protecting your daddy, is what I think. But who knows? I hate to say this, but whatever happened that night, Ben needed to be in prison. He even says so. He had something inside him that wasn't right for the outside world. A violence. He does so much better in prison. He's very popular in there. He penpals with all these women, the women are so crazy about him. He gets a dozen proposals of marriage a year. Every once in a while, he thinks he wants back outside. But he doesn't."

"How do you know this?"

"We keep in touch," she snapped, then smiled sugar. The yellow-orange light of the sunset rayed across her chin, her eyes suddenly in the dark.

"Where's the baby, Diondra? The baby you were pregnant with?"

"I'm here," said the Day Girl.

Ben Day

B en opened the door into the dark living room and thought, *home*. Like a hero-sailor returning after months at sea. He almost shut the door on Diondra—*can't catch me*—but let her in because. Because he was scared what would happen if he didn't. It was a relief at least they left Trey behind. He didn't want Trey walking through his home, making his smart-ass remarks about things Ben already knew were embarrassing.

Everyone was asleep now, the whole house doing a collective breath-in-breath-out. He wanted to wake his mom, willed her to turn around the corner, blurry eyed in one of her clothes cocoons, and ask him where in the world he had been, *what in the world had possessed him?*

The Devil. The Devil possessed me, Mom.

He didn't want to go anywhere with Diondra, but she was behind him, rage fuming off her body like heat, eyes wide—*hurry up, hurry up*—and so he started to quietly sift through the cabinets, looking in his mom's hiding places for cash. In the first cabinet, he found an old box of wheat flakes, opened it up, and swallowed as much as he could of the dry cereal, the flakes sticking to his lips and throat, making him cough just a little, a baby cough. Then he stuck his whole hand in and grabbed the flakes by the fistful, jamming them into his mouth, and opened the fridge to find a Tupperware container packed with diced peas and carrots, a skin of butter on top, and he stuck a spoon in them, put his lip to the plastic rim and shoveled it all in his mouth, peas rolling down his chest, onto the floor.

"Come on!" Diondra hissed. He was still in her purple sweats; she was in nice new jeans, a red sweater and the black menswear shoes she liked, except her feet were so big they were actually men's shoes. She did not like this acknowledged. Now she was tapping one. Come on, come on.

"Let's go to my room," he said. "I definitely have money there. And a present for you." Diondra brightened at that—even now, her eyes blinkering on and off, swaying with the drugs and liquor, she was distracted by presents.

The lock to his room was snapped off, and Ben got pissed, then worried. Mom or police? Not that there was anything to find. But still. He opened the door, flipped on the light, Diondra closing the door behind him and settling on the bed. She was talking, talking, talking, but he wasn't listening, and then she was crying and so he stopped his packing and lay down next to her. He smoothed back her hair, and rubbed her belly and tried to keep her quiet, tried to mutter soothing stuff, talking about how great their life was going to be together and more lies like that. It was a good half-hour before she calmed down. And she'd been the one telling him to hurry up. Classic.

He got back up, looking at the clock, wanting to get out of here if they were really going to get out. The door had opened a crack and he didn't even stop to go close it, wanted it open, the danger making him move faster. He threw jeans and sweaters in a gym bag, along with his notebook filled with girls' names he'd like for the baby—he still thought Krissi Day was the leader in that, that was a good name, Krissi Day. Krissi Patricia Day or else, after Diane, Krissi Diane Day. He liked that because then her friends could call her D-Day, it'd be cool. He'd have to fight Diondra though, she thought all his names were too plain. She wanted names like Ambrosia and Calliope and Nightingale.

Gym bag on his shoulder, he reached into the back of his desk drawer and pulled out his hidden cash pile. He'd been tucking away fives and tens here and there, had convinced himself he had three hundred, four hundred dollars, but now he saw he had not quite a hundred. He jammed it in his pocket, got down on his hands and knees to reach under his bed, and saw only space where the bag of clothes had been. His daughter's clothes.

"Where's my present?" Diondra said, a guttural sound because she was lying flat on her back, her belly aimed up, belligerent, like a middle finger.

Ben lifted his head, looked at her, the smeared lipstick and dripping-black eyes, and thought she looked like a monster. "I can't find it," he said.

"What do you mean, can't find it?"

"I don't, someone's been in here."

They both stood in the glare of his single lightbulb, not knowing what to do next.

"You think it was one of your sisters?"

"Maybe. Michelle is always nosing around in here. Plus I don't have as much money as I thought I did."

Diondra sat up, grabbing her belly, which she never did affectionately, protectively. She clutched it like it was a burden he was too stupid to offer to carry. She was holding it now, out at him, and saying, "You are the father of this goddam baby, so you better think of something fast, you are the one who got me pregnant, so you better fix this. I am almost seven months pregnant, I could have a baby any day now, and you—"

A flicker at the door, just a swipe of nightgown, and then a foot jutting out, trying to keep balance. An accidental bump and the door swung wide. Michelle had been hovering in the hallway, trying to eavesdrop, until she leaned in too far and her whole moony face popped into sight, those big glasses reflecting twin squares of light. She was holding her new diary, a dribble of pen ink coming from her mouth.

Michelle looked from Ben to Diondra, and then pointedly down at Diondra's belly, and said, "Ben got a girl pregnant. I knew it!"

Ben couldn't see her eyes, just the light on the glasses and the smile beneath.

"Have you told Mom?" Michelle asked, getting giddy, her voice a goading hint. "Should I go tell Mom?"

Ben was about to reach for her, jam her back into bed with a threat of his own, when Diondra lunged. Michelle tried to make it to the door, but Diondra got her hair, that long brown hair, and yanked her to the ground, Michelle landing hard on her tailbone, Diondra whispering *not a word, you little cunt not a fucking word,* and then Michelle twisted away, pushing against the walls with slippered feet, leaving Diondra holding a clutch of hair, which she threw onto the floor, going after Michelle, and if Michelle had only run for Mom's room it may have been all right, Mom would take care of it all, but instead she went straight for her own room, the girls' room, and Diondra followed, Ben trailing her, whispering *Diondra, stop, Diondra let it go.* But Diondra was not going to let it go, she walked over to Michelle's bed where Michelle was cowering against the wall, whimpering, and she yanked Michelle down by a leg, straightened her out on the bed and sat on her, *You want to tell the world I'm pregnant, that your plan, one of your little schemes, some fucking little secret you sell for fifty cents, tell your mommy, guess what I know? I don't think so you little shit, why is this whole family so stupid,* and she wrapped her hands around Michelle's neck, Michelle's feet, cased in slippers that were supposed to look like puppy feet, kicking up and down, Ben watching the feet, disconnected, thinking they really did look like puppy feet, and then Debby slowly waking from her zombie sleep so Ben closed the door, instead of opening it wide, calling for his mom, he wanted everything to stay quiet, no other instinct than to stick to the plan which is don't wake anyone up, and he was trying to reason with Diondra, thinking it would all be OK, *Diondra, Diondra, calm down, she won't tell, let her go* and Diondra leaning deeper onto Michelle's neck, *You think I'm gonna spend my life worried about this little bitch,* and Michelle scratching, then stabbing Diondra's hand with her pen, a glint of blood, Diondra letting go for a second, looking surprised, looking like she just couldn't believe it and Michelle leaned to one side and gulped air and Diondra just grabbed her neck again, and Ben put his hands on Diondra's shoulders to pull her off but instead they just rested there.

Libby Day

NOW

T he Day Girl was slender, almost tall, and as she came into the room, she showed me a face that was virtually mine. She had our red hair too, dyed brown, but the red roots were peeking out just like mine had days before. Her height must have come from Diondra, but her face was pure us, me, Ben, my mom. She gawked at me, then shook her head.

"Sorry, that was weird," she said, blushed. Her skin was dusted with our family freckles. "I didn't know. I mean, I guess it makes sense we look alike, but. Wow." She looked at her mom, then back at me, at my hands, at her hands, at my missing finger. "I'm Crystal. I'm your niece."

I felt like I should hug her, and I wanted to. We shook hands.

The girl wavered near us, twisting her arms around each other like a braid, still glancing sideways at me, the way you glimpse yourself in the glass of a storefront as you walk past, trying to catch a look at yourself without anyone noticing.

"I told you it would happen if it was meant to, sweetheart," Diondra said. "So here she is. Come here, sit down."

The girl tumbled lazily onto her mother, pushing herself into the crook of Diondra's arm, her cheek on her mother's shoulder, Diondra playing with a strand of the red/brown hair. She looked at me from that vantage point. Protected.

"I can't believe I finally get to meet you," she said. "I was never supposed to get to meet you. I'm a secret, you know." She glanced up at her mom. "A secret love child, right?"

"That's right," Diondra said.

So the girl knew who she was, who the Days were, that her father was Ben Day. I was stunned that Diondra trusted her daughter to know this, to keep the secret close, not seek me out. I wondered how long Crystal had known, if she'd ever driven past my house, just to see, just to see. I wondered why Diondra would tell her daughter such a horrible truth, when she didn't really need to.

Diondra must have caught my train of thoughts. "It's OK," she said. "Crystal knows the whole story. I tell her everything. We're best friends." ·

Her daughter nodded. "I even have a little scrapbook of photos of you all. Well, just that I clipped out of magazines and stuff. It's like a fake family album. I always wanted to meet you. Should I call you Aunt Libby? Is that weird? That's too weird."

I couldn't think what to say. I just felt a relief. The Days weren't quite dying out yet. They were in fact flourishing, with this pretty, tall girl who looked like me but with all her fingers and toes and without my nightmare brain. I wanted to ask a flood of nosy questions: Did she have weak eyes, like Michelle? Was she allergic to strawberries like my mom? Did she have sweet blood, like Debby, get eaten alive by mosquitos, spend the summer stinking of Campho-Phenique? Did she have a temper, like me, a distance like Ben? Was she manipulative and guiltless like Runner? What was she like, what was she like, tell me the many ways she was like the Days, and remind me of how we were.

"I read your book too," Crystal added. "*A Brand New Day*. It was really good. I wanted to tell someone I knew you because, you know, I was proud." Her voice lilted like a flute, as if she was perpetually on the verge of laughter.

"Oh, thanks."

"You OK, Libby?" Diondra said.

"Um, I guess, I guess I still just don't understand why you all stayed secret for so long. Why you have Ben still swearing he doesn't know you. I mean, I'm assuming he's never even met his daughter."

Crystal was shaking her head no. "I'd love to meet him though. He's my hero. He's protected my mom, me, all these years."

"We really need you to keep this secret for us, Libby," Diondra said. "We're really hoping you do. I just can't risk it, that they think I was an accomplice or something. I can't risk that. For Crystal."

"I just don't think there's a need for that—"

"Please?" Crystal said. Her voice was simple, but urgent. "Please. I seriously can't stand the idea that they can come any minute and take my mom away from me. She's really my best friend."

So they'd both said. I almost rolled my eyes but saw the girl was on the edge of tears. So she was actually frightened of this specter Diondra had created: the vengeful bogeymen cops who might bust in and take Mommy away. I just bet Diondra was her best friend. All these years, they lived in a two-person pod. Secret. Gotta stay secret for Mommy.

"So you ran away and never told your folks?"

"I left right when I was really starting to show," Diondra said. "My parents were maniacs. I was happy to be rid of them. It was just our secret, the baby, Ben and mine."

A secret in the Day house, how unusual. Michelle finally missed a scoop.

"You're smiling." Crystal said, a matching small smile on her lips.

"Ha, I was just thinking how much my sister Michelle would have loved getting her hands on that bit of gossip. She loved drama."

They looked like I slapped them.

"I wasn't trying to make light, sorry," I said.

"Oh, no, no don't worry about it," Diondra said. We all stared at each other, fingers and hands and feet wiggling about. Diondra broke the silence: "Would you like to stay for dinner, Libby?"

SHE FED ME a salty pot roast that I tried to swallow and a lot of pink wine from a box that seemed to have no bottom. We didn't sip, we drank. My kind of women. We talked about silly things, stories about my brother, with Crystal layering on questions I felt embarrassed I couldn't answer: Did Ben like rock or classical? Did he read much? Did he have any diabetes, because she had low blood-sugar problems. And what about her grandma Patty, what was she like?

"I want to know them, as, you know, people. Not victims," she said with twenty-something piousness.

I excused myself to the bathroom, needing a moment away from the memories, the girl, Diondra. The realization I was out of people to talk to, that I'd come to the end, and now had to loop around and think about Runner again. The bathroom was as gross as the rest of the place, mucked with mold, the toilet perpetually running, wads of toilet paper smeared with lipstick dotting the floor around the trashbin. Alone for the first time in the house, I couldn't resist looking for a souvenir. A glazed red vase sat on the back of the toilet tank, but I didn't have my purse with me. I needed something small. I opened the medicine cabinet and found several prescription bottles with Polly Palm written on the label. Sleeping pills and painkillers and allergy stuff. I took a few Vicodin, then pocketed a light pink lipstick and a thermometer. Very good fortune, as I would never, ever think to buy a thermometer, but I'd always wanted one. When I take to my bed, it's good to know whether I'm sick or just lazy.

I got back to the table, Crystal sitting with one foot on her chair, her chin resting on her knee. "I still have more questions," she said, her flute voice doing scales.

"I probably don't have the answers," I started, trying to ward her off. "I was just so young when it happened. I mean, I'd forgotten so much about my family until I began talking with Ben."

"Don't you have photo albums?" Crystal asked.

"I do. I'd put them away for a while, boxed them up."

"Too painful," Crystal said in a hushed voice.

"So I only just started looking through the boxes again—photo albums and yearbooks, and a lot of other old crap."

"Like what?" Diondra said, smushing some peas under her fork like a bored teenager.

"Well, practically half of it was Michelle's junk," I offered, eager to be able to answer some question definitely.

"Like toys?" Crystal said, playing with the corner of her skirt.

"No, like, notes and crap. Diaries. With Michelle, everything got written down. She saw a teacher doing something weird, it went in the diary, she thought our mom was playing favorites, it went in the diary, she got in an argument with her best friend over a boy they both liked, it went—"

"—odd Delhunt," murmured Crystal, nodding. She swallowed some more wine with slug.

"—in the diary," I continued, not quite hearing. Then hearing. Did she say Todd Delhunt? It was Todd Delhunt, I never would have remembered that name on my own, that big fight Michelle got into over little Todd Delhunt. It happened right at Christmas, right before the murders, I remember she stewed all through Christmas morning, scribbling in her new diary. But. Todd Delhunt, how did—?

"Did you know Michelle?" I asked Diondra, my brain still working.

"Not too," Diondra said. "Not really at all," she added and she started reminding me of Ben pretending not to know Diondra.

"Now it's my turn to pee," Crystal said, taking one last swirl of wine.

"So," I started, and stalled out. There is no way Crystal would know about Michelle's crush on Todd Delhunt unless. Unless she read Michelle's diary. The one she got Christmas morning, to kick off 1985. I'd assumed none of the diaries were missing, because 1984 was intact, but I hadn't even thought about 1985. Michelle's new diary, just nine days of thoughts—that's what Crystal was quoting from. She had read the diary of my dead—

I caught a flash of metal to my right, just as Crystal slammed an ancient clothes iron into my temple, her mouth stretched wide in a frozen scream.

Patty Day

atty had actually drifted to sleep, totally ridiculous, and woken up at 2:02, scooted from under Libby, and padded down the hallway. Someone was rustling in the girls' room, a bed was creaking. Michelle and Debby were heavy sleepers but they were noisy—cover throwers, sleeptalkers. She walked past Ben's room, the light still on from when she'd broken in. She would have lingered, but she was late, and Calvin Diehl didn't seem likely to put up with late.

Ben Baby.

Better not to have the time. She walked to the door, and instead of worrying about the cold, she thought of the ocean, that single trip to Texas when she was a girl. She pictured herself slathered in oil and baking, the water rushing in, salt on her lips. Sun.

She opened the door, and the knife went into her chest, and she doubled over into the arms of the man, him whispering, *Don't worry, it will all be over in about thirty seconds, let's just do one more to make sure,* and he tilted her away from him, she was a dancer being dipped, and then she could feel the knife turn in her chest, it hadn't hit her heart, it should have hit her heart, and she could feel the steel move inside her and the man looked down on her with a kindly face, getting ready to go again, but he looked over her shoulder and his kindly face got mottled, his mustache started shaking—

"What the hell?"

And Patty turned her face just a bit, back into the house, and it was Debby in her lavender nightgown, her pigtails crooked from sleep, one white ribbon trailing down her arm, yelling, *Mom, they're hurting Michelle!* Not even noticing that Mom was being hurt too, she was so focused on her message, *Come on, Mom, come on* and Patty could only think: bad timing for a nightmare. Then: shut the door. She was bleeding onto her legs, and as she tried to shut the door so Debby couldn't see her, the man pushed opened the door, and yelled *Goddamgoddamgoddaaammmmm!* Thundering it into Patty's ear, she felt him trying to pull the knife out of her chest and realized what it meant, that he wanted Debby, this man who said no one should know, no one could see him, he wanted Debby to go with Patty, and Patty put her hand hard on the hilt and pushed it deeper inside her and the man kept yelling and finally dropped hold of the knife, kicked the door open and went inside, and as Patty fell, she saw him going for the axe, the axe that Michelle had propped by the door, and Debby started to run toward her mother, running to help her mom, and Patty screaming *Run away!* And Debby froze, screamed, vomited down her front, scrambled on the tile and started the other way, made it to the end of the hallway, just turning the corner, but the man was right behind her, he was bringing the axe up and then she saw the axe go down and Patty pulled herself up, stumbling like a drunk, not able to see out of one eye, moving like in a nightmare where her feet go fast but she doesn't get anywhere, screaming *Run, Run, Run,* and turning the corner to see Debby lying on the floor with wings of blood, and the man so angry now, his eyes wet and alight, yelling, *Why'd you make me do this?* and he turned as if to leave, and Patty ran past him, picked up Debby, who wobbled a few steps like when she was a fat little toddler, and she was really hurt, her arm, her sweet arm, *It's OK, baby, you're OK,* the knife sliding out of Patty's chest and rattling down onto the floor, blood pulsing out of her more quickly and the man came back this time with a shotgun. Patty's shotgun, that she'd placed so carefully on the front-room mantelpiece, where the girls couldn't reach it. He aimed it at her as she tried to get in front of Debby because now she couldn't die.

The man cocked the gun and Patty had time for one last thought: I wish, I wish, I wish I could take this back.

And then with a whoosh, like summer air shooting through a car window, the blast took off half her head.

Libby Day

NOW

"Sorry, Mom," Crystal was saying. I was semi-blind, could see only a burnt-orange color, an eyes-shut-to-the-sun color. Flashes of the kitchen came back into vision and immediately disappeared. My cheek ached, I could feel it throbbing straight down my spine, into my feet. I was facedown on the floor and Diondra was straddling me. I could smell her—that insect-spray smell—balanced on top of me.

"Oh God, I screwed up."

"It's OK, baby, just go get me the gun."

I could hear Crystal's feet hit the stairs, and then Diondra was flipping me over, grabbing for my throat. I wanted her to curse at me, scream something, but she was silent, all heavy, calm breathing. Her fingers pressed into my neck. My jugular jumped, then began thumping against her thumb. I still couldn't see. I was about to be dead. I knew it, my pulse beating faster and then way too slow. She pinned down my arms with her knees, I couldn't move them, all I could do was kick at the floor, my feet sliding. She was breathing on my face, I could feel the heat, picture her mouth hanging open. Yes, that's right, I could picture where her mouth was. I gave one big, twisting push beneath her, squirmed my arms free, and rammed my fist into her face.

I connected with something, enough to knock her off me for a second, just a small bone crunch, but enough that my fist stung and then I was pulling myself across the floor, trying to find a chair, trying to goddam see and then her hands grabbed my ankle, *Not this time, sweetheart,* and she was holding my foot inside my sock, but it was my right foot, the one with the missing toes and so it was harder to hold on to, the socks never fit right and suddenly I was up and left her holding my sock, and still no Crystal yet, no gun and I was running away toward the back of the house, but I couldn't see, couldn't keep a straight line, and instead I veered to my right, through that open door and fell face-first down the flight of stairs to the cold of the basement, me going slack like a child, not resisting, the right way to fall, and so by the time I hit the bottom I was back up, in the dank smell. My vision flickered like an old TV—off then on—and then I could just make out the shadow of Diondra lingering in the rectangle of light at the top of the stairs. Then she shut the door on me.

I could hear them upstairs, Crystal coming back, "Are we going to have to—"

"Well—*now* we are."

"I can't believe, I just, it just came out of my mouth, so stupid—"

Me running in loops around the basement, trying to find a way out: three walls of concrete and one wall toward the back, covered to the ceiling in junk. Diondra and Crystal were not worried about me, they were jabbering at each other behind the door upstairs, me pulling away at the pile, looking for a place to hide, trying to find something I could use as a weapon.

"—doesn't really know what happened, not for sure—"

I opened a trunk I could hide in, and die in.

"—knows, she's not stupid—"

I started tossing away a hat-rack, two bicycle wheels, the wall of junk shifting with each thing I burrowed past.

"—I'll do it, it was my fault—"

I hit a mountain of old boxes, sagging like the ones I had under the stairs. Push those away and out falls an old pogo stick, too heavy for me to wield.

"—I'll do it, it's fine—"

The voices angry-guilty-angry-guilty-decisive.

The basement was bigger than the house itself, a good Midwest basement made to withstand tornados, made to store vegetables, deep and dirty. I pulled junk out and just kept going, and as I squirmed behind a massive bureau I found an old door. It was a whole nother room, the serious part of the tornado cellar, and yes, a dead end, but no time to think, got to keep going, and now light was illuminating the basement, Diondra and Crystal were coming and I shut the door behind me and stepped into the narrow room, more stuff stored there—old record players, a crib, a mini-fridge, all stacked to the sides, not much more than another twenty feet to run, and behind me I could hear more of the junk pile collapsing in front of the door, but that didn't help much, they'd be through that in a few seconds.

"Just shoot that way, she's got to be that way," Crystal saying and Diondra shushing her, their feet heavy on the last stairs, taking their time, Diondra kicking things out of the way as they moved toward the door, closing me off like I was a rabid animal that needed to be put down, Diondra not even all that focused, saying suddenly: "That pot roast was too salty." Inside my little room, I noticed the faintest light in the corner. Coming from somewhere in the ceiling.

I pushed toward it, stumbling over a red wagon, the women laughing when they heard me fall, Crystal yelling, "Now you're going to have a bruise," Diondra knocking things away, and I was underneath the light, it was the opening of a wind turbine, the ventilation shaft for the tornado shelter and it was too small for most people to fit but not me, and I started piling things to reach it, to get my fingers to the top so I could pull myself up and Diondra and Crystal were almost past the debris. I tried to stand on an old baby buggy, but the bottom gave out, I ripped up my leg, started stacking things: a warped diaper table, and then some encyclopedias, and me on top of the encyclopedias, feeling them want to slide away, but I got my arms up through the shaft, breaking through the slats of the rusty turbine, one big push and I was breathing the cold night air, ready for the next push to get me all the way out and then Crystal was grabbing my foot, trying to pull me back down, me kicking her, scrambling. Screams beneath me, *Shoot her!* and Crystal screaming *I got her,* and her weight pulling me down, me losing leverage, half in and out of the ground, and then I gave one good kick with my bad foot and jabbed my heel right in her face, the nose going, a wolf-wail beneath me, and Diondra yelling *Oh baby* and me free, back up, my arms bearing deep red scratches from the top of the shaft, but up, over and onto the ground and as I was heaving for air, breathing in the mud, I could already hear Diondra going, *Get up top, get up top.*

My car keys were gone, lost somewhere inside, and so I turned and ran for the woods, a limping trot, like something with three legs, one sock on, one sock off, mucking through the mud, stinking of manure in the moonlight, and then I turned, feeling almost good, and saw they were out of the house, they were behind me, running after me—white pale faces each leaking blood—but I made it to the forest. My head was whirling, my eyes unable to hold on to anything: a tree, the sky, a rabbit spooking away from me. *Libby!* behind me. I went deeper into the woods, about ready to pass out, and as my eyes started going dark, I found a gargantuan oak. It was balanced on a four-foot drop-off, gnarled roots radiating out like the sun, and I climbed down in the dirt and burrowed my way into an old animal den, under one of the roots as thick as a grown man. I dug into the cold, wet ground, a little thing in a little hollow, shivering but silent, hiding, which was something I could do.

The flashlights came closer, hitting the tree trunk, the women clambering over me, a flash of skirt, a glimpse of one red freckled leg, *She has to be here, she can't have gone that far,* and me trying not to breathe, knowing if I did it would be a gulp of air that would get me shot in the face, and so I held my breath as I felt their weight nudge the tree roots and Crystal said, *Could she have gone back to the house,* and Diondra said, *Keep looking, she's quick,* like someone who knew, and they turned and ran deeper into the woods and I breathed into the ground, swallowed earthy air, my face muffled against the dirt. For hours, the woods echoed with their screams of outrage, frustration—*this is not good, this is very bad*—and at some point the screaming stopped and then I waited more hours, til dawn, before I pulled myself out and hobbled through the trees toward home.

Ben Day

JANUARY 3, 1985
2:12 A.M.

Diondra was still perched on Michelle's body. Listening. Ben sat in a bundle, rocking himself while from the hallway came sounds of screaming and cursing, the axe hitting flesh, the shotgun and silence and then his mom going again, not hurt, maybe not hurt, but then he knew she was, she was making gibberish sounds, *whh-llalalala* and *geeeeee,* and she was banging into the walls, and those heavy boots came walking down the hall, toward his mom's room, and then the horrible sound of small hands trying to gain purchase, Debby's hands scraping along the wooden floor and then the axe again and a loud release of air, and then came another shotgun blast, Diondra flinching on top of Michelle.

Diondra's nerves showed only in her hair, which twittered around her head in those thick curls. Otherwise she didn't move. The steps paused outside the door, the door Ben had shut after the screaming began, the door he was hiding behind while his family lay outside, dying. They heard a wail—*goddammmmm it*—and then the steps ran, heavy and hard out of the house.

Ben whispered across to Diondra, pointing at Michelle, "Is she OK?" and Diondra frowned like he'd insulted her. "No, she's dead."

Ben couldn't stand up. "Are you sure?"

"I'm totally sure," Diondra said, and unstraddled her, Michelle's head lolling to the side, her open eyes on Ben. Her broken glasses lay next to her.

Diondra walked over to Ben, her knees in front of his face. She held out a hand to him. "Come on, get up."

They opened the door, Diondra's eyes widening like she was looking at a first snow. Blood was everywhere, Debby and his mom in a pool of it, the axe and shotgun dropped along the hallway, a knife farther down. Diondra walked over to look more closely, her reflection dark in the pond of blood that was still flowing toward him.

"Holy shit," she whispered. "Maybe we really did fuck with the Devil."

Ben ran to the kitchen, wanting to vomit in the sink, the heaving feeling comforting, *get it up get it all up,* the way his mom used to say, holding his forehead over the toilet when he was a kid. *Get all that bad stuff out.* But nothing happened, so he staggered toward the phone and there was Diondra, stopping him.

"You going to tell on me? For Michelle?"

"We need to call the police," he said, his eye on his mom's stained coffee cup, some Folgers still at the bottom.

"Where's the little one?" Diondra asked. "Where's the baby?"

"Oh shit! Libby!" He ran back down the hallway, trying not to look at the bodies, pretending they were just obstacles to jump over, and he looked inside his mom's room and felt the chill, saw the breeze fluttering the curtains and the open window. He came back to the kitchen.

"She's gone," he said. "She made it out, she's gone."

"Well, go bring her back."

Ben turned to the door, about to run outside, and then stopped. "Bring her back, why?"

Diondra crossed to him, took his hands and put them on her belly. "Ben, do you not see how all this was meant to be? You think it's a coincidence that we do the ritual tonight, that we need money, and that—pow!—a man kills your family. You will inherit everything for your mom's life insurance now, whatever you want to do, you want to go live in California, on the beach, go live in Florida, we can do it."

Ben had never said he wanted to live in California or Florida. Diondra had said that.

"We are a family now, we can be a real family. But Libby is a problem. If she saw something."

"What if she didn't?"

But Diondra was already shaking her head no, "Clean break, baby. It's too dangerous. Time to be brave."

"But if we need to get out of town tonight, I can't wait around for the life insurance."

"Well, of course we can't leave tonight. Now we need to stay, it would look suspicious if you left. But you see what a gift this is— people are going to forget all about the Krissi Cates bullshit, because you're the victim now. People will want to be good to you. I'll try to hide this," she fingered her belly, "for another month, somehow. I'll wear a coat all the time or something. And then we get the money, and we fucking fly. Free. You'll never have to eat shit again."

"What about Michelle?"

"I got her diary," Diondra said, showing him the new journal with the Minnie Mouse cover. "We're cool."

"But what do we say about Michelle?"

"You say the crazy man did it, like the rest. Like Libby too."

"But what about—"

"And Ben, you can never say that you know me, not til we leave. I can't be linked to this in anyway. Do you understand? You want me to give birth to our baby in prison, you know what happens then, it goes into foster care, you will never see it again. You want that for your baby, for the mother of your child? You still have a chance to be a big boy here, be a man. Now go get me Libby."

He took the big utility flashlight and went out into the cold calling Libby's name. She was a quick kid, a good runner, she could have made it all the way down their road and toward the highway by now. Or she could be hiding in her usual place down by the pond. He crunched through the snow, wondering if this was all a bad trip. He'd go back to the house and it would be just like it was earlier, when he heard the snick of the lock and everything was normal, everyone asleep, a regular night.

Then he saw Diondra crouched on top of Michelle like some giant predator bird, them both shaking in the dark, and he knew nothing was going to be OK and he also knew he wasn't going to bring Libby back to the house. He brushed his flashlight over the tops of the reeds and saw a flash of her red hair amidst the bland yellow and he yelled, "Libby, stay where you are, sweetheart!" and turned and ran back to the house.

Diondra was chopping the walls, chopping the couch, screaming with her teeth bared. She'd smeared the walls with blood, she'd written things. She'd tracked blood in her men's shoes all over, she'd eaten Rice Krispies in the kitchen and left trails of food behind her, and she was leaving fingerprints everywhere, and she kept yelling, "Make it look good, make it look real good," but Ben knew what it was, it was the bloodlust, the same feeling he got, that flare of rage and power that made you feel so strong.

He cleaned up the footprints pretty good, he thought, although it was hard to tell which were Diondra's and which were the man's— who the fuck was the man? He wiped everything she'd touched—the lightswitches, the axe, the counters, everything in his room, Diondra appearing in the doorway, telling him, "I wiped down Michelle's neck," Ben trying not to think, don't think. He left the words on the walls, didn't know how to fix that. She'd gotten at his mother with the axe, his mom had strange new gashes, deep, and he wondered how he could be so calm, and when his bones would melt and he'd collapse, and he told himself to pull it fucking together, *be a fucking man, do it be a man do what needs to be done be a man,* and he ushered Diondra out of the house and the whole place already smelled like earth and death. When he closed his eyes he saw a red sun and he thought again, *Annihilation.*

Libby Day

NOW

I was going to lose toes again. I sat outside a closed gas station for almost an hour, rubbing my ringing feet, waiting for Lyle. Every time a car went by I ducked behind the building in case it was Crystal and Diondra, out searching for me. If they found me now, I couldn't run. They'd have me and it'd be done. I'd wanted to die for years, but not lately and definitely not by those bitches.

I had called Lyle collect from a phone outside the gas station I was sure wouldn't work, and he'd started the conversation before the operator even got off the line: *Did you hear? Did you hear?* I did not hear. I don't want to hear. Just come get me. I hung up before he started in with his questions.

"What happened?" Lyle said, when he finally pulled up, me in full bone-chatter, the air frosted. I threw myself in the car, my arms in a mummy wrap from the cold.

"Diondra's definitely not fucking dead. Take me home, I need to get home."

"You need to get to a hospital, your face is, it's. Have you seen your face?" He pulled me under the dome light of his car to take a closer look.

"I've felt my face."

"Or the police department? What happened? I knew I should have gone with you. Libby. Libby, what happened?"

I told him. The whole thing, letting him sort it out between my crying jags, ending with, *and then they, then they tried to kill me . . .* the words coming out like hurt feelings, a little girl telling her mom that someone was mean to her.

"So Diondra killed Michelle," Lyle said. "We're going to the cops."

"No we're not. I just need to go home." My words were curdled with snot and tears.

"We've got to go to the cops, Libby."

I started screaming, nasty things, slamming my hand on the window, yelling til spittle ran out my mouth, and that only made Lyle more sure he was taking me to the police.

"You'll want to go to the police, Libby. When I tell you what I need to tell you, on top of this, you'll want to go to the police."

I knew that's what I needed to do, but my brain was infected with memories of what happened after my family was murdered: the long, washed-out hours going over and over my story with the police, my legs hanging off oversized chairs, cold hot chocolate in Styrofoam cups, me unable to get warm, just wanting to go to sleep, that total exhaustion, where even your face is numb. And you can say all you want, it doesn't matter because everyone's dead anyway.

Lyle turned the heater on full blast, aimed every vent at me.

"OK, Libby, I have some, some news. I think, well, OK I'll just say it. OK?"

"You're freaking me out, Lyle. Just say it." The dome light didn't cast enough glow, I kept looking around the parking lot to make sure no one was coming.

"Remember the Angel of Debt?" Lyle began. "That the Kill Club was investigating? He's been caught in a suburb of Chicago. He got nailed in the middle of helping some poor stockmarket sucker stage his death. It was supposed to look like a horseriding accident. The Angel got caught on one of the riding trails, going at the guy with a rock, bashing his head in. His name is Calvin Diehl. Used to be a farmer."

"OK," I said, but I knew more was coming.

"OK, so it turns out he's been helping to kill people since the '80s. He was smart. He has handwritten notes from everyone he murdered—thirty-two people—swearing they hired him."

"OK."

"One of those notes was from your mother."

I bent over at the waist, but kept looking at Lyle.

"She hired him to kill her. But it was supposed to be just her. To get the life insurance, save the farm. Save you guys, Ben. They have the note."

"So. What? No, that doesn't make sense. Diondra killed Michelle. She had her diary. We just said it was Diondra—"

"Well, that's just the thing. This Calvin Diehl's playing himself off like a folk hero—I swear, there's been a crowd outside the jail the past few days, people with signs, like, Diehl's the Real Deal. They'll be writing songs about him soon: helping people in debt die so the banks won't get their property, screwing over the insurance companies to boot. People are eating it up. But, uh, he's saying he won't confess to murder on any of the thirty-two people, says they were all assisted suicide. Die with dignity. But he's taking the rap for Debby. He says he'll confess to Debby, says she wandered in, got in the middle, things went bad. He says that's the only one he's sorry for."

"What about Michelle?"

"He says he never even saw Michelle. I can't think why he'd lie."

"Two killers," I said. "Two killers the same night. That would be our luck."

SOMEWHERE BETWEEN THE time I was hiding in the woods, then whimpering at the gas station, then bawling in Lyle's car, and finally convincing a sleepy local sheriff's deputy I wasn't crazy (You're *who's* sister?), I wasted seven hours. Diondra and Crystal were clean gone by the morning, and I mean clean. They'd doused the place with gas, and it had burnt to the ground before the fire trucks even got out of the station.

I told my story a lot more times, the story taken with a mix of bemusement and doubt, and then finally a dash of credence.

"We'll just need a little more, you know, to link her to your sister's murder," one detective said, pressing a Styrofoam cup of cold coffee in my hand.

Two days later, detectives appeared on my doorstep. They had photocopies of letters from my mom. Wanted to see if I recognized her handwriting, wanted to see if I wanted to see them.

The first was a very simple, one-page note, absolving Calvin Diehl of her murder.

The second was to us.

Dear Ben, Michelle, Debby and Libby,

I don't think this letter will ever reach you, but Mr. Diehl said he'd hold it for me, and I guess that gives me some comfort. I don't know. Your grandparents always told me, Make a useful life. I don't feel I've really done that, but I can make a useful death. I hope you all forgive me. Ben, whatever happens, don't blame yourself. Things got beyond our control, and this is what needed to be done. It seems very clear to me. I'm proud in a way. My life has been determined so much by accidents, it seems nice that now an "accident on purpose" will make things right again. A happy accident. Take good care of each other, I know Diane will do right by you. I'm only sad I won't get to see what good people you become. Although I don't need to. That's how sure I am of my kids.

Love you,
Mom

I felt hollowed out. My mom's death was not useful. I felt a shot of rage at her, and then imagined those last bloody moments in the house, when she realized it had gone wrong, when Debby lay dying, and it was all over, her unsterling life. My anger gave way to a strange tenderness, what a mother might feel for her child, and I thought, At least she tried. She tried, on that final day, as hard as anyone could have tried.

And I would try to find peace in that.

Calvin Diehl

It was stupid, how wrong it had gone, so quickly. And here he'd been doing her a favor, the redhead farmgirl. Goddam, she didn't even leave him enough money; they agreed on $2,000, she left an envelope with only $812 and three quarters. It was petty and small and stupid, the whole night. It was disastrous. He'd gotten lax, cocky, indulgent and it had led to . . . She'd have been so easy, too. Most people were picky about how they died, but all she asked was not to drown. She didn't want to drown, please. He could have done it so many simple ways, like he'd always done. But then he'd gone to get a drink at the bar, no big deal, truckers went through here all the time, he never stood out. But her husband was there, and he was such a piece of shit peckerhead, such a little worthless rat man, that Calvin found himself listening pretty hard for what this Runner guy's deal was, and people were telling all sorts of stories, about how the man had ruined the farm, ruined his family, was in debt up to his shirt-collar. And Calvin Diehl, a man of honor, had thought, why not?

Stab the woman through the heart on her doorstep, make this Runner guy sweat some. Let the cops question him, this sorry shit who took no responsibility. Make him take some. Ultimately it'd be written off as a random crime, as believable as the other stuff he'd pulled, car crashes and hopper collapses. Down near Ark City, he'd drowned a man in his own wheat, rigged it to look like a turnover. Calvin's killings always worked with the seasons: drowning during spring floods, hunting accidents during autumn. January was the season for house robberies and violence. Christmas was over, and the new year just reminded you of how little your life had changed, and man, people got angry in January.

So stab her through the heart, fast, a big Bowie hunting knife. Be over in thirty seconds and the pain wasn't bad at all, people said. Too much shock. She dies and it's the sister that finds her, she'd made sure her sister was coming over early. She was a thoughtful lady that way.

Calvin needed to get back to his house, back over the Nebraska border, and clean his hair. He'd wiped himself down with chunks of snow, his head was smoking from the cold. But it was still sticky. He wasn't supposed to get blood on him, and he needed it out, he could smell it in the car.

He pulled over to the side of the road, his hands sweating inside his gloves. He thought he saw a child, running in the snow up ahead, but realized he was just seeing the little girl he'd killed. Pudgy thing, her hair all still in braids, running, and him panicked, seeing her not as a little girl, not yet, but as prey, something that needed putting down. He didn't want to do it, but no one got to see his face, he had to protect himself first and he had to get her before she woke the other kids up—he knew there were more, and he knew he didn't have the heart to kill all of them. That wasn't his mission, his mission was to help.

He saw the little girl turn to run and he got that axe suddenly in his hand—he saw the shotgun too, and he thought, the axe is more quiet, I can still keep this quiet.

And then, maybe he did go insane, he was so angry at the child—he chopped up a little girl—so angry at the redhead woman, for screwing this all up, for not dying right. He killed a little girl with an axe. He shot off the head of a mother of four instead of giving her the death she deserved. Her last moments were horror, nightmare in her house instead of him just holding her while she bled onto the snow and died with her face against his chest. He chopped up a little girl.

For the first time, Calvin Diehl thought of himself as a murderer. He fell back in his seat and bellowed.

Libby Day

NOW

Thirteen days after Diondra and Crystal went missing, and the police had still not found them, had still not found any physical evidence to link Diondra to Michelle. The hunt was dissolving into an arson case, it was losing steam.

Lyle came over to watch bad TV with me, his new habit. I let him come if he didn't talk too much, I made a big deal about him not talking too much, but I missed him on the days he didn't come. We were watching some particularly grotesque reality show when Lyle suddenly sat up straighter. "Hey, that's my sweater."

I was wearing one of his too-tight pullovers I'd taken from the back of his car at some point, and it really did look much better on me.

"It really does look better on me," I said.

"Man, Libby. You could just ask, you know." He turned back to the TV, where women were going at each other like angry pound dogs. "Libby Sticky Fingers. Too bad you didn't leave Diondra's with, like, her hairbrush. We'd have some DNA."

"Ah, the magic, magic DNA," I said. I'd stopped believing in DNA.

On the TV, a blond woman had another blond woman by the hair and was pushing her down some steps, and I flipped the channel to a nature show on crocodiles.

"Oh, oh, my God." I ran from the room.

I came back, slapped Diondra's lipstick and thermometer on the table.

"Lyle Wirth, you are goddam brilliant," I said, and then I hugged him.

"Well," he said, and then laughed. "Wow. Huh, brilliant. Libby Sticky Fingers thinks I'm brilliant."

"Absolutely."

DNA FROM BOTH objects matched the blood on Michelle's bedspread. The manhunt ignited. No wonder Diondra had been so insistent she was never remotely connected to Ben. All those scientific advances, one after another, making it easier and easier to match DNA: she must have felt more endangered each year instead of less. Good.

They nailed Diondra at a money-order dive in Amarillo. Crystal was nowhere to be found, but Diondra was nabbed, although it took four cops to get her in the car. So Diondra was in jail and Calvin Diehl had confessed. Even some skeevy loan agent had been rounded up, his mere name giving me the willies: *Len.* With all that, you'd think Ben might have been released from prison, but things don't go that quickly. Diondra wasn't confessing, and until her trial unfolded, they were going to hold on to my brother, who refused to implicate her. I finally went to visit him at the end of May.

He looked plumper, weary. He smiled weakly at me as I sat down.

"Wasn't sure if you'd want to see me," I said.

"Diondra was always sure you'd find her out. She was always sure of it. Guess she was right."

"Guess she was."

Neither of us seemed willing to go past that. Ben had protected Diondra for almost twenty-five years, I had undone all that. He seemed chagrined but not sad. Maybe he'd always hoped she'd be exposed. I was willing to believe that, for my own sake. It was easy not to ask the question.

"You'll be out of here soon, Ben. Can you believe it? You'll be out of prison." This was by no means a sure thing—a strip of blood on a dead girl's sheets is good, but a confession's better. Still, I was hopeful. Still.

"I wouldn't mind that," he said. "It may be time. I think twenty-four years may be enough. It may be enough for . . . standing by. Letting it happen."

"I think so."

Lyle and I had put together pieces of that night from what Diondra had told me: They were at the house, ready to run away, and something happened that unraveled Diondra, she killed Michelle. Ben didn't stop her. My guess is, Michelle somehow learned of the pregnancy, the secret baby. I would ask Ben one day, ask for the details. But I knew he'd give me nothing now.

The two Days sat looking at each other, thinking things and swallowing them. Ben scratched a pimple on his arm, the *Y* of the Polly tattoo peeking out from his sleeve.

"So: Crystal. What can you tell me about Crystal, Libby? What *happened* that night? I've heard different versions. Is she, is she wrong. Bad?"

So now it was Ben wondering what happened in a lonely, cold house outside of town. I fingered the two tear-shaped scars on my cheekbone, imprints from the iron's steam ducts.

"She's smart enough to duck the police all this time," I said. "Diondra will never say where she is."

"That's not what I asked."

"I don't know, Ben, she was protecting her mother. Diondra said she told Crystal everything, and I think she meant it. Everything: *I killed Michelle and no one can know.* What does it do to a girl who knows her mother is a murderer? She gets obsessed, she tries to make sense of it, she clips photos of her dead relatives, she reads her dead aunt's diary until she can quote from it, she knows every angle, she spends her life ready to defend her mom. And then I show up, and it's Crystal who blows it. And what does she do? She tries to fix it. I kind of understand. I give her a pass. She won't go to prison because of me."

I'd been vague with the police about Crystal—they wanted to speak with her about the fire, but they didn't know she'd tried to kill me. I wasn't going to snitch on another member of my family, I just wasn't, even if this one happened to be guilty. I tried to tell myself she wasn't that disturbed. It could have been momentary madness, born out of love. But then, her mom had had a case of that, and it left my sister dead.

I hope to never see Crystal again, but if I do I'm glad I have a gun, let's put it that way.

"You really give her a pass?"

"I know a little bit about trying to do the right thing and fucking up completely," I added.

"You talking about Mom?" Ben said.

"I was talking about me."

"You could have been talking about all of us."

Ben pressed his hand against the glass, and my brother and I matched palms.

Ben Day

NOW

Standing out in the prison yard the other day, he smelled smoke. Smoke was floating on a current of air about eight feet above his head, and he pictured the field fires of autumn, back when he was a kid, flames marching across the soil in flickering lines, burning away what's not useful. He'd hated being a farm kid, but now that's all he thought about. Outside. At night, when the other men were making their sticky sounds, he'd close his eyes and see acres of sorghum, rattling at his knees with those shiny brown beads, like a girl's jewelry. He'd see the Flint Hills of Kansas, with their eerie, flattened tops, like each mound was waiting for its own coyote to howl from it. Or he'd close his eyes and picture his foot, slopped deep in mud, the feel of the earth sucking him in, holding on to him.

Once or twice a week, Ben had a giddy moment where he almost laughed. He was in prison. For life. For murdering his family. Could that be right? By now he thought of Ben, fifteen-year-old Ben, almost as his son, an entirely different being, and sometimes he wanted to throttle the kid, the kid who just didn't have it in him— he'd picture shaking Ben until his face blurred.

But sometimes he was proud.

Yes, he'd been a whimpering little worthless coward that night, a boy who just let things happen. Scared. But after the murders, something fell in place maybe. He would be quiet to save Diondra, his woman, and the baby. His second family. He couldn't bring himself to bust out of that room and save Debby and his mom. He couldn't bring himself to stop Diondra and save Michelle. He couldn't bring himself to do anything but shut up and take it. Stay still and take it. That he could do.

He'd be that kind of man.

He'd become famous because he was that kind of man. First he was the bad-ass Devil-daddy, everyone twitching to get away from him, even the guards spooked, and then he was the kindly, misunderstood prisoner. Women came all the time, and he tried not to say too much, let them imagine what he was thinking. They usually imagined he was thinking good thoughts. Sometimes he was. And sometimes he was thinking what would've happened if that night went different: He and Diondra and a squealing baby somewhere in western Kansas, Diondra crying mean tears in some tiny, food-grimed cell of a motel room they rented by the week. He'd have killed her. At some point, he might have. Or maybe he'd have grabbed the baby and run, and he and Crystal would be happy somewhere, her a college graduate, him running the farm, the coffee maker always on, like home.

Now maybe it was his turn to be out and Diondra's turn to be in, and he'd get out and find Crystal wherever she was, she was a sheltered kid, she couldn't disappear for long, he'd find her and take care of her. It'd be nice to take care of her, to actually do something besides shutting up and taking it.

But even as he was thinking this, he knew he'd have to aim smaller. That's what he learned from his life so far: always aim smaller. He was born to be lonely, that's what he knew for certain. When he was a kid, when he was a teenager, and definitely now. Sometimes he felt like he'd been gone his whole life—in exile, away from the place he was supposed to be, and that, soldier-like, he was pining to be returned. Homesick for a place he'd never been.

If he got out, he'd go to Libby, maybe. Libby who looked like his mother, who looked like him, who had all those rhythms that he just knew, no-question knew. He could spend the rest of his life begging forgiveness from Libby, looking out for Libby, his little sister, somewhere on the outside. Somewhere small.

That's all he wanted.

Libby Day

NOW

The curlicues of the prison barbed wire were glowing yellow as I reached my car, and I was busy thinking of all the people that had been harmed: intentionally, accidentally, deservedly, unfairly, slightly, completely. My mom, Michelle, Debby. Ben. Me. Krissi Cates. Her parents. Diondra's parents. Diane. Trey. Crystal.

I wondered how much of it could be fixed, if anyone could be healed or even comforted.

I stopped at a gas station to get directions, because I'd forgotten how to get to Diane's mobile park, and goddam it, I was going to see Diane. I fingerbrushed my hair in the station's bathroom mirror, and applied some chapstick I'd almost stolen and bought instead (still not feeling entirely good about that decision). Then I drove across town, into the white-picket-fenced trailer park where Diane lived, daffodils yellowing up everywhere.

There is such a thing as a pretty trailer park, you know.

Diane's home was right where I remembered, and I rolled to a stop, giving her three honks, her ritual when she visited us way back when. She was in her small yard, poking around the tulips, her broad rear to me, a big block of woman with wavy steel hair.

She turned around at my honks, blinked wildly as I got out of
the car.

"Aunt Diane?" I said.

She strode across the yard in big solid steps, her face tight.
When she was right on top of me, she grabbed me and hugged me
with such force it pushed the air out of my lungs. Then she patted me
hard twice, held me at arm's length, then pulled me in again.

"I knew you could do it, I knew you could, Libby," she mumbled
into my hair, warm and smoky.

"Do what?"

"Try just a little harder."

I STAYED AT Diane's for two hours, til we started running out of
things to say, like we always did. She hugged me again gruffly and ordered me to come back out on Saturday. She needed help installing a
countertop.

I didn't get straight on the highway, but slowly rolled toward
where our farm had once been, trying to find myself there by accident. It had been a shaky spring, but now I rolled the windows down.
I came to the end of the long stretch of road that would lead to the
farm, bracing myself for housing developments or strip malls. Instead I came upon an old tin mailbox, "The Muehlers" in cursive
paint on the side. Our farm was a farm again. A man was walking the
fields. Far down by the pond, a woman and a girl watched a dog
splatter in the water, the girl windmilling her arms around her waist,
bored.

I studied it all for a few minutes, keeping my brain steady, staying away from Darkplace. No screams, no shotguns, no wild bluejay
cries. Just listen to the quiet. The man finally noticed me and gave a
wave. I waved back but pulled away as he started to wander over,
neighbor-like. I didn't want to meet him, and I didn't want to introduce myself. I just wanted to be some woman, heading back home to
Over There That Way.

ACKNOWLEDGMENTS

Growing up in Kansas City, Missouri, where a twenty-minute drive can get you to wide, open fields of corn and wheat, I was always fascinated by farms. Fascinated, but not, shall we say, knowledgeable. Huge thanks to the farmers and experts who instructed me on the realities of farming, both during the '80s farm crisis and now: Charlie Griffin of the Kansas Rural Family Helpline; Forrest Buhler of the Kansas Agriculture Mediation Service; Jerrold Oliver; my cousin Christy Baioni and her husband David, a lifelong Arkansas farmer. A giant debt of gratitude goes to Jon and Dana Robnett: Jon not only let me play farmer for a day on his Missouri lands, he answered endless questions about farming—from grain elevators to bull castration. He stopped short of advising me exactly how to sacrifice a cow in a satanic ritual, but I forgive him that bit of good taste.

My brother, Travis Flynn, one of the best shots in the Missouri-Kansas region, was incredibly gracious with his time, advising me on both the period and personality of guns and taking me out to shoot everything from a 10-gauge shotgun to a .44 Magnum—thanks to his wife, Ruth, for putting up with us.

For my crime-scene questions, I turned once again to Lt. Emmet B. Helrich. For rocking, I turned to Slayer, Venom, and Iron Maiden. My cousin, lawyer Kevin Robinett, answered my legal questions with his signature mix of wit and brains. Huge thanks to my uncle, the Hon. Robert M. Schieber, who has suffered my gruesome, strange *Dark Places* queries for two years, and always takes the time to talk out what could happen, what might happen, and what would likely happen when it comes to the law. His judgment has been invaluable. Any errors regarding farming, firearms, or the law are mine; I hope my fellow Kansas Citians will indulge my few fictional liberties regarding good ole KCMO.

On the publishing side, thanks to Stephanie Kip Rostan, whose good humor, smarts, and sensibility I rely on. Cheers to my editor Sarah Knight, who both challenges and trusts me—a lovely combination—and knows how to show a girl a good night on the town. In the United Kingdom, Kirsty Dunseath and her gang at Orion are endlessly kind. A final thanks to the inimitable Shaye Areheart, who took a chance on me a few years back!

I have a lovely group of friends and relatives who offer constant encouragement. Special thanks to Jennifer and Mike Arvia, Amie Brooks, Katy Caldwell, Kameren Dannhauser, Sarah and Alex Eckert, Ryan Enright, Paul and Benetta Jensen, Sean Kelly, Sally Kim, Steve and Trisha London, Kelly Lowe, Tessa and Jessica Nagel, Jessica O'Donnell, Lauren Oliver, Brian Raftery, Dave Samson, Susan and Errol Stone, Josh Wolk, Bill and Kelly Ye, and the delightful, talented Roy Flynn-Nolan, who helped craft beautiful sentences like: nfilsahnfiojfios343254nfa.

To my big Missouri-Kansas-Tennessee family: the Schiebers, the Dannhausers, the Nagels, the Welshes, the Baslers, the Garretts, the Flynns, and my grandma Rose Page. My aunt Leslie Garrett and my uncle Tim Flynn offer particular support and a lot of illuminating thought to my "gonzo feminist" writing.

To my in-laws: James and Cathy Nolan, Jennifer Nolan, and Megan and Pablo Marroquin, for always being so nice about the book, for making me laugh at unexpected times, and for letting me eat all your desserts. I couldn't have lucked into a funner family. And no, *funner* is not a word.

And to my super-friend writing group: Emily Stone has a brilliant eye for detail and reminds me to celebrate during the sometimes-sloggy act of writing. Scott Brown reads and then reads more, and always makes me feel quite brilliant. Plus he knows when to stop writing and go visit haunted chicken houses in Alabama.

To my parents, Matt and Judith Flynn. Dad, your humor, creativity, and kindness keep me in awe. Mom, you are the most gracious, generous person I know and someday I will write a book in which the mother is not a) evil or b) killed. You deserve better! Thank you both for the company on various Missouri-Kansas road trips, and for always letting me know I make you proud. A kid couldn't want more than that.

Finally, thanks to my brilliant, funny, giant-hearted, super-hot husband, Brett Nolan. What do I say to a man who knows how I think and still sleeps next to me with the lights off? To a man who asks me the questions that help me find my way? To a man who reads voraciously, makes a mean gumbo, looks smart in a tux, and whistles better than Bing? To a man who's as old-school cool as Nick Charles, for crying out loud! What do I say about us? Two words.